Harold Coyle, a graduate of the Virginia Military Institute, has seen fourteen years of active duty with the U.S. Army that includes assignments ranging from tank platoon leader in the Federal Republic of Germany to assistant operations officer with the Combined Field Army in the Republic of Korea. He, his wife Pat and their three children currently live in Texas.

CODE OF HONOUR

Harold Coyle

POCKET
B O O K S

LONDON · SYDNEY · NEW YORK · TOKYO · SINGAPORE · TORONTO

First published in Great Britain by Simon & Schuster, 1994
First published in Great Britain by Pocket Books, 1995
An imprint of Simon & Schuster Ltd
A Paramount Communications Company

Simon & Schuster Ltd
West Garden Place
Kendal Street
London W2 2AQ

Simon & Schuster of Australia Pty Ltd
Sydney

A CIP catalogue record for this book is available from the
British Library

ISBN 0-671-85266-3

Typeset in Times 10/12pt by
Hewer Text Composition Services, Edinburgh
Printed and bound in Great Britain by
HarperCollins*Manufacturing*, Glasgow

ACKNOWLEDGMENTS

In writing this book, I was ably assisted by a number of people from various walks of life who took time from their busy schedules to read the rough drafts and help me make this book a reality.

Lieutenant Jeff Givens, the executive officer of a 1st Infantry Division brigade, used much of his precious free time to plow through the manuscript and comment on it as well as pass it on to others in the Big Red One for their comments. Thanks, Jeff.

Captain Kristine K. Hayter, a JAG officer with the 1st Infantry Division, was kind enough to review the manuscript and comment on legal matters. Besides thanking her, I would like to apologize to her and just about every JAG officer in the United States Army for taking my liberties with the Manual for Courts Martial as well as the conduct of the investigation and court martial I have depicted. However, as Captain Hayter herself acknowledged, this is a novel and not a supplement to the Manual for Courts Martial.

Chet Burgess, my media expert, took time to go through the material I sent him despite the fact that he was knee deep in remodeling his new home and moving into it.

The New York City connection, Michael Korda and Paul McCarthy, as usual, tolerated my fits of passion and my incredibly creative spelling as they worked with me to make this a finished product. Good editors, I am told, are hard to find, which is why I am thankful that I have been blessed by two of the best.

A new addition to my circle of helpers is Melanie M. Martin, a dear friend who, from the start of this project to the very end, helped me in innumerable ways.

In the course of writing this book, I lost a dear friend, a man who helped me on this book and others, for he knew no bounds when it came to a friend. Lieutenant Commander Gerry Carroll was a naval aviator, a veteran, a writer, and a man dedicated to his family, his friends, the United States Navy, and his nation. He died this past September, leaving a hole that no one will ever fill. Gerry, here's to you, kid.

CONTENTS

War is the unfolding of miscalculations.

— Barbara Tuchman

It is better to die on your feet than to live on your knees.

— Emiliano Zapata

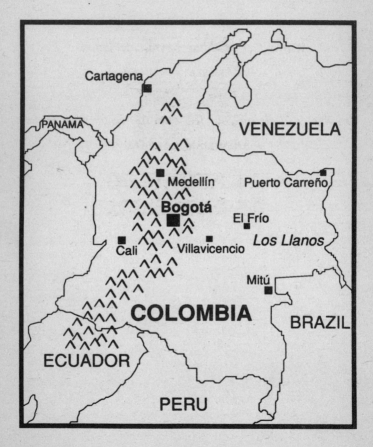

PART ONE

A GATHERING
OF DARKNESS

CHAPTER 1

September 21

Looking down at her watch, Captain Nancy Kozak decided that it would probably be a good idea to go over and check with her battalion commander. Though nothing had changed in the past thirty minutes, she was doing nothing where she was, and doing nothing was something that Nancy Kozak had never been able to do well.

Taking a deep breath, Kozak brushed from her face the stray wisp of hair that always managed to escape from the tight bun she put her hair into before an operation like this. Ready, Kozak set the butt of her rifle on the ground upright between her legs and grasped its forward grip with both hands. With a single heave, she pushed herself up and out of the dirt she had been lounging in. Her grunts and exertions caused none of the other eleven soldiers she had been waiting with to stir or follow suit. They were used to her need to be doing something, even if it was just trooping, checking things for the umpteenth time. With nothing more than a casual glance, if that, the men and women who made up Kozak's battle staff withdrew back into their own thoughts as they waited for the helicopters to arrive, provided, of course, they did arrive.

At the edge of the clump of trees she paused. From there she looked out toward the dirt runway, if the bare scraping of earth could be called a runway. To one side of it, closest to her, sat the soldiers of Company A languishing in the oppressive late-morning sun. They were the assault company today, the first in. Followed by Company C in support, the unit she had been waiting with, the battalion had the mission of seizing and securing a suspected arms cache located in the Cauca River Valley some ninety-five kilometers from where they sat. Like most of their operations to date, it would be, as one of her sergeants put it, 'a walk in the woods and a nice break from this hole.'

For the briefest of moments she considered the wisdom of leaving the relative shade of the tree line just to go trotting out on a fool's errand. But then she shook her head and stepped off. She figured if she had put out this much effort already, she might as well follow through, and she headed directly for the first group of soldiers waiting at the edge of the runway.

As she approached, no one in the group she was headed for paid her much attention. It wasn't that the twelve people, mostly members of the command group for the first wave, were ignoring her. It was simply that after sitting in the hot Colombian sun for over an hour waiting to start an operation that was hopelessly behind schedule, all the energy and enthusiasm that they had been able to muster earlier in the day to psych themselves and their soldiers up for this operation had melted away. Even her battalion commander, Lieutenant Colonel Hal Cerro, merely looked up at her without speaking when she finally reached them. He was, she knew, like her, doing his utmost to contain the anger and frustration that he felt whenever he thought about the manner in which operations had been conducted in the last few months.

Stopping just in front of Cerro, Kozak mumbled something that Cerro didn't hear. He didn't bother to ask her to repeat it. Had it been good news, he knew Kozak's pace and tone of voice would have been far more animated. Her leisurely, almost sullen manner and subdued greeting told him all he needed to know; nothing had changed, everything was still proceeding as normal, late and getting later.

Looking up while she stood before him, the sun at her back, Cerro watched Kozak rearrange her gear and dust herself off as she looked down the line of waiting clusters of soldiers. She was, he thought, like everyone else in the 3rd Battalion, 511th Infantry Regiment, tired of waiting in the oppressive heat for the helicopters that were late and getting later by the minute. But rather than waste his time pondering what his operations officer was about to do, Cerro turned away and went back to thinking about the timetables and schedules Kozak's operations section had developed and published for the battalion's orders that were supposed to be driving this operation. Now, like so many other such efforts, those wonderful little schedules were worthless. Instead of being a well-synchronized effort, today's operation, like most of the operations the 11th Air Assault Division had conducted since arriving in Colombia, would have to be conducted on the fly. Not that either he or Kozak minded doing things that way. If the truth were known, both secretly preferred to operate on the run, for they were both part of that rare breed of soldier that not only thrived on chaos but could make that chaos work for them.

Looking down at Cerro, Kozak was about to ask if there had been a change in the estimated time of arrival for the aviation company that was supposed to be supporting them that day. Kozak stopped, however, when she realized that she had asked him that very same question not thirty minutes before. His answer now no doubt would be the same: 'Brigade will call us as soon as they have any word.' She looked down at her boots and shook her head before looking back at Cerro. 'Sir, I'm going to take a walk down the line. Want to join me and kill some time?'

Though he knew that he should accept her invitation, at that moment Cerro had no drive whatsoever. After ensuring that everything that could be done in the way of planning and coordination had been done, he had finally managed to turn in just after midnight. Up three hours later, due more to the heat than nerves, Cerro had bounced about the battalion's base camp checking those things that a good battalion commander should. At dawn both he and Kozak had gone over the plan one more time with each of the company commanders and then from a distance watched the pre-combat inspections. In the process, Cerro, like Kozak, had skipped breakfast, believing, or more correctly hoping, that this operation would get off on time.

But it didn't. Like many others before, delays due to the overcommitment of the division's aviation assets in support of multiple operations left the 3rd of the 511th baking in the hot tropic sun along the flat dirt landing zone like lizards on a rock. After having been physically and mentally pumped up and then let down, Cerro had little energy or drive to spare for another inspection that would only serve to kill a few more minutes. Squinting as he looked up at Captain Nancy Kozak, Cerro shook his head. 'If it's all the same to you, Nancy, I think I'll sit this one out.'

Feeling much the same way he did, Kozak nodded. 'Okay. No problem. I'm sure the XO back at the command post will give us a hoot as soon as he hears something.'

Still squinting, Cerro didn't even nod his head. 'Roger that.' With that he let his head drop as if there were a lead weight tied to the brim of his helmet and allowed his mind to wander off in search of a thought or sleep, whichever came first.

With no need to say more, Kozak turned, held her rifle at her side by its charging handle, and began to walk down the line. That line consisted of groups of soldiers, numbering ten to twelve per group, spread every thirty meters parallel to the dirt runway. Like the command group, each of the small circle of soldiers represented a helicopter load, at times referred to as a slick. The distance between each group was based on the fact that each UH-60 utility helicopter with its blade unfolded measured about sixty-five feet, or approximately twenty meters. With ten meters added for separation between aircraft, the line of twelve groups that made up the first lift extended almost a quarter of a mile.

As Kozak approached each group, no one stood, though her appearance did cause a slight stir as the first soldier in each group to see Kozak would tap the senior man on the shoulder. If the sergeant or officer was too far away to reach, the soldier would throw a small rock to get his attention and let him know that the battalion S-3 was coming. Alerted, the senior soldier would prop himself up, look in the direction that Kozak was coming from, and prepare to greet her. Normally the greeting consisted of a glib comment such as 'Mornin', Captain. Nice day for the beach,' or 'Doesn't brigade know that exposure to the sun too long causes skin cancer in lab rats?' While the officers' comments were for the most part less caustic, everyone who spoke found some means of conveying their displeasure. Though many of these comments were just this side of disrespectful, the quips and remarks Kozak heard that morning and on many other mornings were the only way her soldiers could legally let Kozak know that they were not at all happy with their predicament.

The fact that they were making them, however, often

with a smile, was enough for Kozak. Had they simply sat there as she went by, glaring at her and saying nothing, then Kozak would have been concerned. For her part, Kozak would pause and return the comment with one of her own. To the sergeant who joked, Kozak shot back, 'Well, Sergeant Wells, that's why they sent us out here instead of the lab rats. We wouldn't want to be guilty of being cruel to animals, would we?' This caused the soldiers in Wells's squad to crack up. One specialist toting a squad automatic weapon slapped the side of his weapon as he laughed out loud before he joined the exchange. 'Yeah, Captain. We wouldn't want those animal rights activists coming down on us. Them folks from division is bad enough.'

Not interested in any long-drawn-out conversations, especially when they involved any mention of the division or its bloated staff, Kozak would respond with a light laugh, make a comment or two, and move on to the next group. Because she was not the commander, Kozak could move about with greater freedom and less hassle. In Cerro's own words, she moved through the battalion area with the ease of a cat, while he could only do so with the grace of a bull. Being an astute commander, Cerro used this to his advantage, since he knew that the officers and NCOs would freely tell her things that they would hesitate to tell him. That, coupled with an incredible eye for detail and a knack for working with people, allowed her to see things that he couldn't. Since she had assumed the full responsibilities as the operations officer, after the major in that slot had been killed in a freak accident, Cerro had come to value Kozak's observations as much his own.

Knowing this, Kozak tried hard not to miss anything. As she walked among the groups of waiting soldiers, her eyes would move from one soldier to the next, looking at his or her face, uniform, weapon, even boots. For often it was the condition of the soldiers' boots that betrayed how long they had been with the battalion. The newer the boot, the greener the soldier. This morning as she was parrying comments with her own and trying to gauge the condition of the battalion, the number of new boots Kozak saw served to remind her that the battalion was changing. It was no longer the well-trained and tight-knit group of professionals that had left Fort Campbell four months earlier. It was now a hodgepodge of tired veterans fast approaching burnout and new, partially trained soldiers fresh out of training centers in the States. A full 25 percent of the command now consisted of people who had joined them after they had arrived in country. With another eight months to go and the tempo and cost of operations increasing, Kozak was beginning to wonder how many of the soldiers she was looking at would make it to May, when they were due to pull out of Colombia.

Finished with Sergeant Wells's group, Kozak waved to Wells and slowly made her way to the next group without saying another word. Private Andrew Hayman watched her go by. New to the unit, Hayman found it difficult to relate the training and indoctrination he had received in his infantry training at Fort Benning to what was going on here. Nothing, from the manner in which the officers and sergeants conducted themselves to the way in which Staff Sergeant Wells ran the squad, bore any resemblance to Fort Benning. Everything, including the Army he was now serving in, was foreign. Of course, Hayman thought, with less than three days in a line unit under his belt, it wasn't surprising that things would be confusing. Still he was hoping that something, anything, that he had learned in basic and advanced infantry training would be of use. But so far this battalion seemed to do everything different. Looking over at the specialist with the squad automatic weapon who had spoken to the captain, Hayman longed for the day when he could face an upcoming operation with such casual disregard.

Kozak was deep in thought, her head slightly bowed, when she came up to the group that included Second Lieutenant Gerald T. Horan. A graduate of West Point and only recently assigned to the 3rd of the 51th, Horan jumped to his feet when he saw Kozak approaching and saluted. Surprised by Horan's sudden move, Kozak stopped in her tracks and looked up to see what the problem was. The image of a second lieutenant dressed in new camouflage that hadn't faded and boots that still betrayed a hint of polish beneath the thin covering of dust caught Kozak off guard. Not that there was anything wrong with Horan. It was just that Kozak hadn't been expecting such a display of military etiquette. As she looked Horan up and down, it finally dawned on Kozak how long it had been since a young officer in this battalion had behaved in such a manner. Were they, she wondered, getting too casual, too slack?

While Kozak stood there looking at Horan with a blank stare as if she were pondering what to do next, Horan's platoon sergeant jumped to his feet, glaring at his new officer and barely able to contain the muted obscenities that he was mumbling below his breath. While Horan was somewhat bewildered by Kozak's reaction, Sergeant First Class Timothy Banks knew exactly what was going on. Taking charge, as was his style, Banks gave a quick salute so as not to further embarrass his platoon leader and reported. 'Good morning, ma'am. Second Platoon, Company A, at your service.'

Shaken from her thoughts by Banks's response, Kozak looked away from Horan over to Banks and gave a rather casual hand salute in return. She began to say something to Banks, then paused, remembering that the Second Platoon, for the first time in well over a month, had a lieutenant as a platoon leader. Turning back to Horan, Kozak looked at the eager young officer. Again she did not speak. Rather she allowed her mind to stumble over a series of disjointed thoughts. The first that came to her was Kozak's regret that her battalion commander had agreed to accept Horan and another second lieutenant into the battalion while they were still deployed forward and involved in operations. Though she knew that eventually they would have to accept these officers as well as senior noncommissioned officers to replace losses that were beginning to accumulate, Kozak, like the other battalion operations officers in the 11th Air Assault, preferred to wait until their battalion had been pulled back to Eagle Base outside of Bogotá. There, as the division reserve and without the pressure of back to back operations, Kozak thought, the company commanders could spend the time necessary to properly integrate and indoctrinate the new people into the ranks properly. The idea that new soldiers, officer and enlisted, could be sent to them straight from the States and plugged into units without additional training or time to acclimate to the country, the climate, the unit, and the level of operations that they were conducting was in Kozak's mind worse than ludicrous. It was, as her brigade commander had once put it during a fit of anger, akin to being an accomplice to murder.

Still Kozak, like her brigade commander, was a soldier, and they had their orders. They would accept and integrate individual replacements into their ranks as quickly as they arrived in country in accordance with the division's policy. So young Horan, along with another lieutenant whose name Kozak couldn't remember at the moment, was out there along with the rest of the battalion waiting in the sun for helicopters that never seemed to arrive on time. This led Kozak to her next thought or, more correctly, observation. Horan was young, frighteningly young. As she stood there staring blankly at the nervous young platoon leader, Kozak couldn't help but think that Horan didn't look at that moment old enough to graduate from high school. The fact that Horan wasn't much older than

the bulk of the platoon he was about to lead into combat
didn't make Kozak feel any better.

Nor did it make the members of Horan's platoon feel too
comfortable. To them, Banks was a known commodity.
He had been their platoon sergeant back in Kentucky
before the deployment. When their platoon leader came
down with malaria six weeks prior, Banks had assumed
command. To the soldiers of the platoon this was no big
deal. They, the old-timers in the platoon, knew Banks and
trusted him. They knew what he would do in a tight spot
and had come to depend on his judgment. They knew that
when he said do something, it was the right thing to do. In
four months of operations they – Banks and the members
of the platoon – had become a single entity. It came as
no surprise to Kozak, therefore, that the assignment of
Horan would be greeted with hostility. Only the direct
intervention of the A Company commander had quieted
their discontentment. Still, based on the looks on the faces
of the old-timers, and even Sergeant Banks's, Kozak could
tell that their company commander's efforts had not been
100 percent effective.

Shaking her head slightly, Kozak brought her hand up
and with a casual flip swept from her face the stray wisp of
hair that had fallen out of place again. Looking in Horan's
eyes, she noticed that he was staring at her, waiting for her
to say or do something. Her presence and her failure to
say anything up to now was, she realized, unnerving this
young officer.

Still she said nothing as her mind wandered off again.
Had she, Kozak wondered, been like this? Though only
seven years separated her date of graduation from West
Point and Horan's, the difference between the two seemed
incredible. That she could stand there, the author of an
order that was about to propel two rifle companies into
battle, a battle in which she would function as the fire
and air support coordinator, with no more on her mind

than fleeting thoughts about the age of another officer, was to her unnerving. Had she, Kozak wondered, become too casual about all of this? Had war, and the agony and destruction that it visited on everyone and everything that it touched, become so much a part of her that she didn't even give what she was doing a second thought?

How terrible, Kozak suddenly realized, to be twenty-nine and so hardened to pain and suffering that your only measure of human worth was whether the person in front of you could stand up in combat or not. Perhaps, Kozak thought, that had been on the mind of her former boss, the operations officer she was filling in for. At about the same time that Horan's predecessor had been evacuated, the operations officer, a major with a bright career ahead of him, had gotten up from his desk one day and walked out of the battalion command post. Without a single word to anyone, he casually strolled over to the flight line and right into the rotating blades of a liaison helicopter that was preparing to take off. Had he, Kozak wondered as she stood there staring blankly at Horan, become so casual about death that even his own meant nothing?

Unable to contain himself, Horan finally took the initiative. 'Captain Kozic, is there something that you need?'

Kozak blinked, looked at Horan, and finally spoke. 'It's Kozak. Pronounced co-zack.'

Though she hadn't meant to make it sound like a reprimand, her response stung Horan. 'Oh, sorry, ma'am. I . . . well . . .'

Realizing that she had only shaken him further, Kozak forced a smile. 'It's okay. Everyone screws it up the first few times.'

Looking down at the ground between them, Horan sighed. 'Well, I do apologize. It won't happen again.'

My God, Kozak thought as the faint smile disappeared from her face, it had been a mistake to plug this lieutenant into the line so soon. Maybe, she thought, she could talk

the battalion commander into leaving him behind. Maybe
it wasn't too late. But as soon as that thought came to
mind, she pushed it aside. It was too late. If Horan
was pulled out of his platoon right now, it would be an
embarrassment that he would never live down, with either
his own men or the other officers in the battalion. No,
she thought. As cruel and cold as it seemed, Horan was
committed to this operation, ready or not. Besides, maybe
she was being too cautious. Thousands of other officers,
she thought, had had to face the same thing Horan was
now facing, or worse, and had survived. Why should this
young officer be treated any different? Without a pause
Kozak's smile returned. 'No, there's nothing I need. I'm
just trooping the line one more time. Now if you excuse
me, I need to be going.'

Horan smiled and saluted. 'Yes, of course, ma'am. By
all means.' He was in truth glad to be rid of Kozak, an
officer who had a reputation and combat record that was
the envy of every junior officer in the battalion.

Without acknowledging his salute, Kozak turned away
and began to tread her way down the line again. She was
halfway to the next group when she heard the faint sound
of helicopter blades off in the distance beating the humid
midmorning air. Instinctively Kozak stopped and turned
to face the direction from which the sound was coming.
Quickly slinging her rifle over her shoulder, she lifted
both hands up to the brim of her helmet to shield her
eyes from the sun as she searched for the source of the
noise. When she finally caught sight of a small black dot
on the horizon, she shifted her head first to the left then
to the right as she prepared to count the number of other
helicopters that were inbound. Only after watching for
several seconds did she finally realize that there was only
one inbound helicopter, and that one as it grew closer
appeared to be only a light liaison aircraft.

Dropping her hands to her sides, Kozak was about

to despair when the first happy thought of the morning popped into her mind. Maybe, she thought, Aaron was flying the inbound bird. The idea of seeing Captain Aaron J. Pierce, whom everyone called AJ, brought a smile to Kozak's face. For AJ was the first man that Nancy Kozak had allowed herself to become involved with. Though Kozak was by no means an advocate of celibacy, all of her affairs before AJ had been more or less purely physical. In her efforts to make it or break it as an infantry officer, Nancy Kozak had gone out of her way to avoid becoming involved in a relationship that could endanger her standing in the eyes of her superiors, peers, and even her subordinates. After all, she had reasoned, the image of a love-struck female fawning over her lover didn't quite fit the role model that infantry officers were expected to follow. So it was in the image of Iron Mike, the statue that stood in front of Building Four at Fort Benning, Georgia, the home of the infantry, that Kozak patterned her lifestyle.

It was only after she had met AJ that Kozak realized that living in the shadow of Iron Mike was perhaps overdoing things a bit much. Even Iron Mike, she thought, must have had someone that he went home to after a hard day of yelling 'Follow me' and toting his rifle about. So when Kozak first gazed into AJ's pale blue eyes and found herself blushing, she decided it was time to reassess her position on the issue of love, men, and relationships.

Intently, Kozak watched and followed the approach of the inbound helicopter, just as everyone else scattered around the pickup zone did. While everyone, even the most hardened veteran in the battalion, could feel their pulse begin to quicken in anticipation, the reasons differed from one soldier to the next. For the old-timers, the increase in the heart rate and accompanying awareness had become as much a part of their pre-combat preparation as checking their weapons. When the time came for the final run into the LZ, each soldier who had been there knew they had to be ready for anything and everything, from jumping right into the middle of a firefight to a crash landing.

When it became obvious that there was only one helicopter coming in, the veterans of the two line companies waiting grunted or mumbled before turning their attention back to whatever they had been doing. The new men, including Horan, however, hadn't learned yet how to turn their emotions on and off with such ease. For them the sensations they felt as they watched the lone helicopter approach varied. For some it was akin to the sudden fear one feels when riding a roller coaster for the first time as it is slowly being cranked up the first long incline. Like the ride on a roller coaster, just beyond that incline, now clearly in sight, lay all sorts of unknown terrors that the rider had no control over. To others the thought of battle brought only images of a vague, unfathomable darkness.

Regardless of what they thought, the sudden realization that they were about to go over the top and there was nothing that they could do to stop it struck each new soldier to some degree. Every trooper in the battalion knew that, despite all their physical and mental preparation, only when they had reached the end of the ride would they know for sure that they could deal with it. Even the old soldiers, those who had been with the battalion since the beginning, wondered. No man or woman, after all, could be expected to be a hero every day.

Not everyone in the battalion, however, felt the strange grip of fear, excitement, and anticipation as they watched and waited. Of the soldiers waiting and watching, Kozak alone felt joy in her heart. Unable to restrain herself, she inched her way onto the runway in an effort to get a closer look.

Seeing Kozak wander out from the edge of the runway, the pilot of the helicopter assumed that she wanted him to land near her. With measured ease he slowed his aircraft and prepared to land near Kozak. Only when the helicopter finished its approach and slowed down just before landing in front of her did Kozak suddenly realize that AJ wasn't flying this aircraft. Always the cocky aviator, AJ never missed the chance to show off his skill and daring when he thought that Kozak might be watching by coming in a little too fast and far too low. Whoever was flying this helicopter, Kozak decided, was doing it by the book. Heaving a sigh of disappointment, Kozak watched as the pilot lightly touched down and allowed his single passenger enough time to dismount from the left door and walk away before he pulled up and away from the landing zone.

Crestfallen, Kozak was still watching the helicopter fly away when the passenger it had left behind called to her, 'Expecting someone else, Nancy?'

The familiar voice, which she had not heard in a long time, caught her off guard. Whipping her head around to face the owner of the voice, Kozak quickly brought herself to a position of attention when she caught a glimpse of the lone black star centered on the front of the helmet approaching her. Rendering the best hand salute she could manage, Kozak greeted Brigadier General Scott Dixon. 'Yes, sir. But I'm sure he's busy.'

As Dixon closed the distance between them, Kozak could see the sly smile shaded by Dixon's hand as he returned her salute. 'Jan told me that you finally found a romantic interest that was worthy of your attention.'

Kozak's eyes widened. 'My God, does everyone know, sir? Excuse me, but did Jan, I mean Mrs. Dixon, report on my love life during a prime-time news show or something?'

Reaching up with his right arm, Dixon put his hand on Kozak's left shoulder and gave a slight shrug. 'Jan, Captain, is a reporter, a female, and my wife. She told me that she came across you out here in never-never land, and brought me up to date on everything you were doing.'

That comment caused Kozak's eyes to grow wider. 'She told you everything?'

Understanding the meaning of Kozak's question, Dixon smiled. 'Well, almost everything. At least everything that a broken down old tank general from the Pentagon would be interested in.'

Taking a deep breath, Kozak tilted her head down but kept eye contact with Dixon. 'Which brings up the next question, sir. Exactly what is a general officer assigned to the Army General Staff doing out here in the middle of nowhere?'

'The chief sent me down here to find out what you sky warriors were up to.'

It was only with a great deal of effort that Kozak kept herself from replying that the only thing that they were up to was eye deep in bullshit, but she held her tongue. For although she had known Dixon and his wife for years, and theirs was a relationship that transcended the formal military boundaries, there had always been a fine line between maintaining a comfortable and relaxed professional relationship and being too familiar. After all, Dixon, Kozak reminded herself, was a general and the chief that he was so casually referring to was the Chief of Staff of the Army, General Paul M. Fulk. That he had sent Dixon didn't surprise Kozak. Of all the senior officers she had known, he always managed to stand head and shoulders above the rest when it came to calling the shots as he saw them and speaking his mind, damn the consequences. Such an attitude would have cost a lesser man his career long ago. But Dixon had in his own lifetime become something of a legend. It was said by those who knew him that he could do no wrong in the eyes of those who counted.

While the general and the captain stood in the middle of

the dirt runway talking, the soldiers of Kozak's battalion looked on, wondering who the general was and more importantly why he was being so chatty and informal with Kozak. Of all the people watching, only their battalion commander, Hal Cerro, who was now making his way to where they stood, knew. Almost from the day Kozak had reported to her first unit at Fort Hood Texas, an unusual friendship had sprung up between Dixon and Kozak as their careers and their lives became intertwined. Cerro knew all about this because he too was part of that relationship that merged professionalism and friendship. That Scott Dixon, who Cerro knew was assigned to the Pentagon, was standing here dressed for battle rather than sitting in an air-conditioned office overlooking the Potomac didn't surprise Cerro. Dixon was never one for staff work. He was a field soldier. That wasn't to say Dixon couldn't do what was necessary when he was serving on the staff. In fact he had a knack for it. But when the choice came down to going out and doing something in the field with a unit or sitting in an office moving papers about a desk, in Dixon's case the papers never stood a chance.

As he approached, both Dixon and Kozak turned to face Cerro. Smiling as he saluted, Cerro spoke first. 'I heard that you were down here on some kind of fact-finding tour. What brings the newest general in the Army to our humble little corner of the earth, sir? General Staff need some fresh coffee and decided to send its junior general to find and secure Juan Valdez?'

'No, not quite, *Colonel* Cerro. Fact is, we need someone to empty the trash cans in the chief's office and he asked if I knew a lieutenant colonel who could handle the job.'

Cerro said, 'Oh, no, sir. I don't need to do time in the Pentagon. I've been a good boy. Ask my S-3. She'll tell you.'

Kozak backed off, putting one hand up and waving it. 'Sorry, sirs. I'd prefer to stay out of this one.'

After an exchange of handshakes, Cerro got around to the same question that Kozak had asked Dixon minutes before, namely, What was he doing there?

Though there was still a hint of a smile, both Cerro and Kozak could tell that Dixon was getting serious now. 'I thought that my last day in country would best be spent in the field with a unit on an operation. When I saw your unit was slated to hit a suspected weapons cache, I decided to join you.'

Cerro, now slowly turning serious, shook his head. 'Well, I'm sorry to disappoint you, sir, but if the reports from division intelligence are to be believed, this will be a real sleeper. The report, based on information provided by informers, *claims* that this is a Class B logistic site, small arms and sustenance only. All the Class A sites with the big stuff, heavy weapons and all, are up in Norte de Santander or Vichada. The rebel insurgents are active around here but not like to the north and east.' After a slight pause, Cerro added, 'Fact is, I think this is just going to be a drug bust.'

Betraying no surprise, Dixon cocked his head to one side. 'What makes you say that?'

Looking down at the ground for a moment, Cerro considered his answer. Though he suspected that Dixon already knew the truth, since the division commander's preference for drug-related targets was common knowledge, Cerro still hesitated. No one had ever offered him any proof, though the number of missions that the battalion had been given that had been labeled as FARC but instead turned out to be drug-related were too numerous to ignore. Looking back at Dixon, Cerro decided, What the hell! He had asked. Besides, Cerro knew of Dixon's knack for detecting BS in all its forms. It would do no good to attempt to bluff him.

'Well, to start with, the "informers" usually turn out to be DEA agents. When these Rambos gone astray find something belonging to the cartel that they can't handle, they pass the word onto the local CIA. The CIA translates cartel into FARC and passes the information directly to the division G-2. Well briefed on their roles, the intelligence analysts in G-2 accept the CIA information as gospel and pass it on to division operations, who then task the brigades. This allows the division commander to tell the Colombians that he's going after the Farcees every chance he gets, while he's actually getting more druggies.'

As Cerro spoke, Dixon nodded. He already had found out much of this on his own and had pretty well figured out the rest. The 'Farcees' Cerro spoke of was the popular name used by American forces when discussing the Revolutionary Armed Forces of Colombia. Officially known as the FARC, based on a shortening of the Spanish name, which stood for Fuerzas Armadas Revolucionarios de Colombia, the Farcees were the chief opponent of the 11th Air Assault Division. An aborted military coup nine months prior and the resulting purge of officers had left the Colombian military disorganized, dispirited, and incapable of dealing with both the drug cartel, which had never been under control, and a resurgent socialist movement aimed at ridding Colombia of a corrupt government, an oppressive military, and the drug cartel. Though the Colombian government tried to deal with its problems on its own, the President of Colombia finally was forced by circumstances to either accept defeat at the hands of the FARC or request American military intervention.

Through the use of strict controls and limitations, the Colombian President was able to convince the majority of his government that the Americans were the lesser of two evils. There was in his estimate little choice. As he told his confederates, in order to save their regime and their way of life they would have to risk alienating portions of their population and suffer the righteous and overbearing

Americans for a while. So with great trepidation, the President requested that the United States dispatch a small expeditionary force to Colombia for a period of no more than one year to hold the line against the FARC while the Colombian government rebuilt its own military machine, starting from the top.

The United States, seeing an unparalleled opportunity to put a sizable military force that would have relative freedom of action into the heart of a nation noted for its illegal drug industry, decided the invitation was too good to pass up. Hence, while it was the avowed mission of the 11th Air Assault to protect the regime in power from the FARC while it put its own military house in order, the 11th Air Assault was under special orders to do as much damage as possible to the drug cartel while it was in country. With only one year to do it, the division commander, Major General Charles B. Lane, was determined to become known as the man who won the war on drugs for the United States.

While few people had a problem with going after the drug lords, it soon became obvious that the 11th Air Assault couldn't perform both its mission to suppress the FARC and tackle the druggies as well. That, of course, didn't keep Lane and his staff from attempting to do so. Thus started the vicious cycle of mixed priorities, overextension of divisional resources, and botched missions as the Colombian government put pressure on the American military to go after the FARC rebels, while the commanding general of the division and the DEA did everything they could to find and destroy the infrastructure of the drug industry. The problem here was that the industry they sought to destroy was far more resilient than anyone had suspected. While inroads had been made into the drug industry, the efforts by the 11th Air Assault against it were proving to be of little consequence, especially since the drug cartel had become, shortly after the coup and the resurgence of the FARC threat, the main supporter in Colombia of the ruling government. That Lane or anyone else in the military chain of command, not to mention the DEA or CIA, failed to appreciate this, was understandable.

That, however, only accounted for a small part of the problem facing the 11th Air Assault. Its biggest problem was internal. For it was becoming more and more obvious to the American media, as they freely roamed the battlefield and spoke to soldiers who were being worn thin by operations that never seemed to end, that they weren't accomplishing anything. That the mission of the 11th was not to win the war but just to keep the FARC from doing so until the Colombian Army was ready to resume its own burden had been lost to both the media and the general public as American men and women killed in the line of duty started coming home in body bags.

General Fulk, the Chief of Staff of the Army, decided that to allow the impression that the Army was wasting men and money in pursuit of a hopeless cause was not only inexcusable but detrimental to the American Army as a whole. Which was why Dixon found himself standing in the middle of a dirt runway on a hot September morning in Colombia. Fulk was tired of overoptimistic reports and muffled responses, coupled with statistics that showed that American casualties were on the rise. That was why he dispatched Scott Dixon down to Colombia to look at the situation for him. General Fulk's only instructions to Dixon were 'Scotty, I don't want any goddamned Vietnams on our own watch. Go down there, find out what is going on, figure out what we need to do to fix it, and report back to me, ASAP.'

There was silence for several seconds while both Cerro and Kozak waited for Dixon to continue. Finally Dixon, looking over at the troops, spoke. 'Well, regardless of

where you're going, I'm going. After all, how would it
look if I spent two months without ever getting my boots
dirty.' Turning back to Cerro, he added, 'Provided you
have room.'

Cerro, relieved that the subject had been changed,
turned to Kozak. 'Well unfortunately every seat on my
aircraft is taken. But I'm sure Captain Kozak can find an
open seat with the second wave.'

Dixon leaned over toward Kozak. As she was looking
over a listing on the manifest, he whispered so that Cerro
could hear, 'Correction to that last transmission, Captain.
First wave. Your boss's last message should have read first
wave, not second.'

Kozak grinned as she looked up at Cerro. Cerro rolled
his eyes. 'I stand corrected. First wave.'

Nodding her head in acknowledgment, Kozak looked
down the listing of helicopters and the number of troops,
referred to as paks, assigned to each one in the first
wave. Finding what she was looking for, Kozak called
out her answer without thinking. 'The fifth aircraft has
two open slots.'

'Perfect!' Dixon exclaimed. 'More than enough room
for a general officer and his ego.'

While Cerro laughed, Kozak frowned when she saw
that the fifth aircraft was the same one Second Lieutenant
Horan was on. Fearing that putting Dixon in the same load
as Horan might unhinge the young officer further, she was
about to recommend another aircraft when the sound of
numerous inbound helicopters broke the morning stillness.
In unison, Dixon, Cerro, and Kozak turned toward the
sound. 'Well, General, looks like show time. I'll take you
over to where you need to go while Captain Kozak trots
on over to the command group and notifies Brigade we're
on the way.'

Without another word, both Cerro and Dixon turned
and began to walk away, leaving Kozak to look over

to where Horan was standing, then at the approaching aircraft. This was going to be a simple raid, Kozak reasoned, a good first mission for him. There really wasn't any reason to make a big deal over where the general sat or whether or not Horan was ready to go on an operation. General Dixon was never one to make a big to-do about protocol. If he said riding with the Second Platoon was fine by him, he meant it. And if this indeed was a simple anti-cartel raid, then an easy operation would be perfect for Horan's initiation. Nodding, Kozak pushed her concerns about Horan's and Dixon's presence aside as she headed down the line of troops back to where the command group was beginning to stir. There were other things she needed to deal with that were critical to the success of this operation, and they had nothing to do with general officers or second lieutenants.

Kozak had just begun to turn her full attention to the operation that was about to begin when she suddenly turned around to face the incoming helicopters. Perhaps, she thought, AJ was flying one of them. The idea of seeing AJ, regardless of how briefly, was never far from Kozak's mind these days and always managed to soften a face that was becoming too old too fast from holding up a burden that had broken lesser people. Only the shouts of sergeants and officers rousing their men from their slumber broke Kozak's concentration, pulling her mind away from her forlorn hope and back to the task at hand. With a sigh, Kozak turned once more toward the waiting command group and began to make her way toward them. Still, every few feet she slowed and glanced over her shoulder, looking and hoping.

CHAPTER 2

September 21

The soldiers of the 3rd Battalion, 511th Infantry, weren't the only combat troops waiting to get on with it that morning. Nor were Nancy Kozak and the officers of that battalion the only leaders chafing at the unexpected delay in the operation.

Not far from the Cauca River, near a level patch of ground that broke up the steep slopes that rose from the riverbed, Hector Valendez looked at his watch, then scanned the skies. The Americans were late. According to his calculations, they should have been here a long time ago. Though recent experience showed that this was becoming more the norm rather than the exception, the uncomfortable delay was not welcome. There was too much at stake here, too much time and energy invested in this operation to have it compromised by simple ineptitude.

Turning his head this way and then that, Valendez debated what he should do while he waited. The idea of sitting there in the cramped confines of his covered observation bunker, which was nothing more than a small scooped-out hollow with heavy overhead cover in the side of the mountain, was not appealing. He could, he knew, leave its relative safety and concealment and walk among the waiting soldiers of the Revolutionary Armed Forces of Colombia one more time. As with Cerro and Kozak, the unwelcome idleness weighed heavy on Valendez. He found the gap of time that existed between his final instructions and the commencement of a battle intolerable.

This feeling, Valendez knew, was not uncommon. He had first become aware of it as a problem for commanders when he had read Clausewitz's book *On War*. The passage in that book left little impression on Valendez at the time he had read it. Only later, as he himself became involved in military operations and rapidly moved up the chain of command within the FARC, did Valendez begin to appreciate what Clausewitz had been saying. Understanding of a problem, however, is only the beginning. Even now, though he knew that it was impossible to change anything, Valendez found himself fighting the urge to get up, go out, and do something. What that something was didn't matter.

But he didn't. Instead, he sat there looking out over a landscape that had in the past few days become as familiar to him as the garden of his former home in Bogotá that he had once tended with such care and love. In an effort to turn his mind away from the fears and apprehensions that were nagging him, Valendez carefully analyzed his own thoughts, an ability that made Valendez unique among the leadership of the FARC. He knew that all he was interested in doing was occupying his mind. A diversion, he decided, was what he needed. It didn't matter what it was. Just something to fill the time and keep his mind busy until the Yankees arrived. Behind him he noticed that the deputy company commander who shared the bunker with him was becoming impatient. 'You are anxious, my friend?'

The young man nodded. 'Yes, Jefe. I was just wondering whether the crew of the number-two machine gun finished clearing that brush in front of their position as you told them. Do you think there is time to go down there and see if it was done?'

Though that thought was at that moment rather seductive, Valendez knew that his tromping about would cause his men to become more nervous than they already were. And the last thing that Valendez wanted to do was rattle his soldiers. 'No, my young friend. Little would be gained from going out now other than perhaps betraying our own positions, or maybe getting caught in the open. Best we stay here.' Still, as he turned away from the nervous deputy commander, the urge to leave continued to be overpowering. He did not like the confinement of his observation post. Only the steel nerves that had led Valendez to this place kept him where he was.

That and of course American technology. After all, there was no telling when the helicopter gunships equipped with their all-seeing thermal sights would make their final sweep of the area before the troop-carrying helicopters came in. Of all the problems that Valendez faced, dealing with American technology was for him the most difficult. Though the FARC had sufficient funds with which to tap into the vast arsenals of the former Soviet Union, his force was and always would be a light force that had to rely on man-portable systems. That left them with few options other than ingenuity and cunning with which to counter the mobility, agility, and technology of the Yankees.

Not that this bothered Valendez. After all, he reasoned, the Yankees had often held the upper hand in weapons and technology and had more than once been embarrassed by a smaller force that had something that technology could not replace – determination. That and a blind belief in their cause were the primary tools that propelled not only Valendez's soldiers but Valendez himself. He was in fact becoming to many the personification of the movement.

From behind him he could feel the presence of someone else very close. Glancing over his shoulder, he noticed it was Rafael Dario, his radioman. Like the deputy company commander, he was becoming impatient. 'Jefe, I was wondering are we ready for this?'

Valendez liked Dario. A young man not much different in age than the deputy company commander, Dario had become more than a radioman. He was his traveling partner, orderly, bodyguard, and at times like this a friend. Dario in turn looked up to and admired Valendez, seeing in him more than a military commander. 'Well, Rafael, while it is true that the magnitude of what we are about to do dwarfs anything that the FARC has tried before, we can do it. After all, every man out there is a well-trained, hand-picked volunteer. For months now I have been telling those people in the central committee that it was time that we had the courage of our convictions. It is time for the FARC to come out of the shadows and start to apply pressure directly on the Yankees.'

Valendez paused. To get to where they were now he had been forced to argue, sometimes quite strongly, to convince the rather conservative members of the FARC's ruling council that he was right. Finally after repeated efforts he had prevailed. No one in the end could seem to refute his arguments or his record of successes that belied his background and amateur status as a soldier.

For Valendez was by nature an intellectual, a man who had once been content to spend his days in the confined spaces of the classroom. At five feet, six inches, with dark hair and a pinched face that accentuated his lean, almost skeletal frame, Valendez looked like a schoolteacher. And for years that was exactly what he had done and had for the most part been content to do. Since joining the FARC, however, Valendez had found the experience of living in the jungles and mountains of Colombia among the people both enjoyable and liberating. Out here, free of the trappings of civilization, the restrictions of a man-made world, and a self-deluding society, Valendez found himself closer to the idealized world that his favorite philosopher, Karl Marx, had written so much about. He had quickly, with the drive of a zealot but the disciplined mind of an intellectual, found his place in the world.

Pushing through these idle thoughts one more time, Valendez again felt the need to suppress his nervousness. Finally resigning himself to the idleness resulting from the failure of the Yankees to adhere to their own schedule, Valendez moved over to the corner of the dugout and sat down on an empty ammo box. Folding his arms across his chest, he lowered his head and tried to close his eyes.

Following him, Dario asked if he would like some warm coffee. Without looking at him, Valendez shook his head. 'No, not right now. If I drink anything else, my bladder will burst, and that,' he said with a chuckle, 'would be quite embarrassing in battle.'

Turning his mind back to the pending battle, Valendez thought about doing what he had just told the deputy company commander he didn't want him to do. There was no point in going out into the open again. All had been set and ready since dawn. Nothing had changed. The soldiers of the provisional company that he had helped to train and the night before to emplace about the perimeter of the plateau jutting from the mountainside were ready. None had moved. He knew that. None needed to be reminded of their individual and collective tasks, for they had been well briefed and rehearsed in them by him and their company commander. All was set. All was ready. There was nothing useful that he could do but wait quietly and patiently for the Americans to come. For the moment they held the initiative, they set the time. But Valendez, the deputy military leader of the Revolutionary

Armed Forces of Colombia, was determined to change all of that today.

One of the runners, new to this company, looked over to where Valendez sat. He was a farmer, or more correctly, the son of a farmer, who had left home and joined the FARC. Though he wanted to be a fighter like his brother, he had been assigned to this company as a runner. While he didn't much care for that duty, it did have certain advantages, including meeting men like Valendez. Screwing up his nerve, he began to speak in a faltering voice. 'Jefe?'

Valendez looked over at the young man. He was still not very comfortable with the title El Jefe, which meant leader. Not that it wasn't deserved. At age thirty-seven Hector Valendez had become in a shockingly short time a very powerful figure within the FARC. It was just that he hadn't set out to become El Jefe. 'Yes, my young friend. Is there something you need?'

'I have been told, Jefe, that you had been a professor at the university in Bogotá, and that when you left, instead of becoming an officer, you chose to be a common fighter, like I wanted to be. Why?'

'Yes, it is true. I was a professor of economics at the university, with a strong interest in military history, a hobby.'

'That hobby,' Dario said with a smirk, 'has cost the government in Bogotá dearly these last few months.'

Valendez looked up at his radioman and smiled. 'Yes, well now that hobby has become my vocation. You see, though I had been successful and well liked at the university, I, like many thinking men such as you, became more and more disheartened by what I saw. In my case it was class after class of students, bright with the flame of social and economic reform while sitting in my classroom, who within a matter of years after graduating forgot those ideals. Instead they became a part of the system, which is corrupt, heartless, and socially depraved.'

A student of Karl Marx, a man he felt who was badly misunderstood, Valendez had chosen to combine the study of economics with history. In the classroom he had endeavored to lead his students, through the use of well-documented historical failures, to discover not only what had worked and what had succeeded in the combination of economics and society, but why. He had hoped since his early days as a student himself to be part of a peaceful revolution from within the system by enlightening and stirring the social conscience of the children of the privileged class themselves. But the students, when freed from the confines of the classroom, were mesmerized by the benefits and luxuries of power and money that their fathers commanded and defended. In their transformation he saw his dream of using education as the key to the salvation for the people of Colombia slowly wither and die. Discouraged, Valendez walked out of his classroom at the university on his thirty-fourth birthday and went into the jungle, where he offered his services to the Revolutionary Armed Forces of Colombia as a rifleman.

'My choice to become a soldier pitted against the establishment does not come from any deep desire to save our people or to change their fate. I have already tried that and failed. Instead, in the beginning all I wanted to do was to destroy those who had destroyed my dream. I left the university with an overwhelming belief that I had been betrayed. In my eyes I had been betrayed by a system that preached that there was a future for our people when there was none. We have all of us been betrayed by the realization that our dream of true social and economic change was merely a shimmering mirage, not a vision, held out by men who only want to line their pockets with money earned though our labors. And I felt betrayed by students I had hoped would become the agents of social and economic change but who instead used their education to reinforce the bands that bound an oppressive system together.' Slapping his knee to add emphasis to his point he concluded his impromptu speech. 'So it was the destruction of what was, and not an effort to work for what could be, that drove me to want to be a fighter.'

Looking about the bunker, he saw that everyone was watching him, mesmerized by his explanation. Not wanting to leave things there, he looked down, bringing his hands together. When he spoke again his voice was calm, softer. 'In the process of seeking to destroy, I was reminded that when destructive forces are given free rein, darkness enshrouds everything that it touches. From being a man of enlightenment working for true social reform for a system he believed in, I found myself becoming the foremost agent of the forces that threatened that system's very existence. Though I, in truth, do not really relish the notion of being known only for my powers to destroy, if that is what is necessary to bring the criminals who rule this country to justice, then so be it.'

While the men gathered in the small bunker looked at him and each other, Valendez reflected upon his climb to power within the FARC. It had been his talents as a military strategist and trainer, together with his burning desire to lash out, at times with an abandon that was both blind and total, that had caught the attention of the FARC leaders. When they attempted to direct Valendez's fury, they found there was more to him than they had at first thought. Upon closer examination of this new and fanatical fighter, every leader that came in contact with Valendez found he commanded a useful wealth of military knowledge that he wielded like a weapon. Coupled with the disciplined and logical mind of a teacher of economics and the skills of a professional teacher, his hobby propelled Valendez into the inner circles of the

FARC military command at a time when new problems and issues demanded new answers, answers that Valendez seemed to have.

He was quickly elevated to the position of squad leader, then deputy company commander, where his unique ability to combine the realities of his country and its people with his vast pool of military knowledge brought life to a military revolution that had for years been little more than an annoyance to the Colombian government. Though he was politically naive, none of the old-line leaders of the FARC could find fault with Valendez's methods or the results those methods yielded. He was, they thought, an important tool that with a little guidance could be very useful.

Somewhere during this almost meteoric climb the man was transformed. As praise and promotions were heaped upon him, Valendez came to the realization that he had never been mistaken about the revolution or his need to be part of it. The only error he had made had been a choice of means with which to pursue his goals. Now that he was on the right track, there was no stopping him. With the enthusiasm of a lost soul who had finally seen the light, Valendez redoubled his studies of military history while throwing himself into every task and assignment he was handed. So it came to pass that after much debate among those who made up the ruling council Valendez was recalled from the FARC's training base in Venezuela, where he had been serving as an instructor, back to Colombia, where he became the deputy and chief adviser to the FARC's military chief.

The debating did not stop with Valendez's appointment to such an important position. In fact that debate was only the beginning. For, once back in Colombia, Valendez moved the FARC's military campaign against the Colombian government forward with all the drive and energy that he could muster. Such drive, long absent in an organization that had grown old and set in its ways, caused concern among the more conservative members of the ruling council. Everything that Valendez did was aimed at one thing and one thing only: pulling down the Colombian government. He gave little thought these days to what would happen after that. 'Those were issues,' he told close associates, 'best left to those with a knack for dealing with the trivialities of politics.' While such statements might have been sincere, they did nothing to endear Valendez to many of the old-timers who wanted a country left after the revolution.

So it was, when Valendez pushed his boss into presenting to the central committee of the FARC his long-range plan for discrediting the Colombian government, that a major crisis erupted. Though the nominal head of the military arm of the FARC mouthed the words, few listening doubted that Valendez had been their author. 'We have been presented a unique opportunity,' the preamble of the paper stated, 'with the involvement of American forces in Colombia. For us the conditions and the terms dictating their use could not be more favorable. First, the number of combat units and their support troops have an upper limit which the American President dare not exceed. Second, their commitment is also limited in duration and is not contingent on either the internal conditions or events in Colombia. Repeated assurances by the American President and a pledge by the American Congress to hold him to this deadline leaves us little fear of a protracted conflict with the Americans. Third, the Colombian military recovery is being hamstrung by relatively low-ranking officers who were not purged by the government after the aborted military coup and in secret are looking for an opportunity to exact revenge for the injustice of the government when it decimated the ranks of the Army's officers corps.'

At home before a group, Valendez's mastery of oral

presentation and his ability to draw his listeners into his way of thinking made him a powerful force to be dealt with. Even the hard-core members of the central committee were just so much clay in his hands as he molded their thoughts with the skill of an artisan. 'This feeling, never far below the surface, is manifesting itself in many ways, in particular the reluctance of the officers of those units ready for field operations to use those forces against us, preferring to save their manpower for what they feel is the inevitable showdown with the government. Finally, the American media, as they invariably do, have followed American forces into Colombia and provide us with a source of propaganda which we could never muster ourselves. By drawing the American forces into heavy engagements that produce casualties which cannot be hidden by the American military high command, we will be given a spotlight into which we can present our case to the world and at the same time mobilize the anti-government sentiment that has been simmering below the surface of our country for years.'

The plan, or more correctly the campaign, that Valendez presented to the council through his superior was hotly debated. While everyone had an opinion, no one had a good counter to the campaign. It seemed that the FARC, which had worked to overthrow the Colombian government for years, was finally being handed a set of circumstances and a plan designed to exploit those circumstances. In the end those with wise and cool heads recognized that they had become too accustomed to defeat, failure, and fear. It was time perhaps, they reasoned, to take big risks. And Valendez's plan was certainly a big risk. When the decision was made to give Valendez his way, the vote was unanimous, though for many different reasons. While there were those on the ruling council who felt that Valendez might be right, there were those who knew he was wrong or who simply feared him. The failure of such a high-risk and costly plan, they reasoned, would allow them the opportunity to do away with this upstart. They had without saying so told Valendez that it would be for him victory or death.

Slowly he shifted his weight as he sat on the ammo box and looked toward the small aperture of his dugout, listening for the telltale signs of American helicopters. Valendez could almost feel the cold invisible hand of the ruling council on his shoulder. This operation, though only the first of what he expected to be many, would make or break him and, he believed, the future of the revolution.

Sitting next to the open door, Dixon tried to occupy his mind by looking down at the landscape as it flew by him. Though he worked hard at studying the terrain, his mind was cluttered with self-recriminations and admonishments. It had been a mistake, he realized minutes after lifting off, to have come along with the lead element of Cerro's assault force. The idea that he was a general officer now, a rank that is surrounded by a mystique and aura that few understand but most are intimidated by, had not hit him until then. Even the platoon sergeant, who had seated himself next to Dixon so that one of his soldiers didn't wind up in the hot seat, couldn't ignore Dixon. General officers, after all, are the closest things to a god that most soldiers ever come to know, and gods, as we all know, are seldom friendly folk.

Often generals appear to move about without their feet touching the ground. The mere mention that a general officer might be in the area is often enough to send every officer and noncommissioned officer into a low hover. It is, after all, seldom a simple task to prepare for the divine visit. This feeling that general officers are demigods is not without foundation in reality. The fact of the matter is that generals, because of their position and their ability to make decisions that can only be overridden by bigger generals, have in their hands the power of life and death. Every soldier knows this. It is ultimately the generals who decide who will go where and when. It is the generals who give the orders to close with the enemy and decide when to pull back. While staff officers may draft the orders of battle and more junior officers lead their men and women into combat, the person who like a Roman emperor sits on the sidelines and gives the modern American gladiator the thumb up or the thumb down is without exception a general.

It wasn't that any of this was new to Dixon. He too had once gazed upon generals with that same spellbound look of awe that the young second lieutenant catty-corner from him now viewed Dixon. From the reaction that he had received, Dixon imagined that the soldiers of this rifle squad would have preferred having an alien from another world travel with them than a general. It wasn't that Dixon hadn't been warned. Even before he went to the special course for newly promoted general officers dubbed the charm school, Dixon had been watching, listening, and thinking about how generals acted and what sort of response those actions created. In a sort of naive way, Dixon had been able to convince himself that when his time came, if the gods in power smiled upon him and chose him to join their ranks, he wouldn't act any different as a general than he had as a captain, major, or lieutenant colonel. Before Jan Fields-Dixon and General Fulk had pinned the single star of brigadier general onto Dixon's shoulders, he had been able to believe that he could do so. And even after that landmark event, an occasion that had reminded Jan more of a religious ceremony than a civil procedure, Dixon had been able to continue to act as if the star he wore hadn't changed anything.

But that had been in the Pentagon, a place where one's value is measured by the number of stars one wore or in the case of mere mortals the number of stars one's boss wore. Until General Fulk had sent Dixon to Colombia in an effort to figure out what was going on down there, Dixon had not had the occasion to be with soldiers, real soldiers, as a general. Only after he had boarded the helicopter he now rode in and introduced himself to the squad he would be traveling with did it hit him that he was no longer one of them, a simple soldier. In the past he had always been able to move about and conduct himself in a manner that put those around him at ease and allowed his abilities and personality to transcend rank and position. The glaring sheen from his general's star, even the single black subdued star he wore on each collar of his battle dress uniform, however, now blinded the soldiers he was traveling with. They could not see Dixon as a man. They could not even see him as a fellow soldier. All they could see was a general, a person who had sent them there and in their minds had the power to take them away from this hell on earth. None of them could imagine that Dixon was as nervous as the rest of them as they drew near the landing zone. None of them even considered Dixon vulnerable to the same dangers and hazards that threatened their lives. He was, after all, a god.

A tap on his shoulder caused Dixon to look away from the lush green and red of the Colombian landscape. It was the crew chief. He was reaching over the heads of the soldiers across from Dixon and holding up two fingers. Over the whine of the engine Dixon could barely make out the words he repeated, 'Two minutes, two minutes.' They were two minutes from the landing zone. Nodding that he understood, Dixon looked down to check his personal gear, what little he had, without thinking that the crew chief, like the other soldiers on the helicopter, was so conscious of Dixon's presence that he made a special effort to tell Dixon first of their approach before informing the rifle squad Dixon was traveling with. They were, after all, just riflemen. Dixon was a general.

*   *   *

Even before Hector Valendez's radioman could say, 'They're here!' the whine and sudden rush of noise and wind created by a scout helicopter flying low and fast over Valendez's dugout told him battle was about to be joined. At first Valendez simply looked up, first at his radioman, then past him at the blinding daylight that streamed through the aperture of his dugout. For a second it seemed as if Valendez was frozen in place, unable to move. In truth he was briefly overcome by the significance of the moment. All the planning and preparation that he had put into this operation was about to be put to the test. Everything that he had worked for since joining the FARC, from the hardening of his own heart, body, and mind to the demanding training he had run his specially recruited companies through, was about to be tested. Everything, including the future of the revolution, was about to be risked in battle, one that would pit two dissimilar forces, each led by dynamic, thinking humans, against each other.

Standing up as best he could in the cramped confines of the dugout, Valendez moved over to the aperture. Without a word passing between them, the radioman stepped aside and allowed Valendez full use of the aperture. Valendez, after all, was the deputy military commander for all of the FARC. Though he lived with his soldiers, eating the same food at a common table in camp, sharing the hardships and burdens of long marches and demanding training, Valendez's position demanded respect and along with that a deference by subordinates that was never demanded but always shown.

From the narrow aperture Valendez could see two small scout helicopters buzzing about both the landing zone and the camouflaged arms-cache site like dragonflies searching a pond for prey. The scouts, themselves armed to the teeth, were in fact doing just that. They were looking for trouble, becoming bolder by the minute as nothing below them moved or showed any sign of responding to their presence. They had, Valendez knew, been sitting several kilometers away for some time watching for signs of his forces. Only when they were satisfied that there was no apparent danger did the scouts come charging in at treetop level in an effort to stir a reaction. Even this seemingly foolish move was not made without the presence of attack helicopters hovering off in the distance watching and waiting to intervene if necessary. Now, as Valendez watched, the scouts slowed down and began to circle areas where they feared the enemy might be hiding. With no outward show of fear or concern, Valendez watched as the helicopters flitted about from one place to another, turning this way then that as they made sure all was clear for the troop-carrying helicopters.

To his radioman, the deputy company commander, and the two runners that shared the dugout with Valendez, his calm demeanor was almost unnerving. They of course did not realize that he, like them, had his own fears. Unlike them, however, his were not of death, something that he had often wished for after he had thought himself a failure as a revolutionary at the university. Rather, his greatest fear was that his plan would not yield its desired results. He wanted to smash things, to destroy. After years of patiently trying to work within the system in order to reform it and seeing all of his efforts come to nought, he had resolved that he would spend the rest of his life if necessary trying to level that system. Destruction, complete and utter destruction, was his chosen tool now. And today his target, a mere stepping-stone to his goal, was the Yankees, the Yankees who belonged to the 3rd Battalion, 511th Infantry.

After the long and uneventful flight from the base camp to the LZ over the peaceful countryside, the sudden rush of events at the landing zone came on like a blur. Because he was sitting at the door, Dixon would be the first out on his side. To make sure that he didn't embarrass himself or slow things down by trying to exit the aircraft with his seat belt still on, Dixon undid his seat belt long before the wheels of the UH-60 helicopter even got near the ground. This response was not an imaginary fear. Dixon had, in the rush of events, tried to get up and out of a helicopter without undoing the seat belt a few times too many.

With that out of the way and prepared to spring up and out, he was still careful to hang on to the frame of the seat just in case the pilot made a sudden turn. Watching, Dixon saw the ground draw near as the helicopter coming in at a steep angle prepared to land. It was almost as if the ground itself was rising to greet them. As he braced himself for action, Dixon considered drawing his pistol, but then decided not to. That, he decided, would be a little too melodramatic even for him. All he waited for now was the thump of the wheels digging into the dirt to cue him and he would be gone.

The riflemen he was traveling with, however, weren't waiting for that. From behind him, Dixon heard the platoon sergeant yell, as much for Dixon's benefit as for his troopers, 'EVERYONE OUT. NOW!'

Without so much as a pause, the platoon sergeant got Dixon moving and out the door with a nudge that was more of a shove before Dixon even had a chance to determine how far off the ground they still were. It was a good thing that he hadn't, for had he seen how high they were when the troops started exiting, Dixon probably would have stiffened up and really hurt himself after falling six feet from the helicopter to the ground.

Almost before he realized what was happening, it was all over. In a blur he went tumbling out of the helicopter, hit the ground, and instinctively allowed his body to collapse as he had learned a long time ago at airborne school.

Though his intent was good, Dixon's form was terrible. Even before he stopped rolling, he knew that he had hurt and bruised at least a half a dozen spots on his body and would no doubt find more after he had time to think about it.

But there was no time to think about his personal injuries or anything else for that matter. The riflemen he had been traveling with, used to this kind of punishment, had already scampered past where Dixon still lay on the ground. Propping himself up on an elbow, he watched his traveling companions clear the landing zone and disappear into the waist-high brush and bushes that surrounded it to begin the process of deploying into a rough perimeter. Only the young lieutenant paused long enough to ask Dixon if he was all right, and even then he kept one eye on his platoon sergeant lest he lose track of the one man in his platoon who knew what he was doing.

Dixon, still too stunned to say anything, just waved the lieutenant on. By the time he had managed to get himself onto his feet and headed for the brush, the helicopters had already disappeared. The whine of their engines, now barely audible, had been replaced by the shouts and orders of officers and sergeants as they got their troops in hand and ready to move on. Off to his left, Dixon heard Cerro's clear and distinct voice driving on the company commander of the assault force. Officers and sergeants hearing Cerro didn't wait for their company commander to relay the order. They immediately redoubled their efforts and, trusting that their riflemen would follow, plunged forward into the brush and toward the arms cache.

As he watched, a silly thought popped into Valendez's head. As effortlessly as a cooling breeze it quickly replaced the nervous apprehension that he had felt earlier. While he stood there watching American troops sweep through the dummy arms cache a few hundred meters below them, the strange and silly vision pushed aside Valendez's conscious thoughts and removed him from that time and place. Rather than viewing the Yankee riflemen moving forward by short rushes and bounds from the lee of one covered spot to the next with concern or foreboding, Valendez's mind drifted back to his childhood.

For several moments Valendez felt the same giddy feeling that he would get when playing hide-and-seek with his brothers. It was, he remembered, such an exquisite feeling knowing that all your searching for the right spot, efforts at burrowing yourself into place just so, and supreme patience were about to pay off. He could tell as a child when he had his brothers dead to rights. He could tell by the look of concern that would creep upon his brothers' faces, a look that was poorly masked by a stern and falsely confident expression. When he saw that look, Valendez's own excitement would multiply. He would almost jump up and down with joy, knowing that regardless of what his brothers did he, Valendez, would win.

As important as the selection of the site and his patience had been, however, Valendez knew that timing was everything, both in the past when playing with his brothers and now as he prepared to kill Yankees. As a child he had learned that if he timed it right, he would be able to scare the devil out of his brothers, causing them such confusion and shock that he would be able to do anything he wanted for seconds, sometimes minutes, before his brothers would be able to recover sufficiently to react and make him pay for his trickery.

As he struggled to restore clear and conscious thinking, Valendez realized that what he and his soldiers were doing was nothing more than a grown-up game of hide-and-seek! They were playing now the same games that he and his brothers had played when they had been children. This action today, Valendez knew, would be no different. When he and his soldiers sprang their ambush, there would be a period where Valendez would be in control. How long that period would last Valendez did not know. He was prepared, as were his men, to wait until sundown before breaking and running, if they could last that long. But that, Valendez knew, was only one possibility. If the Yankees were well led, resolute, and able to quickly regain their balance and bring their overwhelming firepower to bear effectively, then Valendez and his men would need to break off the action sooner. For Valendez knew that, as terrible as the initial results of the ambush would be, psychologically as well as physically, the impact of fighting a hard battle that had been costly in lives would be greater if at the end of the fight the Yankees had few or no enemy bodies to drag before the cameras of the world and display like so many trophies. To bleed without having the opportunity to draw an equal or greater amount of blood was to a soldier a defeat of the worst kind.

Slowly the images of his childhood began to fade back into the recesses of his mind. Before they disappeared completely, Valendez the university professor wondered if the games he had learned as a child such as hide-and-seek had been nothing more than preparation for adulthood, or if what he, his soldiers, and the Yankees were doing at this very moment was simply an extension of childhood games. As interesting as this philosophical question was, Valendez realized that this was no time to deal with it. Leaning forward, he began to watch for the mystical cue he had used so well as a child, the subtle cue that would tell him it was time to initiate the firefight. That – and the need to start dealing with the next problem that he, the leader of his men, El Jefe, would need to address, which was deciding when they had done enough killing for the day – wiped the last vestiges of childhood memories from his mind.

The anger that Dixon felt over his treatment at the landing

zone was finally beginning to subside when they stumbled upon the arms cache. While there had been a high level of tension as Cerro's lead company moved from the landing zone to where they were now, that tension seemed to redouble itself, almost becoming a real and tangible commodity that Dixon imagined he could touch as the squad he traveled with began to move in between the camouflaged huts and sheds. Hanging back ten to fifteen meters, Dixon conformed as best as he could to the movements of the rifleman to his front. As he did so, the fact that he didn't have a weapon worth mentioning other than his holstered pistol heightened Dixon's anxiety and nervousness. Not wanting to get in the way and wanting to create the smallest possible target, Dixon moved against a tree at the edge of the arms cache site and eased himself into a squatting position.

Effortlessly the riflemen of Cerro's battalion changed from the formation they had used during the approach march to the site of the arms cache into one that allowed them to begin the methodical process of clearing and securing it. From where he sat, Dixon could only see a relatively small number of people. But what he saw pleased him. Few commands were given. There was no need to. The soldiers were well trained and often anticipated the command before the squad leader or the platoon sergeant gave the order either by word or with a simple signal. Automatic riflemen eased into positions that afforded them the best field of vision and fire. Riflemen designated to lead off were up and moving forward without hesitation or confusion, headed for positions they had already selected that would allow them to cover the next group of soldiers to advance.

Here and there Dixon could tell who the leaders were by the manner in which they moved and acted. He could also tell which ones were new to all of this, like Second Lieutenant Horan, the young officer he had traveled with who had been so unnerved during the flight. Horan, Dixon concluded, was doing no better down here on the ground than he had in the helicopter. Though he was going through the motions no doubt just the way he had been taught at Fort Benning, Horan was always one or two steps behind his platoon sergeant, Sergeant First Class Banks, in thinking and acting. At least, Dixon thought as he watched Horan move up to Banks and hold a hushed conversation before issuing his next order, Horan had the common sense to use Banks's talents and experience.

Now that the lead or point elements had penetrated well into the site and the troopers who had been giving them cover from the tree line were moving forward to new positions to cover further advances, Dixon pulled himself up from his squatting position, using the tree he had been next to for support. In the process of doing so he imagined that he could distinctly hear several bones and joints crack and pop. This, Dixon realized, was no longer an easy game to play at. Activities and motions that had come to him so easily as a junior officer and those being displayed by the sky troops before his very eyes were neither easy nor came naturally anymore. The idea that he could not make the one hundred and seventy-two pounds that his five-foot, ten-inch frame supported perform like it used to often bothered Dixon, especially at times like this. Perhaps, he thought as he finally managed to straighten himself out, Jan, his wife, was right. Perhaps it was time that Dixon stopped playing cowboys and Indians and let what she called the younger lads do all the fun stuff while he did the thinking.

Ready, Dixon followed the last of the troopers into the site, looking closely at the huts and lean-tos for the first time. Ignoring the sound of helicopters heralding the arrival of the next wave of Cerro's battalion, Dixon began to wander through the site barely keeping track of the squad he had traveled with. Slowly Dixon began to realize that the huts and lean-tos were not very impressive up close. Nor were they well laid out or camouflaged. That last item, he thought, goes without saying, for if this site had been well laid out and camouflaged, no one would have found it. Only small, seemingly insignificant errors or omissions that Dixon himself had been able to discern in the aerial photos had allowed the division intelligence officer working with the CIA to pinpoint the arms cache so quickly and accurately. It was, he thought, almost as if the FARC had wanted the 11th Air Assault Division to find this cache and come here. It was –

Like being hit in the face by a ball bat, the sudden realization of what was happening struck Dixon. Like a bird of prey's, his eyes darted from one item to the next as he quickly sought confirmation of his worst fears. There were no trails, no beaten paths leading from one hut to the next or through the site that men carrying arms would have left. There were no signs around that soldiers, even highly disciplined soldiers, would have left behind as they worked, such as discarded scraps of paper, cigarette butts, bits and pieces of equipment. And even in the lean-tos, stacked high with boxes that should have held weapons and ammunition, Dixon saw that the boxes were old and weathered, stacked in a rather indifferent manner, and had no tarps or plastic coverings to protect them from the cruel jungle humidity and rains. This site, this supposed arms cache, was bait designed to draw them in.

Realization of course is one thing. Doing something with that knowledge, however, is entirely different. Having come along on this operation on a whim and merely as an observer, Dixon really didn't fit into the chain of command. To simply yell out, 'AMBUSH,' at the tops of his lungs might cause more problems and confusion than the ambush itself. With that thought, Dixon looked for an officer who was in the chain of command. Unfortunately the first one that his eyes fell on was Second Lieutenant

Horan, a lad already overwhelmed by all of this. Rejecting that idea, Dixon next decided to find Cerro, Kozak, or the company commander. By going to them and working from the top down he could be sure that whatever Cerro's lead company did in the few seconds that it had left before the trap was sprung would be productive and orderly. At least that's what Dixon hoped as he turned and prepared to head for where he thought he would find the battalion command group.

For some reason Valendez had noticed the lone soldier wandering about the dummy arms cache behind the advancing line of Yankee infantrymen. This soldier, unarmed and unburdened by field pack or gear, struck Valendez as looking and acting different from the others. There was something special about him. His actions, his aloofness from the action, his detachment from the others all marked him as some kind of special observer. Though Valendez could not explain to himself why this special observer, whoever he was, wasn't traveling with the command group, a cluster of officers and radiomen he could clearly see gathering on the far side of a hut away from the lone soldier, Valendez suspected that this lone soldier was significant in some way. While keeping one wary eye on the command group as it milled about for a moment, with some officers talking on radios while others looked down at maps, Valendez studied every move the lone soldier made. He therefore was able to see the sudden reaction, the quick jerking of the lone soldier's head, and the rapidity with which he began to move toward the command group. Whoever this man was, he had, Valendez knew, figured out their game and was about to alert the others.

Taking a deep breath, Valendez began to give his orders as he continued to watch Scott Dixon. 'Let us begin with the mortars now, if you would, please.'

At once Valendez's radioman keyed the handset of his radio and called out, 'Eagle, commence firing. Eagle, commence firing.' With that the radioman released the push-to-talk button and waited. Over the earpiece of the handset, Eagle, the call sign for the leader of the mortar section, responded. 'Eagle acknowledges. Firing now.'

With that done, there was for the moment nothing that Valendez, the deputy company commander who stood next to him, or their radioman behind them could do but wait, watch, and pray.

The distinct thud of half a dozen mortar rounds being pushed out of their tubes broke the hushed stillness just as Dixon caught sight of Cerro talking on the radio. Both Cerro and Dixon, knowing the significance of the thuds, didn't try to determine where the noise came from. They knew that it would be a foolish waste of time. They therefore reacted appropriately by dropping to the ground and making themselves as small as was humanly possible. With few exceptions every soldier in or around the arms site did so, for they had been in Colombia long enough to have heard that terrible sound before. The only exceptions were the new troopers, the soldiers who had just joined the battalion and were, if they survived the stupidity of those who sent them into battle before they were ready and their own ignorance, about to become veterans.

CHAPTER 3

September 21

Even before the first mortar round slammed into the midst of the soldiers of Alpha Company at the arms-cache site, Charlie Company, still going through the motions of forming up in preparation for movement to the arms site, was engulfed in a withering fire that swept the landing zone and the area around it. The surprise was complete and the effects for a unit that had sustained less than a dozen casualties in its first six months in Colombia were devastating. Before the commander and soldiers of Charlie Company really understood what was going on, half a dozen of their number were hit, including the company commander himself.

Nancy Kozak, who had been talking to him just before the firing had started, had turned away looking toward the arms cache when she had heard the mortars being fired. When she realized what was happening, Kozak had spun her head around to order Terry Kaplin, the Charlie Company commander, to get his unit on the move fast. But Kaplin wasn't there. Bewildered, she looked to her left, then to her right. Only when she heard the gurgling sound of Kaplin as he tried to spit up the blood that filled his mouth did Kozak look down at her feet. Then it all hit at once. The sound of automatic weapons firing, the zing and snip of bullets cutting through the air and vegetation around her, and the screams of wounded soldiers shocked and panicked at being hit mingling with the shouts of officers and sergeants to get down and open fire.

Without any further conscious thought other than being careful to avoid falling on Kaplin, Kozak threw herself flat on the ground. For a moment she lay there pushing her face down into the mud that smelled of stagnant water and rotting vegetation and tried to overcome her own shock and surprise and collect her thoughts. The sound of Kaplin lying next to her drew her full attention. Turning her head to face him while keeping it down, Kozak was appalled by the sight that greeted her less than two feet away. Kaplin, lying face up, was arching the small of his back up while clawing at the empty sky with wild and disjointed motions. His eyes were all but popping out of their sockets, fixed in an unblinking look of panic and fear as he spit blood from his gaping mouth. To see a fellow officer, a man who was little more than a year younger than she, reduced to such a state in a matter of seconds was as unnerving at that moment as the sudden hail of gunfire had been. For what seemed like an eternity Kozak lay there and looked at Kaplin, mesmerized by the sight before her eyes. In those seconds there was no feeling of fear, no conscious thought. Only horror, a horror that almost paralyzed her mind and body.

That feeling, however, only lasted a moment. As quickly as it had overwhelmed her it was gone, replaced by a flurry of action as she pushed her body along the ground closer to Kaplin and began to look for the wound that had felled him. This task, given that she could not raise her head up off the ground for more than a few inches, was difficult.

The fact that Kaplin's face was intact and that he was spitting up blood ruled out a wound above the neck. That meant that he either had a chest wound, a stomach wound, or had been shot in the neck. Laying her rifle on the ground next to her, Kozak took one hand and began to feel Kaplin's abdomen and chest while she reached for Kaplin's throat with her other one.

As soon as her hand closed around Kaplin's neck, she knew she had found the wound. Ignoring the sticky warmth that coated her hand, Kozak felt for the actual site of penetration while feverishly working to free the compression bandage that hung on Kaplin's web belt with the hand she had been using to check his torso. The first small pouch she found and ripped open turned out to contain a compass, which fell out on the ground. Kozak ignored that and moved her hand further around the web belt until it came upon another small pouch that felt about the right size. Pulling the cover open, she found the plastic-encased bandage and pulled it out just as the fingertips on her other hand found the broken flesh on Kaplin's neck.

Working as fast as she could without fumbling, Kozak ripped the plastic pouch open with her teeth, pulled the bandage out with one hand, opened it up, and reached around with it until she had it over the wound her other hand had discovered. Quickly Kozak pulled the hand that had found the wound out of the way and pressed the bandage down over the wound. Using her bloodied but free hand, she slid it under Kaplin's neck. Once she had managed to reach all the way around the back of his neck, she put the hand over the top of the bandage and began to apply all the pressure on the wound that she could with both hands. Whether this would do any good was anyone's guess. It was all, however, that Kozak could do for Kaplin at the moment.

From behind her Kozak felt a slap on her thigh. Without

letting up on the pressure she was applying to Kaplin's wound, she turned her head to see who it was. It was, to no surprise, Sergeant Andy Pender, the assistant operations sergeant who was serving as her radiotelephone operator that day. Pender, his body pressed flat against the ground and his face showing no sign of fright, was holding the hand mike of the radio out toward Kozak. 'Captain, the old man's on the horn. He wants to know Charlie Company's status.'

Kozak was perplexed. Forgetting for the briefest of moments that her hands were wrapped around the Charlie Company commander's neck in an effort to keep his life from oozing away, Kozak shouted back, 'Hasn't anyone from Charlie reported in yet?'

In a matter-of-fact manner, one that appeared more suitable for a training exercise than close combat, Pender shook his head. 'I haven't heard anyone other than the colonel on the radio since the shit hit the fan, ma'am.'

Glancing back at Kaplin, whose eyes and expression showed no change, Kozak thought for a moment. Then she turned back to Pender. 'I can't let go of this bandage right now. Get yourself around here so you can keep pressure on this wound while I check in with the colonel.'

Ignoring Cerro's frantic call over the radio, Pender clipped the radio's hand mike to his web gear and began to crawl over Kozak's legs and around Kaplin's head. As he was doing so, Kozak lifted her head slightly so that she could look around. Cerro, she knew, would want to know what their situation was when she finally was able to talk to him. That she couldn't do so at the moment caused her to curse. She had become so involved in dealing with Kaplin's wound that she had lost track of everything around her. It would take her several seconds, all the time that it took Pender to complete his maneuver, to figure out that Charlie Company for the moment was leaderless and pinned in place, unable to move and barely returning fire at assailants that up to now had been unseen.

The ringing in Scott Dixon's ears caused by the detonation of a mortar round that impacted less than twenty meters to his right was quickly replaced by a piercing scream. For a moment Dixon, stunned by the suddenness of the attack, simply lay there wondering if he was the one producing the horrible scream. Slowly, ever so slowly, he managed to regain control of his senses by slowing his breathing and simply letting himself relax, despite the impact of a second volley of mortar rounds. As each sense came back into play, Dixon was able to start piecing together the scene around him.

Even as he worked at that, the one thought that began to dominate his still rattled brain was that he was stupid. It had been wrong for him to come along on this operation, to place himself in the middle of a combat unit without prior notice, and to add to the burden of a commander, one he had always held in high regard and had a special relationship with. As heroic as the image of a general officer out front with the troops might seem in a cheap novel, Dixon knew the Army hadn't made him a general so that he could go running about like a rank second lieutenant absorbing shrapnel and bullets.

The screaming, which had subsided only for a moment, started up again with a vengeance. Taking care to make sure that he didn't lift his head off the ground more than a few inches, Dixon turned his head toward the screaming. A few meters away, ten, maybe fifteen, to Dixon's right, a soldier lay on the ground flailing his arms and legs madly as his head jerked from side to side, screaming with all the strength he had left and throwing off sprays of blood from numerous wounds as he did so. The motion of his head jerking from one side to the other gave the scream a strange warbling effect like the siren on a police car. The sight of a small pillar of smoke rising lazily up from the ground a few feet from where the wounded soldier lay told Dixon that whoever the poor bastard was he had taken almost the full blast of a mortar round. Odds were, Dixon knew, there was little that he or anyone else for that matter would be able to do for the wounded man other than put him out of his misery. And that simply was not the way the Americans did things normally.

That the body Dixon was watching belonged to Private Andrew Hayman, newly assigned to the 3rd Battalion, 511th Infantry, meant nothing to Dixon. Hayman was, as far as Dixon was concerned, just another image of war that would burn itself into his brain, where it would wait patiently with all the others he had collected over the years until the quiet hours of some night. Then like other images and sights, the vision of Hayman's death throes would come back in all its fury to rob Dixon of his rest and sanity.

Turning his head away from Hayman, Dixon forced himself to think about something else, like getting out of the open and under cover. At first he thought about heading to where he had last seen Cerro and his command group. To do so, however, would have forced him to move across open ground to a spot that was even more exposed than the one he was in. Besides, as he surveyed the route he would need to take, Dixon noticed clods of earth being kicked up by concentrated machine-gun fire stitching its way this way and that. No, he decided. First things first. Get out of the open and then take it from there.

Looking to his left, he spotted two soldiers crouching behind a slight rise of ground thirty meters to his front left. One of the soldiers had a radio whip antenna sticking up out of his rucksack, a sure sign that the other had to be an officer or at least a senior sergeant. Without another thought Dixon slowly began to push himself forward toward the antenna. Even if one of the pair he was headed toward wasn't an officer or sergeant, the cover offered by an otherwise insignificant dirt mound was a lot more inviting than his present position. As if to drive that point home, a stream of bullets cut their way across his path, throwing dirt up into his face and into his eyes, blinding him and causing Dixon to flatten himself on the ground.

While Brigadier General Scott Dixon was wiping the dirt from his eyes and preparing to restart his long and arduous trip across the thirty meters that separated him from the mound of dirt and the antenna, Second Lieutenant Gerald T. Horan finally began to look around. The only person he saw at first was his radioman next to him. Everyone else in his platoon it seemed had disappeared. Shaken by his first taste of combat, his current predicament further unnerved him. Were he and his radioman, Horan wondered, the only survivors of his platoon? Had the jarring mortar barrage and the ceaseless hail of small-arms fire killed everyone? Though commissioned and trained as an infantry officer, Horan suddenly found himself in a position that he realized he was not ready to deal with. Fortunately, he thought, he had his platoon sergeant. He'd be able to get a handle on this mess and give him, Horan, a chance to sort himself out.

As suddenly as that thought came to mind, Horan flashed back to his original thought: Is everyone else dead? As if to answer his question, the screams of Private Andrew Hayman caused Horan to look out across the open ground behind him. Immediately behind him he saw one soldier lying flat on the ground busily rubbing his eyes. Though exposed, this figure didn't appear to be in serious distress. Not far from him, Horan saw Hayman, still thrashing about madly, though not as much as he had been when Dixon had first set eyes on him. Even from where he lay, Horan could see that Hayman was severely

wounded and needed assistance. For a second all thoughts
of his platoon were pushed aside as Horan lifted his head
higher off the ground and began to yell, 'MEDIC,' just
as he had seen it done in dozens of war movies. Though
he had no idea who the wounded man was, he was an
American soldier who needed help.

Though many heard Horan's call for assistance, only
one man responded. Noticing a head pop up from behind a
mound of dirt, followed by yells that he didn't understand,
the gunner behind a Russian-made PKM machine gun
shifted the barrel slightly to his right, made a quick
estimate of the range, tilted the barrel down slightly as
he had been taught, then pulled the trigger.

While not every round fired by the FARC gunner
found its mark, and the flak jacket and kevlar helmet
that Second Lieutenant Horan wore deflected or absorbed
most, enough found exposed portions of Horan's upper
torso and head to do the job. Watching from where he
lay, Horan's radioman found watching the death of his
lieutenant both fascinating and horrifying. As he watched,
the impact of bullets fired from very close range kept
Horan's body propped up. It was almost as if they were
working together, the first bullets holding the body in a
vulnerable pose so that their brothers could catch up and
do their job tearing into those portions of Horan's head,
chest, and shoulders that were exposed above the mound
of dirt. Only when the bullets stopped did Horan's lifeless
corpse simply flop down into the pool of blood that was
already beginning to form at the base of the dirt mound
in front of the radioman's face.

For a second the radioman continued to stare wide-eyed
at the shattered mass of bone and flesh that had once been
a face. This sight, combined with the fear, the smell, and
the strain of battle, was all at once overpowering, crippling, and numbing. In a single moment of spontaneous
revulsion, the involuntary convulsion of the radioman's

stomach muscles forced him to turn his own head to the side away from his shattered lieutenant and throw up with all his might. Though he had yet to be touched physically by the battle that continued to ebb and flow all around him, the radioman was as dead at that moment as his lieutenant. The fact was, though he didn't know it and wouldn't for years to come, that every bullet that had ripped into his lieutenant had in its own insidious way made its mark in his brain, a mark that time would never wash away.

From his bunker, Valendez darted his eyes from the scene before him to the sky above. Below him, on the small patch of level ground that jutted out of the mountainside where the dummy arms cache was located, all was going well. Actually, things were going better than well. As he watched in silence, Valendez could see individual American officers and sergeants scurrying about in an effort to organize a response to the devastating fire that rained down on them from an unseen ring of bunkers. Those responses, however, were being frustrated time and again as the Americans discovered that, rather than facing a single line of enemy positions, their tormentors were deployed in a series of well-placed positions that ringed the arms-cache site on three sides. Each FARC fighting position, the Americans were finding, was well placed, expertly camouflaged, and covered by at least two other positions. Any effort to isolate and deal with a single position would draw fire from two and sometimes three other bunkers to either flank or further back. It would take, Valendez knew, a well-coordinated force lavishly supported by fire support to crack the lines of bunkers his men occupied. And so far the Yankees had yet to recover from their initial beating and put together such an effort.

Satisfied with all that he saw before him, Valendez turned his attention for a moment in the direction of the landing zone. Off in the distance, further down the hill on another level patch of ground, he could see only faint signs that the ambush on the landing zone was still in progress. Like the commander of the company conducting the ambush, Valendez relied on radios for reports from the platoon leader at the landing zone. At that moment that platoon leader, like the two platoon leaders at the main site, reported all was going well. Report after report confirmed what Valendez himself could see, that return fire was sporadic and poorly directed, leaving their own firepower undiminished. Only the mortar platoon had ceased fire, and that was only because of the necessity of moving the mortar tubes to new locations, lest they become detected from the air and attacked by the Yankee gunships.

Thinking about those gunships caused Valendez to look up and search the sky again. Where, he wondered, were the vaunted American attack helicopters? Why hadn't they struck? Was the surprise so complete that the Yankees had been caught off guard and unprepared to react? How nice, Valendez thought, that would be. But this, he knew, was no time for such dreams and fantasies. They would come and attempt to extract revenge for the punishment that his men had rained down on the Yankee ground troops. But until they did, there was nothing he could do about it. The new trap was set, and all he could do was wait for the Americans to come rushing into it as their ground troops had done earlier. Still Valendez could not help but wonder and worry. Looking up, he whispered, 'Where are you?'

Little more than two hundred meters away, down on the small level area that Valendez was watching between his incessant scans of the sky above, Lieutenant Colonel Harold Cerro was thinking the same thing. Though he and his command group had like everyone else been taken aback by the suddenness and severity of the FARC attack, the officers, sergeants, and the soldiers serving as radiotelephone operators with him recovered quicker than most and began to respond to Cerro's orders and their training. Under the dubious cover of the lee of one of the huts, some of the members of the battalion command group worked on the two wounded troopers they had pulled to safety. At the same time, Cerro and the fire support officer, a young captain named Peter J. Crippen, were attempting to get a handle on the situation so that they could bring in the attack helicopters, which were busily trawling about several kilometers away in search of targets that weren't there.

While Crippen, on the ground inches from Cerro, attempted to contact the commander of the attack heli-copters loitering off somewhere north of them, Cerro's own radioman alternated his attempts to contact the commander of Alpha Company or Kozak, who was with Charlie Company back at the landing zone. Neither answered the radioman's call. Though Cerro understood that both were in tight if not tighter situations than his own at that moment, his inability to exercise anything resembling command and control infuriated him.

As bad as this was, the fact that he had been cautioned about going in with the lead element during such opera-tions added to the anger that Cerro felt welling up in him. At least if he had taken his brigade commander's advice and used one of the helicopters he had been offered as a command and control bird, he would be able to get a picture for himself of what was going on, with or without reports from the elements in contact. Other battalion commanders in the division, flying just over the heads of their people on the ground, were doing so effectively. Except for an odd angry shot, the light weapons of the FARC had done little to discourage this practice. Only Cerro's determination to lead from the front, as his mentor Scott Dixon had always done, caused

Cerro to reject the idea of commanding from above. Even if Cerro had known that less than fifty meters away his mentor was having similar thoughts and regrets, he would have still felt the anger that continued to well up inside of him. Both Kozak, at the landing zone, and Frank Spelvin, the Alpha Company commander, should have reported in already. They knew better. They damned sure knew how Cerro felt about reporting, and that to Cerro made all of this harder to tolerate.

Revelations as to the true nature of their situation at that moment were coming fast and furious. Already Kozak had a firm grasp of several important pieces of information. For one, they had not been subjected to the mortar fire that the main force with Cerro had been. This made it easier to look about and gather more information and assess the situation. Next, the volume of fire, the noise of battle, and the manner in which the troopers of Charlie Company were deployed led her to believe that they were faced by a FARC platoon, probably no more, deployed in a simple L-shaped ambush. Though this didn't make things easy, it could, she began to realize, be worse. On the debit side, the wounding of the company commander and the failure of the company executive officer to seize immediate control of the company left the three small platoons of Charlie Company on their own for several critical minutes. During those minutes only one platoon leader, Second Lieutenant Elie Tibbetts, was able to pull his platoon together and do something quite on his own that would set the pace for the rest of Charlie Company's fight.

That Tibbetts and the Third Platoon were able to do so was more an accident than good planning. Upon landing, Tibbetts had hustled his platoon out and away from the exposed landing zone, rapidly deploying them into a hasty defensive line. Though he had gone further than he should have, and he was about to correct this when the firing began, the effect of this misjudgment meant that a large portion of his platoon, including him, was outside of the kill zone. Free from the imminent danger, Tibbetts was able to take a moment to assess the situation. This was not his first firefight, since he was one of the 'originals' who had been with the battalion before it deployed from Fort Campbell to Colombia. Though the volume of fire was greater and far more accurate than anything he had seen to date, the solution to the problem that he applied here was the same that had worked so well before.

With little more than a quick overview of the area from where he stood, Tibbetts ordered the one squad in contact to stay in place and keep up a good return fire. Correctly guessing that his one squad had found the extreme flank of the enemy positions, he would use that squad as a base of fire and a guide. With his other squads, now forming up to his left and right, he would pull further away from the ambush site before moving around and to the rear of where he thought the last enemy positions were. With luck, he could then take the enemy positions from the front, flank, and rear. If that succeeded, then it would, he knew, be a relatively easy matter of rolling up the entire enemy line by taking on one position after another using similar tactics.

While the squad leaders with him prepared their people for this, Tibbetts decided that he'd best inform his company commander of his plans and maneuvers lest the other platoons or attack helicopters mistake the movement of his men for the enemy. When Captain Kozak answered the radio instead of his own commander, Tibbetts didn't hesitate to render his report to her. He knew that Kozak had been traveling with Kaplin, and his own commander no doubt was listening in on his report.

When Tibbetts was finished, Kozak threw the radio hand mike back at Kaplin's radioman, who had given it to her when he had seen his own commander was wounded.

It wasn't that Kozak was being disrespectful or anything. It was just that throwing the hand mike happened to be the quickest and most efficient, not to mention safest, method of returning it. Looking at her own radioman, Sergeant Andy Pender, Kozak considered Tibbetts's report before deciding that she had best get this situation in hand before doing anything else. Tibbetts's report and initiative were both encouraging and gave her something to work with. Ready, she began to issue her orders. 'Sergeant Pender, drag Captain Kaplin over there in that stand of trees. We'll collect the wounded there and set up a command post. When you're set, contact Colonel Cerro and let him know what's going on here.'

Pender, unsure of what Kozak had in mind and wanting to make sure he got it right, shot back to her, 'What exactly is going on here, ma'am?'

His question was not meant to be funny or critical. Only after Pender had asked did she realize that she hadn't taken the time to tell him. Quickly she blurted her plan. 'Third Platoon is looking for the enemy's right flank. When they find it, they'll start rolling it up. I'm going to rally the rest of the company. If I can, I'm going to pull one of the other two platoons back and throw them around the right flank to reinforce Tibbetts while the platoon left in contact lays down a base of fire and pins the enemy in place.'

Pender was about to comment that as far as he could see it was them and not the Farcees that were doing all the pinning down, but he didn't. Though Kozak enjoyed a little humor now and then, this was not one of those times. So Pender merely nodded that he understood and turned his full attention to dealing with Kaplin, his rifle, his radio, and keeping himself as close to the ground as the buttons on his uniform allowed him while Kozak turned away and began her search for whoever was in charge of the First and Second platoons.

*   *   *

Lieutenant Horan's radioman was still heaving when Dixon came up next to him. Dixon, not noticing what the radioman had been doing, suddenly found himself running his left hand through a vile pool of vomit. Jerking his hand back, Dixon cursed as he shook it. 'Jesus! Damn you!'

Looking up at Dixon and noticing that the general was next to him, the radioman cleared his throat. 'Sorry, General, I, I . . . The lieutenant, he's dead. All shot to shit.'

For the first time, Dixon took the time to study the shocked, numbed expression that the radioman wore. Carefully lifting his head so that he could see over him, Dixon looked over to where Horan's corpse lay. The sight that greeted him explained without any need for words the radioman's reaction. Two feet beyond the radioman Horan's head was turned toward Dixon. One couldn't call what Dixon saw a face, not anymore. Rather it was a beaten mass of pulp framed by the kevlar helmet that now served as a bowl that collected the blood, gray tissue, and bone that had once been Horan's head.

Without any further thought, Dixon allowed his head to drop down on the ground, where he let it lie for a moment while he sucked down several deep breaths in an effort to calm his own stomach. Watching, the radioman began to feel better about himself. If a general could be shaken by looking at a corpse, then he didn't need to worry about being embarrassed by tossing his lunch.

Blinking his eyes as if this would magically cancel out what he had just seen, Dixon turned his attention to his next concern. 'Is your radio on the company or battalion radio net, trooper?'

'Company, sir.'

'Give me the hand mike.'

Fumbling about his web gear, the radioman pulled the

hand mike free of the metal hook that it had been hanging from and handed it to Dixon.

'What're the call signs for your company commander and your platoon leader?'

'Alpha Six is the old man. The LT is, was, Alpha Two Six.'

The use of such simple call signs, a violation of operational security, angered Dixon, but he let it pass. This was no time to bother about such trivial matters. Besides, since he had no call sign for himself within this unit, he would have to throw OpSec out the window himself as soon as he began transmitting. While the zing of bullets passing close overhead reminded Dixon of the need to keep low, he pressed the rubber-covered lever called the push-to-talk button on the side of the hand mike and began speaking. 'Alpha Six, Alpha Six, this is Oscar Seven. Over.'

At first, there was no response. Then a voice came back. 'Unknown station, this is Alpha Six Romeo. Get off this net. Out.'

Realizing that he had reached the Alpha Company commander's radio-man who didn't recognize the ad hoc call sign Dixon was using to identify himself, Dixon decided to use the direct approach. Re-keying the mike, he tried again. 'Alpha Six Romeo, this is the general officer that was traveling with Alpha Two Six. Inform your Six that Alpha Two Six is dead and that the Alpha Two Six element is pinned under heavy fire. Over.'

Releasing the push-to-talk button, Dixon closed his eyes and tried to think. What, he wondered, would he do now? Before he came up with an answer, the speaker on the hand mike blurted, 'Oscar Seven, this is Alpha Six Romeo. Alpha Six wants to know if you have contact with Alpha Two Six Alpha. Over.'

The platoon, Dixon realized, was out of touch with their commander. With this lieutenant dead and the company commander asking about Alpha Two Six Alpha, who should be the platoon sergeant, things had to be really bad. Keying the mike, Dixon responded without thinking. 'Negative. I've no contact with any of the leaders of this element. I'll get the senior man up on the radio as soon as possible.'

Quickly the response came back. 'This is Alpha Six Romeo. Alpha Six would appreciate that. Anything else? Over.'

'This is Oscar Seven. Negative. Out.'

Handing the hand mike back to the radioman, Dixon lifted his head in an effort to look about some. Off to his left he heard the familiar pop-pop-pop of several M-16s close at hand. Someone from this platoon, he decided, was over there and returning fire. That meant that he had to go over and find out who, if anyone, was in charge. Though the task of chasing platoon sergeants and squad leaders during firefights was definitely something that didn't fall within the job description of a general officer, Dixon justified his actions without much thinking about them by the seriousness of the situation. He began to back away from the dirt mound in order to crawl around the radioman. As he did so, he slapped the radioman on the bottom of his boots and yelled, 'Okay, trooper, follow me.'

Without giving the radioman another thought, Dixon continued, following the mound of dirt as closely as possible while keeping his entire body pressed to the ground as best he could. This was no easy task, especially for a man in his late forties who had never counted low crawling as one of his specialties. He had and had always had a particular problem keeping his butt down, even when he was a somewhat spry young cadet at VMI. Still, for not having done anything like this for some time, Dixon was able to establish a rhythm of sorts. That, with the added motivation provided by an occasional burst of small-arms fire overhead, allowed him to make good time, reaching a point where he could finally see the line of troopers he had been following earlier. Confident that their platoon sergeant was among them, Dixon turned on his stomach slightly and began to crawl toward them, oblivious to the fact that the dirt mound that had protected him had long since disappeared.

It took Scott Dixon a few seconds to realize this. The fact was that he had become so oblivious to his surroundings, concentrating instead on maintaining as low a profile as possible while at the same time keeping an eye open for the platoon sergeant, he hadn't noticed that the mound that had been protecting him had diminished in height and thickness to the point where it ceased to exist. When belatedly he noticed that it had disappeared, he froze in place, carefully looking wide-eyed to his left and then his right to see if his error had drawn any unwanted attention to him. After several seconds that dragged on forever, Dixon let out a sigh of relief. Anxious to correct his oversight, Dixon prepared to move back behind the mound of dirt. Before doing so, however, he glanced back to make sure that the radioman wasn't in the way.

Only then, while he was lying flat on the ground totally exposed to enemy fire and sweating from every pore in his body, was Dixon startled by a second revelation: He was alone. There was no radioman behind him. At first he feared that the radioman had been hit and he hadn't noticed. Carefully Dixon twisted his head around further and looked back along his route. There was no sign of the radioman. Not until he saw a pair of boots, partially obscured by the dead lieutenant's boots, move, did Dixon realize what had happened to the radioman. He hadn't budged an inch. The bastard, Dixon realized, had simply lain where he had found him and had made no effort to follow. Though angry, Dixon did his best to suppress it. The last thing he wanted was to lose his temper, get excited, and draw attention to himself while he was in the open. With great care Dixon slowly began to reverse his direction. As hard as crawling forward had been, doing so backwards was slower, more awkward, and given Dixon's anger at being abandoned by the radioman, more nerve-racking. Still, propelled by his anger, an anger that had started the moment he had toppled unceremoniously out of the helicopter at the LZ and was now multiplied with every burst of small-arms fire that tore overhead or kicked up dirt nearby, Dixon made record time.

Dixon found the radioman in the same position he had left him. He was still lying next to the dead lieutenant with his head turned away. The only difference was that his eyes were closed. They were in fact being held shut so tightly that Dixon could see wrinkles in the corner of the man's eyes from the effort. For a moment it reminded him of a child who had seen something terrible and hoped by closing his eyes he could make it go away. That this was exactly what was going on inside the radioman's head didn't, however, occur to Dixon at that moment. Rather, Dixon's anger blinded him to any consideration other than the fact that he, a general officer, had given a soldier in combat an order and that the soldier, for whatever reason, had disobeyed him. It wasn't that Dixon was an unreasonable man. On the contrary, those who knew him and had worked with him knew him to be one of the most understanding human beings that had ever put a uniform on. But the fact was that Dixon was a human being, and as such he was as susceptible to all the frailties of human nature as the next man. At that moment anger and fear, and not compassion and understanding, were the emotions that were driving Brigadier General Scott Dixon. For not only had he given an order that had not been carried out promptly, he had in a very real sense been abandoned by this radioman, left alone to face the dangers of moving about in a firefight.

In the heat of the moment very little of this occurred

to him. There was no time for rationality or compassion. Only later on, after the heat of passions and emotions flamed to a fever pitch by battle had cooled, would Dixon be able to understand and be reasonable. But with men dying all about and his own life in danger, reason was a scarce commodity. Dixon, already embarrassed at putting himself in an awkward situation that he knew had been a mistake from the beginning, could think of nothing else but doing something that would correct that error in judgment. His immediate response, getting the platoon sergeant of the unit he had been traveling with in contact with his company commander, was the only beneficial thing that he could think of. And a radioman, no matter how scared or shaken he was, was not going to stop him from doing so.

Reaching out, Dixon grabbed the radioman's shoulder and gave him a violent shake. This had the desired effect, causing the radioman's eyes to fly open. When he had eye-to-eye contact, Dixon lit into him. 'I told you to follow me. I *ordered* you to follow me! Now get your shit together and do it. Understand?'

The radioman's eyes that had moments before been squeezed shut now grew to the size of saucers. His lips parted slightly, and he gave the appearance he was going to speak, but nothing came out. Instead the radioman closed both his mouth and eyes and ignored Dixon.

This reaction served only to multiply the anger that Dixon had already been building up, pushing rational thinking further and further from Dixon's mind and replacing it with blind fury. Letting go of the radioman's shoulder, Dixon took hold of his collar, gave it a twist, and jerked the soldier as close to his own face as he could. As before, this violent action caused the radioman's eyes to open wide. 'Damn you, soldier. I gave you an order and you're going to comply. Do . . . you . . . understand?'

When the radioman finally answered, there was a slight quiver, almost a pleading quality to his voice.

'I . . . I can't, General. Jesus, I can't deal with this shit.'

As contorted with fear as the radioman's face was, Dixon's was just as twisted and disfigured with anger and rage. The real reason for having the radioman follow him no longer entered into Dixon's thinking. Dixon could have ripped the radio off of the man's back and taken it himself. But in the rage of passions that consumed Dixon's mind, the fact that a soldier in combat was steadfastly refusing his orders overrode all logic and reason. Twisting the soldier's collar tighter, to the point where he was beginning to choke the man, Dixon lowered his voice and hissed in the most menacing tone he could, 'You're going to move your ass and follow me or you're going to die right here, right now.' Dixon was about to add, Or I'll shoot you myself, but didn't, though that's exactly what he thought. Soldiers, after all, were fighting and dying around the two of them, and getting the radioman in contact with his platoon sergeant was to Dixon the only thing that he could do to stop it. And if that took radical and even illegal means to make it happen, then he was prepared in his current state of mind to follow through.

As dramatic as the confrontation between Dixon and the radioman was, another incident that would have far greater consequences was beginning to be played out. Cerro, between ducking every time a burst of small-arms fire struck near his command group and shouting orders and instructions to the soldiers around him, had managed to put together a reasonable picture in his mind of what was happening to his command. It was not at the moment a good one, but it at least gave him some hope. In addition, Pete Crippen had managed to raise the commander of the attack helicopter company supporting them and was waiting to hand off the radio hand mike to Cerro so that he could personally give them an update on the situation and issue them instructions.

When he was finished talking to Kozak, Cerro tossed the hand mike back to his own radioman and reached out toward the fire support officer for his. As he pulled the hand mike to him, Cerro muttered a curse, damning the division commander for insisting that attack helicopters in support of ground operations would operate on the artillery support net and not the battalion command net of the unit they were supporting. Had the helicopters been on the command net of the 3rd Battalion, 511th Infantry, Cerro and his fellow battalion commanders wouldn't have to waste valuable time telling the attack helicopter commanders what was happening on the ground. The attack helicopter commanders and pilots would already know simply by listening to the reports. Still there was no changing that, at least not now. Keying the hand mike, Cerro called the helicopters. 'Bravo Five Two, this is Mike Seven Six. Over.'

With the quick situation report that Crippen had given him, Captain Allen A. Bryson responded to Cerro's call with as much information as he had so that Cerro didn't have to play a thousand questions. 'Seven Six, this is Five Two. I have four snakes coming in from the southwest. We can see two firefights in progress, one at the LZ and one at the arms site, but cannot identify who's who down there. Over.'

For a moment Cerro wondered how best to guide Bryson in without exposing his own positions. This was especially critical, since the enemy mortars in new locations were picking up their barrage where they had left off. Ready, he pressed the push to talk button on the hand mike. 'This is Seven Six, the situation at the LZ is pretty much in hand. They are in close contact and rolling up the enemy bunker line now. We're still pinned, however, at the arms-cache site and cannot maneuver. I need you to locate and take out their mortars. From those platoons I've been able to contact and what I see here, none of my people are more than fifty meters from the outer edge of the arms site. The other people are in bunkers and beyond the fifty-meter mark. The greatest volume of the enemy fire appears to be coming from positions on the high ground north of the arms site. At this time, that's the best I can do for you. How copy? Over.'

Bryson, serving as the gunner for his own aircraft as well as the company commander and senior aviator on the scene, looked up from his sight and surveyed the unfolding battle before him. He did not like going in with such skimpy information concerning friendly dispositions and target data. This fear was a natural one given the amount of drilling that he and every attack helicopter pilot and gunner in the Army had been given concerning engagement criteria. After the First Persian Gulf War, with the numerous incidents of 'fratricide,' the modern term given to friendly fire, the need to have positive controls and clearly marked friendly front line traces had been driven home to them in the classroom and on the live fire range. This was not, Bryson realized, a classroom drill or a live fire exercise. This was the real thing with real men and women, American men and women, dying before his eyes. And unlike past engagements that he had been involved in since his arrival in Colombia, the enemy was standing fast, toe to toe with the Americans, giving apparently better than they were getting. Taking a deep breath, Bryson pressed his radio button. 'Roger, Seven Six, I understand your people are in the open and all within fifty meters of the arms cache. I will split my flight, using two snakes to work over the area between the LZ and the arms site and the others concentrating on the forward slopes above the arms site. Over.'

Not knowing what else to say, Cerro looked at Crippen as he responded. 'Roger, that sounds good to me. I'm turning you back over to my Eight Nine. Work with him for further guidance. Over.' Without waiting for a response, Cerro handed the radio hand mike over to Crippen. 'He's all yours. Just keep him in the game. Okay?'

Crippen, who had been watching and listening to Cerro, nodded. As an artillery man Crippen would have felt much more comfortable dealing with a tube artillery battery than with an understrength attack helicopter company. But given the fact that there was no way that the limited range of the field howitzers could reach every corner of the 11th Air Assault Division's area of responsibility, they had to make do with helicopter gunships in those areas where friendly guns couldn't reach. Besides, the only other alternative was relying on Colombian Army artillery units, something that no American ground commander in his right mind would do if he could avoid it. So as much as he disliked it, the helicopters were better than nothing, especially in situations like this.

Alerted to the presence of the incoming American attack helicopters, Valendez shifted his attention from the fire-fight on his immediate front to the horizon beyond. From the bunker apertures, built so as to give him a clear and unrestricted view of the river valley and skyline to the south, Valendez could barely make out the approaching attack helicopters. Though they were mere dots in his binoculars, their speed and the range of their weapons made them more than deadly, even now. Still the danger they presented didn't seem to bother Valendez. The truth was he was relieved to see them coming up the river valley. All was, Valendez suddenly realized, in order. Without betraying any of the excitement that he felt, Valendez began giving orders to his radioman, Rafael Dario. Dario in turn relayed them over the air as Valendez spoke. 'Contact Eagle. He will cease fire and shift his mortars to their next position immediately. Once there, he will notify me when they are ready and stand by for my order to fire again. Next notify Falcon. When they have all targets within range, he is to engage the enemy at will. All positions around the arms site are to begin reducing their volume of fire until Falcon has engaged.'

Having given his orders, Valendez went back to watching and waiting. He had no need to monitor Dario as he passed the orders to the various leaders scattered about the mountainside. Of all the men in his command that day, Dario was the one man he could depend upon no matter what. For Dario, a young man who had known nothing but poverty and deprivation, was more than a simple radioman. He was in fact a jack of all trades, serving as an aide, cook, driver, and personal bodyguard to Valendez, a man whom Dario saw as more than a military commander. He was in Dario's eyes the father that he had never had. For his part Valendez, a man who had never married, returned the affection and loyalty, taking Dario into his confidence and taking him by the hand as a father would a son. And like a son Dario followed Valendez, from the first day when Valendez as a deputy company commander met Dario, the raw recruit. When he had finished relaying all of the orders and had received acknowledgments from the recipients, Dario leaned forward and softly informed Valendez of that.

With a slight nod Valendez in turn acknowledged Dario's message. It was back to waiting, always waiting, Valendez thought. How well, he realized, the old German military philosopher knew war. Why, he wondered, had so few listened to what he had said? Indeed why?

Reaching a point where he felt that he could safely engage the Farcee positions without exposing his aircraft to their small-arms fire, Bryson ordered his pilot to slow down to a hover. His wingman, just to the right and rear of his aircraft, conformed to Bryson's actions. With little more than a quick glance over his shoulder to reassure himself that the other aircraft was ready, Bryson turned his attention to fighting his own aircraft. Putting his head down onto the sight that sat before him, he switched to the thermal viewer mode and began to look for targets. Identifying friendly ground troops, given that they were for the most part still exposed, was not difficult. Finding the mortars, however, was more of a challenge. Though he detected several hot spots out beyond the fifty-meter perimeter that the battalion commander had defined, Bryson passed them by in his search for something that looked like a mortar tube or a mortar firing position. Thus engaged, neither he nor his pilot noticed the telltale back blast and bloom of white smoke as a volley of Russian-made surface-to-air missiles leaped out of the jungle behind them and began to reach up for them. The only warning Bryson had that they were in trouble was the sudden scream of surprise from his pilot when he saw their wingman suddenly blow up. Bryson was so absorbed in opening his engagement that he didn't even have time for this before his own multimillion-dollar helicopter disappeared in a fireball that dwarfed everyone and everything below them.

Seldom in a war can a person, either during the war itself or even after it, point to a single incident and say with any degree of certainty that such and such a moment was a decisive moment, that after a particular incident the face of a war was changed forever. In modern history one such incident occurred on June 4, 1942, when Navy Lieutenant Clarence W. McClusky led his thirty-seven Dauntless dive bombers into a dive that wrecked three Japanese aircraft carriers off the Pacific island of Midway. Another moment, only slightly less dramatic but often ignored, took place near a small Vietnamese village named Ap Bac on January 2, 1963, when Lieutenant Colonel John Paul Vann, an American adviser with the South Vietnamese Army, watched helplessly as the Viet Cong for the first time stood their ground against overwhelming South Vietnamese ground forces and destroyed in quick succession three American helicopters and repelled a mounted attack by a Vietnamese mechanized infantry unit.

The destruction of the American attack helicopters above the dummy arms cache, both those searching for the mortars and those working over the area between the LZ and the arms site, by a section of Valendez's command code-named Falcon caused everyone on the ground to pause in whatever they were doing and look up. Although the angry explosions were ominous, they meant little to Nancy Kozak and her efforts to break the back of the enemy platoon engaging Charlie Company at the LZ. To Cerro, still pinned against the wall of a dummy arms shed, the loss of the attack helicopters meant that the firefight his command was engaged in would continue unchecked until the pinned remnants of Alpha Company finally were able to make a dent in the enemy bunker line or the enemy simply got tired of killing his men. For Dixon, still locked in his own personal struggle to motivate a soldier who had lost all ability to function, the destruction of the helicopters was another inconvenience, another incredible stroke of bad luck that like all the others that day was conspiring to rob him of his self-esteem.

Only Hector Valendez standing before the aperture of his observation bunker fully appreciated what he was seeing and what it meant. The shock waves created by the destruction of those four attack helicopters would not only continue to ripple their way across the valley where he had so carefully set up his ambush, they would sweep from the banks of the Rio Cauca at the bottom of the valley and reach eventually the banks of the Potomac River itself. And behind those shock waves Valendez felt, for the first time with a degree of confidence he had not felt before, the sound of victory for his cause would come. For he knew that even if he and every member of the FARC with him that day died, their achievements would change the face of the war against the Yankees and the reactionary Colombian government forever. From that day on, he, his men, and the FARC were fighting a new war, one in which they could not lose. For now they, and not the government in Bogotá or the commander of the 11th Air Assault Division, would choose the time and place of their battles. They had in their hands the most necessary commodity to victory that an army could have, initiative. And Hector Valendez was determined never to relinquish it.

CHAPTER 4

September 22

Had he been a Roman general at the height of the Empire, Major General Charles B. Lane would never have entered a meeting with less than six trumpeters to announce his presence. But he was not. Rather he had been doomed by fate to being an American general commanding at a time when pomp and circumstance, at least for the military, were viewed as both frivolous and too expensive. So Lane had to content himself with a crisp, sharp shout of attention as he walked into the briefing room for the 0700 daily update.

Still Lane refused to be totally denied what he considered to be his due. What little he could have and still be considered within bounds he took. This attitude resulted in making the headquarters of the 11th Air Assault Division a sort of showpiece within the Army when it came to proper procedures and military correctness. While everyone who had ever worn the uniform of the United States Army knew from day one that lack of order equaled failure and defeat, Lane's ideas and views bordered on compulsiveness. Everything in the division had a proper place, and every action and task had an established routine that was mandated and supported by reams and reams of policy statements, checklists, and standard operating procedures. Not that anyone expected anything less from a man who had from the beginning been referred to in the ranks and behind his back as Conan the Bureaucrat.

With the punctuality of a train pulling out of the station, the rituals surrounding the morning update briefing ran their course. As Lane made his way to his seat, his aide slipped into the room, heading straight for a small table where he set down his notebook and a metal coffee thermos. While Lane took his place between the assistant division commander for maneuver seated on his right and the chief of staff to his left, exchanging small talk with these two officers, his aide poured a cup of coffee for him.

Even this action was conducted with a ritualistic quality not unlike that of a Japanese tea ceremony. The thermos used to convey the general's coffee itself was part of the ceremony. It was covered with stickers that represented the division's shoulder patch and Lane's name and rank in large, neat black block letters running down the side. When the aide had filled the cup three-quarters full, he made his way to where Lane sat, holding the cup aloft as if it held sacred nectar for the gods. After handing his boss the cup over Lane's right shoulder, the aide disappeared, his role in the ceremony at an end. Without looking, Lane brought the cup up to his lips, took a sip, then brought the cup down until the arm holding it rested on the arm of the overstuffed leather chair that he sat in. Having thus partaken of the ceremonial coffee, Lane looked up at the assistant division intelligence officer, already standing at the front of the briefing room with pointer in hand, and nodded, letting him know that the briefing was now in session.

From the rear of the room came a click as a sergeant turned on the overhead projector. Every day when he heard this, Colonel Christopher Delhue, the division's chief of staff, watched the briefing officer. For as soon as the projector clicked on, the briefing officer sprang to life, whipping the long pointer he held in both hands horizontal to the floor across his body, bringing it to rest on the screen at the front of the briefing room within inches of where he wanted it. Without fail, this caused Delhue to smile, for it was as if the briefing officer was somehow connected to the overhead projector and switching on the projector served to activate both the projector and the briefer. The only thing that tempered Delhue's sense of humor was the realization that the briefing officer now presenting and the others that would follow spent more than an hour rehearsing this routine briefing every morning in an effort to achieve the level of perfection that Lane demanded of his staff.

As with all morning briefings, this one started with the same preamble. 'Good morning, sir. Enemy activity in the past twenty-four hours has been moderate,' or light or heavy, as the case may be. The intelligence officer would then point to various locations on the map of Colombia and in order of occurrence describe each contact or sighting made by a U.S. unit that involved an FARC squad or larger unit, starting with just after midnight of the previous day and ending at midnight of that same day. Though this left a seven-hour gap in reporting, no one felt that this was of any major significance. The division intelligence officer felt it was necessary to have such an early cutoff so that his analysts could sift through the information that was coming in and package it for the briefer in plenty of time for him to prepare himself adequately. Besides, the midnight-to-midnight reporting period fit nicely into Lane's way of thinking, with each reporting period equaling one twenty-four-hour day.

Though things did occur after midnight that were of importance, they were never allowed to interfere with the delicate routine that had become the standard. Once when an American infantry platoon on ambush patrol was engaged by a superior enemy force estimated to be at company strength after the midnight cutoff, the briefing officer on his own added this item to the morning briefing. Before the briefing officer finished, Lane turned to face Delhue. When he spoke, it made Delhue think of what it would be like to be a snake's prey as the snake looked into the eyes of its victim before consuming it. With measured ease and never bringing his voice above a quiet conversational tone, Lane in a mocking voice asked Delhue, 'Is it too much to expect, *Colonel*, for the staff officers under your charge to follow established procedures?' Without waiting for a response, Lane rose to his feet, looked about the room, and announced, 'When you people have your act together, have someone contact my aide.' Finished, he turned and walked out of the room, leaving the gathered staff confused, embarrassed, and somewhat insulted that a senior officer would behave in such a manner. Still, C. B. Lane got his way, as he always did, and broke the will of his subordinates, giving them the choice of conforming to his views or facing professional suicide.

So despite the fact that the battle between Hector Valendez's special action company and Cerro's battalion was the only operation of any significance during the reporting period being briefed, it waited for its chronological turn. When, after a detailed description of six questionable sightings and three minor squad-sized confrontations between units of the 11th Air Assault and elements suspected of being FARC, the officer giving the intelligence update turned to the fight at the arms cache, everyone in the room sat up and began to pay close attention. 'At approximately 1145 hours, two companies of the 3rd Battalion, 511th Infantry, made contact with an

FARC force here, estimated to be a reinforced company. The enemy were – '

Before the briefing officer could finish, Lane interrupted. 'Who said that the enemy force was a reinforced company?'   ·

Caught off guard by Lane's question, the briefing officer looked at Lane for a second before glancing over to the division G-2 intelligence officer. There was in his face a pleading request for salvation, or at least some guidance. Before the G-2 could respond, Lane asked his question again, a little more forcefully this time. 'Who said that the enemy force was a reinforced company?'

Turning his face back to the division commander, the briefing officer began to field the question, groping about for the right answer as he did so. 'Well, sir, the information concerning this particular incident was generated by the unit in contact and sent up the chain. To the best of my knowledge, there has been no effort made to re-evaluate this data.'

'So,' Lane pronounced as he stuck his right index finger in the air, 'we have no independent confirmation concerning the size of the enemy unit.'

Confused, the briefing officer looked at Lane for a moment before responding. 'Well, yes, sir, that is, I suppose, correct. I don't know that there was – '

Again Lane cut off the briefing officer, this time by turning in his chair to face the division intelligence officer himself. 'Please correct me if I'm wrong, but didn't your office generate an assessment of enemy capabilities three weeks ago stating that the Colombians were incapable of conducting military operations above platoon level?'

Uncomfortable with the sudden attention of his superior, the G-2, who had been lounging in his seat, sat upright and shifted this way and that as he threw his hands out in front of him. 'Well, yes, I believe we did make that assessment three weeks ago.'

'Has anything,' Lane continued, 'developed or come to light, other than this farce the commander of the 3rd of the 511th calls a battle, to change that assessment?'

Though he had known, like all the other officers on the division staff, that mention of FARC units of company size was a no-no, the division G-2 had included the assessment of the forces that had engaged the 3rd of the 511th in his briefing. 'How much trouble can I get into,' he had asked in a rather cavalier fashion, 'by telling the truth for once? Besides,' he added, 'the assessment is the 3rd Brigade's, not ours. If Lane doesn't like it, he can hammer *them*.' Now with Lane glaring at him, the bravado the G-2 had displayed evaporated. Shaking his head more as a reaction than as the result of careful thought, the G-2 looked down at the floor like a puppy being scolded and muttered, 'No, not that I have seen.'

Casting his eyes across the assembled staff, Lane feigned a look of confusion. 'Then I don't understand? How can one of our battalions get thumped so soundly by an enemy force the size of a platoon and then right here in my own headquarters have my own staff support the fantasies of an ill-informed and confused battalion commander?'

As Lane spoke, Delhue felt his stomach knot up. He already knew that Cerro had only two companies on hand, not his entire battalion as Lane was implying. Even worse, through his manner and pronouncement Lane was instructing his staff in so many words that any discussion of an enemy force in company strength or larger would not be tolerated. The reason for this, as he and every officer in the room knew, was that to admit that the enemy capability was improving rather than diminishing would be to cast doubt on the effectiveness of the division and in turn on the division commander. Lane himself had stated in the narrative of the monthly summary of operations sent to the Pentagon via SOUTHCOM less than a week ago that 'the military balance in Colombia has tilted irreversibly in favor of U.S. and Colombian forces.'

Had this been true, Lane's diversion of effort to deal with the drug cartel and his emphasis on those operations would have been appropriate. But since the FARC was not declining in power but on the contrary increasing its capability, Delhue knew that every trooper and weapon taken away from their efforts against the FARC was a dangerous weakening of their position. 'We're failing to do what we were sent here to do,' he told another officer. 'Instead we're off playing cops and robbers while the Farcees are sharpening their knives and jockeying their people about for the big kill.'

Delhue was pondering the consequences of what Lane was doing when Lane ended his visual sweep of the room by staring directly into Delhue's eyes. The sudden direct and piercing stare of Lane's narrowing eyes less than two feet from his own was as unnerving to Delhue as Lane meant it to be. When he saw that his gaze had achieved its desired effect, Lane smiled slightly but narrowed his eyes. 'Chief, we need to get to the bottom of this. I want you to contact 3rd Brigade and have the battalion commander fly up here today to see me. Until then, make sure that all reports concerning this incident, including press releases issued by the public affairs officer, are screened to ensure that they conform with the reality of the situation. Understood?'

Caught off guard like everyone else, Delhue nodded and murmured, 'Understood.'

Satisfied that his point had been made and that nothing more needed to be said, Lane settled himself back into his large overstuffed leather chair, took a sip from his coffee, nodded to the briefing officer, still visibly shaken from being on the spot for so long, and smiled. 'You may proceed, Major. We've wasted more than enough time on this incident.'

*   *   *

Although she didn't need to be escorted to the restaurant or even to her table, Jan Fields-Dixon didn't object. It would have done no good, since every time she did so, the member of the hotel or restaurant staff escorting her, always a man, would offer profuse objections. Each man was quick to point out that it would be inappropriate for a woman of such beauty and importance to be allowed to go about in public unaccompanied. 'There are many men,' one maitre d' with a toothy smile had remarked to her when she objected, 'who would take advantage of a woman in your situation.' Knowing full well that she could count that particular maitre d' among them, along with scores of other Colombians and American businessmen in Bogotá, Jan had said nothing and followed, as was expected.

About the only class of males in Bogotá that seemed to leave Jan alone were those in U.S. Army uniforms. The fact was they gave her a wide berth, since most knew she was the senior correspondent for the World News Network in Colombia. Though Jan had never betrayed the confidence of a source, no one assigned to the military mission in Bogotá or the 11th Air Assault Division wanted to be the first. Equally intimidating, at least to the officers, was the fact that Jan was the wife of Brigadier General Scott Dixon. Conventional wisdom left little doubt that making a pass, or anything resembling a pass, would in short order be brought to the general's attention. 'I would just as soon,' one lieutenant colonel cautioned a major who had seemed interested in buying Jan a drink one night, 'do a root canal on a hungry tiger. Odds of surviving that are considerably higher.'

Still, Jan would not be ignored and she knew that. There were simply too many young men in and out of uniform who enjoyed the thrill of twisting a tiger's tail just for the hell of it. So when Jan was informed that Scott hadn't arrived yet, she decided to be seated at a table alone in the middle of Army officers and go into what Scott called her Mrs. Robinson mode. In a playful mood, despite having been stood up by Scott the previous evening, Jan had even dressed for the occasion on the off chance that Scott would be late, as he usually was. The time alone would allow her to have a little fun.

Wearing a short-sleeved white cotton dress with a full skirt that reached mid-calf, Jan stood out like a shining beacon in a sea of green uniforms. Simple gold jewelry sparkling in the radiant morning sun that streamed into the room drew her spectators' attention to all the right places. Her long lustrous brunette hair, pulled away from her face by a white hairband but left falling about her shoulders, nicely framed an oval face that was high-lighted with a light application of makeup that accentuated her big brown eyes. Jan demanded second looks, and despite the decorum of the moment she got them.

Assured that she would draw the attention that she desired, Jan followed the maitre d'. Before taking her seat, Jan carefully gathered her skirt at the sides and brought it around to her front, pulling it tight across her rear as she did so. With a measured grace befitting her performance, she seated herself and allowed the maitre d' to push her chair in to the table. As she turned to thank him with a smile, she casually glanced around the room, knowing that somewhere in such a target-rich environment an adventurous heart was waiting for the right moment to come up and open a conversation with her on some pretext or other. Taking up her menu, Jan pretended to carefully study it, even though she already knew every entry on it by heart and knew what she would have. Selection of her meal was not her interest. Rather, this gave her the opportunity to look up from the menu every now and then and catch one of the officers at another table staring at her. When she did, Jan would divert her eyes while smiling before returning to her careful study of the menu.

She was still engrossed in looking the menu over when a voice from behind startled her. 'You know, Jan, such antics are not in line with your public image.'

Spinning her head about to see who belonged to the voice, she smiled when she recognized Colonel Chester Thomas, the military attaché assigned to the American embassy in Bogotá. Besides being one of the few military men who would talk to her, he was a genuinely friendly man, just a few months away from retirement. Thomas had not only been instrumental in helping Jan get her feet on the ground when she had arrived in Colombia, he had taken care to keep an eye on her, playing the role, as Jan liked to claim, of her surrogate father. Looking up at him, she smiled. 'Is there nothing better for you to do, Chester, than prowl the local restaurants looking for people to scare?'

'Jan, you should know by now that I am very, very discriminating about whom I scare. You, for example, one of the most successful television coreespondents in the world, with a list of credentials longer than my right arm, make a wonderful target of opportunity.'

Jan blushed. Though she was proud of her achievements, she took even greater pride in the fact that she, a woman, had achieved them in a still heavily male-dominated field.

'You realize, Chester, that if you don't go away, my public image, the one that my superiors in Washington have so carefully cultivated and are so concerned about, is going to be placed in jeopardy.' This comment, which caused both of them to chuckle, was said only half in jest. At times it really bugged Jan that her credibility and appeal were tied by the producers of her news broadcasts to their network ratings. To protect her they often placed Jan in a bubble that she was not comfortable in. Hence she used every opportunity to be a little naughty in a rather harmless way. Though not an exhibitionist by any stretch of the imagination, Jan did enjoy being the center of attention as well as the object of admiring glances and mesmerized stares. While Scott found her behavior amusing, Jan, despite being the very portrait of sophistication and a role model for so many young female correspondents, found it nothing less than erotic.

'Would you care to join us, Chester?'

Making a great show of looking about, Thomas finally asked, 'Us?'

'Yes, Scotty and me. I'm expecting him any minute.'

The mention of Dixon's name caused the expression on Thomas's face to change. 'I think, Jan, it would be better if you two were alone.'

Noting the sudden change, she was about to ask why he had said that but decided not to. 'Well, I guess you're right. This is, after all, his last day in town and I'd like to spend some more time with him. He missed our dinner date last night.'

'Yes, I know.'

Seeing that Thomas now appeared to be anxious to go, Jan missed the tone of his last comment. Had she thought about it, she might have been a little better prepared for the unexpected, but she didn't. Making his apologies, Thomas turned and left Jan's table to go over and join another group of officers. Jan, finished with the menu and after placing her order sat back to enjoy her coffee and the show that she was putting on. While she sat there looking about with a carefully measured casualness, a sadness caused her brow to darken momentarily. The source of the unhappy thought was Scotty's absence the previous night. It was to have been, as far as she knew, his last night in Colombia before he departed for Washington and she remained behind searching for all the news that was fit to be reported. Since they often found that their separate careers took them in opposite directions, both Jan and Scott took great pains to make their times together meaningful and enjoyable. Last night was to have been a special night, just the two of them. Jan had arranged for a nice intimate dinner for two at a restaurant few Americans frequented, after which they would spend some time at a rather romantic establishment where they played old tango records, then . . .

Such thoughts caused Jan to forget about the leers and stares directed at her. In the bright sunlight amid the clatter of plates and silverware and light breakfast conversation. So involved had Jan become with her fantasies that she did not notice Scott when he approached her.

When she became aware of his presence and turned to greet him with a smile, her mood turned from pleasant surprise to stunned silence. The man standing in front of her was not the same man that she had said good-bye to the day before. Instead of smiling eyes and a warm smile that enhanced his usual confident and commanding expression, Jan was confronted by a man who looked like he had been dragged through a rat hole. While both his face and uniform were clean, Scotty had the look and demeanor of a man who had not slept all night and carried with him the burdens of the world to boot. Even more disturbing were the cuts and scratches, still red and swollen, that marked his face. Without having to be told, Jan realized that her husband had been involved in something serious.

Though concerned, Jan said nothing. Instead, as soon as she could recover her poise, she flashed the best smile she could muster, stood up, and reached out to embrace Scott, who for his part responded by stepping closer to her. Taking her in his arms, he gave her a stiff and somewhat perfunctory hug, breaking it off as soon as he could do so. Stepping back, he avoided her stare as he mumbled an apology for not being able to keep their date last night. With that he reached down, held Jan's chair, and motioned for her to sit. Sensing that he either wasn't in the mood to expand on why he missed last night's meeting or couldn't at the moment, Jan remained silent as she took the offered seat, watching Scott while he seated himself but doing so without staring.

For his part, Dixon dropped into his seat across from Jan with the grace of a sack of potatoes. Without looking over at Jan, he took the napkin, placed it on his lap, and immediately began to fiddle with the silverware. He was nervous, Jan thought. Very nervous and edgy. She had seen him like this before, too many times before. Normally this behavior came when something was troubling him, something that was to him very important and he had been unable to find a way of dealing with it, or it was one of those things that dwarfed him and threatened to overwhelm him. It wasn't that Scott Dixon was the strong silent type. On the contrary, Scotty could be very vocal and outspoken when he had something to say and the issues at hand needed to be addressed. He even had the reputation of being quite emotional in a violent sort of way.

What Scotty Dixon lacked, Jan had learned years before, was the ability to vocalize those thoughts and concerns that played upon his personal emotions and beliefs. Like most men of his age and position, he had been carefully trained by his parents, his society, and the Army to stuff his personal feelings and bear in silence those internal struggles and issues that had nothing to do with the performance of his assigned tasks and duties. In a way, Jan could understand the need for this. He had, after all, in his lifetime seen many things and participated in many actions that to a normal person would be unendurable. Scotty as a combat commander not only had to deal with such issues as death, fear, privation, physical discomfort and suffering, and the unknown, he was expected to inspire and lead others to not only endure these things but to willingly confront more of them. Men and women who allowed themselves to show their true feelings and allowed those feelings to dictate their actions could not do what the Army expected Scott Dixon and thousands of others like him to do. So men and women who considered themselves combat leaders, including Scott, were left on their own to learn how best to deal with their own human frailties in private while doing what needed to be done.

Knowing this, however, never made being with Scotty any easier for Jan. The only thing that she could do at times like this was to start a simple dialogue on a subject that was comfortable for the two of them and hope that Scotty would eventually respond to her and at least for the moment let the worries of the world go. Choice of topic at a time like this was critical, for Jan knew that being too frivolous would turn Scotty off. At the same time she wanted to ensure that she didn't accidentally stray into a subject that would only deepen Scotty's somber mood.

After taking a long sip from her coffee, Jan smiled. 'I got the official word yesterday that we'll be working with some new equipment down here in Colombia, a new mobile transponder. It's the size of a small suitcase and has everything, including satellite dish and power supply, that a camera team needs to beam back a live report to Washington from practically anywhere in the world. The whiz-bang kids back at WNN headquarters call it a manpack satcamstay, which is short for man-portable satellite camera station. Of course, the first question I asked was whether this man-portable unit could be converted to a woman-portable unit.'

The last part of her announcement caught Dixon's attention. Looking up at him, Jan saw a slight smile begin to creep across his face. She had his attention. Letting her last statement hang for a moment, Jan took another sip of her coffee. Scotty, not knowing whether she was serious or not, couldn't allow the comment to go past without finding out for sure. Finally he shrugged and asked, 'And?'

Wanting to keep the conversation light for a moment, Jan set her cup down. 'And what, my dear?'

'Is it or isn't it?'

'Is it or isn't it what, dear?'

Taking a deep breath, an exasperated expression lit across Dixon's face. Jan was doing it to him again, he thought. She liked to play these games, starting a conversation, getting his interest, and then dropping the matter before she finished. Sometimes he imagined that she did this just to piss him off, though he knew it was her own weird and twisted idea of fun. Playing along with her, Scott leaned forward. 'Is your new man-portable camera unit – ' Stopping in mid-sentence, he suddenly realized how silly his question was. She had gotten him again. Jan enjoyed creating elaborate stories, capturing his interest, and then getting him to either lose his patience or make a fool of himself by asking silly follow-up questions. Though most of the time he didn't know why she did it other than to engage in her own perverted form of fun, Dixon knew what she was after this morning. With a shake of his head, Dixon looked at Jan and smiled. Yeah, he thought, he was not being very good company this morning, and Jan was doing the best she knew how to draw him out of his gloom. Finally he asked her, in an effort to avoid dwelling on his concerns and issues, how she was doing.

This caused Jan to raise an eyebrow. 'Well, if you must know, I'm quite horny at the moment, thank you very much.'

Ordinarily Dixon would have responded with a quip of his own. Though he tried hard to come up with an appropriate comeback that would equal Jan's off-color comment, he just didn't have it in him this morning. Instead he looked down at his cup of coffee. 'Sorry about last night, Jan. I know how much it meant to you.'

Dropping her playful smile, Jan reached across the table and touched the back of Scotty's left hand. As she did so, she noticed that it too bore several cuts and scratches. 'The real question, trooper, is how are you?'

Lifting his cup midway to his mouth, Scotty brought his right elbow up onto the table and held the cup thus supported as he returned Jan's stare. 'To tell you the truth, Jan, I don't know. I don't know what to tell you, even if I knew how to tell you. Fact is, right now I'm supposed to go back to Washington and in five days submit a report to General Fulk along with recommendations concerning our operations here in Colombia; and at this moment I don't know what I'm going to say.'

'What about telling the truth?'

No sooner had she asked that question than she was sorry that she had, for Dixon's expression turned from concern to anger. When he responded, his words were short and sharp. 'Whose truth, Jan? My truth? His Lord High Majesty Major General C. B. Lane's truth? Hal Cerro's truth? Private Andrew Hayman's truth? Whose truth do I report?'

Though Jan had no idea who Andrew Hayman was, she realized that she had hit upon the raw nerve that Scotty had been trying to protect. And now that she had done so, she had to find some way of calming Scotty or changing the subject. Already his voice, louder with the sudden rush of emotions, had caused several of the diners sitting close to them to stop their own conversations and turn to look at her and Scotty. While she glanced around the room flashing a somewhat apologetic smile, Jan reached across the table and clasped Scotty's left hand between her own two. Looking over into his eyes, still showing red from lack of sleep, Jan tried to calm him. 'I'm sorry, dear, if I've upset you. I didn't mean to meddle in your concerns.'

Blinking his eyes, Scotty returned Jan's gaze and for the first time realized that he had lost it for a moment. Putting his cup of coffee down, which he had held suspended all this time, he took his right hand and put it over the top of Jan's two hands as they held his left hand. 'I'm sorry, Jan, for snapping like that. It's just that . . .'

Jan tilted her head sideways and gave Scotty a sympathetic smile. 'No need to apologize, dear. I understand.' She didn't of course. She seldom did. But it helped to say so, she knew, when they both needed a quick out from an uncomfortable moment.

Accepting what Jan said at face value, Dixon saw this as a good out and used his right hand to pat their hands that were still joined together on the table. 'Thanks, Jan. I appreciate that.' Then with the awkward scene closed, he pulled both hands away and settled back into his chair. 'Have you ordered yet?'

Taking her cue, Jan nodded her head. 'Yes. I'm having the usual. One egg, toast, and fresh fruit.'

With a quick glance at the menu, Dixon made a face. 'That sounds good. I think I'll have the usual too, pancakes and sausage.'

Though what he had just said wouldn't have made any sense to someone else, Jan understood him perfectly. Satisfied that the moment of crisis was over, Jan settled down and did the best she could to enjoy the rest of breakfast with her husband and make it equally enjoyable for him.

To the southwest, and almost two hundred air miles away, Captain Nancy Kozak was just sitting down to eat her breakfast. Finding a nice quiet spot not far from the dummy arms-cache site that they had hit the day before, Kozak dropped to the ground, crossed her legs, and took off her helmet. As she moved her head around in a slow circular motion, she realized that this was the first time she had had that damned thing off in almost twenty-four hours. The sensation that one experiences after taking such a burden off your head is one of wonderful light-headedness. For several moments it almost seems as if your head is floating. For a combat infantryman such feelings are as close to pleasure as one can get while in the field. At that moment Kozak was determined to enjoy her moment of pleasure regardless of anything else that was going on around her.

There was in fact a great deal going on. After having engaged in a bitter firefight throughout the afternoon the day before, the soldiers of Companies A and C of the 3rd Battalion, 511th Infantry, held their ground unsupported throughout the night in a tight perimeter. Only after dawn, when it became clear that the FARC units that had contested control of the area with the 3rd of the 511th so fiercely had slipped away under cover of darkness, did helicopters venture in to bring reinforcements in and evacuate the wounded out. Though this was accomplished quickly and efficiently, it was much too late as far as the soldiers of the 3rd of the 511th were concerned. They had, they felt, been left in the lurch, abandoned by everyone outside the small fire-swept circle of death.

While Nancy Kozak unsnapped her web belt and reached into her pants pocket for her Swiss Army knife, she looked about in an absentminded way. Off to her front several meters away a small squad of soldiers were carefully picking their way through the underbrush searching for enemy emplacements. Despite the fact that the battalion had been at this since dawn, not all the enemy bunkers had been located yet. Those that had been found showed beyond any doubt how badly misinformed the battalion had been about the enemy's strength and intentions.

On the hillside above the dummy arms cache Kozak could see markers used to tag each position uncovered arranged in a series of concentric rings layered one above the other. The FARC commander had arranged his position like an amphitheater, using the arms cache as the stage. It was, she thought, no wonder that Company A wasn't able to effectively mount any type of effective drive from the arms site against their assailants from below. Every move was visible and every inch of ground was covered by more than one position. She and Company C had been lucky at the landing zone, where all they had faced was a single horseshoe ring of positions. Yet even those had been a bear to roll up, requiring nothing less than a full-scale platoon effort to crack each one. By the time they had finished their own fight and were able to reach Company A, the sun was already setting and the danger of fratricide was, in the battalion commander's mind, too great to warrant any further action that night.

In that, Nancy Kozak had concurred. What she couldn't abide, though, was the failure of brigade or division to commit additional attack helicopters in their support or even to send medevac birds in to dust off their wounded. Insistence that the battalion secure the high ground before any aircraft would be sent in by division aviation meant that the wounded spent a painfully long night on the field with only medics available to tend to their needs. Though the medics did more than could have been reasonably expected, their limited training and woefully inadequate aid bags could do nothing to help soldiers who had wounds that only skilled surgeons operating in well-equipped hospitals could have effectively dealt with. In the end several had died. Though most did so quietly, a few could not be quieted. One trooper, his bowels and intestines torn open and exposed by a mortar round, lingered on throughout the night. Only a single well-aimed bullet delivered at close range by a friend at the trooper's request brought him peace.

Like the other survivors of the night Kozak continued to do what was necessary in a rather mechanical manner. With the large blade of her Swiss Army knife she slit open the top of the brown plastic bag that contained her breakfast. Ignoring the detail of soldiers twenty meters away who were busy laying out their dead comrades in body bags, Kozak spilled the contents of her plastic bag on the ground before her. Sorting through it, she looked at each item, putting it either in her lap or throwing it over her shoulder into the undergrowth. Only after she had finished sorting out her breakfast in this manner did she begin to tear into the separate pouches of those items she had kept and eat whatever came out. There was no thought needed to accomplish this particular feat, for there was no enjoyment to be gained from what the Army passed off as food. It was a simple mechanical process, not unlike the one used by the soldiers filling the body bags. For them it was simply a matter of sorting too. After finding a body all they needed to do was drop it in the bag, mark the tag, and pull up the zipper. No thinking necessary. In fact the less thinking the better.

When she was halfway through her meal, Sergeant Andy Pender, her radioman, came trudging up next to her. Looking down at his captain while she ate, he waited for her to acknowledge his presence before speaking. When finally she looked up, he spoke, using the same slow, almost slurred speech that everyone seemed to be using that morning. 'Colonel Cerro's looking for you, ma'am. Says that he will be catching the next helicopter out and needs to turn operations here over to you.'

Kozak waited a moment to clear her throat before speaking. 'Did he say where he's going?'

'Something about him having to go to division head-quarters in Bogotá to see the CG.'

When she let her head drop, it reminded Pender of a puppet collapsing after its strings had been cut. After a moment Kozak let out an audible sigh. 'Well, Sergeant Pender, the Inquisition begins.'

'Pardon me, ma'am?'

Looking back up at Pender as she reached for her helmet, Kozak just shook her head. 'Nothing, Sergeant

Pender. It was nothing. Now do me a favor and inform the colonel that I'll be with him in a minute.'

'Okay. Will do.'

Without saluting, Pender turned away and headed back to where he had left Cerro.

Entering the World News Network offices at a brisk pace, Jan headed straight for her office without pausing to enjoy the usual morning greetings. The only person she spoke to or acknowledged en route was her secretary, and even then it was just a quick 'Have everyone in my office, right now' before she disappeared into it herself.

'Everyone,' of course, didn't mean everyone who worked for WNN in Bogotá. The people Jan called for in her own verbal shorthand were the correspondents and heads of the sections working for her. Being a slow news morning, Jan's wish was easily and quickly accomplished.

When everyone was crowded into her small office, Jan got right to the matter at hand. 'Something's gone down in the last twenty-four hours concerning U.S. forces. Anyone have any ideas what it was?'

For those who knew Jan, her announcement that something had happened delivered in such a positive manner was a signal that she had a lead on something but nothing solid to back it up with. What she was after at this moment was a pooling of rumors and observations from her staff in an effort to come up with a scheme for pursuing her lead. Though few knew where she got her information from, no one doubted that she was right. Her track record and careful methodical methods of developing a story made any doubt a noncontender. All they had to worry about was digging in the right places and finding the information that she and the other correspondents would need to support Jan's lead, whatever it was. And that, she knew, would be only a matter of time. For whatever had shaken Scotty, she told herself, couldn't be hidden from the prying eye of the news camera for very long.

From his desk Colonel Delhue watched through the open door of his office as the commander of the 3rd Battalion, 511th Infantry, left Lane's office and headed off toward the corridor. Even from where he sat Delhue could tell that Cerro had been through hell, both out in the field and in Lane's office. His hangdog look of exhaustion was now accentuated by a mix of shock and anger. Cerro, he knew, would stop and take advantage of a warm shower and change of clothes at the BOQ before fleeing back into the field and away from division headquarters. Bogotá under the best of circumstances was not a good place for a field soldier to hang around. It was, Delhue knew, even worse when Lane was angry at you.

The voice of the division commander coming over the intercom broke Delhue's train of thought. 'Chief, could you come in here a minute?'

Reaching down, Delhue depressed the speaker button. 'On the way, sir.' But rather than jump up and bolt for the door, Delhue eased back in his seat for a moment. Damn, he thought, the bastard is going to can that poor battalion commander. Instead of trying to figure out what went wrong and learning from his experience, Conan is going to bury him and his battalion in a dung heap. After taking another moment to compose himself, Delhue stood up and strolled out of his office to the commanding general's office across the way.

Upon entering, he closed the door and remained standing, waiting for Lane's signal to take a seat. Lane, however, didn't give the signal. Instead he leaned back into his seat and looked at Delhue through partially closed eyes. 'The 3rd of the 511th is due to rotate into Bogotá and assume the division reserve mission soon, isn't it?'

Looking down as if he were mentally checking notes

attached to the front of his skull, Delhue thought a moment before responding. 'Yes, sir. They are, in fact, overdue. The 3rd of the 511th should have been replaced by the 2nd of the 188th Infantry two weeks ago, but that move was delayed at the request of the 3rd Brigade commander.'

'Well, as much as I hate to do it, we're going to have to bump the 3rd of the 511th back down the reserve rotation list again. Tell the G-3 to alert the next unit on that list to begin preparation for assumption of the division reserve mission.'

Delhue waited for an explanation. When none was forthcoming, he asked, 'Sir, why is the 3rd of the 511th being bumped? They have yet to be given a break from the field. We have even had to send their replacements forward to join them out there rather than wait for the unit to come back here. And if the initial reports from yesterday's actions are accurate, they need the time out of the line to pull themselves together.'

Delhue's last comment caused Lane to bolt forward, slapping his hand on the desk. 'The last thing they need, Colonel, is to be taken out of the field. If we pull them back now while they are shaken from yesterday's fiasco, they'll lose their cutting edge. No, they need to stay in the field at least for the foreseeable future and soldier on.' Having vented his anger, Lane eased back again. 'It's like falling off a horse, Chief. If you don't get right back on you never will. You understand, I'm sure.'

Of course Delhue understood. He understood that if the 3rd of the 511th came back to Bogotá, the home base of every news agency covering their little war in Colombia, word of the battalion's ambush by a reinforced FARC company would eventually leak its way into the news. It wasn't the officers Lane was concerned about. Most of them were still sufficiently concerned about their careers not to jeopardize them by saying something that might upset the division commander or Army high command. No, it would be a rifleman at first who would spill the beans. Somehow one of the enlisted men or women, perhaps even a sergeant, disgusted with what they considered pointless operations that wasted lives, would wind up in front of the camera telling the correspondent and the whole world about the dumb-ass mistake that had cost a friend his or her life. It had happened too many times before concerning other issues and operations the soldiers considered botched to expect something of this magnitude, regardless of precautions, to go unnoticed or commented on. No, Delhue knew, Lane couldn't take that chance.

Without any further comment, Delhue acknowledged Lane's order and left, headed to the G-3's office to personally relay the order. When he was alone, Lane reached out and hit his intercom. When his aide responded, he ordered him to put a call through to the deputy chief of staff for operations, a personal friend of his in the Pentagon. It was best, Lane knew, to start squelching Brigadier General Scott Dixon's story of the incident before he had a chance to tell anyone.

While Lane tended to the immediate task of preserving his career, Delhue slowly, almost ponderously, walked down to the division's G-3 operations section. He was dejected. He had been ever since the morning briefing and nothing that he had seen or heard that day had done anything to relieve him of his somber mood. That this required a visit to the operations section didn't lighten his dark mood.

He was, he knew, impaled on the horns of a dilemma, held in check by a code of honor that advocated loyalty to one's superior and devotion to duty above all else. But what was one to do, Delhue asked himself over and over again, when one's superior no longer abided by the same code that he himself so ruthlessly imposed upon his subordinates? And who, he wondered, would or could sit in judgment of such a man? After all, Delhue reasoned, nothing that Lane had said or done, either today or in the past, was technically wrong or inappropriate. As he had before, Delhue turned everything over in his mind two, three times, looking at every word, every order Lane issued in an effort to . . . To what? Delhue thought. What was he trying to do in his own mind? Build a case against his own commanding general? Collect information to present to someone in an effort to prove that Lane had acted and was acting inappropriately? To collect facts so that if the hammer fell, he would be able to cover his own ass? What exactly, Delhue thought, was he doing?

As he came to the end of the corridor where the G-3 operations section started, Delhue hung his head, looking at the floor tiles as he walked, shaking his head while he pondered these bothersome thoughts. Two enlisted members of the division staff headed in the opposite direction paid him no heed. They didn't even comment on Delhue's absentminded shaking of his head. Senior officers, everyone knew, were a rather strange breed of human being and it was best for an enlisted man to simply leave them alone. Passing into the offices where the G-3 and his officers worked, Delhue was stopped by the division operations sergeant. 'Is there something I can help you with, Colonel?'

Looking up, Delhue stared at the sergeant major for a moment before answering. 'No, Sergeant Major, no thank you. I need to see the G-3 on a matter.'

Without any change in expression, the sergeant major shook his head. 'I'm sorry, sir, but the G-3 is in a meeting right now with all of his staff officers. Professional development or something like that.'

Glancing about for the first time, Delhue noticed that except for the Colombian Army major, a Major José Solis, who was assigned to the G-3 section as an adviser and liaison officer, all the officers were absent. Turning his head back to the sergeant major, he was about to ask exactly what 'something like that' was but decided not to. Odds were the sergeant major didn't know. To ask him would only have borne that out and would have embarrassed him. Delhue, like the division G-4, agreed that the operations section was nothing more than a clone farm where Lane was raising a new generation of officers who saw Lane as the personification of the perfect general and slavishly patterned themselves after him. The idea of another generation of Lanes made Delhue shudder.

Deciding not to waste any more of his time, Delhue walked over to Solis, the Colombian officer. As Delhue approached his desk, Solis jumped up and flashed a broad smile on his face, causing Delhue to respond in kind. 'How are you this afternoon, Major?'

When he spoke, there was only a hint of an accent. 'We are doing quite well, Colonel. How may I help you?'

That Solis was not part of whatever kind of meeting the G-3 was holding didn't need to be explained. Lane had more than made it clear that he didn't like the Colombian Army officers, considering them lazy, incompetent, and untrustworthy. He therefore had as little to do with them as he could, and that attitude pervaded the division, especially those who felt the sun rose and set on C. B. Lane. 'I have a message, Major, for the G-3. He is to revise his rotation plan for the division reserve battalion. The 3rd Battalion, 511th Infantry, will be bumped from the top of the list back down into the order someplace.'

Solis nodded. 'Yes, sir, I see. Is there anyplace on the list that the 3rd Battalion, 511th Infantry, should be moved to?'

That he hadn't considered that question surprised Delhue. He was letting his mind get too cluttered with trivial personal concerns and petty politics. He needed to forget about his misgivings and concentrate more on the business of running a division. That decided, he looked into Solis's eyes and thought for a moment. He had to give this officer an answer. Understanding Lane's intent, Delhue worked the issue over in his mind in an effort to come up with a good compromise. If left to Lane, the 3rd of the 511th would never be rotated into the reserve position just outside of Bogotá. That, however, would not do. Eventually the battalion would need to come in and be afforded the opportunity to stand down and rest. Even Lane, Delhue knew, would eventually have to agree to that. Knowing that six to eight weeks would be more than enough time for this issue to blow over and allow another one to creep in and dominate Lane's mind, Delhue told Solis to instruct the G-3 to arrange it so that the 3rd of the 511th would not assume the division reserve mission for at least six weeks. When Solis asked if there was any particular reason why this battalion was being held back from coming in, Delhue didn't provide an answer. He merely shook his head. 'The G-3,' he responded, 'will know the reason.'

With that, Delhue left. For a moment Solis stood there and watched the colonel as he slowly shuffled out of the office. There was something bothering him, Solis thought. There is more to this change in rotation than he is willing to tell. With that thought in mind, Solis sat down and pulled a notebook out of his right breast pocket. He would make a note of this. Perhaps, Solis thought, Hector Valendez would be able to use this information. Then, as he was writing the unit number down, it stuck him like a thunderclap. This was the battalion that had been involved in the ambush the day before. Solis smiled. Yes, he thought, he must include this information in the daily update he fed his FARC contact.

CHAPTER 5

September 29

In Washington, the reaction of the men who made up the Army's senior staff was about what General Fulk had expected. He could tell by their reactions, subtle though they were, that they were not comfortable with what Dixon was saying about the situation in Colombia, especially Lieutenant General Richard Knol. Knol, the deputy chief of staff for operations, became particularly animated when Dixon spoke in terms that made the commander of the 11th Air Assault, one of Knol's fair-haired boys, appear incompetent or at best simply negligent. Dixon, of course, didn't use those words in his briefing. He didn't need to. All he needed to do was lay out the bare facts as he found them and let them speak for themselves. Perhaps, Fulk thought, that was what bothered Knol the most, the fact that what Dixon was saying was so self-damning that he or anyone else didn't need to add any embellishments to paint a clear and accurate picture of what Lane was doing to his division.

As Dixon approached the conclusion of his briefing, he

paused for a moment and looked around the room. There before him, with few exceptions, was every senior officer on the Army staff and major Army command. What he had said up to this point he knew did not sit well with many of these men, men who took great pride in their personal integrity and ethics and those of their institution. To be told that one of their own had submitted reports that were misleading to the point of being false was painful to them. To realize in their heart that it was true was devastating. Dixon, who had been tagged to be one of them someday, understood this. That is why before he concluded his somber presentation he hesitated ever so slightly.

In those few moments of silence he could almost hear himself sweating. From around the room the gathered generals returned his stare, their personal feelings hidden behind masks of stone. Even the man who had sent him on the mission that he was now reporting on, General Fulk, gave Dixon no sign of encouragement, no warm, friendly nod of approval. He was on his own. For the conclusion, unlike the main body of the briefing which contained cold, hard facts, was mostly suppositions, his thoughts and views on what would happen if nothing changed. Suddenly the image of Ebenezer Scrooge standing before the Ghost of Christmas Future popped into Dixon's head. These officers, he realized, for all the confidence that comes with the attainment of high rank and their garnet-like veneer, were afraid of what he was about to show them. For he knew that no one, especially Americans, liked being told that they were going to lose.

Unable to postpone the moment any longer, Dixon looked down at his notes and began. 'Based on the briefings I received from the commander and staff of the 11th Air Assault, discussions with commanders of troop units, both U.S. and Colombian, a thorough review of all pertinent records, reports, and studies, coupled with my personal observations, I have come to the following conclusions. First, the capabilities of the FARC's military arm have not been diminished by the presence of the 11th. On the contrary, the FARC has improved in all areas during the past six months despite the efforts of the 11th. This becomes all too clear when you consider the fact that when the 11th Air Assault first arrived in country, operations by FARC units in greater than squad strength were unheard of. Now there is no denying that they are not only capable of but willing to engage in company-level pitched battles with U.S. forces. This point stands in sharp contrast to the capability or apparent lack of improvement of the Colombian Army. Based on reports and studies from our military assistance teams in Colombia submitted before the deployment of the 11th, I can find no appreciable change in the combat readiness of those units which I inspected. This is even more devastating when you add the fact that most of the units which I did see were supposed to be their showpieces.'

For the first time in the briefing, Fulk interrupted Dixon. He already knew the answer, since Dixon had pre-briefed the chief on everything the day before. Fulk, however, wanted to emphasize Dixon's next point, as well as give him some support, regardless of how minor it was. 'You mentioned that the Colombian units you saw were supposed to be their best. Why do you think otherwise?'

'Well, sir, records show that we have been transferring huge amounts of weapons and equipment to the Colombians, more than enough as of last week to completely re-equip fifty to sixty percent of their Army. I could not find any evidence, however, that this equipment was being issued to those units considered to be their most reliable and best-trained. During my first visit to the brigade they have just outside of Bogotá, a unit they refer to as their Presidential Guard, I saw no new weapons or equipment. Vehicles, weapons, even the soldiers' web gear in that brigade were old and obviously well used.

Before going to their next unit, one deployed in the most sensitive area of the country, I reviewed exactly what we had given them. Again I saw no sign of any new or modern equipment. When I asked the second brigade commander about this, he shrugged and smiled, telling me that the Presidential Guard Brigade had first priority on everything and his unit nothing.'

Leaning forward and folding his hands on the table before him, Fulk looked at Dixon. 'Then where, Scotty, do you suppose all of this equipment is going?'

Relieved that Fulk had called him Scotty, a sure sign that he was on solid ground, at least with the chief, Dixon responded, looking at Fulk as he ignored everyone else in the room. 'That, sir, brings me to my last point. Our efforts and those of the Colombian government have done nothing to relieve the tensions that existed before the military coup of 28 February. The ambassador and his staff made sure that I understood that the economic and political reforms that were introduced shortly after that coup have without exception failed to take hold. If anything, our operations and the efforts of the FARC have brought their reconstruction of the rural infrastructure to a standstill. Key crops such as coffee and cocoa have shown a steady decline since June of this year, one month after we arrived in force.'

Cocking his head back, Fulk looked into Dixon's eyes. 'Which means?'

'I believe, sir, that the Colombian Army is in fact rearming, but not in preparation to fight the FARC. Rather I believe that they are using the equipment we are sending them to outfit units that in a second coup attempt would be used against forces loyal to the government, provided, of course, there are any.'

'Scotty, you're asking me to believe that the Colombian government doesn't know what its own Army is doing. Do you expect us to accept that their own Army is arming itself to the teeth in preparation to get rid of them, and they can't see that?'

Taking a deep breath, Dixon prepared to throw out an answer that he knew would bring the briefing to a close. 'Why not, sir. For the past six months we have been accepting everything coming out of Colombia from our own people as gospel. I have no doubt that the Colombian government has the same capacity to believe whatever it chooses despite the facts.'

From out of the corner of his eye, Dixon saw Knol sit bolt upright in his seat. He didn't need to look over to where Knol sat to know that his last comment had the chief of operations on the edge of his seat, nostrils flaring and blood in his eyes. Turning his full attention back to Fulk, Dixon saw what he thought was a faint smile on the chief's face. Only slowly did Dixon realize that the chief had used him and his briefing to bring Knol down a peg or two in a high-profile Pentagon power game. Though he didn't like internal politics, especially in an institution such as the Army, where soldiers' lives and national security were at stake, Dixon knew that they were part of the landscape. The fact was it took some serious behind-the-door maneuvering by several senior officers who liked Dixon to get him his star, and Dixon knew it.

Pushing those bitter thoughts from his mind, Dixon turned his full attention back to the matter at hand. Fulk gave him the high sign to continue. 'In conclusion, sir, based on what I now know, I believe that there is nothing that we can do, now or in the next six months, to save the Colombian government.'

'Rather bleak outlook, isn't it?'

'It is, sir, more than bleak. I am assuming that the Colombian Army is simply waiting for us to leave before they decide to go into round two with their own government. And even that is assuming that the weight of FARC successes in the field and the failures of the Colombian government to deliver promised reforms don't beat the Colombian Army to the punch. In my opinion, sir, we'll be lucky if the current Colombian government holds up long enough for us to get out of there.'

He was about to pick up his briefing where he'd left off, but Knol interrupted. 'General Fulk, pardon the intrusion here, but I've heard enough.' Jabbing his index finger at Dixon while he faced Fulk, Knol's voice betrayed his anger. 'Just who in the hell does he think he's talking to. I have seen nothing to support one allegation – '

Without saying a word, Fulk cut Knol short. A simple gesture of his head and a glance about the room so subtle that Dixon missed it told Knol that it was time to cease and desist. This also served as a warning to everyone present that another such outburst would not be tolerated. When he was satisfied that he had restored order, Fulk turned his attention back to Dixon. 'Scotty, I would like to thank you for your report and observations. Now if you would excuse us, I have a few items I want to cover with these gentlemen before we all break for the day.' With that Fulk turned away from Dixon, leaving him to slip quietly out the door and away from the firestorm that he suspected his briefing was about to generate. Pausing only long enough in the anteroom to stuff his notes and supporting documents into his briefcase, Dixon was about to flee out the door when Fulk's aide came up to him and touched him on the arm. 'General Dixon, General Fulk would like to see you in his office as soon as he's finished here.'

Damn! he thought. Damn it, now what? Then, without having to think about it, Dixon realized that his involvement with the war in Colombia wasn't over. It was, he feared, if anything, just beginning.

To his surprise, Dixon didn't have long to wait. Fulk, his head down and muttering to himself, burst into the outer office where Dixon sat waiting and charged straight forward toward his door. His secretary, used to such entrances, shouted out as fast as she could while he stormed by, 'General Fulk, a reminder that you're scheduled to meet with the Secretary of the Army and Sec Def in twenty minutes.' The slamming of Fulk's door served nicely to punctuate the end of the secretary's announcement. Fulk's aide, unable to keep up with his boss, came trotting in a second later. As he came in, the secretary shot a knowing glance at him. The aide sighed. 'Lions ten, Christians nothing.' With that, the secretary shook her head once before going back to filling in the next day's schedule while the aide went over to his desk and began to sift through the pile of messages that had gathered in the center of it during his absence.

For the next minute or so the three of them, Dixon, the secretary, and the aide, sat in their own little corners, keeping to their own thoughts or busy work. To Dixon this lull was both a blessing and a time of apprehension. It was a blessing because for the first time since Fulk had given him the task of finding out what really was going on in Colombia he had nothing pressing to do. Dixon had hoped that the briefing he had just concluded and the written report on which it was based finished that project. But as he sat there watching the secretary and aide go about their separate jobs while waiting for him to leave so that they could gossip about what had happened at the briefing, he knew in his heart that that wasn't going to be.

'Martha, send General Dixon in.' Fulk's sudden barking over the intercom that sat on the secretary's desk startled no one but Dixon. He looked at them for a second, then shook his head. They must be used to this sort of thing, he thought as he stood up, adjusted the coat of his uniform, and prepared to go in. Dying to see him go so that she could talk freely to the aide about what had gotten their boss in such a huff, the secretary smiled and pointed to Fulk's door. 'The chief will see you now, General.'

With the same dread as that of a schoolboy going to see the principal, Dixon walked into Fulk's office. The chief, his uniform jacket unbuttoned, sat behind his desk slouched down in his seat, surrounded by a haze of cigarette smoke, madly puffing away on a cigarette. This surprised Dixon, who had grown used to the anti-smoking campaigning of the Army. The surprise obviously showed in his face, for Fulk took the cigarette, held it at arm's length, and looked at it for a moment. 'My wife will give me hell for starting again.' He turned his gaze to Dixon as he took another puff. 'She always knows. That woman has a nose like a blood hound.' He chuckled. 'Of course, whenever I start again, I always try sneaking into the house in an effort to get upstairs and change before she gets a good sniff of my uniform. You'd think after thirty-two years of marriage I'd finally get my act together, but no. There are just some things that never seem to change.'

At a loss as to what to do and how to respond, Dixon simply stood there and nodded. Seeing that his efforts to put Dixon at ease were failing miserably, Fulk decided to drop the chase and get down to the matter at hand. Motioning to Dixon to take a seat, Fulk sat up, snubbed out the cigarette, and leaned across his desk, folding his hands and thrusting his head toward Dixon. 'Scotty, in fifteen minutes I'm going to have to go into the Secretary of Defense's office and tell him that we are involved in another war that we cannot win.' Fulk let that thought hang in the air for a second before he pushed himself back into his seat and looked up at the ceiling. 'I don't like that. Not one bit.' Looking back at Dixon, 'And he isn't going to like that either, especially since he was the stupid son of a bitch who thought of sending combat forces to Colombia in the first place. The idea that a simple military show of force, that the image of American combat troops alone will solve the world's problems has been tried one time too many. And I'm the schmuck who's going to have to tell the administration that, in terms that even the Sec Def can understand.'

As Fulk spoke, Dixon at once felt a sense of relief and one of sympathy. Relief that the chief himself was going to serve as the bearer of bad tidings to the Secretary of Defense, something that he had been afraid Fulk would require him to do. With that burden lifted, Dixon was free to feel a little sympathy for Fulk for having to do so.

'You know what the first thing the Secretary is going to do, Scotty?' Without waiting for an answer, Fulk continued. 'He's going to say, "Well, perhaps the Joint Chiefs of Staff were right. Perhaps we do need to send in Air Force ground attack units and use the Marines to deal with the Caribbean provinces." I can see it all now. Jet jockeys with big watches and little penises zooming in at four hundred miles an hour dropping a couple of tons of ordnance on villages all over the place while the media have a heyday filming the jarheads splashing ashore like John Wayne in the *Sands of Iwo Jima*. Christ, in a month it will be a regular three-ring circus.'

While the chief vented his anger and frustration, Dixon simply sat watching him, nodding his head, and going over all the arguments in his mind that the Army had used to keep the other two services out of Colombia. The fact that this was in the beginning a low-intensity conflict, a simple guerrilla war and that the Army was trained to deal with it. The fact that only small well-trained, highly mobile combat units were needed to deal with the FARC threat. The fact that a single service with common techniques and a single clean chain of command would best serve our purposes, and finally the fact that we wanted to keep the lowest possible profile. All that had sounded good seven months ago when the intervention into Colombia was first being discussed. There had been, Scotty knew, nothing less than an in-house fight between the services in an effort to determine who got the lion's share of the mission and the funding. In the end it had been the Army's plan, submitted over Fulk's own signature, that had won out. Now Fulk was going to have to go in to the Secretary of Defense, the very man he had convinced seven months ago that the Army could do the job, and tell him that they were failing. Still, Dixon thought, this wasn't all bad. At least Fulk was taking a stand now, while he still had something to stand on. At least, he thought, this wouldn't be another Vietnam.

Then, just as that thought came to Dixon, Fulk shattered it. 'Scotty, I can't go into the Sec Def's office empty-handed. I've got to tell him something that will buy us some time so that we can sort this thing out on our own. That's where you come in.'

Those words, though he had been expecting them, hit Dixon like a sledgehammer. Tensing up in preparation to receive without flinching whatever the chief was about to throw his way, Dixon waited for the other shoe to fall. The wait was mercifully short.

When he spoke this time, Fulk's tone and voice were very deliberate and calculating. 'I've come to the conclusion that Lane and the 11th Air Assault down in Colombia need closer supervision. Jerry Stratton can't do it from SOUTHCOM headquarters. Too far. What we need is someone on the ground representing Jerry and SOUTHCOM who can physically go out and personally verify reports and progress.'

Fulk's obvious solution, as Dixon watched it unfold, both appalled and stunned him. Rather than seek a quick and direct means of resolving the problems as Dixon saw them, the chief was coming up with a solution that was at best a Band-Aid. Lane, Dixon thought, needed to be relieved and pressure from the State Department needed to be applied to the Colombian government in an effort for them to clean up their own house. Though Dixon thought that he might be jumping to conclusions, he feared that he wasn't. Pushing his own thoughts to the background, he continued to listen as Fulk outlined his solution.

'I'm going to have Jerry establish a forward command post for SOUTHCOM on Bogotá.' Looking over at Dixon, Fulk pointed at him. 'You're going to be in charge of it.'

With that brief statement, Dixon's worst fears were realized.

'The mission of this command post, we'll call it SOUTH-COM Forward, will be assisting the 11th Air Assault in coordinating with and reporting to SOUTHCOM. You will serve as General Stratton's personal representative in Colombia and provide whatever assistance to the commander of the 11th Air Assault he deems necessary to facilitate the quick and accurate flow of reports and orders back and forth between SOUTHCOM and the 11th.'

For a moment Dixon waited for additional instructions. But there were none. Rather than do something substantial about correcting the problems that Lane was creating, Fulk was putting a Band-Aid on the whole affair in the hope that it would stem the hemorrhage that Dixon was predicting. Though he didn't like it, none of it, he had spoken his mind and now he had his orders, though they were at this moment far from clear. For the first time since entering the chief's office, Dixon spoke. 'Will this forward command post have any operational control over the 11th Air Assault?'

Dixon's question caused Fulk to think for a second. With a shrug and a slight shaking of his head Fulk responded. 'No, I don't think so. At least not at this time.'

The manner of Fulk's response confirmed Dixon's worse suspicion: Fulk was making this up on the spur of the moment and didn't have a clear idea in his own head what he really wanted. That meant that Dixon would be, as he just had been during the briefing, pretty much on his own. 'When, sir, am I to have this headquarters established and functioning?'

Fulk waved his hand. 'After you finish up with your written report, head down to SOUTHCOM and get with their chief of staff. Find out when he can put together a package using the staff and equipment he has on hand and get it down to Bogotá. When you have a good idea, let me know when you can be on the ground and running.'

The sinking feeling that Dixon had begun to experience was slowly being replaced with one that was a mix of dark foreboding and acute depression. Nothing, it appeared right now, would be changed in Bogotá. Like a tenured professor who had long ago outlasted his usefulness, Lane would be maintained in place simply because there was no clean, graceful way of removing him without causing internal political problems. A compromise solution arrived at by the Army's highest counsel had been reached, and like most compromise solutions this one didn't really solve the problem.

Still General Fulk was the chief, Dixon's boss, and he had made his decisions and issued his orders. All Dixon had to do now, he knew, was to salute and carry on like a good soldier. That he would do so there was no doubt. In his briefing and in his written report Dixon had voiced his opinion and had made his recommendations. That the chief had opted not to listen to all of them was regrettable to Dixon, but there was nothing that he could do. To push the matter further just now would serve no useful purpose as far as Dixon was concerned.

Finished with him, Fulk dismissed Dixon, lit another cigarette, and leaned back in his chair as he pondered how best to deal with the Secretary of Defense.

Under different circumstances, the countryside which the troops of Company B, 3rd of the 511th Infantry, moved through would have been beautiful to behold. The lush green vegetation lining the sides of fertile valleys through which clear mountain streams ran down to empty into the Rio Cauca stood in stark contrast to the commanding mountains that made up the Colombian Sierra. But all of this natural beauty was lost to the men and women of Company B. They were not out there moving along at a snail's pace along narrow trails that wound their way up and down one hill after another for enjoyment. They were, as the orders that originated from Division stated, conducting a show of force, moving about the countryside in an effort to encourage the natives and intimidate the enemy.

Nancy Kozak, as well as most of the B Company troopers, doubted that they could encourage anyone, especially themselves. Nor did they believe that the Farcees would be very much impressed by the show they were trying to put on, not after giving the other two line companies in the battalion a sound beating and then slipping away in the dark. As one sergeant said loud enough for Kozak to hear, 'We couldn't even awe the dullest donkey in these mountains right now if we wanted to.'

Still the operation wasn't a total waste, at least not for Kozak, who marched along between the second and third rifle platoons in the column. The monotony of watching the same rucksack of the trooper in front of her as the file of soldiers snaked their way up one hill, and then down another didn't bother Nancy Kozak. Even the streams of sweat running down her face and soaking every stitch of clothing she wore didn't faze her. It was instead in its own way rather therapeutic. The one thing she was sure of was that it was a damned sight better being out here humping up and down the mountains than sitting back at the brigade base camp listening to the bickering and whining of the troops.

Word that the battalion had been taken out of the rotation for division reserve had come as a shock. Coming as it did, on the heels of the ambush at the arms cache, the men and women of the battalion, both officers and enlisted, couldn't help but draw the conclusion that they were being punished for their conduct during the ambush. The manner in which the troopers themselves reacted varied, depending on where they had been that day. The people who had actually been involved in the ambush and resulting firefight were stunned, then angered. They knew what had happened. They knew that they had done everything that humanly could have been done given the situation they were thrown into. Fact was that most of them came out of it feeling rather proud of the way that they as individuals and units had behaved under appalling conditions. Their battalion commander himself, Lieutenant Colonel Cerro, had in fact congratulated them on their ability to maintain discipline and unit cohesion throughout the day despite appalling losses. Which is why when the word came down that they would remain in the field conducting combat operations instead of going to what the troopers in the 11th referred to as 'The Big City,' their sense of pride turned to one of bewilderment and anger. How they as individuals and squads could have done better was beyond them. Not even Cerro could explain with any degree of satisfaction why they were being forsaken.

Cerro himself was rocked back on his heels by the censure Lane had given him. Though he didn't go into specifics and limited his comments to one-liners like 'That man's incredible' or 'He has no earthly idea what's going on out here,' Nancy Kozak knew that whatever had transpired between the two men had affected her battalion commander as nothing had before. 'He was,' she wrote in a private letter to her grandfather, 'a man transformed, a knight of the realm suddenly exposed to the harshest deprivations of a system he had not only defended but believed in with his heart and soul. Though he continues to soldier, it is clear that this is out of habit now and not out of love for the profession and what it had once stood for. He is, in short, a broken man.'

In the days that followed, and Kozak watched, nothing seemed to revive her sagging spirit as she watched a man she so admired tear himself up from within. In a firefight, the man gave the appearance of being fearless. He conducted himself in the same calm, almost remote manner during an engagement with the enemy as he did on training exercises. Some even commented that he actually appeared to slow down some during a fight, almost as if he were forcing himself to keep from being carried away by the chaos and confusion around him. Even his handling of personnel and administrative issues was almost faultless, a rarity for a combat leader with a background such as his. It had been Kozak's experience that most combat arms officers were either super troopers in the field and wanting in all other areas or they were whiz-bang staff officers who couldn't fight their way out of a paper bag. Cerro seemed to be both, which was why she so admired him and had fought so hard to be assigned to his battalion.

Had he only had to deal with the aftermath of the ambush, given a little time Cerro could have pulled the battalion back together and restored confidence to those shaken by the experience of that battle. But the mindless decision to keep them in the field indefinitely was too much for Cerro's skills as a leader, just as it was too much for the soldiers to understand. Complicating the issue was the fact that a rift within the battalion itself appeared as soon as everyone found out that they were not going to the rear for what they considered was a well-deserved rest. For those soldiers within the battalion who had not taken part in the fight at the dummy arms cache blamed those who had for the mass punishment that the division commander had brought down on them. In the charged environment that existed at the time word got out, there was nothing officers or NCOs could do to stop the fights, sometimes involving whole platoons, from breaking out. This ripped whatever was left of the delicate fabric called unit cohesion to shreds and left Cerro with a situation for which his training and experience had not prepared him.

The brigade commander, Colonel Henry R. Johnson, an individual who was outside of the division commander's circle of chosen favorites, did all he could do to lessen the impact of Lane's seemingly mindless decision. The division operations section, however, anticipating such a move, ensured that Johnson's brigade had more missions than it could handle with the units assigned to it. This move in effect forced Johnson to use the bulk of Cerro's battalion on a daily basis, leaving Cerro no time to sort out his internal problems.

For some people in the 3rd Battalion, 511th, this was fine by them. Kozak was one of those people. She saw what was happening and knew that eventually it would have severe and dire consequences. But, like Cerro, nothing in her training or experience equipped her to deal with the quagmire of internal resentment and self-recrimination that the battalion found itself in. Though she did have the people within her own staff section to deal with, Kozak was a staff officer, the acting operations officer for the battalion. Technically her job as the battalion S-3 had nothing to do with the maintenance of morale and discipline within the battalion. Those areas of responsibility belonged to the commanders and leaders of the battalion, called green tabbers because of the one-inch green felt cloth they wore under the unit crest on the tabs of their dress green uniforms. As a staff officer Kozak could concentrate on dealing only with the problems concerning the missions and tactical operations of the battalion. Though the morale of the battalion and its ability to function as a cohesive force did impact on its combat capability, she didn't need to deal with the factors that contributed or detracted from those delicate and pliable commodities. She didn't need to come up with solutions or become directly involved in efforts to revive them. She could and did put on mental blinders and kept her attention focused solely on doing her job, period.

It wasn't that Kozak didn't care about what was happening to the battalion. Like every officer who was worth a damn, she was very much concerned about the downward spiral of morale and effectiveness that showed no sign of ending. Nancy Kozak was too good an officer not to care. But caring and being able to do something about it were not the same thing. The problem of encouraging soldiers, shoring up flagging morale, and mending fractured cohesion required leaders who themselves were confident and together. While it is possible for someone to go through the mechanical process of producing operational plans or issuing orders without regard to physical or mental state, a leader who was shaken himself, whose face betrayed fear or who spoke with a voice that lacked conviction could do nothing to influence others. That in a nutshell was Kozak's problem and, to a lesser extent but only slightly, Cerro's too.

For they, like the soldiers who had been with them at the arms cache, had felt that the battalion had done well despite the odds. And because Cerro and Kozak were humans, just like their people they too felt the bite of Lane's seemingly arbitrary decision to deny them the rest that was not only well deserved but needed. Kozak in particular had been looking forward to spending time in The Big City with AJ, the aviation captain who had captured her heart as no other man had ever done before. To suffer the trauma of battle like the one that the battalion had been involved in, followed by word that the one thing that had been sustaining her for weeks, her dream leave with AJ in Bogotá, would be denied her was too much.

At a time when everyone around her was suffering the same sense of anger and frustration, there were few that Kozak could turn to for advice and comfort. She had considered confiding her feelings to the one intimate friend that she had at the base camp, another female captain by the name of Jessica Ann Cruthers, who was the assistant brigade intelligence officer, but quickly dismissed that idea. She had, or thought she still had, an image to maintain. To go to an officer on the brigade staff and cry on her shoulder, regardless of what their relationship was, would be in Kozak's eyes unprofessional. Though she suspected that Cruthers would as a woman understand, Kozak had since entering active duty carefully guarded her emotions and feelings, confiding in no one and dealing with her feelings alone as best she could. Now when she suddenly felt the need to turn to someone, someone who could help her by lending her a sympathetic ear and easing her seemingly intolerable burden with a kind word and friendly smile, Kozak not only found that she had no one she could trust, she didn't even know how to.

There was, of course, AJ. Before the fight at the arms cache, Kozak and he would spend hours on the phone late at night when traffic over the military lines was almost nil. The two seemed to be able to talk about almost everything, from their day-to-day experiences in Colombia to memories of growing up and views on the world at large. Such conversations, free-flowing and uninhibited by rank, protocol, or the need to maintain a professional facade, had come to mean a lot to Kozak. After one such conversation that had gone on well into the early morning hours, Kozak suddenly realized how much she had given up in her pursuit of a military career. Like a blind person who had suddenly been given sight, she understood all the misgivings and concerns that her mother, even her own father, a former officer himself, had tried so hard to communicate to her. What she would do about AJ and how she would fit her newfound feelings and love into a promising career were questions still unanswered when they had gone into the arms cache.

Now, like everything else, her affair with AJ was on hold. For not only did she have to fight through the acute depression that hung over her like a gray winter day, she had to sort out how she felt about AJ, who was an aviator. Of all the surprises and shocks that had rocked the battalion during the firefight, the one that had hurt the most was the feeling that the aviators of the division, the people who made an air assault unit what it was, had abandoned them.

Not that it was the fault of the aviators in general or AJ in particular. They, like everyone else, up to the moment that the first surface-to-air-missile, or SAM, had been launched, had been working under the premise that the Farcees didn't have any shoulder-fired SAMs. As with the overly optimistic intelligence summaries that denied the FARC the capability of conducting company-level operations, no mention was ever made, officially or unofficially, about periodic reports of Russian- and French-made SAMs turning up here and there in Colombia. This failure to appreciate the potential danger led to the habit of not arming the helicopters of the division with anti-missile flares dropped by helicopters in their wake to lure away incoming heat-seeking missiles. On the day of the ambush, the flares of the aviation company supporting Kozak's battalion were safely locked away in their storage boxes at the division's main ammunition supply point. When word of the disaster of the arms cache reached the division, orders went out that no aircraft was to be permitted to enter into the battle zone until the FARC forces had broken contact and the area was secured or they had been armed with the flares. The operations officer of the aviation battalion took this order to mean all, to include medical evacuation birds. Thus, during the critical hours when the 3rd of the 511th's wounded needed evacuation and everyone still in the fight needed fire support from attack helicopters, the wings of the division sat idle, unable to respond while a

frantic search of the division ammo dump was conducted
to find the well-packed flares.

In her mind, the logical part at least, Kozak could
understand that AJ had nothing to do with the decision
not to arm the helicopters with the anti-missile flares. He
had no say over the order preventing needed relief and
support flights from reaching the 3rd of the 511th when
they were needed the most. Kozak knew this. Yet, with
the same irrational thought process that allows a woman
who has been raped to blame a husband for not protecting
her, even though he was physically unable to do anything
to protect her, Kozak condemned AJ. She condemned
him by virtue of the fact that he was an aviator and thus
in a convoluted sort of way no better than the operations
officer and whoever kept the choppers from coming to the
rescue.

With her mind busy churning away at this and other
personal concerns, Kozak missed hearing the first few
pop-pop-pops of an M-16 firing at the head of the column
that announced the initiation of a firefight. It was only
when the rucksack that she had been staring at in front
of her disappeared that she realized something was going
on. Startled, she stopped and looked to the left and right
before she understood what was happening. Then without
another thought she threw herself to the side of the trail,
just as everyone in front of her had.

From behind she felt a tap on her shoulder. Without
needing to look back to see what it was, Kozak reached
up with her right hand and let her radioman for today,
Specialist Luis Haya, pass her the radio's hand mike.
Set to the Bravo Company's command frequency, Kozak
listened to the initial contact report from the platoon
leader of the lead platoon to his commander. Like most
young men involved in a sudden and unexpected fight,
the platoon leader spoke just a little too fast and with a
slightly higher pitch in his voice. 'Bravo Six, Bravo Six,

this is Bravo Two Six. My point element ran into a half a dozen armed people at a trail junction about one hundred meters up ahead. The other people didn't return fire. They just took off into the jungle headed northwest. Should I pursue? Over.'

There was a pause. Kozak said nothing as she waited to hear the company commander's decisions. Though technically outranking him by virtue of her position, she had no intention of intervening in the manner in which the company commander ran his company unless of course he did something that was totally inappropriate. Like Cerro, she believed in allowing subordinates maximum leeway in exercising their prerogatives and authority. That she was present that day with Company B was only due to her personal desire to get away from the oppressive atmosphere that permeated the base camp and not from any wish to run the operation at hand.

In the few seconds that stretched between the platoon leader's request for guidance and the announcement of his decision, the commander of Company B had to juggle many considerations and options in an effort to come up with the best one. If he guessed right, he and his company would be successful, winning the day and another battle. On the other hand, if he made a bad choice, all he'd wind up doing was stuffing more body bags. In light of the recent past, the company commander opted on the side of caution. 'Bravo Two Six, this is Bravo Six. Deploy your platoon and form a base of fire. I'll bring the First Platoon up on your right and move forward in pursuit. Third Platoon will follow and be prepared either to swing to your left or follow First. Do you understand? Over.'

Without any hesitation, the Second Platoon leader responded, 'I roger. We'll be set in a minute. Over.' No sooner had that platoon leader stopped transmitting than another voice came over the radio. 'Bravo Six, this is Bravo One Six, I roger your last transmission to Two Six.

I am preparing to move my element around to the right as soon as you give the word. Over.' Again, as soon as the last platoon leader let go of the hand mike, a fourth voice came up on the air. 'Six, this is Three Six. I monitored your instructions to Two Six. I am closing up my people and standing by for further orders. Over.'

Without waiting for any further response, the company commander came back. 'Okay Bravo, let's do it. Out.' As if on cue, the soldier in front of Kozak got up and began to move forward at the double with his rifle held close to his chest and ready. Taking the radio hand mike from her ear and thrusting it back without looking, Kozak yelled to her radioman, 'Let's get moving, Haya, before we get run over.' Once she felt Haya grab it away, she pushed herself up off the ground with the aid of the rifle, brought it up to the ready position, and took off after the platoon to her front. As she caught up, the first reassuring thought in days popped into her head. At least, she thought, the soldiers were still able to react well under pressure. Of course this was just one company, the one that hadn't been involved in the fight at the arms cache. Still it was something.

Up ahead, no more than two hundred meters from the trail junction where Hector Valendez and his small escort had stumbled into a group of American soldiers, Valendez ordered a halt. He had no sooner dropped down to one knee facing to the northwest when the squad leader of Valendez's small escort came up next to him and dropped to one knee next to him. The squad leader, a young man who had left an American-owned coffee plantation to fight for the land that had once been his father's, was winded, more from the excitement of running into the Americans and being fired on than from running.

While the squad leader waited for orders, Valendez looked over his shoulder, cocking his head to listen for a moment in the direction he and his small party had just fled from. In the distance he could hear the orders in English being shouted. When it became evident that the voices were growing no closer, a slight smile began to creep across his face. They were deploying first and preparing to come forward carefully. The Americans, he thought, had learned caution.

Turning to the squad leader, he studied him before he issued his orders. There was a hint of fear in the young man's eyes. Yet there was no panic. Though shaken, he was waiting patiently, as he had been trained, for his orders from the senior commander present. And no one in the entire FARC's military arm was more senior at this moment than Valendez. Without any flourishes or unnecessary embellishments, Valendez spoke. 'You will hold here for five seconds after I leave with my party. At the count of five your men will open fire in the directions of the Americans for two to three seconds. Then, without delay, break and continue to move to the northwest as fast as you can for two to three hundred meters. Stop, turn, and fire your weapons again for several seconds. After that, change directions, moving to the southwest until you reach the river. Once you've done that, cross over, move upstream, and find someplace secure to hold up for the night near the river. In the morning move out and rejoin your unit as quickly as possible. Is that clear?'

There was no thought of questioning Valendez's orders. The squad leader knew where Valendez was headed and understood that he could best protect his commander now by drawing away the Americans so that he could continue to the secret meeting with the ruling council. Nor did he dread telling his men what they were about to do. Whatever apprehension the fighters of the FARC had felt about closing with the Americans in close combat had been eradicated by the fight that Valendez himself had planned and led. With a nod and a confident 'Yes, it shall be,' the squad leader stood up and turned away from

Valendez, signaling his squad by hand to deploy in a firing line facing the direction from which they had just fled.

Finished with the squad leader, Valendez also stood, pointing to his assistant and radioman. With a quick wave of his right hand he signaled them to follow as he pivoted a quarter turn and ran north at a quick trot. After traveling for several seconds, the three came to a halt in a line several meters from the trail. The small party of rebels dropped down to one knee in unison and listened. To their rear they could hear the sound of a volley of gun fire. To their immediate front they heard or saw nothing. Satisfied that the Americans were still taking their time and deploying, Valendez signaled to his assistant. 'Onto the trail and head north on the double.' Though the radioman questioned the wisdom of getting back onto the trail so soon after running into an American force, he followed the assistant without hesitation, trusting the judgment of their esteemed leader.

When they were up and on the trail running north as fast as their loads permitted, Valendez hung back a little and turned around, running backwards as he did. His first instinct back there had been to turn and fight. He had found it necessary to use every ounce of restraint he had to keep from doing so. Not because the Americans they had encountered outnumbered them. Together with his radioman, assistant, and the escort, he had nine men versus the four Americans he thought had been a point element. With both sides equally surprised, his nine could have easily taken the four. But that, he knew, wouldn't have been prudent. For even if they had taken out all four and been able to get away before follow-on forces could come up, there was a good chance that his own people would have taken one or more casualties. That would have meant they would have had to stop and police up their wounded or leave them and face the possibility that they would betray under interrogation the identity of who had been traveling with them, where they had come from, and where they were going. The risking of such consequences wasn't worth the momentary thrill that participating in a stand-up firefight with the enemy would have brought him. So, like the good commander and tactician he was, Valendez looked, thought, decided, and acted appropriately.

Spinning back to face front, he picked up his pace in order to catch up with the rest. As he did so, he also decided that it would have been a shame if he had himself been struck down now when he almost had in his hands everything that he had been working for. At the meeting of the revolutionary council that he was headed for, he expected to be given carte blanche to step up the military pressure on both the American and Colombian forces as he saw fit and conditions warranted. The success of his six-hour battle with the Americans eight days before would be, he knew, more than enough to convince even the most skeptical member of the council that his ideas and plans were sound. Though he expected heated debates and some dissension, a feature of every meeting of the FARC's council, in his heart he knew that they would release control of the newly formed regular forces that he himself had organized and trained.

Though by most standards the twenty-seven companies of the FARC's regular forces were slight, when grouped with the special weapons platoons into nine provisional battalions, they would form a hard-hitting force, one unlike anything that the FARC ever before possessed. Augmented with local rebel forces, the military arm of the FARC would then bring to an end the seeming pointless hit-and-run raids that stung but did no permanent damage and begin to concentrate on carving out permanent rebel enclaves. Such holdings, Valendez knew, no matter how trivial, would serve to discredit the government and force them to come to the FARC and fight them on their terms, in their time, just as he had done on a small scale to the Americans. That he and his forces, molded by his own hands, would ultimately be victorious was never in doubt in Valendez's mind.

Nor was there any doubt about how this would all end in the minds of the few Americans who took the time to carefully read the unmistakable signs of doom that were growing in number like a gathering storm as each day past. Rather than light at the end of the tunnel, all they saw was a gathering darkness. And it frightened them.

PART TWO

THE END OF
INNOCENCE

CHAPTER 6

October 2

Before the first shot was fired in the FARC's new campaign, a different kind of battle had to be fought. It took place at a remote site not far from Armenia, a city located in the Cauca River Valley. The logic of choosing such a site baffled Valendez, since the current leadership of the FARC could come and go just about anywhere in Colombia without fear, but he said nothing. Despite the fact that they were men of strength and character, with few naive illusions left, they, the FARC's chosen leaders, still needed on occasion to indulge their fantasies. One of the fantasies that many of them cherished as fondly as his own manhood was the image of himself as a struggling revolutionary hunted by the government and forced to lead a secret and precarious existence. For each and every one knew that one day, long after their victory had been won and they were nothing but memories, the more heroic and dangerous their lives seemed, the brighter those memories would burn. So Valendez, despite the fact that his travel to this meeting had almost cost him his own life, said nothing. He had other issues that needed to be attended to and he had no intention of allowing trivial concerns to confuse or dilute his agenda.

This meeting, as all of them did, started with rivals on the ruling council heaping praise and platitudes upon their most bitter enemies on the council in an elaborate charade designed to give everyone present the illusion that all was well between the leaders of the FARC. The object of most of the opening day's salutations and acclaim was Valendez, the hero of the moment. First came Simón Mortino, the chairman of the council and sharpest critic of what he called Valendez's mindless war of attrition. He opened the meeting by standing up and summarizing in the most glowing terms the political and propaganda benefits Valendez's ambush had already reaped. 'We have shown,' he crowed, 'that we are men who are not afraid to stand up to the machines and firepower of the Yankees. We have given our people hope and pride. Hope that one day we will in fact prevail despite the odds, and pride that the courage to liberate ourselves from oppression is within our own hands. My good friend Hector Valendez, the man his enemies now call The Jaguar, has shown us the way, the way to victory.'

Mortino's speech did not surprise Valendez. In fact, had he not spoken in such a manner, Valendez would have been concerned. Nor did the following speech, given by Mortino's archrival on the council, León Febres Cordero, contain any surprises or variations from the tired old line that he had been spouting for years. Cordero, a man who viewed political change from within the existing system as the only true way to meaningful success, and therefore an opponent of any form of armed insurrection, nevertheless could not allow his opponent on the council to reap all the fruit of Valendez's labors. No sooner had Mortino sat down than Cordero stood up and continued to heap praise in a backhanded sort of way on Valendez. 'As you all know,' he stated, 'I am a man who has from the beginning advocated change from within, using the government's own laws to destroy it. But I am not a naive fool. I can, like many of you, appreciate the need to hurry things along with a little shove every now and then. Through the recent efforts of our deputy commander of the military arm, we have given the government in Bogotá and the Americans something to think about.' Pausing, Cordero looked at Valendez and then at Mortino. 'But I, as always, advise caution when wielding the bayonet. Pushing too hard too fast might cause our enemies to rally and our friends to shy away. We, the leaders of the revolution, must put our heads together and determine how best to use the victory that our heroic field commander, Hector Valendez, has given us.'

This last sentence, coming from Cordero himself, pleased Valendez for several reasons. The first and most obvious was an admission finally that the FARC's military arm had a viable role to play in bringing down the government in Bogotá. Like many of the pseudo intellectuals that had infiltrated the ranks of the FARC in recent years, Cordero had championed peaceful and legal means of effecting change to the exclusion of all others. To openly admit at a meeting of the full council that there was a place for military operations in his theory of revolution could only be viewed as a last gasp for a failed policy. Though he was tempted to smile as Cordero spoke those words, Valendez did not. Biding his time, he simply nodded in acknowledgment. Besides the moral victory of finally forcing Cordero to admit the need for armed confrontation, a more subtle and far-reaching victory for Valendez had been proclaimed by Cordero's simple statement. When Cordero referred to Valendez as 'our heroic field commander' and no one on the council bothered to remind him that Valendez was only the deputy, Valendez knew that from that moment on his voice and his opinions, when it came to military operations, would dominate. He had without any scheming or manipulation been given everything he needed to carry out his war against his enemies, both here in the council and out there in the forests, streets, mountains, and jungles of Colombia.

Even so, Valendez was rather circumspect about using his newly won power. For despite the praise and joy over the recent victories of the FARC's military arm over both the Yankees and the government forces in the field, there was still some opposition to the notion that it was time to accelerate the military campaign. Early on in the meeting, however, this opposition was easily swept aside. Valendez's success of the twenty-first of September assured that. Talk by the council members themselves that one day Colombians would look back to that date as being the military turning point of the people's war against an intolerably corrupt government gave the twenty-first of September more meaning than Valendez could ever have hoped for and silenced many naysayers.

Of course, the heady joy of an unexpected victory did nothing to end the unnerving practice of holding protracted debates and discussions on every issue and subject presented to the FARC's ruling council, no matter how trivial, before a decision could be made. This did not come as a complete surprise to Valendez. In fact he had counted on it. Still, as the council turned to the selection of which region this campaign would be waged in, he felt a pang of regret that men who considered themselves the leaders of the socialist movement in Colombia could allow their egos and personal agendas to interfere with the business at hand when, in Valendez's eyes at least, the issues at hand and their solutions were crystal clear and irrefutable. But there was no escaping the human and political elements that so complicated his efforts and those of his fighters. Thus resigned to his fate, Valendez leaned back in his seat, folded his hands on the table, and prepared to suffer in silence hour after hour of heroic speeches and discussions that contained more dogma and florid words than substance.

That resignation did not mean that he was abdicating decisions concerning the strategic direction of the upcoming campaign to the political buffoons who called themselves the council. Valendez's silence instead was a tactic, one which he used, like any combat tactic he employed, to achieve his desired objective. In the past it had been necessary to stand and shout toe-to-toe with opponents on many occasions. When his successes in the field followed one after the other, as he had predicted and promised, his need to scream, shout, and argue had diminished to the point where all he needed to do now was clear his throat to silence a speaker he was at odds with. Even his silence, as in this day's meeting, now made itself felt. As the discussions progressed and Valendez said nothing concerning the where and when of their next major move, more and more members of the council cast worried eyes in his direction, wondering and worrying what he was up to. None understood that he was letting them play themselves out with their own indecision and arguments. He was doing what most horse trainers did when breaking a new and undisciplined horse. He was letting the wild beast run itself down before applying a firm and guiding hand to it. As he did with the enemies he faced on the battlefield, he would let his opponents on the council exhaust themselves in pointless efforts before exerting his influence.

From his seat next to the nominal head of the FARC's military arm, Valendez watched the arguments go this way and that with the same deadpan stare that a sophisticated English gentleman watched a tennis game at Wimbledon. First there was the debate between those who wanted to go after the populated urban areas first in order to deny the government major nerve centers and provide bountiful recruiting grounds for the growing military arm, and those who favored a rural uprising. After much discussion it was pointed out that while seizing a city might be relatively easy, running and sustaining it and its population were beyond the FARC's means. The focus of the discussion then turned toward mountainous regions of the country where the FARC had been enjoying its unbroken string of successes in the past few months. Though this was tempting, the proximity of the capital and the heavy concentration of both American and government troops made this proposition risky at best.

It was at this point that Hector Valendez began to become personally involved. For while he listened patiently to the early part of the discussions and nodded when appropriate, he did so out of deference to the speaker and not in approval, since he had already decided not only when he would strike and where but how. Only when Mortino, the council chairman, was about to lose control of the meeting did Valendez decide that the time had come to speak. He announced his intent to do so by standing up and walking over to a map of Colombia displayed at the rear of the one-room country schoolhouse where the meeting was taking place. Without his saying a word, Valendez's simple action brought a hush to the room as everyone present watched and waited for him to speak. To heighten the dramatic effect he had achieved, Valendez stretched the pause for better than a minute. During that time, a time when all eyes and thoughts turned and focused on this former professor, he pretended to study the map. Only when he was ready did he turn to face the council.

'At a time like this it would be very easy to lose our focus, to become mesmerized by our own successes and power.' Valendez lifted his hands up and open as if he were weighing pieces of fruit in each one. 'Nine regular-force battalions and thirty-five local-force companies seems to us now like a powerful force. It is, in fact, the largest, best-equipped, and most thoroughly trained force we have ever had. But,' Valendez continued as he dropped his hands to his sides, 'we could throw it all away if we do not move forward with caution.'

This last statement caused eyebrows all around the conference table to rise. To hear this from Hector Valendez, the man who was always advocating bigger and bolder military operations, was akin to hearing the devil renounce evil and sin. His had always been a shrill voice pleading for increased aggressiveness in all areas when most of the old-time members of the FARC were frightened by their own shadows. Now, when this voice spoke calmly of caution at a time when his bold and seemingly rash policies were bearing fruit, there was shock. Without having to raise his voice above that of a loud whisper, he had captured their undivided attention. Seeing this, Valendez put his hands on his hips and began to move about the room, just as he had done when he had been at the university.

'We have the tools, both military and political, to do much. But they are fragile tools, expensive ones that once broken we may not be able to replace. For each of the regular-force battalions is more than a collection of five hundred men. It is, like our own bodies, a complex organism composed of many specialized parts that when functioning together create something greater than the sum of the parts by themselves. For just as one cannot make a man by simply sewing together two arms, two legs, a head, a torso, eyes, hands, feet, a heart, and so on, so too is it impossible to gather up strangers in one place and call them a unit. Like the human body, the military unit needs the magical spark of life that animates it. For the human, the spark is what we call the miracle of life, given at birth by the mother. For the military unit, leadership, training, camaraderie, common purpose and respect, organization, and shared hardships all work in mysterious ways to make a collection of individuals an effective unit. Weapons and people are only tools. Spirit and determination, that's what makes a unit.'

From his place at the head of the table Mortino interrupted. 'Yes, yes, my friend, this is very interesting, but this is not the time or place for such discussions.'

Raising his finger in the air, Valendez exclaimed, 'On the contrary, Mr. Chairman. This is precisely the time to discuss this. You see, the same rules that apply to our units apply to those of the enemy. The same forces that hold our companies together hold theirs. If we understand this, if we bear this in mind as we plan our strategies, we can use this knowledge to diminish the effectiveness of his units while preserving ours, both physically and psychologically.'

Despite the fact that he had just been spoken down to as if he were a lowly college student in one of Valendez's classes, Mortino said nothing. This pleased Valendez, for Mortino's yielding to him only served to reinforce Valendez's stature in the eyes of the members of the ruling council. Though this was only a minor point, every such point gained reinforced Valendez's growing power.

'I do understand the logic behind each of the proposals presented here this morning concerning where and when to strike next. They all promise a quick gain, gains that can serve our purposes well. But each of them would, in my opinion, cost us too much militarily. The capture of a major city or province capital would secure us many headlines, but the government and the Yankees, with superior mobility, firepower, and manpower, would eventually return and throw us out. All we would have then would be a short-lived victory, a city in rubble, and a fresh defeat with no forces left to repeat such a stunt. To go into the mountains anywhere within two hundred miles of Bogotá as a start would be equally doomed. We would by our own hand be bringing into play a war of attrition in which we would be at a great disadvantage. Every bullet, every replacement weapon, every trained recruit would have to travel hundreds of miles through contested or enemy-controlled territory before it reached its intended destination. We could expect to lose a good percentage of everything, from men to supplies, before it reached the front. Besides, the enemy again would be able to employ its superiority in numbers and firepower. Until such time as the government forces are no longer loyal or become ineffective in the field, we cannot hope to go into the mountains, seize land, and hold it for long.'

'Where then,' Mortino asked, 'do we use this marvelous weapon that you have so carefully crafted? Certainly not in the Amazon region. We have had virtual control over that region in the past without reaping the sort of benefits that we need to ensure a final and unchallenged victory.'

Valendez smiled as he shook his head and circled the table one more time before stopping his wanderings when he reached the map again. 'Yes, quite right. No, I was not thinking of the Amazon. That is where the government would like to see us go and linger about on the fringes as we have done in the past. There we would be isolating ourselves, out of sight and mind, at no cost to them.' Using his hand to indicate the various regions that he spoke of, Valendez continued. 'Instead of along the coast or in the mountains or in the cities themselves, I believe we should concentrate our efforts, now and for the foreseeable future, in Los Llanos.' With that, he slapped his hand, palm down, on the eastern region of Colombia, a vast area of flatlands and rivers, some 250,000 square kilometers that bordered Venezuela. It was, everyone in the room knew, an area which no one really controlled, a region that had hung in a strange limbo of near lawlessness for so long that a sort of peaceful coexistence between the guerrillas, government officials, narcotics growers, and ranchers who lived there had been long established and respected. It had no major cities and few towns worthy of the name. What roads existed were little more than trails. Rivers, instead, provided the only reliable surface travel year round.

'Here in the vast savannas we can let our revolution take root very quickly and with little interference from the government.' As he pivoted about, Valendez's flashing eyes and excited yet deliberate tone spoke of a man possessed. 'The government in Bogotá will not be able to stop us, for they, and not we, will be at the end of a long and tedious supply line. Any efforts will spread them thin elsewhere in critical areas where our local forces will be able to fill the vacuum created by the absence of forces that they will have to send east to challenge us.'

For the first time since Valendez had started speaking, Cordero spoke. 'You seem sure that the government will come to us on our chosen ground when we are ready.'

Without hesitation, Valendez responded, making a fist as he did so. 'Yes! They will come to us as we want them. The government will have no choice. To allow us to hold land that is of some consequence, with easy access to the rest of the world and its all-seeing media, cannot be tolerated. With Los Llanos tamed by us, we will be able to protect the ranchers there and open new lands for farming and ranching to those peasants and Indians that the government has for years forgotten. We will be able to put into effect those reforms that we have discussed for so long but have never had the opportunity to try. And after as little as one season, when the crops of the land are harvested by the new landowners under our guidance and protection, in a land free of drug lords and corrupt governments, we, the FARC, will reap a harvest of popular support anywhere we choose in this country.'

'Provided,' Mortino interjected, 'the government does not destroy that which we have planted.'

When he spoke, Valendez did so with a gleam in his eye, a gleam that told of boundless confidence. 'Yes, the Army will come. And perhaps the Americans too. But they will come slowly in bits and pieces, never large enough to do what needs to be done. We will meet them, each piece the fools in Bogotá offer us, as a raging grass fire driven by the winds meets all who stand in its way and consumes them.' Lowering his head slightly, Valendez allowed a wicked smile to creep across his face. 'Besides, when the government comes attacking us with their big guns and attack aircraft, the government troops will by their own hand be subjecting the very people that they have come to save to the cruelties of war. And as in so many other wars that the Americans have waged or supported, once their television cameras have captured for the American public the horrors of a government waging war on its own people, this war will become unpopular in the United States. In time this unpopularity will give way to protests that will eventually give the current administration in the United States a choice between staying in office or maintaining an unpopular war.'

'You speak with great confidence, a confidence, I fear, that I do not share. To challenge our own government, that is one thing. But to imagine that we can influence another country's, that is in my opinion quite arrogant, not to mention dangerous, thinking.'

Valendez met Mortino's comment with a shrug. He felt like telling Mortino that the reason that he could not share his confidence was summed up in a word he had just used, fear. Like so many of the other men at the table before him, Mortino had neither the stomach nor the nerve to risk all, even when there was no risk. Valendez, however, held his tongue. He had already flamed far too many sparks of anger that afternoon.

Time now, he knew, to finish making his point and let others take up his case, as he knew they would. Yet he still could not resist the urge to take one more swipe at the timid men who called themselves leaders. 'This will not be, my friends, the first time that members of this council have listened and doubted. Fortunately, every time the need to move forward has presented itself to this esteemed body of men, enough men of courage stood up and made their presence felt.'

This insult and direct challenge to the manhood of some of the members of the council did not go unnoticed. Several of them became visibly upset or annoyed. And yet no one said anything. Again Valendez had thrown down a challenge that was not picked up by anyone. Though he knew he was playing a dangerous game, for the very men he was addressing would be in the beginning the heart of the new government once the one in Bogotá was gone, Valendez drove on. He was a soldier, not a politician. In time, he suspected, he would have to become one in order to survive. But for now survival meant little to him. Destroying his enemy was his only concern.

Besides, there was more to his confidence than sheer logic or bluff. His statement concerning the Army was based on solid intelligence that few in the room possessed. As far as he knew, only he and one other man knew how deeply involved the disenfranchised elements of the Army's officer corps were in the success of the FARC in the field. Those officers, though few in number at present, were so well placed that they would be able to influence without suspicion which units came east to challenge the FARC and how they came. When that day did come, and it would, Valendez had no doubt that the first units they would feed into his meat grinder would be those most loyal to the Bogotá government and least likely to support another coup. With little effort on their part, the sponsors of the next coup would be able to eliminate, at no cost to themselves, future opponents. Valendez did not understand how those men could be so disloyal to a government they were pledged to support, and what they hoped to gain from such treason. Yet he also believed that it was wrong to turn away gifts, regardless of bearer, on personal principles alone. War, after all, made strange bedfellows, and right now Valendez was prepared to crawl into bed with anyone who promised to give him what he and the revolution needed.

Having achieved the impact that he had desired, Valendez placed his right hand over his heart and lowered his head in a gesture of apology. 'I have, my fellow patriots, been too long-winded. I hope that my case has merit and will be judged to be acceptable. That, of course, is for you to decide. And I am confident, as always, that whatever your decision, it will be the best.' With that, Valendez returned to his seat to watch and listen as the others discussed his plan.

October 5

Once he had been sentenced to a term in purgatory, Scotty Dixon saw no sense in delaying his departure from Washington, D.C. The fact was, after his briefing to the Army staff concerning the situation in Colombia, the sooner he left the better he and everyone concerned would feel. That briefing had generated a blizzard of annoying questions concerning the conduct of operations and reporting procedures that was proving to be an embarrassment to the Army staff. Even the Secretary of Defense found himself in the awkward position of having to choose between his personal integrity and loyalty to the administration when the threat of a congressional investigation reared its ugly head. So no one was really upset when word was passed around the corridors of the

Pentagon that Dixon, the bearer of the ugly truth, was going south, the term used when assigned to Colombia. It was hoped that with him out of sight the specter of defeat that he had fostered would fade. Though many believed that Lane's reports had been too good to be true, they likewise believed that Dixon's report was too pessimistic. 'The truth,' one general who had attended Dixon's briefing said, 'no doubt lies somewhere in the middle.' Not sure, as a result of the two extremes presented to them, where the truth was, many opted to trust the system. 'All we need to do,' conventional wisdom stated, 'is to wait out the next six months, pull out the 11th on schedule, and we can all go back to business as usual.'

Dixon, on the other hand, was faced with anything but business as usual. Rather than hide behind the conventional, he was now faced with the task of creating a job, not to mention a staff, out of nothing. This task included everything imaginable, from such simple considerations as where he would literally hang his hat once in Colombia, to where he and his tiny staff would get the phones and communications equipment that they would need to carry out their assigned tasks, whatever they turned out to be.

Such an assignment for a man of Dixon's talents and reputation was not impossible. He had found himself in similar circumstances before. During the First Persian Gulf War he and the tank battalion he was serving in as the operations officer found themselves thrown into an area of the world where the United States Army had never before trodden en masse, dangling precariously at the end of a long and vicarious line of communications. There they faced an enemy force that was numerically superior and fighting on its home soil. A few years later in Egypt when the United States found itself faced with a resurgent Russia bent on making its mark on the world scene, Dixon was given the command of a tank battalion at the last minute and ordered to lead it into battle. Following that, during a war with Mexico that was often referred to as 'an unfortunate misunderstanding,' he was charged with planning a mission that if it had failed would have put both him and his commander in the military prison at Fort Leavenworth, Kansas. And recently in Germany he had been cast into the eye of a storm that had set into motion political changes in Europe that were still being sorted out.

During his trip from what his wife, Jan, called Sodom on the Potomac to SOUTHCOM headquarters, Dixon pondered all of this and tried hard to find something from his past that he could use to guide him or at least provide solace. This effort, however, yielded nothing. The more he searched for some sort of parallel or a simple glimmer of hope, the more precarious and lonely his current situation seemed. There was nothing, no matter how far back he reached into the dark days gone by, that he could use to steel himself for the ordeal that lay ahead. The trials which he had passed through before bore no comparison to the one he now faced. Always in the past he had been in the company of friends or serving with soldiers who, though they were strangers, were skilled professionals. That he was leaving a hostile camp behind him and traveling into an even more hostile one depressed Scotty Dixon to a degree that he had never felt before.

Nothing at SOUTHCOM did anything to disperse his gathering gloom. If anything, it added new dimensions as he was bounced from one staff section to another, hat in hand, seeking the necessary personnel, coordination, and equipment that he and his staff would need in Colombia. The principal staff officers, brigadier generals themselves, inevitably fell back to the same position. 'Sorry, Scotty, but we're already stretched to the max now with no prospect of getting any better anytime soon.' Dixon, having reviewed the entire Colombian adventure from top to bottom, understood this, since the administration had opted to fight this dirty little war on the cheap, with no mobilization of reserves and no increase in the end strength of an already undermanned Army. This understanding didn't make Dixon's task any easier. In fact, it only served to heighten his anger and deepen his depression. After three days of walking into brick walls, Dixon threw up his hands and walked into the office of General Jerry Stratton, the SOUTHCOM commander-in-chief.

The meeting was brief and to the point. Though respectful, Dixon made sure that Stratton understood his frustrations. 'We both have been in the Army long enough to know,' Dixon stated, 'that an order can be dodged only so long before someone gets bent out of shape, stops accepting excuses, and starts looking for results. Unless you know something that I don't, sir, this mission of mine isn't going to be canceled.'

To his surprise, Stratton not only agreed with Dixon, he expressed a sincere and unabashed sympathy for Dixon's plight. 'Scotty, I'm quite concerned about what is going on down there. Since your briefing I've done a lot of serious soul searching and have come to the same conclusion that you have; the 11th Air Assault is an accident waiting to happen. I've closed my eyes to what's been going on down there, hoping that we could make do with Lane, but as you have pointed out, that's not going to work anymore. Of course, knowing that Lane is not up to the job and as a result something bad is going to happen is one thing. Accurately predicting what that bad thing is going to be, let alone when it's going to happen, makes doing something about it difficult. Though I don't agree with the chief that sending you and a tiny staff down there to play 'I Spy' will solve our problems, I have my orders just like you. With that matter settled in my mind, I've come to the conclusion that you can be very valuable to me up here, and despite the grief that Lane and his staff are going to give you, you may, when push comes to shove, quickly find yourself in the position of being their savior.'

'Or,' Dixon quickly added, 'their scapegoat.'

Stratton took a deep breath as he looked down at the blotter on his desk. 'Yes, that too.'

Though he still had another two weeks before he would be able to leave for Colombia, and his mission was still far from clear, let alone satisfactory, those weeks went fast. The doors of SOUTHCOM were slowly pried open to Dixon, allowing him to scavenge among the meager resources available to that staff in search of the men and material needed to build his own staff. In those weeks, during long conversations with Stratton, Dixon began to appreciate that Stratton was coming to view Dixon's forlorn hope mission in a new light. Dixon's newly created SOUTHCOM Forward, as his tiny staff was officially designated, was being designed to be a bridge across the gaping abyss that both he and Stratton found themselves peering into. Failing that, Stratton hoped in private that Dixon and his people would be able to provide him with a safety valve to stave off disaster.

October 15

Had Scotty Dixon and his wife, Jan Fields-Dixon, compared notes, they would have been hard put to tell who had to deal with more stonewalls and frustrations. Like Scotty, Jan was finding herself dealing with a situation that bore no resemblance to anything that she had faced in the past as she tried to put together a story that she knew was out there somewhere, but for now was simply beyond her grasp. The differences between the problems each faced were like night and day. While the issues and people that Dixon found himself up against were rather straightforward and upfront, the roadblocks that were faced by Jan were very circumspect and subtle. In fact, had she not known intuitively that the line of bull she was being fed by the public affairs officers at the embassy and the 11th Air Assault was just that, bull, she would have shrugged off her hunch as just another dry hole and left the issue alone.

But she knew that all was not well. There was something going wrong, seriously wrong, in Colombia. She had seen it in the eyes of her own husband the day he left in September. Though he was, as always, careful to keep his thoughts and feelings to himself, Jan had spent too many nights easing her husband back from the brink of recurring nightmares to know that what he had seen during his visit to Colombia had shaken his very soul. In itself Scotty's behavior could have been ignored. But when it was linked by Jan the next day to a sudden change in policy regarding the announcement of U.S. casualties, her suspicions grew. Rather than give information concerning losses and injuries on a daily basis, as had been the practice to date, it was announced from the Pentagon that only weekly totals would be provided, totals that did not separate battle and non-battle losses. One of the more astute correspondents observed dryly that this was what happened in Vietnam when the high personnel losses became an embarrassment. 'Much better,' he said, 'for the public-affairs officer to have to waffle an answer during a press briefing only once a week than seven times.' Finally, and most telling to the media gathered in Colombia, the policy imposing restrictions on the travel of correspondents and the pooling of them to cover military operations was revived and immediately enforced by both the U.S. military and the Colombian government.

Suspecting something and being able to build a story, however, were two different things. And Jan knew it. Being confined by a very stringent code of ethics that she followed, and insisted that everyone who worked in the Bogotá bureau conform to, didn't make it easy for her or her staff. Still she had no intention of compromising her professional integrity and would not tolerate anyone around her who did. 'Nothing,' she told her people, 'leaves this office unless we can verify it using reliable sources and facts.' Unfortunately, their efforts so far to discover what exactly Scotty had seen which had resulted in the gathering cloak of secrecy that was now obscuring military operations in Colombia had yielded nothing of substance. The weekly press briefing given by a member of the American embassy staff concerning military operations provided little information. Though facts and figures concerning those operations conducted the previous week were shown in large multicolored graphs and charts, the nature of those operations, let alone their locations and results, was withheld due to what the military labeled operational security.

Jan Fields-Dixon would not be denied. There was something going on, and she knew it. Travel restrictions, non-informative briefings and press releases, and military commanders who made themselves unavailable for comment be damned. She was going to get to the bottom of this story no matter what. And those veterans of the press corps in Bogotá who knew Jan knew what that meant. So it was with a certain amount of humor that her fellow correspondents looked upon Major General C. B. Lane and expressed their sympathy for him. Eddie Bauer of CNN summed it up best when he said, 'Unless he mends his ways and starts giving Jan a little something of substance, the Farcees are going to be the least of Lane's troubles.'

Bauer, of course, was like every other American in

Bogotá. Used to the small-scale operations that had become the accepted pattern of life for the 11th Air Assault since their arrival, they, like the American public, had come to view the activities of the FARC as little more than dangerous entertainment. That view was about to change forever.

CHAPTER 7

October 20

Watching the ancient C-130 transport plane roll to a stop, Major General C. B. Lane felt a twinge of apprehension. He was not accustomed to such a feeling. Though he had felt it before, usually when he was faced with a situation which he did not completely control, he had always managed to find some way of attacking the cause of his apprehension head-on and crushing it. Which was why he was here at the military airport waiting on this particular C-130. He would, as soon as Brigadier General Scott Dixon stepped off it, roll over him like a steamroller, leaving no doubt in Dixon's mind that he, *Major General* C. B. Lane, and nobody else was calling the shots down here, the Chief of Staff of the Army be damned.

Lane liked being in control; he needed to be in control. Where and how this obsession with dominating everything and everyone that came into his life originated was buried deep inside of Lane's psyche. Only the physical manifestations of that need mattered anymore to those around him and, to an extent no one appreciated, to Lane himself.

With the rank of lieutenant general assured and that of full general within his grasp, he really didn't care anymore, if he ever had, what drove him. The why no longer was an issue. Only the how, the process that had gotten him this far, mattered. After all, he rationalized, it had gotten him this far. There was no reason, none at all, to imagine that it wouldn't get him the rest of the way. So control and domination, always the strong suit in Lane's limited repertoire of skills, became so prevalent that any others that he might have possessed at a younger age were pushed aside and lost.

But the current situation was not his to dominate, at least not for the moment. Things had changed and were still changing fast. In the beginning the opportunity that the deployment of his division to Colombia had been was to him a gift. Added to this gift, as a benefit, were restrictions imposed by the Colombians governing every aspect of American military operations in Colombia. These restrictions included the number of troops, the duration of their commitment, the rules of engagement under which they would operate, where they would operate, and even the manner in which they were controlled. The 11th Air Assault was so tightly regulated by the terms of the agreement that governed their use that many in the military, including Lane himself at first, felt they were unworkable. But the administration had made its decision, and General Fulk, despite his better judgment, had saluted the President and issued the necessary orders.

Especially galling to the Army had been the decision made by the State Department to place the operational control of the 11th Air Assault Division in the hands of the Colombian Ministry of Defense. In part this was a sop given by the Colombian President to his senior officers. After the military coup the previous spring and the brutal purges that followed, the government had to give something back to the military, if only their pride.

Seizing any opportunity offered to them, the generals that had survived the coup and the purges insisted that only those U.S. officers and control headquarters that were absolutely essential would be allowed to enter and operate in Colombia. They did not want American generals coming into their country, taking over everything and telling them how to do things, a habit, most noted, that was as American as McDonald's. It wasn't that they didn't like the Americans or that the American generals were evil. It was just that their manhood would not tolerate having a foreigner, especially a Yankee, sitting in their capital, telling them how to defend it. Such a practice, the generals had told their President, would only serve as grist for the FARC's propaganda machine. Besides, there was the need to make sure that when the time came for the military to re-exert its influence over the conduct of internal politics there would be no interference from anyone, foreign or domestic.

For Lane this arrangement was ideal. In theory he received the orders that governed his tactical operations from the Colombian Minister of Defense. The Minister of Defense, however, was a former lawyer who was chosen for his personal loyalty to the President of Colombia and not his military knowledge. In the past the Minister of Defense had always been an Army general. The coup by the Army, however, had made that practice seem unsafe to the new President. So he had chosen from his ranks of loyal supporters a man he could trust to assume that post.

Though he had picked as wisely as he could have, the new Minister of Defense, José de Contrilla, was not up to the task. He had no experience with military tactics of any kind, let alone those used by an air assault division. Seeing an opportunity, Lane used Contrilla's shortcomings to his advantage. At their first meeting, before the 11th Air Assault even began deploying, Lane suggested that it would be to the advantage of all concerned if Contrilla,

rather than trouble himself with the grimy details of
day-to-day operations, simply assigned areas of responsibility and general guidelines to the 11th Air Assault.
His staff and subordinate commanders, Lane assured
Contrilla, would handle the planning and execution of
their operations. Pleased to be relieved of such a burden
and left free to deal with the final decimation of officers of
questionable loyalty from his own Army, Contrilla readily
agreed.

For four months that arrangement had suited Lane just
fine. He was, as a result of the State Department's efforts,
the senior American military officer in Colombia, commanding the only major American military headquarters.
He controlled his own operations and his staff, chosen as
much for personal loyalty to him as for their skills. He
also controlled the flow of information concerning those
operations not only to the Pentagon but also to the media.
Such an opportunity, Lane knew, came only once in a
lifetime. So he, with the help of his staff, was determined
to make the most of it while it lasted. During the first
few months, when the war in Colombia was new, popular,
and going all his way, Lane and his staff made even the
simplest search-and-destroy mission appear to be a heroic
epic planned and controlled by Lane's hand-picked staff.
The media, as a result, became an unwitting partner in
Lane's campaign of self-promotion.

But somewhere, unnoticed at first, things started to go
wrong. Without any fanfare, with no true warning, a new
element, one that no one had planned on, began to enter
into Lane's carefully orchestrated march to promotion. In
a way, the success of the American forces in the first few
months was responsible for the change. As long as it was
just an all-Colombian affair, the leadership of the FARC
had seen no need for any changes in its tried and true
methods. They had in fact become as much a part of
the political landscape of Colombia as the government

itself. And like the government, the FARC was always there but never quite fully in control. The presence of the 11th Air Assault Division, viewed by most Colombians as nothing less than an invasion from the north, brought forth a hue and a cry from many. It was, many Colombians shouted during riots in Bogotá, a surrender of the nation's manhood. The same type of rebellion that rocked the capital shook the ruling council of the FARC. Those members of the FARC who had been restrained by the old guard broke free of their former leaders and in a matter of days joined in fanning the flames of discontent. 'How can any man,' one popular FARC slogan that began to appear just as the 11th Air Assault began to arrive read, 'who considers himself a man freely submit to a government that must be propped up with Yankee bayonets.' The wave of enthusiasm that swept away the FARC's old line brought forth new faces, methods, and ideas. Foremost among them was the former university professor Hector Valendez.

Unfortunately, the G-2 intelligence section of the 11th Air Assault and the CIA in Colombia never suspected that the increasing change in fortunes of the FARC in the field paralleled the ascendancy of Valendez through the ranks of the FARC's military arm. Though they were able to note changes, both the G-2 and the CIA credited those changes to other people or circumstances. Valendez, never rising above the position of deputy to the military chief, remained hidden from the view of the American intelligence network.

But his efforts didn't. Slowly, almost unperceived, things began to change. There were no sweeping announcements, no single striking event that heralded the altering of the tactical and strategic balance. The presence of platoon-sized FARC units where only squads had operated before was easily dismissed at first as nothing more than exaggerated reports made by hysterical or nervous commanders in the field. This 'error,' like so many others, was easily remedied. For example, in the case of reports of platoon-sized units, the division G-2 adopted the practice at division headquarters of halving the number of enemy forces that American troop units reported contacting and doubling the number of dead FARC soldiers every contact yielded. Thus a thirty-man FARC platoon that had suffered six casualties in a firefight with an 11th Air Assault unit became a reinforced squad that was all but wiped out by the time the report was briefed to Lane. This good news, of course, was duly passed on to both the Pentagon and the media. 'The troopers of the 11th,' Lane would tell reporters, 'can put another notch in the stocks of their rifles,' meaning that another FARC combat unit had disappeared.

Of course when it became evident that FARC units were not only failing to disappear but were in fact multiplying, the gears of the 11th Air Assault Division's reporting system had to be thrown in reverse. By the time the division had been in country for three months, both the G-2 and the G-3 found themselves working to downplay rather than magnify the level of operations that the division was involved in. Soon it became the policy of the division's public-affairs officer to discount any contacts that involved less than a company of American soldiers or a battalion of the Colombian Army. And even when reported, the size and nature of the units involved were not given, 'in the interest of operational security.' To further tighten up the flow of information, reporters and correspondents found the free rides to units in the field becoming harder and harder to get. Only when they had the permission of the public-affairs officer were selected members of the media, members who were still considered pro-Lane, allowed forward to brigade or battalions in the field. Jan Fields-Dixon, of course, was not one of them.

Still, had everything continued to run at the pace

that it had been going, Lane could have survived the Colombian experience not only unscathed but with his career enhanced. September, however, put an end to that. First came Scott Dixon, sent by the Chief of Staff of the Army on a fact-finding tour. There'd been little time to prepare for him when Dixon came waltzing into Lane's private theater of operations. Then at the tail end of Dixon's visit the 3rd Battalion, 511th Infantry, stumbled into a massive ambush and got its nose bloodied in the single costliest operation to date. On the heels of this disaster, and partially as a result of it and his unsuccessful efforts to cover it up, the media turned on Lane and his division. These elements, all of which Lane had thought he controlled, became unglued at the same time and left him with a handful of problems. That they could be dealt with effectively was never in doubt. In a meeting of his key staff officers Lane pointed out quite proudly that 'the media can be muzzled, Dixon can be stonewalled, and the tempo of our operations can be regulated so that we can ride out the next few months without a care.' Lane's chief of staff, Colonel Delhue, sitting opposite him, was about to add, Well, that only leaves the FARC to deal with, but did not. Lane had a vision, and no one, no matter what his rank or position, was going to be allowed to obscure it with facts.

Even before the C-130's foot ramps were in place, Lane saw the figure that he knew to be Scott Dixon come bounding down from within the aircraft. Not wanting to wait until Dixon had his feet, so to speak, firmly planted before confronting him, Lane had decided to meet him here in person on the very first day. Another meeting of the two was inevitable, he knew, and Lane had decided to make it at a time and place of his choosing. What better way, he thought, to throw Dixon off than to hit him in person right between the eyes as he was stepping off the bloody airplane.

The image of Major General C. B. Lane taking long and measured strides had greeted the tiny staff of SOUTH-COM Forward before they had finished filing off the plane. At the rear of the C-130, Scott Dixon and Lieutenant Colonel Jeffrey K. Worsham were talking when Lane and his aide-de-camp came out of the building where they had been waiting. Worsham, who was serving as the chief of staff of Dixon's small staff, saw the two of them coming over Dixon's shoulder and motioned in their direction. 'Looks like the welcome wagon is acomin', sir.'

Twisting his head about in the direction Worsham was pointing, Dixon drew in a deep breath when he saw who it was. 'Well, he sure as hell isn't wasting any time coming out to mark his territory.'

When Dixon had recruited his small staff of officers and NCOs, he made sure that they understood that the reception and cooperation that they could expect would be at best strained. So his comment to Worsham came as no surprise. With one eyebrow cocked, Worsham volunteered, 'Would you like me to stand fast or make myself scarce?'

Without looking back at his chief of staff, Dixon responded with a dry halfhearted order. 'Best you check on the unloading of the gear and equipment. If we lose it here at the 11th Air Assault's airhead, we'll never see it again.' Then, turning to him, Dixon added, 'And, Jeff, if you see me fold my arms and start tapping my right foot, do us both a favor and come over and rescue me.'

'From Lane?'

'No, from myself. You see, the Army takes a dim view of generals striking other generals in public.'

Giving Dixon a wry smile as he saluted, Worsham added before he turned to leave, 'Well, sir, I wouldn't worry too much about that. In Major General Lane's case, I'm sure if you plead temporary insanity, you'll get no argument from the judge and little more than a verbal reprimand.'

Putting on a stern face, Dixon returned Worsham's salute. In the past he would have been upset if a subordinate had spoken of a general like that to him. But after having met and spent the better part of a week trying to work with Lane, Dixon didn't feel the slightest urge to correct Worsham or defend Lane. Of all the general officers he had ever met or known of in his career, Lane was in Dixon's eyes without doubt the least worthy of the respect and honors that his rank accorded him. With Worsham disposed of, Dixon spun about to face the man who would be for him the real enemy.

As Lane closed the distance between them, Dixon studied the person. He always thought of Lane as a person, since he didn't consider him fit to bear the title general or even that of man. In stature, Lane was exceedingly unspectacular. Of medium build, he stood at six foot one and appeared to be in good physical trim. His starched BDU uniform, spit-shined boots, blocked BDU hat with the two large stars centered in the front, and a well-polished general officer's belt and holster tagged this person as an officer who was more at home in an office than in the field. None of this in itself set Lane apart from any other officer who believed that exaggerated uniform standards were the mark of a good soldier. Not even the dark sun-glasses, the kind that hide the wearer's eyes, marked Lane as anything other than a simple martinet.

What gave Lane his distinct personality traits, the ones that automatically set people he met to disliking him, were his carriage and stride. He walked with an exaggerated casualness, the type that is not casual at all but that requires much practice, not too unlike the one that Douglas MacArthur had used. This casual stride and carriage were meant to show that he, C. B. Lane, was confident and in control, that he didn't need to worry about trivial worldly concerns because the world around him was his to command. The only detraction from his almost carefree image was Lane's habit of slowly sweeping his head from side to side, looking at all around him. He did this, Dixon imagined, not to survey and take in information but rather to detect dangers and threats in much the same way that a search radar automatically scans the horizon for the enemy. For Dixon knew that Lane viewed him as nothing less than a direct and immediate danger to his career. Which was why Lane was there that afternoon to greet Dixon and his staff. It made sense to Lane and it made sense to Dixon, since both men, from their earliest years in the Army, had been taught that when dealing with an enemy victory can best be achieved by seizing the initiative and striking when your foe is off balance.

When Lane was within six feet of him, Dixon brought himself to a rigid position of attention and rendered a sharp hand salute. 'Good afternoon, sir. I hadn't expected to see you so soon. It was my understanding that I had an initial office call with you tomorrow morning.'

Returning his salute, Lane closed the gap between him and Dixon. 'Well, yes, that's true. But, you see, we have a major operation scheduled for the morning that my aide neglected to consider when he was making up my schedule. A two-battalion sweep south of Medellín. Since I'll be tied up keeping an eye on that, and I didn't want to wait for several days before talking to you, I thought I'd pop on out here and get this over with now so that we both understand each other from the start.'

Since he couldn't see Lane's eyes because of the dark glasses, Dixon watched his mouth. Though Lane wore a smile, Dixon imagined it was like the one the wolf had when he was speaking to Little Red Riding-Hood.

When he dropped his salute and stopped in front of Dixon, Lane planted his feet shoulder width apart and grasped the front of his leather general officer's belt with his hands on either side of the shiny brass buckle.

Seeing that Lane had no intention of offering him his hand, Dixon likewise spread his feet apart. But instead of putting his hands in front of him, he placed them in the small of his back, sticking them palms out under his own leather belt.

Puffing out his chest and rocking forward on his heels slightly, Lane exaggerated his commanding height. 'Let me get right to the point, General Dixon. The Colombian Minister of Defense is not at all thrilled with the idea of SOUTHCOM establishing a headquarters here in his country. He feels that this is a clear violation of the status of forces agreement that his government and ours agreed to months before.'

This statement threw Dixon, and the smile on Lane's face told Dixon that his expression had betrayed his surprise. To get around the status of forces agreement, the Colombian government had been told that Dixon and his staff, who would be housed in the American embassy's compound, were nothing more than an augmentation of the ambassador's staff. The real purpose of Dixon's small staff, their role as the forward element of SOUTHCOM, had been classified secret, no foreign dissemination. Since only a handful of senior officers and members of the embassy staff knew of Dixon's real mission, the only conclusion that Dixon could come to was that someone violated the U.S.-only restriction on revealing the nature of his headquarters and told someone in the Colombian government. Not having any use for this person, Dixon naturally jumped to the conclusion that if Lane hadn't himself been the perpetrator of this security violation, he at least was involved in making it so. Yet with no proof of any type, Dixon could say nothing. Instead he took a deep breath. 'Well, sir, I guess the first order of business for me and my people is to put the Colombians' mind at ease and let them know that we are not coming down here to expand our presence or role.'

The smile on Lane's face grew larger for a moment when Dixon said this. Then, feigning concern, Lane looked down at his boots and shook his head. 'Well, Dixon, I'm afraid that's going to be quite a chore.' Looking back up at Dixon, Lane began to give a little lecture to the new kid on the block. 'These Colombians, General Dixon, are quite suspicious of us. They're proud people who really don't want us here at all and see everything we do as a potential threat to their sovereignty. It's taken me quite a while to convince them that we're not here for any other reason but to help them hold the line against those socialist guerrillas that are threatening them and their people. I hope that your presence doesn't interfere with the ability of my division to work in harmony with the Colombians. It would be too bad if it did.'

What Lane was telling Dixon, or at least alluding to, rocked Dixon even more than his initial announcement. If he was taking Lane's meaning right, Dixon saw him, C. B. Lane, hard at work making Dixon and his headquarters the scapegoat for any and all failure in joint U.S.-Colombian operations from this point on. The fact that Lane's over-bearing attitude and his barely veiled contempt for the abilities of the Colombian military had already doomed any hope for effective and meaningful combined operations would be lost to most. One Colombian general staff officer had confided in Dixon during his last visit that most Colombian officers would rather link arms with the FARC than join Lane's American forces in the field. Of course Dixon didn't know that some Colombian officers were already doing that. All he knew at that moment was that he now had two major foes to contend with before he even got started. Besides Lane and his loyal staff, who no doubt would only grudgingly cooperate with his own staff, Dixon now had a hostile host nation to deal with, which meant a possible international incident to boot.

Recovering his poise, Dixon looked into the dark lenses

of Lane's glasses. 'Well, sir, I'm sure that we'll be able to muddle through this problem somehow.'

Lane smiled. 'Yes, General, I'm sure you will. Just as I'm sure you and your people will remember that you are here to serve the commander-in-chief of SOUTHCOM as nothing more than a sort of clearinghouse of information needed by my divisional staff and his staff.'

Carefully picking his words and watching his tone, Dixon slowly responded. 'I can assure you, sir, neither I nor my staff have any intention of doing anything that would interfere with the conduct of your operations. We're here to ensure that the information needed by both you and General Stratton gets to all the right places.'

Taking his right hand away from his belt, Lane raised it chest level and jabbed his index finger at Dixon. 'Good! And make sure you don't forget that, General.'

With all his strength, Dixon pressed his jaws together, almost as if he were locking his mouth down for fear of saying something he would regret. The only action he could safely bring himself to take at that moment was to bring his arms up and fold them slowly, across his chest.

Seeing that Dixon had no intention of responding to his intentional provocation, Lane put his right hand back on his belt, looping the thumb behind it. He was preparing to continue to lecture Dixon when a lieutenant colonel quickly came up behind Dixon and tapped him on the shoulder. In a whisper that he was sure Lane could hear, Worsham spoke to Dixon. 'Excuse me, sir. Hate to bother you with this trivial matter but . . .' Not having thought of an excuse that seemed reasonable enough to interfere in the conversation between Lane and Dixon, Worsham stopped in midsentence.

Lane, looking into Dixon's eyes and seeing the anger, knew that he had done what he had set out to do. He had served him notice that he, Major General C. B. Lane, was the only bull in this pen that mattered and he had no intention of letting go of anything to anyone. Seeing no need to stay any longer, he used the interruption to make his exit. 'Well, I see you have housekeeping matters to tend to. I have an air assault division to run. If you need anything, have your chief of staff contact my chief of staff, and I'm sure we can do something to help.'

Still struggling to keep his tongue in check, Dixon was barely able to utter the words 'Yes, sir' as he saluted Lane. With that, Lane smiled and walked away, proud of the way he had put Dixon in his place.

When he was out of sight, Dixon relaxed his stance, though Worsham could see that he was still shaking from his anger. Finally, though he kept watching the door behind which Lane had disappeared, Dixon spoke. 'Jeff, this is going to be a *looong* seven months.'

Looking at the same door, Worsham thought about Dixon's comment. 'We have met the enemy and he is him?'

Cranking his head around toward his chief of staff, Dixon let a smile light across his face. 'Yeah, something like that. Now let's get this show on the road.'

With that, both men turned and began to walk toward the C-130, now disgorging its cargo. Standing at a respectful distance, far enough to be out of the way yet in a position where both his staff NCOs and the Air Force ground crewmen could see them, Dixon and Worsham watched. Worsham informed Dixon that their senior sergeant had already left with the officer serving as the headquarters commandant to check on the quarters they had arranged for before arriving, leaving the senior operations sergeant in charge of the off-loading of the C-130. At the moment, with all of their communications equipment bundled up on huge pallets, there wasn't much he or anyone else could do. It was at that moment that Worsham remembered what he really needed to tell Dixon. 'Oh, by the way, sir, I checked with the ground crew. There's a phone over in the air-ops shed that you can use to call to any commercial line here in Bogotá.'

In all the haste and associated stress of preparing his staff, Scott Dixon had neglected to call Jan and tell her that he was coming. Though he had meant to many times he had just never made the time. When finally he thought of doing so and had the time, a funny idea began to rattle about his head. Why not just pop in unannounced after he had arrived in Bogotá. That, he thought, would really make Jan's day. Pleased that he had come up with such an idea and had stuck to it, Dixon smiled as he began thinking to himself that this time it was going to be his turn to surprise his wife with a sudden and unexpected entrance.

In the town of Puerto Carreño, located on the eastern fringe of the region known as Los Llanos that jutted into the western border of Venezuela, Colonel Marco Agustin of the Colombian Army was waiting for a different kind of surprise. The town, a small provincial affair with a population of a little over five thousand wedged into the far eastern corner of Colombia, was about to become the subject of an experiment in terror in which the soldiers of the commander's garrison were to be the test subjects.

That something was about to happen in his area of responsibility had only slowly become evident to Colonel Agustin. The commander of the region that encompassed most of the province of Vichada and the brigade that garrisoned it, Agustin had recently been made aware of subtle changes in the habits of the people of the region. It began after the first week of October, when his senior sergeants and junior officers began to comment that the local people were starting to act strangely. They were, most of his other sergeants and officers agreed, becoming less friendly, more reluctant to engage in conversation, or even trade with them. Concerned about this, Agustin traveled to the outlying police stations and outposts in his area of responsibility. At each stop he heard the same thing from all of his subordinates. By the time he finished his tour, he knew. Something was about to happen, and soon.

Knowing that something was going to happen and being able to predict with any kind of accuracy exactly what was going to happen, let alone where and when, was a different matter. Agustin's intelligence officer, a young and dedicated major, the son of a wealthy hotel owner in Cartagena, was alerted to his commander's concerns. His efforts to gather information, however, yielded nothing positive. After several days of trying his usual methods, the major reported back that all of his otherwise reliable sources seemed to have disappeared. 'No one,' he told Agustin, 'even my contacts with the drug cartel, can be found. It is as if they had been gobbled up by the earth itself.'

With nothing but negative intelligence, which often can be as valuable as solid information, Agustin flew up to the headquarters of the division responsible for the region in which Puerto Carreño was located. That trip, however, was for Agustin wasted. Though the division commander and his staff listened intently to everything that Agustin reported, and they all agreed that the signs indicated that something was astir in Agustin's region, there was nothing, he was told, that they could do for him until he had something tangible to report, or actual contact. 'We cannot,' the division commander told him, 'target and attack shadows generated by a man's fears and suspicions.' Besides, as the division chief of staff pointed out over lunch, all indications were that the FARC's new efforts were being concentrated in the Cauca River Valley. 'Ever since the eighth of October, the enemy has become very, very active between Cali and Medellín. Both the Ministry of Defense and the Americans have been shuffling forces into that region in the hope of drawing the FARC into a major fight.'

That the date of the increased activities to the west coincided with the change in attitude of the people in his region Agustin considered for a moment before he answered. When he did, he was careful in his choice of words. 'What, my friend, if the real threat was here in our own backyard and all the noise along the Cauca was nothing but a diversion?'

A frown swept across the division chief of staff's face. Leaning back in his seat, he looked at Agustin and thought for a moment before answering. Reaching out, he took his drink, swirled the glass, and took a long sip. The thought of an offensive in their region had never dawned upon him. Still, right now it was nothing more than that, a thought, a formless and unfounded fear. Ready, he reached over, slammed the glass down on the table, and spoke. '*If* that is the case, *if* our area and not the western mountains is to be the scene of the next battle, then we must in the beginning make do with what we have. We will hold until the government in Bogotá can decide where the real danger is and shift their attention and whatever forces they can afford to us here in the east.'

The chief's answer did little to mollify Agustin. 'And if we cannot hold on?'

This last comment brought a smile to the chief's face. 'We are talking about the FARC here. They have been around so long, like our own politicians, that their methods have become institutionalized and somewhat ossified. Though things could become a little rough for a few days, there is nothing out there that we cannot handle on our own until help arrives.'

The efforts of the division chief of staff to calm Agustin's apprehensions failed miserably. If anything, the attitude of the division's commander and his staff only served to heighten his own suspicions. If, as Agustin feared, the FARC's operations in the western mountains were a diversion, then the FARC had already won the first half of the opening battle. Everyone, it seemed, accepted the obvious, and there was nothing that he could do to change that.

Thus, when he returned to Puerto Carreño, Agustin threw himself into a frenzy of preparation. He began by increasing the readiness of his command, especially the small garrisons in the outlying areas. These, he felt, would be the first to feel the pressure of a new enemy drive, a drive he expected would open with small probes against weak points and numerous ambushes through the region. To meet this threat he encouraged all of his subordinate commanders to increase the number of patrols and their own ambushes along likely routes of infiltration out of Venezuela and along the few roads and many rivers of Vichada. To augment the efforts of those units already deployed, Agustin stripped Puerto Carreño of most of its garrison. This allowed him to establish new company-sized outposts at key points along major transportation arteries. Like the others, the commanders of these new garrisons were instructed to keep alert and not to disperse their command.

Agustin's drive, however, was not shared by many of his subordinates. They, like the chief of staff, felt that there was little need to worry too much over the prospect of battle with the FARC. One company commander even told him that he was reluctant to do anything out of the ordinary for fear of spooking his own men. 'Even if they come at us in the dead of night,' he told Agustin, 'we will be able to hold them and still have a reasonably peaceful breakfast.'

Ignorance, of course, is often the basis of confidence. Agustin thought of this as he stood in the open doorway of his office and looked out across the enclosed square that served as a parade ground for the last two companies in Puerto Carreño that were co-located with his own headquarters. One of those companies, broken down into platoons, had been deployed to small blocking positions and strongpoints around the town of Puerto Carreño. The other company, serving as a reaction force not only for Puerto Carreño and the immediate area but for Agustin's entire region, was scattered about the parade ground in small squad-sized groups. The men of the company, cleaning their weapons and sorting through their gear, were preparing for another evening of patrols, ambushes, and waiting, just as they had been doing every night for the past week. In the growing shadows of late afternoon, here and there the sergeants and officers of the company moved about singly or in pairs checking on their men's progress. None of them, Agustin thought, were moving with any real sense of purpose. They, like everyone else, were infected by the status quo. When, Agustin thought, the FARC come, heads will roll. They will start here, he knew in his heart, and continue to roll until they topple every self-serving politician in Bogotá.

Mired in these grim thoughts of the future, Agustin stood in the doorway and watched his men slowly go about their daily chores. Neither he nor his men heard the deep yet distant thud of a dozen 120-millimeter mortars firing the opening volley of Hector Valendez's offensive to seize Los Llanos. In the span of a second, perhaps two, the entire scene before Agustin's eyes was transformed. Everything – men, equipment, trucks, buildings, even the ground itself – was torn apart and heaved into the air by blinding explosions that were magnified by the strong outer walls of the courtyard. Never having been exposed to such an attack, no one, not even Agustin himself, had any idea what to do. While some of the soldiers instinctively threw themselves flat onto the ground, others dropped what they were doing and attempted to run for safety.

There was, however, no safe haven for the company.

As if to underscore this point, a volley of small-arms fire, partially drowned out by the second volley of mortar rounds impacting on the parade ground, announced the commencement of the ground attack. Even before he knew exactly what was happening, Agustin somehow understood that there was no way that he would be able to rally his forces there in the compound and beat off an attack. Picking himself up off the floor of his headquarters building, Agustin turned away from the unfolding horror that the parade ground had become and turned to head out the rear door of the building just as the FARC assault teams forced their way into the open gate of the compound. Shouting as he ran through the building for his staff to follow, Agustin made it to a side entrance seldom used by anyone that had once been a sally port meant for just such an occasion. Prying the heavy metal door open with the help of a sergeant who had followed closely behind him, Agustin shouted to the few members of his staff who had managed to make it this far to head out of town to the westernmost platoon strongpoint. There he would rally his forces, assess the situation, and do what needed to be done.

Just as Colonel Agustin had already found out, there was absolutely no subtlety about the manner in which Hector Valendez threw the FARC's military arm into its new task. Across the entire length and breadth of Los Llanos, from Villavicencio in the west to Puerto Carreño in the east, dozens of small police detachments and military garrisons located in the villages like the one Agustin had commanded were eradicated in a single night. Striking an hour before sunset, six of Valendez's main-force battalions, many of them operating as whole units for the first time, swept all before them. The government forces, dispersed into small garrisons with few of them company strength or greater, withered under the combined impact of the FARC's total surprise, their unexpected firepower, and the boldness of their daytime attacks. In those cases where stunned survivors of this initial onslaught managed to escape death or capture, few would manage to make it through the night, for the night belonged to the FARC's local-force companies supporting Valendez's main-force battalions. Together with the task of policing up the battlefield after the main-force battalions had done their duty, the local-force companies established control of their own home regions and prepared to provide security for the political, governmental, and administrative branches of the FARC as they moved in behind the combat forces. Thus in the span of a few days the FARC was able to make the transition from being a clandestine guerrilla organization of little note to being a sovereign power in its own right and a serious contender for control of Colombia.

It was just like Scott Dixon, Jan thought as she rushed through the last few stories that she needed to review. Damn him! To show up just like that and expect her to fall all over in a rush to hop into bed with him was, was . . . Nervy, that's what it was, pure and simple. That man, she thought as she tossed a finished piece into her out box and reached over to her in box for another, had got more nerve than he knew what to do with. And his weak, wimpy excuse of, 'Well, you do this to me all the time.' That to Jan was even more contemptible. What made him suppose, she fumed, that just because she had the habit of popping in and out without notice he could do that to her at a time like this. As she told her assistant editor, a young woman by the name of Genny Conners, after Dixon had gone storming off that afternoon, she couldn't help it if her job suddenly snatched her up and then just as suddenly dropped her back home on a moment's notice. She didn't do it for fun. At least most of the time she didn't.

From the doorway, Genny called out, 'Well?'

Looking up from a draft story that she had been staring at for a few minutes and yet had no idea what it was about, Jan shot back, 'Well what?'

'Well, Jan, are you going to go meet him tonight?'

'What do you think? My God, with all the increased activity in the western mountains, the shifting of more and more of the 11th Air Assault's combat battalions into the Cauca River Valley, and reports of threats against Medellín itself to deal with, the last thing I need to do is go running about Bogotá chasing an arrogant, inconsiderate fool who thinks playing "Guess Who?" is romantic.'

Genny smirked. 'Oh, come on, Jan. You've got to admit it was sort of funny. I mean the look on your face and everything.'

'Funny? You think being made a fool of in front of everyone on the staff is funny?'

'Oh, not everyone was here. Remember, Frank and Eddie were out making arrangements for your piece on the Ministry of Defense.'

Jan glared at Genny. 'Very funny. Am I the only one here interested in doing her job?'

'Okay, boss lady. Without looking, tell me what the piece in your hands, the one you've been studying so intently for the last five minutes, is about.'

Jan cocked her head to the side and looked up. 'It's about . . . it's the one Carol did on the, ah.'

'I thought so. Your mind is so befuddled by that man you keep referring to as the last of the Neanderthals that you have no idea what you're doing, do you?'

Narrowing her eyes, Jan gave Genny a dirty look before looking down at the pages of copy she held. As her friend had guessed, Jan had no idea what the piece was about. The story she had supposedly been working so hard on was one done by Terry Freeman, not Carol. Genny was right. Her mind was on Scotty, and there was no getting around it. Dropping the paper on the desktop, Jan leaned back in her seat and looked up at Genny, her expression softening to one of complete puzzlement. 'You know the most infuriating thing about this, Genny, is the fact that Scott knows I'll be there. The bastard knows.'

With a sly smile, Genny folded her arms. 'Well, you know the old cliché.'

Jan shook her head and waved her hand at Genny, 'Yes, yes. You're right. You're absolutely right. Can't live with them, can't live without them. But damn,' Jan mused, 'I'd sure like to try someday.'

Dropping her hands to her side, Genny cocked her head. 'Honey, I've tried it. Believe me, I've *really* tried. If I found a way of doing that, I'd copyright it and make a couple of million on the secret.'

Folding her hands in front of her on the desk, Jan surveyed the folders and files and draft stories that hung out of her boxes and cluttered her desk.

'I don't imagine I'm going to make it through this mess tonight. So I might as well throw in the towel.' Standing up, she shuffled a few more papers about the desk, then gave up completely. Looking at her watch, then over to her friend, Jan sighed. 'Well, I guess I'd better go get ready for Hagar the Horrible.'

'Jan, be nice. That man loves you.'

She thought about that for a moment. Then with an impish grin on her face and a gleam in her eye, Jan looked up at Genny. 'Yeah, I know.'

CHAPTER 8

Evening, October 20

While he sat at the table playing with his drink and waiting
for Jan, Scott Dixon thought about his love for her and
their life together. How terrible, he thought, that they had
so little time together. It seemed, as he looked about the
dining room, that most of their lives in the past year had
been spent in dining rooms not unlike this one, here and
in Washington, D.C. There always seemed to be a reason,
he knew, why they couldn't spend more time together at
home like a normal couple did. What with Jan being
a world-renowned reporter, in demand to cover every
major hot spot in the world, and him a newly promoted
general officer with the promise of more stars to come
if, of course, he measured up and punched all the right
tickets. Still, excuses now didn't make up for all the lost
time that they individually and collectively let slip away.

For a while, when his name had come out on the list for
promotion to brigadier, Dixon had considered turning in
his retirement papers and taking a job with a consulting
firm in the Washington area or going back to finish his

degree and look for a job teaching history in college. Though Jan would still be up to her eyeballs with the World News Network, at least one of them would have his feet on the ground and be there, when the opportunities made themselves available, for the other. He would even be able to bring his sons home from their military boarding school in Virginia for the first time in years and give them a real home. Both boys would soon be in college, and there was little time for him to create the father and son bond that he had for so long been postponing due to 'the needs of the Army.'

But when decision time came, when he had to pick between fading into the background or pressing on higher and higher up the career ladder, Dixon found he couldn't do it. He couldn't leave the Army and start his life again as second fiddle to Jan. He wondered how much of that was nothing more than male pride and how much the need, his need, to keep pitting himself against the system and taking on new and more interesting challenges. It wasn't that every job in the Army was a challenge. Far from it. Many of his past duty positions, like the one he had just left at the Pentagon, were nothing more than staff positions in which he did the stubby pencil work for a more senior officer who made all the decisions. The only challenge Dixon found in those jobs, he had once told Jan, was keeping his sanity, biting his tongue at the appropriate times, and preventing his mind from turning into mush. The Army, of course, considered each and every duty position critical to the overall mission of the Army, and Dixon's superiors had always taken great pains to ensure that they frequently expressed to Dixon how important his contributions were to the success of the unit, the section, the Army, etc., etc., etc. Like everything else, Dixon reasoned, you had to take the good with the bad. And in the Army that often meant enduring no-mind jobs as you marked time and waited for a good, meaningful assignment to come your way.

So Dixon stayed and took the promotion. Jan was, he knew, a little disappointed. For she too had hoped that one of them would hang up their spurs and become the continuity in the relationship. Jan, however, had faced the same dilemma more often than Dixon did. It seemed that every time a new assignment in her news agency was offered her, she would ponder whether this was the time to call it quits or stick it out for another year, maybe two. For she was very much like Dixon, a person who loved challenges and had made a living by meeting them head-on and when necessary defying conventional wisdom and practice to do a job that she believed in. She, like he, lived for the thrill of being there out front, doing something that meant so much to her and gave her life meaning and purpose. Alive, Jan had once told Dixon when she was defining how she felt when she was hard at work on a tough assignment. 'I feel alive.' And so the two of them made the necessary accommodations in each of their own lives as they learned to live together while spending so much time apart.

Lost in his private reflections, Dixon didn't notice Jan's grand entrance. Nor did he bat an eye as she approached the table slowly, doing her best to give him something to think about. He didn't need anything more to think about, Jan realized as she watched him stare in her direction without seeing her. With a sigh she realized that his mind, as usual, was lost in space. Though the body was here, the look on his face told her that the thoughts were out there somewhere far from this room, maybe even this country. Perhaps, she feared, the momentary playfulness that had been such an embarrassment to her that afternoon was gone, beaten out of him by a hard afternoon dealing with C. B. Lane and the staff of the 11th Air Assault. Trying to do anything with those morons, Jan knew, was enough to depress a hyena. With this in mind, Jan decided to soften her desire for revenge somewhat as she came up next to Scott.

It took Dixon a moment to realize that someone was standing next to him. It was a scent, her scent, that finally jogged him out of the depths of his own mind. Turning slightly and looking up, a halfhearted smile lit across his face. 'Hello, Jan. I'm so glad you were able to make it.' Almost as an afterthought he stood up, took her hands in his, leaned over, and gave her a light peck on the cheek. Stepping back a bit, he looked at her, head to toe, before he spoke again. Her brown hair, normally worn down about her shoulders or held back with a barrette or bow, was pulled up and held in place on her head with decorative combs. She wore a black cocktail dress with a scooped neckline that went from her barely covered shoulders and dropped to where her breasts began to rise. A simple rhinestone necklace was all she wore to decorate her soft exposed skin. Sheer black lace sleeves encased her arms, their delicate elegance standing out in contrast to the simple dress that curved about her figure and stopped two inches above her knees and left her smooth, shapely legs exposed for all to see and enjoy. Scott gazed into her eyes. It was those eyes that made Jan who she was. For those large brown eyes could both penetrate to the very soul of a person and in the same instant speak louder than any words he had ever heard. At that moment he saw a warm, gentle, and loving look in those eyes. Without a word having been said, he knew that he had been forgiven. Leaning forward again, he gave her a kiss, this time on the lips, and moved his hands up her lace-covered arms to her shoulders. Any lingering thoughts Jan had of exacting revenge for the crummy way that he had come into her office that afternoon and made a fool of her disappeared in the warmth of that moment.

Pleased that she had been able to shake him out of his deep meditative state without having to play any mind games, which she was in no mood to engage in, Jan returned Scott's warm kiss for a moment and then pulled away and looked at him. He was wearing his Class A's tonight, his green uniform with all the badges. She flashed a shy smile. With her cheeks now highlighted by a redness that told all who were crass enough to stare that her passions were rising, Jan leaned into his embrace slightly and brought her hands up and rested them palms down on his chest. When she spoke, it was a warm, quiet breathy tone meant to arouse rather than chide. 'Scotty, please. Not here and now, at least not until we've eaten. I'm starved.'

The mood was broken, but the passions remained. Dixon smiled and shook his head. 'I've never seen a woman who could eat so much and keep her shape like you do.'

Placing her hands lightly on her hips, Jan smiled. 'This figure ain't what it used to be, Scotty. Not by a long shot.'

Pulling her back to him, he gave her another light peck on the lips and then eased back. 'Woman, to this broke dick tanker, that body of yours is heaven.'

With a flourish, he stepped back. Using exaggerated motions, he pulled out her chair and bowed at the waist, motioning her to be seated. 'Madam, your table is ready.'

The evening, despite Dixon's clumsy and aborted attempt at humor that afternoon, was turning out to be a pleasant one. Their conversation was light and engaging as they discussed everything and anything that had nothing to do with Colombia, the Army, or the World News Network. It was, Jan realized, as if they both had by unspoken mutual consent agreed that this night would be theirs and theirs alone and nothing, not job or country, was going to change that.

Finished with the main course, Jan and Scott were busy

weighing the pros and cons of whether it would be more enjoyable to sit there together and enjoy a cup of coffee and dessert or if they should just chuck romance to the wind and run upstairs to the room he had taken for the night when Jan saw Scotty sit upright in his seat. A concerned look that quickly turned to one of despair flashed across his face as he looked at someone in the distance behind her. Sitting up, Jan turned, asking as she did what was wrong. Dixon growled, 'Well, it didn't take long for them to find me.'

Across the room Jan could see the headwaiter, his eyes fixed on their table, headed toward them. He moved like a man with a mission, and the expression on his face told her that it wasn't a social call he was about to pay them. Turning around to face Scotty, Jan reached out with her right hand and grabbed Scott's. 'I suppose you told whoever your number-two man is where you could be reached?'

Sheepishly he looked down. 'Of course I did. Jan, I'm a general officer. I can't go running about in the middle of a war zone disappearing like a kid playing hooky.'

Shaking her head, Jan squeezed his hand. 'Damn you and your dedication.'

Just then the headwaiter arrived at their table, placing himself at the corner of the table opposite from where Jan and Dixon sat. Facing Dixon, he bowed slightly and apologized for having to interrupt their meal. When Dixon nodded and said that he understood, the headwaiter smiled and then turned to Jan. 'Señorita Fields, there is a call waiting for you in the lobby from a Señorita Conners. She says it is very, very important and you must talk to her immediately.'

For a moment Jan didn't think. She thanked the headwaiter and turned to Scott, wondering what Genny found so damned important to call here about. She was pondering this question when she saw her husband looking

at her with an incredulous stare. 'It would seem,' he said
dryly, 'that I'm not the only one at this table suffering from
a severe case of dedication to duty.'

Jan winced a little. 'Sorry, Scotty, but you do understand how it is. I am, after all, the bureau chief here
in Colombia.'

Reaching up with his right hand and sandwiching the
hand she had laid upon his left hand, he smiled and
nodded. 'No need to apologize. You never promised me
a rose garden, et cetera, et cetera. Now best you go tend
to business and I'll settle up with the waiter.'

For a moment she held his gaze and allowed herself
to feel the warmth of his two hands clasping hers. Then
without another word she pulled it away, stood up, and
followed the headwaiter to where her phone call was
waiting.

The FARC's progression from guerrilla force to political
power, or any other concerns other than simple survival,
was the furthest thing from Colonel Agustin's mind that
night. Like many other officers commanding tiny garrisons
throughout eastern Colombia in similar circumstances at
that moment, he assumed that his command alone had
been the target of a brief yet determined raid. In the
beginning he was confident that, as bad as things seemed
then, the situation would stabilize and with a little help
from division he would be able to re-establish control.
Only after being turned away from two of his own
platoon strongpoints by enemy gunfire did it begin to
dawn on him that what had happened at the garrison's
compound was something more than a raid. It wasn't
until he reached the third and final platoon strongpoint
east of Puerto Carreño that Agustin and his small band
of survivors found sanctuary.

The relief he and the men who had come out of Puerto
Carreño with him felt was short-lived when the terrible

truth of the whole situation became apparent. Upon entering the strongpoint shortly after midnight, Agustin was greeted by the commander of the company that had been manning the strongpoints around Puerto Carreño. 'Thank God, Colonel Agustin,' the young captain shouted when he ran up to meet his brigade commander and embraced him. 'You have made it. I knew that it was only a question of time before you would lead a relief effort and save us from annihilation.'

Shaken by his experiences of the day and the physical exertion of moving about in the dark cross-country in an effort to avoid FARC patrols, Agustin didn't respond to the captain's greeting at first. Only after he was led to the command bunker of the strongpoint and handed a canteen of water, which he all but drained with a single swig, did he speak. 'Relief effort? I am leading no relief effort, Captain. What you saw follow me into this post were the only ones who made it out of Puerto Carreño alive.' Seeing the expression of joy on the captain's face turn to shock, Agustin hurriedly continued. 'What is the status of your command?'

It was a minute, maybe more, before the captain was able to shake himself out of the sudden panic that swept over him when his brigade commander announced that there was no relief force coming. Finally in halting sentences he rendered his report to Agustin. 'Not long after we heard the sound of explosions coming from the direction of the compound, the platoon commander of my First Platoon, holding the strongpoint on the west side of town, made one frantic call over the radio. He reported that his unit was under attack. When I tried to contact him to find out more information, I got no response. Two hours later, after nightfall, the platoon commander of my Third Platoon, charged with manning the northern strongpoint, informed me that his positions were under heavy mortar fire. He told me that the bunkers his men were manning, built to withstand only small-arms fire and light mortars, were collapsing under the weight of the enemy attack. From here we could see the flashes on the horizon and hear the explosions of the attack he was reporting.'

The young captain paused, sat down on the ground in front of Agustin, and let his head droop between his shoulders before he continued. In the dim light of the cramped bunker, Agustin could see that the captain's shoulders were shaking. When he spoke again, he was barely able to choke back the sobs that stuck in his throat. 'The enemy shelled the Third Platoon's positions on and off for an hour. After each attack the platoon commander would report, adding the names of more of his platoon to the list of dead and wounded. Finally, after one particularly long mortar attack, the platoon's senior sergeant radioed me and informed me that his lieutenant was dead, along with better than half of the men in his platoon, and that enemy assault parties had penetrated the perimeter of their strongpoint. Only the command bunker and two others were still resisting at that time. He asked for instructions. By the time I responded, the Third Platoon went off the air. That was an hour or two ago.'

'And here,' Agustin asked, 'what has happened here?'

Looking up at his colonel, the captain was about to speak when a sergeant came into the small bunker. Ignoring the presence of the colonel, the sergeant dropped to his knees behind his despondent company commander. 'Excuse me, Commander. But is it true? Has the garrison of Puerto Carreño been wiped out just like the other platoons?'

At first the captain did nothing. He simply sat there before Agustin. For several minutes the silence in the bunker was as oppressive as the hot, humid air. Finally the captain looked at the sergeant with tearful eyes. He tried to answer him, but no words came out. None, however, were necessary. The look on his face and his inability to answer him told the sergeant all that he needed to know. 'What are we going to do, then? Sit here, like the Third Platoon, and wait for them to come and kill us?'

Again the captain did not answer. This time he turned his mournful face toward Agustin and stared at him. He was, Agustin knew, looking to him for the answer to the sergeant's question. It was only natural that he do so, for Agustin was the senior officer present and he alone would make the final choice as to what they would do. But, he wondered, sitting there in the cramped confines of a bunker filled with frightened men, what choices did they have, realistically? Since this had been a platoon strongpoint, the only communications that it had were two short-range radios and a single land line, now useless, that had connected the strongpoint with Agustin's headquarters in Puerto Carreño. There was no news from the outside world, nothing other than what the company commander had already reported, none of which was encouraging.

Given this pittance of information, Agustin forced himself to think in a logical manner. The enemy, it seemed, had struck the compound in town first, destroying it with both mortar fire and ground attack. That meant that they had been able to infiltrate sizable forces past the platoon points. Now, with the company in the compound eliminated, the enemy could move about as they pleased. After achieving this freedom of action, they had begun the methodical elimination of the platoon strongpoints. Starting in the west, then moving to the north, the enemy were toppling them like dominoes. The fact that the Third Platoon, alerted and ready, wasn't able to resist the enemy attacks left little prospect that this position would be able to do much better.

With as firm a grasp of what the enemy was doing as he could hope for, Agustin turned his attention to what he and his diminished command would do. There were, he realized, only three options to choose from. First, he and the tiny garrison of this strongpoint could stand and fight in place. This would, of course, be a last stand. And like most last stands it would be an empty gesture, one that would do no one outside of Puerto Carreño any good and would simply hand the FARC another victory.

If that was true, the next logical thing would be to surrender. Such a thought, however bad the situation was, was quickly cast aside. Agustin had little doubt that if he offered himself up to surrender, he would not live to see the next dawn. His reputation as a fierce and uncompromising anti-guerrilla fighter was well known. There were too many incidents of brutalities visited by men under his command in his past to be ignored by the enemy. Besides, Agustin reasoned, there was still too much pride and too much fight left in him and many of his soldiers. While it was true that everyone was at the moment despondent because of what appeared to be their impending doom, positive leadership and the hope of survival could motivate them to carry on. But carry on and do what?

That question led Agustin to the last and in his mind only reasonable choice they had. Ready, he looked at the captain and the sergeant. 'There is nothing to be gained by staying here and dying. We will therefore abandon this post and make our way west, where I expect we will be able eventually to link up with either relief forces sent to save us or other garrisons still holding.'

Though he was thankful that his commander had given them a solution to their dilemma, the captain was not instantly carried away with enthusiasm. His first response instead was one of skepticism. 'But the enemy, they are to the west of us and no doubt coming our way.'

'Yes,' Agustin snapped, 'they are. That is why we are going go east, away from the enemy, before attempting to make our way back to the west and safety.'

'Into Venezuela?'

'Yes, Captain, into Venezuela. That is where the FARC have operated from for so long and, I'm sure, where the forces that attacked us came from. We will do what they have been doing for years, only in reverse. Once in Venezuela, we will move south along the border and re-enter Colombia.'

Still unconvinced of the feasibility of his commander's plan, the captain continued to pelt him with questions. 'Won't the Venezuela border patrols be alerted and on guard due to the attacks against us here today?'

Losing his patience, but still determined to show his shaken subordinate that his plan was a reasonable one, Agustin leaned over and lowered his voice before responding. 'Look, Captain, we know most of the FARC's old infiltration routes in and out of Venezuela, right?' The captain nodded. 'Yes, and tonight we will use one of them to slip past them and the Venezuelans, just as they have done so many times before. Now do you have any more questions?'

Looking over at his sergeant, then back at Agustin, the captain shook his head. 'No, sir. No questions.'

'Good! For there is much to do, and not much time. Sergeant, pass the word that we will be breaking out of here in the next thirty minutes. Have your men load up as quickly as possible as much food and ammunition as they can reasonably carry. No personal gear or effects. No heavy weapons either. Machine guns and rifles only. We must travel fast and that means traveling light.' When the sergeant left, without turning to verify Agustin's orders to him with his own company commander, Agustin turned his attention to the captain. 'Now I need you to pull out your map of the area between here and the border that shows all the FARC's infiltration routes and bring it to me. We must be quick, for I doubt if they will leave us alone for much longer.'

Just as he'd expected, the two men, given a reasonable

mission and orders that made sense, responded as they were trained. Though Agustin himself was starting to have doubts about their chances of even getting out of the strongpoint without being torn apart by the FARC, he knew in his heart that he had to try. He was, after all, a soldier, and it was his duty to fight as long as he could. Though the thought of fleeing this battlefield now began to bother him, he reasoned that this was only the beginning of a new and more deadly war. And if that was true, if the FARC was now as strong as he feared, there would be many more battlefields on which he could avenge his honor and this defeat. How many more, or where they would be, he had no idea. Only one man that night knew with any degree of certainty. And Hector Valendez was not about to tell anyone, at least not for the moment.

In the quiet hours after midnight, when Captain Nancy Kozak found that she could not sleep, she took up the habit of wandering about the brigade base camp, going from one unit's operations center to the next. In each of them she would stay awhile, sharing information with the officer and sergeants on duty while sipping coffee and, when the mood took them, digressing into swapping war stories and news from back home. The men and women who made up the night shifts in command posts, Kozak had found, were a breed apart. Freed from the stringent protocol that the presence of senior officers dictated, the people who ran the war and maintained the vigilance for their units from dusk to dawn were a more easygoing, sociable lot. This was especially true for the night crew manning the 3rd Brigade's tactical command post, where Nancy Kozak's closest friend in the entire brigade, Captain Jessica Ann Cruthers, ran the S-2 shop from seven in the evening until seven the next morning.

Cruthers, nicknamed Jack because of her initials, was only a few months older than Kozak and in many respects her opposite. Four inches shorter than Kozak, Cruthers was petite. Even her fingers, thin without being bony, were small. She wore her mousy blond hair short and cropped close to her head, unlike Kozak, who despite the misery kept as much of her flowing auburn hair as possible. This was a source of much amusement for Cruthers, who never missed an opportunity to hassle Kozak. Every time she came into the brigade tactical operations center and removed her helmet, Kozak would automatically reach up with her right hand and begin to vigorously scratch her head, causing the hair piled high and held down by legions of bobby pins to start to unravel. As soon as Kozak uttered a word of complaint, Cruthers would start on her from wherever she happened to be standing. 'Girl,' she'd call, 'when are you going to realize that no living mammal worth mentioning is going to give you a second look. Get with the program and lose those long stringy locks.'

Proud of her hair, Kozak would often shoot Cruthers a glance of feigned anger. 'My hair is not stringy. It happens to have quite a bit of body. I just need to wash it and comb it out some.'

'Some!' Cruthers would exclaim. 'You have more knots and snags in that mop of yours than a four-quart pot of spaghetti. It would take a whole platoon of parachute riggers a week to sort them out. Why do you insist in keeping all of that hair? Trying to provide a home for orphaned bugs?'

Looking about before answering, Kozak would give Cruthers a shy glance. 'Jack, you know damned well why I keep my hair this long.'

Like the rest of the ritual, repeated time and time again, regardless of the time of day or night or the presence of others in the operations center, Cruthers would let out a decidedly unfeminine laugh. 'Nancy, who are you kidding? What, with those two bars on one collar, the crossed rifles on the other, and those baggy-ass BDUs you wear, do you really think any man around here is going to give you another thought?'

Sometimes this would anger Kozak. Sometimes she would give a sly smile. With a twinkle in her eye, she would remind Cruthers, 'Ah, got you there, girl. AJ likes my hair.'

The mention of Captain Aaron J. Pierce would cause Cruthers to put her hands on her hips and laugh louder. 'Ha! AJ Honey, let me tell you something. AJ's an aviator, and like all male aviators, the hair he's interested in isn't on your head.'

If Cruthers hadn't managed to anger Kozak up to this point, her making fun of AJ in this manner would push her over the edge. Usually all Kozak needed to do was simply flash a look that told Cruthers that she had gone too far. When she saw that look, Cruthers would quickly change the subject and not mention hair or AJ for the rest of the day. Yet inevitably the next night, when Kozak came into the brigade operations center, removed her helmet with her left hand, and began to claw away at her itchy scalp with her right hand, Cruthers would start the whole routine again.

That was how Cruthers knew that something was wrong when Kozak came into the operations center this evening and plopped down in a chair next to her. Seated half on and half off the metal folding chair, Kozak held her rifle between her knees so tightly that her knuckles began to turn white. She said nothing, did nothing as she stared vacantly at the Intel map on the wall across from her that a sergeant was working on. Even from the side, Cruthers could tell that Kozak's brown eyes were puffy and red. Though everyone in the brigade had bloodshot eyes, especially those who worked the graveyard shift, Cruthers could see that her friend had been crying.

After Kozak sat there for several moments without comment or even removing her helmet, Cruthers decided that whatever it was that was bothering her friend couldn't wait. She had something, Cruthers guessed, that she wanted to talk about, but either didn't know how to start or, for whatever reason, was embarrassed about. Setting aside the list of moving target indicator grid coordinates that she had been calling off to the sergeant who was plotting them on the Intel map, Cruthers looked over at Kozak and studied her for a second. Between the look in her eyes, the despondency that she was displaying, and her failure to initiate what other members of the brigade staff referred to as the Jack and Nancy comedy show, Cruthers knew she had a real problem on her hands. Moving her head around so that it was in Kozak's line of sight, Cruthers looked her in the eye. 'You okay?'

Without breaking her expressionless stare, Kozak nodded. 'Yeah, I'm fine.'

Laying her right hand on Kozak's shoulder, Cruthers shook her head. 'Sure, like you expect me to believe that. I know you better and you know that I do. Feel like talking?'

Looking up into Cruther's eyes, then around the room, and finally back to her friend, Kozak tried to answer, but the word 'yes' got caught in her throat as she fought back a sob. Moving her hand across Kozak's back and giving her a slight reassuring pat between the shoulder blades, Cruthers called over to the sergeant at the map board that she was going to take a break. Having watched what had been going on without making it look too obvious, the sergeant nodded and turned back to the map where he continued to work cleaning up stray marks here and there. Neither he nor any of the other officers or NCOs of the night shift paid the two female captains any heed as they left the brightly lit operations center and wandered into the still night air.

Though there was no breeze to push the sullen night air about, the two women at least were able to escape the stuffiness of the blacked-out command post. Though no brigade base camp had yet been attacked by guerrillas, the brigade commander wasn't taking any chances. Unlike other senior commanders, he took heed of what had happened to 3rd of the 511th. Since the twenty-first of September he had been taking every prudent precaution he could think of to ensure that he and his command weren't surprised like that again. Still, many unwarlike conveniences dotted the brigade area. One of them was a crude wooden picnic table banged together by some soldiers after setting up the brigade base camp months ago. Sitting under a drooping camouflage net that needed tightening, the picnic table was used by members of the brigade when eating lunch or taking smoke breaks away from their posts. It was for them the nearest thing to a sanctuary where they could for a moment forget about their duties, their responsibilities, and most of all the war.

Blinded by their emergence from the bright lights of the operations center into the deep darkness of the night, the two women slowly half walked, half shuffled about in the moonless darkness, searching for the table where they had shared a lunch many times before. Cruthers found it quite by accident when she hit her shin against the weathered board of the bench. After she let out a short damn, they seated themselves on the bench, facing away from the table, side by side. Though there were others somewhere out there, pulling their tour of guard duty or manning operations centers, the darkness and the camouflage net made Cruthers and Kozak feel very much alone. As they settled down, Cruthers wrapped her right arm across Kozak's back while her friend placed her rifle off to one side. Without a word, Kozak slumped and began to cry. Placing her left hand on Kozak's left shoulder and squeezing her tightly, Cruthers tried as best she could to comfort Kozak as she sat there, her face buried in her hands, and began sobbing.

As Kozak let herself go, Cruthers tried to imagine what exactly had finally brought this on. She and just about everyone else outside of Kozak's battalion had seen it coming, not only in Kozak but in just about everyone associated with that battalion. Harold Cerro, the battalion commander, best reflected in appearance and conduct what was happening. He was fast becoming a psychological basket case. The once proud and cocky infantry officer had as a result of the grind of war and the aftermath of the twenty-first of September become sullen and withdrawn. His gaunt face, need to avert his gaze when addressing people, and halting conversation when he did made everyone on the brigade staff uncomfortable. Even his physical stature was changing. Daily his sagging shoulders seemed to sink closer and closer to the ground under the weight of untold worries and concerns that he kept locked in his mind. 'It's only a matter of time,' Cruthers had heard her boss tell the brigade operations officer, 'before Cerro goes off the deep end. Let's just hope he doesn't take too many of his people with him.'

Cerro, of course, wasn't Cruthers's concern. Hers was a more personal stake. Right now in her arms the one person that she really cared for was sitting there falling apart. What to do to help right now was foremost in her mind. Of course, being the intelligence officer she was, Cruthers immediately reverted to her training. It was, after all, only natural. With eleven years of service behind her, Cruthers's way of thinking and reacting had become instinctively military. To really be able to help Nancy, she knew she had to find out what it was that was bothering her the most. So as she tried hard to comfort Kozak and wait until her crying jag had run its course, Cruthers began to assess the situation and determine what evil forces were arrayed in Kozak's mind against her sanity.

Was it the cold and mindless manner in which the division had dealt with 3rd Battalion, 511th Infantry, after the twenty-first of September? This, of course, was a very real possibility. Her own battalion commander, after all, was demonstrating his inability to deal with that event. Was it the trauma of war? Had Kozak allowed all the nightmares of past battles to gang up on her and steal her ability to cope? That possibility sounded reasonable, especially given her recent bout of nocturnal wanderings. Perhaps there was bad news from home, a sickness, a divorce in the family, or other such problem. Such a thing, combined with the stress and strain of the recent month, would be, Cruthers reasoned, enough to cause a Marine to cry. Or maybe, she thought as she began to exhaust her list of possibilities, it was that silly bastard that she had been pining for during the last few months, the aviator with straight teeth and no brain. Though Cruthers hoped that this wasn't the case, the more she thought about it the more she began to suspect that some way, somehow, AJ the throttle jockey was the root cause of Kozak's current state. It wouldn't be the first time, Cruthers sighed, that she had had to sit by and watch as an intelligent, capable female officer impaled herself on the love of a man who had no idea what the word love meant.

Noticing that Kozak was beginning to wind down some, Cruthers leaned over and moved her face close to Kozak's. Softly, calmly, she spoke. 'Feel like talking or would you rather just sit awhile?'

With nothing to blow her nose into, Kozak sniffed back the liquid that was threatening to gush down the front of her face. Sitting upright, she used the index finger on her right hand to wipe away the drop of mucus that had managed to escape. Wiping her hand on the pants leg of her BDUs, Kozak turned, faced Cruthers, but then froze as the thought of her mother popped into her head. For the briefest of moments Kozak imagined what her mother would say if she had caught her wiping snot on her own clothes. Strange, Kozak thought before dismissing that idea. Here I am, a full-grown woman, a combat infantry officer, and I'm still paranoid about my mother. But then, she reasoned, right now she was a little paranoid about everything, including the future. When the vision of her mother's disapproving face was gone, Kozak began to talk in a mournful, shaky voice that warned Cruthers that more tears were only a breath away. 'It's AJ, Jack. We . . . I had a fight with him.'

Drawing in a deep breath herself, Cruthers didn't try to disguise the look of disgust that flashed for an instant across her face. She knew it! Damned if she hadn't guessed right. That weasel, with his oversized watch and an ego to match, had either picked a fight with Nancy or had dumped her now, at a time when she needed his love and understanding the most. Pulling Kozak closer to her and comforting her for a moment, Cruthers looked over Kozak's shoulder, her face contorted with anger. Damn him! Damn them all. Nothing, she had decided a long time ago, could fuck up a good woman and her career faster than a fickle lover boy whose maturity hadn't managed to keep pace with his chronological age. Though she had tried to warn Kozak many times that this was neither the time nor place to be getting involved in a romance, Kozak had ignored her friend and had allowed herself to drift into an affair that now, from all outward signs, was coming to an end. This was not the time, Cruthers knew, to tell her, 'I told you so.' No, not the time at all. Later maybe. But tonight the best she could hope for was to find some way of calming her down, getting her mind off the shit-for-brains boy scout that had gotten her into this state, and give her friend something positive to look forward to. It was, she knew, a tall order, but one that she had to try to fill.

Pulling back out of their embrace, Cruthers looked into Kozak's eyes. Taking Kozak's hands, still moist with her tears, into her own, Cruthers tried to sound as empathetic as possible. 'You ready to talk about this yet, or do you just want to sit here quietly for a while and settle down?'

Without any further prompting, Kozak let it all come gushing out. 'Oh, Jack, I don't know what to do, who to turn to, or even what to think anymore. I'm even beginning to question whether I can think straight anymore.'

'Nancy, in case you haven't noticed, you and your unit have been through a rough month.'

'I know. I know that. I keep telling myself, "Girl, you've seen worse." But then I look around and I realize that I haven't. In the past there was always someone there to prop me up when I needed it or give me a kick in the butt when I deserved it. Colonel Cerro and I go back to the Mexican incident when he was a captain on division staff and I was a fresh lieutenant, and he has been sort of an inspiration to me. When I needed an ideal infantry officer, one that I could model myself after, he stepped into my life and gave me that.'

Taken aback by this oration on her battalion commander, and not the person she had previously indicated as being the guilty bastard, Cruthers gave Kozak a questioning look. Realizing that her friend wasn't making heads or tails out of where she was going with this conversation, Kozak tried again. 'After the twenty-first of September, when the colonel started getting, well, funny, I began to feel a little lost myself. I mean, after all, here's the one person that I had held up as being the personification of the infantry combat leader going to hell in a handbasket right before my eyes. I was beginning to feel . . .'

Noticing her hesitation, Cruthers shook Kozak's hands and moved her head closer to Kozak's. 'Feeling what? You can tell me. Please, what were you feeling?'

With her eyes wide open and her face drooping in the saddest expression that Cruthers could ever imagine, Kozak reminded her at that moment of a little girl. 'Jack,

I felt lost. Lost and vulnerable. There wasn't anyone in the battalion that I could turn to and talk to this about. Everyone, from the XO on down, was either feeling sorry for themselves or angry as hell, sometimes both.'

'Well, why in God's name didn't you come to me? Nancy, I would have listened.'

Kozak looked into her friend's eyes and thought for a moment before responding. No, she thought, it wouldn't do to tell her the truth. She just wouldn't understand. While Jack was a good friend and they were close, Cruthers wasn't a combat arms officer. She hadn't been there! She hadn't seen what Kozak and Cerro had seen, felt what they had felt, or suffered inside as they did for every failure, real and imagined, that combat arms officers suffer after losing people entrusted into their care. Kozak had needed another officer, another combat veteran who had been there in battle and knew what she felt without her having to say anything. Cruthers, for all her friendship and good intentions, could never fill that role. So, shaking her head and averting her eyes, she lied. 'I don't know, Jack. I guess . . . I guess I just wasn't thinking straight.'

'But you told AJ.'

Looking back at Cruthers rather sheepishly, Kozak nodded. 'Yes, I went to AJ.'

'And he didn't understand. He didn't understand what you told him and he didn't understand the pain and suffering you were feeling, did he?'

Kozak took a couple of deep breaths, looked down at their hands clasped and resting on her thigh, and simply nodded her head.

Releasing Kozak's hands, Cruthers half turned, leaned forward, and embraced Kozak again. 'Nancy, Nancy, Nancy. How many times do I have to tell you. AJ's a fool. The only thing he's capable of understanding is that damned machine of his. He's like most men. They have little idea what makes women work and even less inclination to find out. Comprehension of anything that doesn't run on electricity or liquid fuel is beyond them.'

Though Kozak felt that Cruthers, now as always, was being a bit too negative about men and the way they acted, she said nothing. Breaking their embrace, she pulled away from her friend slightly. 'It's not only that, Jack. I think I could have dealt with his lack of compassion. He is, after all, an aviator and he doesn't appreciate what it's like to lead soldiers into battle. What really got me . . . Well, what I mean to say, the thing that I found the hardest to deal with was me and my own thoughts.'

Oh, God, Cruthers thought. Here she goes blaming herself and making excuses for that moron. When's she ever going to learn?

Not noticing the incredulous look in her friend's face, Kozak went on without pause. 'Although I knew that he wasn't involved in this operation, I couldn't get it out of my mind that he didn't, that he couldn't, do anything to help me. All afternoon as we inched our way through the enemy positions, cracking one bunker at a time, losing people all the way, I kept looking up at the sky, hoping that he would come in like the cavalry and save us. When finally we were able to contact the brigade aviation officer and call for med evacs and resupply and he informed us that division aviation was not able to fly any missions in until they had found their decoy flares and mounted them on the helicopters, I felt betrayed. I felt like the man I loved, even though he was a hundred miles away and unable to change anything, had deserted me. Even after we got back. Even after I had been able to push those silly thoughts out of my head, when I saw him for the first time last week, the same ugly feelings of betrayal and abandonment came back.'

'Did you tell him, Nancy, how you felt? Did you explain any of this to him?'

She shook her head. 'I tried. I really tried. But all he

could talk about was how much of a bummer it was that the battalion had been taken out of the reserve force rotation and how he had been looking forward to spending time with me in Bogotá. Imagine that, Jack. Here I am on the edge, with no one to turn to, and all he can think about is how terrible it is that he didn't get to shack up with me. To hell with me. To hell with my problems. I . . . I just . . . I just couldn't . . .'

As Kozak began to get choked up, her voice trailing off into a sob, Cruthers, now half hanging off the bench while she faced Kozak, put both hands on Kozak's shoulders and smiled. 'Honey, believe me, I understand. I really understand.' She ignored Kozak's comment about having no one to turn to and instead sat back on the bench, pulled Kozak's head down on her shoulder. Then slowly she began to run her fingers along the side of Kozak's face and neck, telling her as she did so that everything would be all right, everything would be fine.

The two women sat there like that for a minute, maybe two, with Cruthers's right arm around Kozak's back and the hand on that arm gently playing about on the side of Kozak's face and neck. It felt good to Kozak to feel another person's warm body close to hers. To have a shoulder to lean on and to have a sympathetic ear to talk to. Unburdened, at least for the moment, of her dark thoughts and pain, she was for the first time in a month beginning to feel at ease, at peace with herself. God, she thought, this feels so, so . . .

Slowly, almost unperceived at first, Kozak began to feel uncomfortable. Despite the warmth of Cruthers's embrace, or, more correctly, because of the warmth, Nancy Kozak began to realize that sitting here, with Cruthers like this wasn't . . .

Wasn't what? Kozak wondered. Right, or appropriate, or normal? What was it that was bothering her? she wondered. Was it that she didn't want anyone to see her like this in the dark with Cruthers, a woman that everyone more or less knew was lesbian? Or was her uneasiness due to the fact that she had allowed herself to give way to her foolish emotions and cry like a silly girl in the presence of another officer? Or was there something else? Perhaps, Nancy thought as she felt Cruthers's fingers gently stroking the back of her neck, she was beginning to enjoy this too much. Perhaps, she was . . .

Like a thunderclap, Kozak jumped up, brushing Cruthers's left hand from her and moving out of her embrace. The suddenness of Kozak's reaction startled both women. Spinning around wide-eyed, Kozak stared down at Cruthers still sitting on the bench. She in turn stared up at Kozak. Kozak opened her mouth to speak, but no words came out. Only air, as she began to pant, passed her lips. Disgusted, frightened, and very much shaken, Kozak turned and began to rush off into the night when she heard Cruthers call out. 'Nancy! Your rifle.'

Stopping in place, Kozak clenched both of her fists and shut her eyes. In her rush to get away she had run off without taking her rifle. Pivoting about, she opened her eyes and saw Cruthers standing there in front of the bench holding Kozak's rifle out. Though she knew she had to go get it, she hesitated. What do I say? she thought. What can I say?

Slowly, hesitantly, Kozak inched forward. With great reluctance she reached up and grasped the offered rifle. For a moment Cruthers held on to it, looking into Kozak's eyes as she did so. Neither woman said anything, neither woman moved. They just looked at each other, one frightened and badly shaken, one surprised and embarrassed.

Kozak tried to pull her rifle away from Cruthers, but she held on. As their eyes met, Cruthers began to speak. 'Nancy, I . . .'

It was at that moment when a voice from the direction of the operations center called out to Cruthers, 'Hey,

Captain. Hot stuff coming in from division. You better get here quick.'

Glancing back, she saw her sergeant at the entrance of the operations center. 'I'll be there in a moment.'

'Better hurry, Captain. The ops people have already sent for the old man. The Farcees have lit up the entire eastern part of the country and are hammering every military airfield in and around Bogotá.'

'I said I'll be there in a minute.' The sharpness of her response was enough for the sergeant. He had done his duty. He had passed on the word, given her a warning, and that, he figured, was all an officer deserved. Satisfied, he disappeared back into the operations center. When he was gone, Cruthers looked at Kozak, a sheepish, apologetic look replacing that of surprise in her eyes. 'Nancy, I'm sorry. Believe me, I'm terribly sorry. I thought . . .'

She didn't finish. Letting go of Kozak's rifle, she turned and hurried off, disappearing into the brigade operations center. Behind her she left Nancy Kozak still standing in front of the bench, staring straight ahead into the darkness, alone, more alone and lost than she had ever felt in her life.

CHAPTER 9

October 21

A former boss of Scott Dixon's had once told him that it was far more advantageous to add to those whom you can count on as friends than to multiply one's own enemies. Though not always successful, since people such as C. B. Lane seemed to make it a hobby of alienating those who did not share their views, Dixon worked hard to be cooperative, open, and friendly, or at least to avoid intentionally pissing someone off when the more open approach failed. In Colombia this policy was to prove its worth in spades.

Colonel Chester A. Thomas, whom everyone called Cat or the Cat because of his initials, had been serving in Colombia as the military attaché for close to three years when Dixon arrived there to begin his fact-finding tour for the Chief of Staff of the Army. Thomas, a man who was fast approaching the end of his career in the Army, had found himself on the outside when C. B. Lane and his staff arrived in Colombia. During a meeting not unlike the one that took place between Lane and Dixon, Lane had informed Thomas that his thoughts, ideas, advice, and presence were not welcome in his division. 'We have a job to do,' he told Thomas, 'and we don't need a limp-wristed colonel from the embassy poking around here.' Though appalled by this mindless rebuff, Thomas said nothing. Instead he decided right then and there that if that's the way Lane felt, fine. He'd get his wish. With less than a year to retirement, Thomas decided to do something he had never done in his twenty-seven years in the Army; he'd start taking it easy. Though he would do his job and serve the ambassador as his adviser on military affairs, Thomas had no intention of beating himself up trying to force his views and observations on Colombian affairs on Lane or his staff.

That changed, however, when Dixon had first arrived in country. Dixon, like Thomas, was rebuffed and stone-walled by Lane despite his credentials. Even the staff of the 11th Air Assault Division ignored and stonewalled him when they thought they could. That was why Dixon found Thomas to be an invaluable source of information, a guide through the Byzantine labyrinth of Colombian politics, and a key to unlocking countless doors for him throughout the country. Any difference in rank was quickly put aside as Dixon and Thomas worked side by side whenever poss-ible to fulfill General Fulk's mandate to find out what was really happening in Colombia. 'General,' Thomas had told Dixon when he was departing in late September, 'you're ever down these parts again, you know you have a place to rest your head and a sympathetic ear you can chew on.'

So it was no surprise that when Thomas found out that Dixon was coming to Bogotá as the head of SOUTHCOM Forward, he went out of his way to do everything he could to make sure that the embassy and its staff were ready and willing to accommodate them. He even badgered the ambassador until the ambassador put in writing an agreement that placed Thomas on Dixon's staff as adviser

and liaison officer for the ambassador. Thomas, despite
having been given such a backwater assignment, was still
in every respect a good soldier who simply wanted to do his
duty. By aligning himself with Dixon, he had the chance to
be productive and make a meaningful contribution.

It was the Cat's efforts and preparations that allowed
Dixon's staff to be operational and ready to deal with the
crisis that was enveloping the eastern part of the country
one day after stepping off the aircraft. Even more vital
than the physical accommodations and the rapidity with
which Dixon's communications became operational were
the sources of information, both formal and informal, that
Thomas was able to share with Dixon's intelligence and
operations staffs. For while Lane and his division staff
openly scorned and ignored the wealth of information
that Thomas used to augment the normal U.S. intelligence
sources, Dixon's young and energetic intelligence officer,
Major Herman M. Hagstrom, reveled in the wealth of
information offered by Thomas like a child let loose in
a toy store.

Hagstrom was, as one staff officer at SOUTHCOM
stated mildly, a real piece of work. When Hagstrom was
introduced to Dixon as a candidate for his staff, Dixon all
but rejected him out of hand. Dixon told Jeff Worsham,
his chief of staff, that Hagstrom looked too much like a
cartoon character rather than a G-2 intelligence officer.
At five feet eleven and one hundred and forty pounds,
Hagstrom had the physique of a stick person drawn by
a four-year-old. His head, topped by a tuft of hair that
looked too small to cover it, was almost egg-shaped.
Even his glasses, the black plastic-framed type issued by
the Army that everyone referred to as 'no fuck' glasses,
added to Hagstrom's image as a certified card-carrying
nerd. While Worsham agreed that Hagstrom was far from
being a picture-perfect model of an officer, he countered
that Hagstrom had a unique talent. 'When it comes to

pulling diverse bits and pieces of information together with seemingly meaningless information and producing an accurate estimate,' Worsham told Dixon, 'no one does it better.' Still leery, Dixon had done some checking of his own. What he found out more than supported Worsham's claim, for when no one else in SOUTHCOM could make sense of something, Hagstrom got it. 'The kid,' said the deputy chief of staff for intelligence at SOUTHCOM, 'treats a challenge like that as a game. Behind those godawful glasses is a brain that's as close to a Cray computer as a human being can get.'

Now as he sat in the early-morning briefing and staff brainstorming session listening to Hagstrom go through his paces, Dixon was pleased he had been able to overcome his dislike for the man based solely on appearance. Hours before the CIA's chief analyst was even ready to sit down and start sifting through the mishmash of information on his desk, piecing together the scant information that his sources had made available to him, Hagstrom, drawing off the same sources, which were supplemented by Thomas's connections, had a full estimate of the situation prepared and on Dixon's desk.

That estimate and his briefing did not paint a very bright picture. 'Were I to make a historical comparison of the magnitude and scope of this offensive,' Hagstrom stated at the beginning of his briefing, 'I would have to use the Tet offensive of January 1968. The main difference, however, between the VC in 1968 and the FARC yesterday is that, to the best of my knowledge at this hour, the FARC has succeeded in destroying every target they hit and secured all the objectives that they have attacked. As of oh six hundred hours this morning, it's the FARC ten, Government forces zip.' While hedging slightly by stating that bad news in situations like this is often exaggerated and has a tendency to overwhelm any good news that may be coming in, he warned Dixon and the rest of the staff not to hold their breath.

Continuing his briefing, Hagstrom turned his attention to the western part of the country for a moment. 'The recent operations being conducted by the FARC in the western mountains along the Cauca River now appear to have been nothing but a deception whose aim was to draw the government forces and our own 11th Air Assault away from the true area of operations.' Using a map that covered all of Colombia and large tracts of neighboring nations, he then began to explain the flow of FARC operations, as best he could, based on the fragmented reports, observations, and downright assumptions in the eastern zone. For each major incident he gave the location, the time it started and ended, if known, the government forces involved, the size and nature of the FARC units involved, and the nature of the attack, such as a mortar barrage only, or sapper teams, or ground assault accompanied by mortars. The area in which these operations took place, now being referred to as the Eastern Zone of Operations, was quite extensive. It measured some 230 miles east to west and anywhere from one hundred to one hundred and fifty miles in width, north to south. The defining terrain feature in the north was the Rio Meta, which ran northeast from the eastern mountains near Bogotá to the Venezuelan border. To the south, another river which, like the Meta, originated in the eastern mountains, ran more or less to the northeast also. A tributary of this river, the Rio Ariari, created the western boundary of the zone while the Venezuelan border itself, the eastern. In all, some 54,000 square miles.

In his efforts to piece together some type of coherent picture in his mind, it wasn't until Hagstrom was midway through his briefing that Dixon stopped him and asked him to clarify a point. Putting up his hand, Dixon called out, 'Woo, Herman. Hold up there, lad. For the past ten minutes you've been talking about local and regular forces. Where did that difference come from?'

Surprised, Hagstrom looked at Dixon for a moment and blinked his eyes as if he were changing programs in his mind before he answered. 'Oh, well, I was going to get to that later in the briefing, sir. But I guess now's as good a time as any, if you would like.'

Dixon nodded. 'Yes, Herman, I would like.'

Shuffling through the stack of note cards that he was using for his briefing, Herman looked for those concerning the enemy's order of battle. When he found them, he looked at the first one for a moment, cleared his throat, blinked his eyes, and began to speak without looking up at Dixon. 'Well, sir, as soon as I knew I was coming down here with you, I started going over all the reports that I could get my hands on. You know, after-action reports, spot reports, Intel updates, the works. As I was going through them trying to create my own order of battle for the FARC, I noticed that the nature of some of the enemy units was beginning to change. It wasn't until last night, when I was able to go through Colonel Thomas's files, that I was able to confirm my theory.

'Starting back in late June, stray reports of FARC units, all wearing the same pattern of camouflage uniform and armed with the same type and caliber of weapon, began to crop up. By mid-July the reports of these well-equipped and uniformed units started to increase, coinciding with reports of platoon-sized forces used in quick raids against well-defended Colombian outposts, or in large ambushes. It was the reports from August, however, with the sightings of company-sized enemy forces, supported by mortars in most cases, which convinced me that we were dealing with well-equipped regular forces that were different from the ragtag part-time warriors that had been the mainstay of the FARC up to then. For lack of better terms, I adopted the same terms used in Vietnam to differentiate VC forces. In my opinion, the FARC now has two distinct categories of forces in the field. Local forces, as before, are made up of people from a community who support the FARC but on a part-time basis only and seldom if ever leave their home region. The new forces, which I have been calling main-force units, are mobile shock troops. Well armed, the main-force units are trained to fight as platoons, companies, and maybe, if these reports are to be believed, battalions anywhere in Colombia.' Finished, he looked up at Dixon and waited for the general to say something.

There was a pause as Dixon weighed the information that he had just been given. How in the hell, he thought, could he and everyone else who had studied the same reports have missed something as obvious as the information that Herman had just briefed? Still thinking as he spoke, Dixon asked Hagstrom why he hadn't mentioned this to him before.

An embarrassed smile flickered briefly on Hagstrom's face as he looked down at the floor and shuffled his right foot. 'Well, sir, to tell you the truth, it wasn't until early this morning, at about zero two-thirty, that it hit me. I mean, I had been writing all the information down as I saw it, but it never all came together for me until just a few hours ago. When the idea sort of fell on me, I went back, looked at my notes again, and blam, there it was, clear as a bell. The enemy the government forces are trying to deal with today is not the same one that they have been trained to fight. This is, in my estimate, day one of a new war.'

Slumping in the seat next to Dixon, Worsham let out a low but audible 'Oh, shit! Katy bar the door.'

Without even bothering to glance over at Worsham, Dixon mumbled, 'Jeff, I concur.' Twisting halfway about in his seat, Dixon scanned his entire staff, speaking as he did so. 'Ladies and gentlemen, based on what the G-2 has just stated, I want all of you to begin to adjust your reports and estimates accordingly. Though there may be an outside chance that he's wrong, I don't think so. And,' Dixon added as an afterthought, 'if he is, at least we'll be erring on the safe side.'

Looking back at Hagstrom, Dixon asked if he could hold the rest of his briefing for a moment, indicating that he wanted the operations officer, Major Don Saventinni, to give the staff a quick and dirty overview of how the Colombian military was reacting to the FARC's offensive. Saventinni, at six foot two, one hundred and eighty-five pounds, and a close-cropped ranger haircut, was everything imagewise, that Hagstrom wasn't. An infantryman, Saventinni's uniform was covered with every badge and special skill patch imaginable. From Pathfinder to scuba, he wore them proudly on a chest that filled his BDU shirt and covered chest muscles that gave the appearance of being as hard as marble. With the swagger of a man confident in his ability to take on all comers, day or night, Saventinni moved to the front of the room, dropped his pre-positioned overlay into place on the map, and startled everyone in the room by shouting, 'GOOD MORNING, SIR!' with a sharpness that damned near split Dixon's eardrums.

Feeling good about his staff and how things were going, despite the disasters that were befalling their Colombian allies outside, Dixon turned to Worsham. 'Jeff, if that trooper is on steroids, cut him to half rations. I think he's a little overdone.'

The general's comment caused Saventinni to break out in a grin that ran from ear to ear. Turning his broad shoulders sideways so that Dixon could see the ranger tab on his left sleeve, Saventinni smiled. 'No steroids necessary, General. It's airborne ranger, through and through.'

Looking up at the ceiling, Dixon shook his head and mumbled so that all could hear, 'Lord, save us from the

infantry.' When the laughter died down, Dixon nodded at
Saventinni. 'Okay, Don. What do you have?'

Pointing to the blue symbols that represented the 11th
Air Assault Division's brigades and separate battalions,
Saventinni explained that, as of six that morning, the
division was continuing to conduct operations against
enemy forces that Hagstrom had during his briefing tagged
as nothing more than diversions. When asked if the 11th
had shown any indication that they might be holding back
and preparing to redirect their attention against the new
threat in the east, Saventinni shook his head. 'I spoke to
their operations people just before this briefing started,
sir. At this time there are no plans to suspend, delay, or
cancel any operations in progress or planned for the next
twenty-four hours. The division hasn't even issued a be
prepared warning to the brigades to do so. It is, at this
time, business as usual.' There was in Saventinni's voice
a note of disgust when he made that last statement.

Looking over to Thomas seated to his right, Dixon asked
if the Colombians had asked for any assistance from the
11th yet. Thomas shook his head. 'No, sir, not that I know
of. And even if they need the 11th's help, which I think
they do, it will be a long time before they ask.'

'Why? Pride? The Colombian generals aren't foolish
enough to let simple pride interfere with military necessity,
are they?'

'Yes, sir, they are. You have to remember the new
reformed military has to prove its value and manhood.
We are, after all, dealing with Latinos, proud men who
often value their machismo more than their own lives.'

Dixon thought about Thomas's comments, then looked
at the symbols that represented the 11th and the blue circles and boxes marked on the clear overlay that indicated
unit zones of operations and assembly areas, and said
nothing. After a minute he nodded. 'Okay, while we're
talking about them, what about the Colombians?'

Though he stated from the start that it was still too early to tell, what reports had been received told of, as Saventinni put it, 'nothing but gloom and doom.' Just as Hagstrom had done for the enemy forces, Saventinni briefed Dixon and the staff on what the Colombian Army had done in the past twenty-four hours and what they were planning to do over the next twenty-four. While explaining the former was no easy matter, given the dearth of confirmed information, projecting what the Colombians would do was even harder. 'About the only operation going on, in or outside the Eastern Zone of Operations where the enemy hit, was the dispatch of one battalion of the Presidential Brigade out of Bogotá, early this morning by truck to reinforce the garrison of Villavicencio. A second battalion of that brigade is scheduled to leave within the hour.'

'Villavicencio?' Dixon cut in. 'Why Villavicencio?'

'It is,' Thomas explained, 'the main source of food for Bogotá. Its population of 200,000 makes it the only major city of any value in the Eastern Zone.'

Dixon nodded and looked over to Hagstrom. 'Okay, but except for an attack against the military airfield there, I don't recall you mentioning any real danger posed against that city. Or did I miss something?'

'No, sir,' Hagstrom responded. 'You didn't miss anything.'

Next Dixon looked at Saventinni. 'Why reinforce a garrison that's not in danger, using your only reliable reserve force in the capital? And why trucks? Why not airlift?'

'The last part of the question is easy, sir,' Saventinni stated. 'As the G-2 briefed, sapper teams and mortar attacks pretty well nailed all of the military airfields in and around Bogotá. It's estimated at this time that upwards of two-thirds of the Colombian Army's rotary-winged aircraft and fifty percent of the Air Force's fixed-wing transports have been destroyed or rendered nonoperational. Those aircraft that are still available are being held back to rush forces around to deal with a real emergency.'

With an askew expression on his face, Dixon looked at Saventinni. 'Real emergency? Do they expect things to get worse or are they simply waiting for the situation to stabilize in the east before they rush in reinforcements?'

While Saventinni shrugged and shook his head, Thomas chimed in. 'A coup. You said so yourself, General, in your report to the Chief of Staff of the Army. Up until today the Colombian government has considered their own Army the greatest threat to its existence. We can't expect them, the Colombian administration, to be able to change gears overnight and recognize the fact that we are fighting a new war. After all,' Thomas added by way of example as he pointed to the blue symbols representing the 11th Air Assault Division's positions in the western mountains, 'even an elite professional organization such as the 11th hasn't adjusted to the new realities of the war in the east.'

Though he didn't respond to Hagstrom's reply right away, Dixon shook his head. Then after looking at the entire map one more time, Dixon stood up. Everyone who had been seated jumped to their feet. 'Good job, people. Though I will need to go over the rest of this briefing with you sometime before noon, I really need to get on the horn with General Stratton and give him a quick and dirty rundown on what we know. While I'm doing that, Jeff, how about seeing how fast this motley crew can turn their work here into a coherent report we can zap up to SOUTHCOM.'

Reaching over and rifling through a stack of blue folders, Worsham pulled one out and handed it to Dixon. 'Ready for your review and comments, sir.'

Taking the folder, Dixon opened it, glanced through the report, drafted and ready for faxing, minus the blank section where Dixon would add his own comments. Closing the folder, Dixon cocked his head and gave Worsham a slight smile. Doing his best Humphrey Bogart, Dixon patted Worsham on the shoulder. 'Frenchy, this could be the beginning of a beautiful friendship.' Without further comment, Dixon tucked the folder under his arm and began to leave the room, Worsham calling the staff to attention as he did so. Returning their salute, Dixon had reached the door when he stopped, turned, and faced the staff, who had already began to congratulate themselves.

Caught off guard by this sudden about-face, everyone in the room froze in place and looked at Dixon, half expecting to be chewed out for some infraction that they might have just committed inadvertently. But they relaxed when as Dixon spoke they realized that he had suddenly remembered something. Pointing first to Hagstrom, then to Saventinni, Dixon gave them some additional guidance. 'You two work together. Herman, if what you say is true, that the FARC achieved near total success yesterday, I expect them to conduct follow-up operations today or open up a new series of operations somewhere else. So far those people have been doing everything right. No reason to assume that they'll start dicking things up now. Saventinni, I want you to keep close tabs on the relief force motoring to Villavicencio. Troops in open trucks are just too inviting a target.'

'An ambush, sir?' Hagstrom asked.

'Why not? The VC did it all the time. Threaten an important target with what seems to be a major attack, cause the South Vietnamese Army to react, and blow away the relief force as it comes trundling up the road, fat, dumb, and happy. If you follow your own logic, whoever is pushing those people's buttons for the FARC did some reading on – ' Suddenly it struck him. He himself had started it by using the Vietnam analogy in his report to the Chief of Staff of the Army. The ambush of the 3rd of the 511th, he had stated in his report, was nothing more than the January 1963 battle at Ap Bac revised. Hagstrom's reference to Tet and the division of enemy forces into local forces and main-force units had in turn grown out of Dixon's own observations. The North Vietnamese initial strategy for securing the Central Highlands of Vietnam in 1965 had followed the same script that he had just described. The government's holding back of key elements of the military as anti-coup insurance mirrored the Republic of Vietnam's paranoia. And given the FARC's extensive use of a deception plan to draw attention far away from the main area of battle, just as the NVA had done at Khe Sahn just before Tet '68, the parallels were simply too close, Dixon reasoned as he stood there, not to be a coincidence. It all made sense. Wide-eyed at this sudden revelation, Dixon forgot about Hagstrom and Saventinni and turned his attention to Colonel Thomas. 'Chester, you familiar with the story of Mobile Group 100?'

'Yes, sir. The ambush of a French battalion-sized task force in June 1954 somewhere in the mountains near Pleiku, I believe.' Then Thomas, cued to the danger by Dixon, began to stare back at him. 'I'll be god-damned!'

'Right!' Bounding over to the map through a parting sea of staff officers, Dixon jabbed his finger on the map right on the road that lay between Bogotá and Villavicencio. Thomas, who had followed Dixon to the map, looked at where Dixon's finger was and nodded in agreement. Satisfied, Dixon turned to his staff. 'Gentlemen, the next major fight is going to be there, somewhere along that road.' Dixon glanced back at Thomas. 'Cat, I recommend that you scoot on over to the Colombian Ministry of Defense and explain all of this to them. Maybe they can do something in time to save that battalion.'

'Excuse me, sirs.' Both Dixon and Thomas turned to where Worsham stood. 'Aren't we going a little overboard by making that kind of assumption? I mean, the FARC aren't the most mobile people in the world. They can't be everywhere at the same time. And their ability to pick up and move about, especially the type of units that Herman is referring to as main-force units, is rather limited. How could they know that a government battalion would be dispatched from Bogotá to Villavicencio?'

'Because, Major Saventinni,' Thomas responded, 'during the coup attempt last spring, when the garrison in Villavicencio appeared to be wavering between staying loyal to the government and going over to the rebels, as soon as the capital was secured, a battalion of the Presidential Guard Brigade was dispatched by road to stiffen the resolve of the local commanders. That this happened was no secret. If the FARC military people are half as good as the general gives them credit for, they would have made note of this reaction and taken it into account when they were planning this offensive. Even if you toss that theory aside, the fact that Villavicencio is the gateway into the Eastern Zone and the foodstuffs that come from that area are critical to the survival of Bogotá, one of the standing contingencies is to do exactly what the Colombians are doing now – rush reinforcements to Villavicencio when danger threatens it. There is more than enough evidence available to us that proves that the FARC intelligence network has made its way into the Ministry of Defense. Any plans dealing with operations of the magnitude that we are seeing in the Eastern Zone would never be adopted by any commander worth his salt until he had war-gamed every angle, particularly the reaction of the other people.'

'Like I said, Jeff,' Dixon added, 'whoever is driving the train for the other people is good. This is not the time to assume that there's a flaw in his thinking or that he's going to start screwing up.' Finished, Dixon pointed his finger at Thomas. 'Cat, get going.'

Without needing to hear any more, Thomas headed for the door. 'On the way, sir.'

Looking over at Worsham, Dixon pointed. 'Jeff, first find out when that helicopter we're supposed to have available to us will be ready. Next, have someone get on the line and get a handle on the Colombian Army officer who's been assigned to us as liaison. If you can't find him before the helicopter's ready, have one of our people who's fluent in Spanish standing by.'

'You planning, sir, to head up the road and try to stop the battalion that's out there?'

'I don't know,' Dixon responded. 'But I would like to make sure that at least the man in charge of that unit knows what he might be headed into if the Cat can't get his own people to understand and explain it to him.'

Though Worsham knew that what Dixon was proposing was well outside of the charter of this tiny headquarters, he could see nothing wrong with what they were about to do. While well-defined and prescribed tasks and responsibilities were nice, war, as he and every officer above the rank of captain knew, often demanded the adoption of expedient measures and solutions that often fell well outside previous plans and orders. 'It was the side,' a battalion commander that Worsham had once served under had said, 'that recognized this need for flexibility and did it best that often won.'

Time, circumstances, and luck were not riding with the 1st Battalion of the Presidential Guard Brigade. With three companies of infantry, reinforced with a battery of six 105 mm howitzers and a platoon of armored cars, the 1st Battalion had left the capital just before dawn. The trip from Bogotá to Villavicencio, a straight-line distance of seventy five kilometers or forty-five miles, should have taken no more than four hours, tops. But delays along the route of march caused by local traffic, narrow village streets, and an occasional breakdown made the trip take much, much longer. Although some of the delays were intentional, they were so well conceived and merged so nicely with naturally occurring problems that the obstructions thrown in the 1st Battalion's path by the FARC were never seen for what they were.

These delays did more than simply slow the speed of the column. When the battalion rolled out of Bogotá, it had done so in the manner prescribed by the Colombian Army's regulations governing road marches. The armored car platoon led out, followed by the lead infantry company five hundred meters behind. After them the artillery battery, also at a distance of five hundred meters. Another infantry company, the battalion logistics trains, and the final infantry company all followed in that order at intervals of five hundred meters between company march units. In addition to the distance between companies, there was a distance of fifty meters between each vehicle within the company march units of the battalion. Though this made the length of the entire battalion march column quite long, a little over seven kilometers or four and a half miles in length, these intervals, if maintained, would make it extremely difficult to ambush more than a small portion of the convoy. But those distances, because of the delays, anxious commanders who always pushed on every chance they got, and drivers who were awakened at midnight and on the road for hours, were not maintained. Every time the front of the column slowed or stopped, the following vehicles closed up, reducing or eliminating the intervals. By midmorning, the column had been reduced into a single march unit with less than twenty meters, and in some places ten, between vehicles. Though still large, a little over two kilometers, a reinforced battalion under ideal conditions could ambush most, if not all, of this compressed column. That, of course, was exactly what Valendez had counted on.

Ten kilometers west of Villavicencio the road from Bogotá leaves the valley floor that it had followed most of the way. It goes up over a small mountain, going through a series of twists, turns, and loops before descending on the other side into Villavicencio. Though this was when everyone should have been at their highest state of alert, just the opposite was true. The disturbed night's sleep, the pandemonium of preparing to move out and lining up in the dark, their departure before dawn, and the boring and tortuously slow march had eroded the vigilance of the most dedicated officers and soldiers of the battalion. With the end of the journey literally on the other side of the mountain, the only thought that ran through the minds of the officers and the drivers of the 1st Battalion was to get on with it and get the march over with as soon as possible. With the reduction in speed made necessary due to the steep incline, practically every factor that makes for an ideal ambush was present by the time the column was half-way up the mountain.

As the armored cars at the head of the column finished going around one particularly large loop on the western side of the mountain, a series of explosions to the left, above the roadway, ripped away a large outcropping of rocks. By the time the debris from this rock slide reached the road, it had gained enough momentum and additional material to sweep away into the gully below the first two armored cars, one of which belonged to the platoon leader. Caught totally off guard, the surviving armored car crews, exhausted by the long and difficult march begun before dawn and lulled into a state of inattention, failed to react at all. This, of course, made it easy for the FARC anti-tank gunners on the hillside above to dispatch the only armored fighting vehicles in the column. Having made short work of the escort element, those gunners were free to turn their attention to other vehicles of the column, now brought to a dead halt by the destroyed armored cars and the rock slide further up the road.

The rest of the FARC regular battalion, reinforced by two local-force companies, didn't wait for the anti-tank gunners to finish their initial task. Though each company, fighting from well-prepared emplacements above the roadway, opened fire at slightly different times, based upon when the echo of the initiating blast reached them, the time gaps made no difference for the 1st Battalion. Automatic weapons, light and medium mortars, and machine guns of every caliber ripped through the column, toppling row after row of soldiers sitting in the open rear of the trucks like tenpins. Especially hard hit in the opening minutes were any jeeps or vehicles that had antennas, a sure sign that an officer was riding in them. Though not all officers fell in the opening volley, far too many did to make a rapid recovery possible.

Besides the effects of the bullets, anti-tank rockets, and mortar shells, trucks crashing into each other or rolling over off the road into the gully to the right added to the 1st Battalion's casualties and the chaos. During this confusion the attackers experienced little or no return fire. That which was directed against them was poorly aimed and had no real effect. So the withering fire controlled by FARC platoon and company commanders continued to rain down on the stricken column, becoming more focused as squads and whole platoons began to concentrate their attention on a single vehicle or a cluster of government troops when they appeared to be rallying.

Within minutes the battle degenerated into a long string of separate little fights as the surviving officers, generally young lieutenants who had been riding in the trucks and not jeeps, and senior sergeants began to exert control over the panic-stricken soldiers. Here and there, despite brutal fire from above, small islands of resistance began to form. Though there was no way to form these isolated groups into a single coherent defense, the battle at least began to become a two-way fight. Ten minutes into the fight, a lull seemed to settle as there a was noticeable slackening of fire.

At first the government troops took this decrease in their assailants' volume of fire as a sign that the FARC forces were breaking off the attack. Those officers, sergeants, and soldiers who stuck their heads up prematurely to see what was happening often paid for their curiosity with a bullet through the head or chest. Within each knot of soldiers, one or two casualties inflicted in this manner were more than enough to convince the others that the enemy was still in place and very dangerous. Pulling back behind whatever cover they could, the government soldiers prepared to wait for the situation to develop a little more or for someone to tell them what to do.

They didn't have long to wait. Already the FARC fighters, rehearsed by their leaders in what to do, were preparing to finish the fight quickly and decisively. While sporadic fire held the government troops in place, FARC company commanders, basing their plans on reports from their platoon commanders and their own observations, prepared for the next phase of the ambush. Once the pockets of government troops were accurately plotted, mortar fire was shifted onto them. With a steady rain of mortar rounds pinning the government troops, preventing them from moving or returning fire, FARC commanders shifted their forces. Machine guns were moved from positions that no longer could bring effective fire onto the enemy below to ones that could, while assault parties assembled under cover and prepared to infiltrate down onto the road under the cover of the redirected mortar and machine-gun fire, to physically root out survivors.

Since the situation facing each FARC company commander was different, the resumption of the fight was disjointed. First here and then there the crash of mortars and the chatter of long machine-gun bursts announced the renewal of the attack. Though the officers and sergeants on the road had used the lull as best they could to organize the pitifully few men they had under their control, there were not enough men, heavy weapons, or good positions to fight from. Spread out in a thin line, hiding under or behind their own trucks, the defending government troops were easy prey.

Slowly, methodically the pockets of resistance began to disappear. While the mortars, machine guns, and FARC fighters left in place hammered the government troops, the platoons chosen for the assault infiltrated down onto the road at those places where there appeared to be no government soldiers left alive. Occasionally they would stumble upon one or two men trying to hide or huddled under or behind a truck. Sometimes the frightened soldiers would offer to surrender, sometimes they would resist. Either way, all such individuals were dispatched with a quick volley of fire as the assault teams swept by and began to work their way toward the flanks of the pockets of organized resistance.

When set, the leader of the assault team would make a decision. If he thought he could eliminate the enemy in a single rush, he would radio his commander and have the mortars lift their fire. As soon as the last round impacted, the assault team would be up and charging forward. Hit by fire from above and a sudden attack from the flank, the small pockets quickly crumbled. Again, as before, the government troops had but two choices, try to surrender or keep fighting. Sometimes both reactions would occur at the same instant as one soldier jumped up and raised his hands while his companion next to him continued to fire away at the oncoming foe. As before, the FARC fighters responded the same way to both, killing everyone before them. If, on the other hand, the pocket he was closing on appeared to be too big or too well organized, the leader of the assault team would deploy his men and pour fire into the flanks of the enemy, slowly working his men forward, with the weight of fire from the flanks chewing away at the defenders, one by one, as the fire from above kept the other government troops pinned and unable to react. Only when he was sure that the enemy was about to break or his losses would be small would the leader allow the final assault to go forward. In this manner the pockets went under, one by one, until finally silence returned all along the road.

It took no more than an hour to finish the elimination of all organized resistance. No sooner had the last echoes of fighting ended, to be replaced by the moans and pleas for help from the wounded that littered the two kilometer stretch of road where the 1st Battalion had died, than the third and most brutal phase of the operation began. Teams of FARC fighters flocked down to the road and went to work. Some picked their way through the wreckage of the 1st Battalion searching for weapons and equipment that would be of use to them later. Others went from vehicle to vehicle checking them out, identifying those that could be used to haul away the weapons and equipment being collected and stacked neatly along the side of the road. Medical teams and stretcher parties tended to their own wounded, bringing them to a hasty aid station where they could be given elementary first aid and then in selected vehicles loaded up and driven off along seldom used trails to hospitals awaiting their arrival.

Amid all this activity, four-man teams methodically combed the road in front of each company, checking each government soldier that they came across. Pausing only for a moment, the members of these teams would place the muzzle of their rifles against the head of each government soldier and squeeze off two quick rounds, regardless of whether he was already dead or still clinging to life. By this means Valendez hoped to send a message, a brutally cold message, one which he expected would not only be understood by the relief force that would come but by all those who heard of it. It was, Valendez explained to his field commanders, their way of announcing to the government that this was now a full-scale war, a war which the FARC intended to fight to the finish.

While the field commanders understood this explanation and accepted it with few reservations, few imagined the true reason behind it. Only Valendez, ever mindful of the complexities of war, knew that the introduction of such a level of brutality would bring into play a new level of terror and fear. He expected the government soldiers to repay in kind this terror by overreacting and dropping all pretenses of humanity during this next deadly phase of the war. 'Within a week,' he told a confidant that night, 'Americans will be treated to the images of government artillery pounding every village in their path and heaps of dead civilians stacked high by the indiscriminate use of attack aircraft, artillery, and sophisticated helicopter gunships. In this way we will turn the benevolent government in Bogotá fighting to preserve the freedom of their people into murderers bent on destroying the very people they are supposed to be protecting in order to save their own skins. Slowly we will isolate this government from its own Army, from its own people, from its own allies. In the end, without American support, this corrupt government will die by its own hand.'

PART THREE

BY IRON
AND BLOOD

CHAPTER 10

November 10

Jan chattered with a cheerfulness that reminded Willie Freeman, the senior WNN soundman in Bogotá, of a girl on a school trip. 'You know what I really enjoy about doing work in the field?' she blurted out as they drove from pothole to pothole on the poorly maintained national road on the fringe of the region called Los Llanos. 'Trotting from one troubled spot on the face of the earth to another can be exciting. I don't think I'll ever tire of the adventure of going someplace I've never been before or seeing the world as it really is.' Knowing that all she would get from Willie was a grunt or a perfunctory uh-huh, she turned to JT Evens, her cameraman. 'Don't you just love being able to experience the cultural, ethnic, and social diversity of a new land and its people?' Then without waiting for his answer, for her question roused JT from a fitful sleep, she continued. 'It's like a fringe benefit. Not even the stress and strain of constantly being on the move, having to rush off from one place to another, often on short notice, to cover a breaking story bothers me.'

JT responded with a cynical look. This didn't seem to bother Jan as she continued. 'In fact, I think I rather enjoy the challenge. You know, every situation different, having to be handled in its own unique way. And even when there are similarities between stories, especially ones that involve armed conflict, the background of the war, the history of the people, the principal players involved, and the settings are always different. No, no pat formula or single set of rules applies out here, huh?'

Finally stopping her nervous chatter long enough for JT to respond, the only answer he gave as he shoved his baseball hat further back on his head was a rather halfhearted 'Yeah, right, Jan. You sure are right there.'

JT's apathetic response took some of the wind out of Jan's enthusiastic commentary. Looking over to Willie, she saw that he was busy trying to pretend that he was too absorbed with driving to respond. Without a receptive audience, Jan turned and looked out the window of the van, continuing her thoughts in private. Her professional dedication was coupled with a true love of her job. Together with the recognition that her unique ability to bring the many diverse aspects of a story into play, giving her pieces meaning and impact, Jan was a gem in the eyes of her network and those who heard her stories. Though she had tried different jobs within the World News Network, from being an anchor on one of its prime-time programs to doing shows of her own, she always came back to the work she did best and the assignments that she so loved. As one of the owners of World News Network half jokingly told an associate, 'When the going gets tough, we send in Jan.'

As it was for those who actively pursued a career in the real world, not every aspect of her job was enjoyable. There was in most stories some element of tragedy, suffering, and, as in the case of all wars, death. Though these by-products of the events that made up the news seldom touched her or the crews she worked with, Jan in all of her years as a dedicated, hard-nosed correspondent had never been able to come up with an effective means to shield herself psychologically from the pain and trauma of her stories. It was this element of her makeup and her profession that allowed her to see beyond the coldness and remoteness that her husband often dropped like a shield between them. Often she wondered how Scotty found the strength to go on when she, a mere spectator of this horror, was often troubled by it in her dreams. Though they never spoke of it, this shared experience served as a bond that made their love for each other and their relationship so much more valuable to each of them.

Even before the Land-Rover carrying her and her camera crew reached the village of El Frío, which reportedly had just been wrested away from the FARC, the signs that this would be another one of those occasions when any joy of being a correspondent would be submerged by the sheer pathos of the situation began to manifest themselves. First there was the lingering pillar of black smoke in the distance. Like a marker it stood in stark contrast to the pale blue sky, serving for all to see that another objective in the government's slow, bloody counteroffensive had been achieved. The smoke also allowed Jan an opportunity to steel herself for what she was about to see. Like a ship's crew preparing for a storm at sea, Jan Fields-Dixon started to stuff her emotions away into the deepest recesses of her consciousness where her willpower, like bands of steel, would keep her true feelings in check.

The sight of the smoke and Jan's withdrawal served to end the casual conversation that Jan had been sharing with JT Evens from Athens, Georgia, and Big Willie Freeman from East St. Louis, Illinois. It was said in Jan's office in Bogotá that a more diverse crew couldn't have been picked if someone had wanted to. JT Evens was every bit the southern cracker, in speech, dress, and manner.

He took great pride in being called the last of the good ol' boys. Big Willie was so named because there were two Williams in Jan's office; and Freeman, who towered over the other by better than a head and a half, was a city kid. He was a fighter, a man who had fought, literally, his way out of the ghetto. Even in high school, where his peers regularly beat him up because he chose to study and his high grades set him apart from the other black youths in his class, Willie Freeman had to face adversity on a daily basis. Whereas Evens was laid back and easygoing, everything about Freeman, from the manner in which he carried and expressed himself, to the way he went about his job as a soundman told all who saw him that he was not to be trifled with. And then there was Jan, a self-actualized woman who made her way through life with charm and grace when she could, bluster and blunder when it was necessary, and sheer determination and courage when it was demanded of her. Though not always popular, Jan Fields-Dixon was admired by all who saw her for what she was, a free and independent person, beholden to no human yet a part of the whole, as much a piece of the society that had bred her as any other man or woman, great or small.

Slowly the familiar signs of battle began to unfold as the WNN crew drove on in silence. First they came across a battery of howitzers. Jan watched the Colombian soldiers going about their chores. Near each of the six guns set up on the side of the road in the open was a stack of empty shell casings. This meant that the government forces had found it necessary to use their heavy artillery to overcome the FARC's resistance. Since artillery was rather indiscriminate and men under fire have a tendency to use it too lavishly, Jan thought, odds were that civilian losses were high.

No sooner had she finished that thought than they saw the first of the refugees, led by several soldiers, headed west and away from the place that they had once called home. Their gaunt, vacant expressions told Jan that they had felt the sting of the big guns just as much as the FARC fighters had. Within minutes, this was amply confirmed when another knot of refugees, walking a little slower than the others, came into sight as the van got closer to the village. In this group were the freshly wounded, the crippled, the very old, and the very young. Watching from his window, JT mentioned that none of the soldiers leading them away seemed to be interested in helping the stricken villagers. Willie, driving the van, responded in the same cold, dry manner he always used when he was trying to control his anger. 'What do you expect, cracker? You think they give a damn? You think they care what happens to those people? They're the ones who screwed up those people in the first place. The only thing those soldiers care about is the fact that it's the villagers and not them bleeding all over the road.'

Though Jan wanted to say something, if for no other reason than to keep the two men from opening a fight with each other, she couldn't think of anything. Willie was right. Besides, the sight of a small child, not more than two, crying as she bent over a lifeless form on the side of the road, was enough to silence everyone in the van. It was, Jan knew, an ageless image. She had seen old photos of such scenes from World War II, Korea, Vietnam, and countless other wars. She herself had been witness to such images of tragedy, made more painful by the fact that when she saw them in person they were not images. Rather they were real people, flesh and blood like her, that she could reach out and touch. In the beginning Jan had done that. She had tried to help the people she saw stricken through no fault of their own by a war they did not want and did not understand.

But when you touch someone, they often touch back. In trying to relieve pain, you often absorb more than you can handle yourself. When Jan realized that she was losing her ability to deal effectively with such incidents, she withdrew within herself, not out of callousness but out of the need for self-preservation. When you had no effective means of helping, Jan learned, it is far more cruel to pretend, both to the people you are trying to help and yourself. Hence the need to steel herself beforehand so that she could look upon such things with dry eyes and walk away when she had done what she had come there for. Yet even her best efforts would never be enough to erase the sight of the child and the fallen adult now receding in the rearview mirror of the van. Like so many others, Jan would carry that one with her forever.

From behind her, JT let out a mumbled curse. 'Bastards. Look at that. All these trucks sitting around and they couldn't even shake a few loose to help their own kind. Bastards. Soldiers killing soldiers, that's one thing. This . . . this is too much.'

Shaken from her thoughts, Jan looked around just as Willie started to slow the van. On either side of the road a number of military trucks sat in open fields attended by their waiting drivers and a few stray soldiers. Jan, who had grown used to seeing precision in all things military because of her life with Dixon, always sat up and took note when she saw a sloppy military unit. In this case the trucks that JT had alerted her to were not in any type of order or line. Rather they were scattered about, some parked together in clusters, others sitting quite alone and unattended. Even the drivers, wearing every variation of their uniform imaginable, added to the chaotic scene. Again it was JT who spoke. 'Boy, I hope the grunts in this unit look better than these old boys.'

Jan, still looking about, finally responded. 'Don't hold your breath back there, JT. You've been pounding this beat long enough to know better than that.'

'Yeah, I do. Thing is, Miss Jan, if the Farcees can be

pushed around by a sorry lot like this, then what's the big deal about the Farcees. Seems to me either they're not what they're cracked up to be or someone back in Bogotá is pulling the wool over our eyes, trying to make the Farcees look meaner than they are.'

Turning around, Jan smiled at JT. 'That, friends and neighbors, is why we brought you and your trusty camera along. It's time to play truth or consequences with these good ol' boys now, ain't it?'

JT smiled. He knew Jan was making fun of him and his manner of speaking. But he didn't mind. They all needed a little humor, even if it was at each other's expense, to keep themselves from going crazy in this sick and twisted world. After all, at that moment they were at the less than tender mercy of an Army that had just brutally pounded one of its own villages, people and all, and all they had was each other. So JT smiled and nodded. 'That's right, Miss Jan. Now all we need to do is convince that city boy sitting next to you to take his foot off the brake and drive this thing.'

Unmoved by the levity that Jan and JT were sharing, Willie responded in his deep dry voice. 'I'm afraid those soldiers with the machine guns behind the roadblock up ahead have a different idea.'

Turning to look ahead, Jan saw the checkpoint that Willie was stopping for. Though the weapons they held were menacing in themselves, the manner in which the soldiers held them and their rather lackadaisical stances made the whole scene before them nonthreatening. Popping his head up from behind so that it was even with Willie's and Jan's, JT grunted. 'Um, sleep safely tonight, Bogotá, your Army is on guard.'

Ignoring JT's comment, Jan continued to watch the soldiers at the road-block. 'Okay, Willie, show time.'

Bringing the van to a slow and easy stop off to one side of the road, Jan and Willie opened their doors and began to approach the roadblock, careful to make sure that they didn't do anything that might be interpreted as hostile. When they were several feet away, the two Americans stopped. Without any need to be prompted, Willie called out in Spanish, slowly reaching into the pocket of his equipment vest in search of the government papers authorizing them to be in the forward zone. 'We are a news team, with permission from your government, here to report on your great victory today.'

When the two soldiers heard this, they looked at each other and began to laugh. This caught Jan off guard, since Willie was not known for his humor. Glancing over at him, Jan asked what he had said. When he'd repeated word for word his greeting, Jan cocked her head, then looked back at the soldiers. Since Willie's Spanish was impeccable, there was something wrong here that she didn't quite understand. In Jan's mind the attitude of the soldiers, both here and back down the road, was not that of men who had just finished a hard and costly fight. That thought triggered another as she turned first to one side, then to the other. Not seeing what she was searching for, Jan looked over to Willie. 'Have you seen any wounded soldiers or ambulances headed back up the road?'

Understanding what she was getting at, Willie shook his head. 'None, Jan. The only blood I saw was on those civilians we passed.'

Further speculation was cut short when an officer came around the end of the roadblock nearest Jan and walked up to her. With a broad smile, he introduced himself. With two quick steps to the side, Willie was next to Jan and translating. 'He says he's Captain Emmanual Elmoro, commander of the company that took the village of El Frío early this morning.'

Smiling, Jan offered her hand to the Army captain while she introduced herself and Willie translated. With chivalry more appropriate to the ballroom than a recently contested field of battle, the captain made a slight bow and raised Jan's hand up to his lips. While he was engaged in this little ritual, she studied him. He was clean-shaven, his uniform was neat and almost spotless, and even his hands were free of dirt and mud. 'How long ago, Captain, did you finally secure the village?'

Looking up, though still holding her hand, Elmoro smiled. 'Not more than an hour ago, señorita.'

Lowering her eyes, Jan glanced over to Willie, who nodded. Looking back at the captain, she flashed a shy smile to hide her surprise. Firmly, yet without showing any undue haste, Jan pulled her hand away from the captain's. 'Willie, tell the dear captain who we are and see if you can negotiate our way into the village.'

The idea of having an international news team cover the exploits of his company seemed to excite the young captain. His smile broadened as he quickly responded, reaching out to grasp Jan's arm with one hand and sweeping the other in a wide motion of welcome. Willie had no trouble keeping up with the captain as he announced his intentions. 'Oh, señorita, it would be my pleasure. Come, let me personally escort you and your crew.'

While Jan was being led away past the soldiers at the roadblock, Willie rushed back to the van where JT was already hefting his camera over one shoulder and his battery pack over the other. 'Guess Jan charmed her way past the roadblock, huh?'

Willie, busy pulling his own equipment out, didn't look over when he responded. 'The boss lady smells a rat. According to the captain we were greeted by, his boys just blew into town an hour ago and he looks like he just stepped out of the show, not a firefight.'

Pausing for a moment, JT let his face fall into a reflective stare. 'So you two don't think there's been much of a fight here, huh?'

'JT, I'm not sure what the boss lady's thinking. All I

know is that she wants both of us to be 'on our toes. Watch for her cues and shoot anything that you think she might want.'

Jan, never sure how a story would go, and always looking for the less than obvious, often asked questions that seemed innocent enough at the moment. It was often her commentary, shot afterwards, combined with video and the sound bites caught by an attentive crew that gave what should have been a mundane story power and impact. Seldom did her crew understand exactly what she was looking for or what she was after, since Jan herself was always looking, searching, thinking as they went. That was why anyone working with her had to be able to shoot what she told them to, shoot what she really wanted, and shoot what they themselves saw and felt was important. Though there were occasions when Jan, the cameraman, and the soundman were not in sync, more often than not their efforts were rewarded. Today would be a case in point.

Within minutes Jan's party, led by the fast-talking captain, was in the village. The damage was considerable. What few motor vehicles had been in the village before the attack began littered the streets, shattered and burning. The oily black smoke from burning tires and rubber mixed in with the acrid smoke of homes and shops that were reduced to rubble. Though not every structure was totally demolished, none that she saw escaped damage. Busy explaining how the other two companies of the battalion he belonged to surrounded the village during the night while his command prepared to make the final assault, it was several minutes before the captain noticed Jan's preoccupation with the amount of damage. Waving his finger about in a random fashion at the devastation, the captain explained. 'We started the shelling shortly after midnight in the hope of catching the rebels while they were sleeping.'

JT, filming as he went, held the camera steady while

he leaned over and whispered in the ear Willie had not covered with the headphones, 'Yeah, not to mention the local populace.'

Willie ignored JT's remarks. Following several paces behind, he repeated in English the captain's remarks so that Jan and his mike would pick his words up. Though she was thinking the same thing JT was, Jan simply nodded as she continued to walk alongside the Colombian captain. 'So,' Jan responded, 'most of this was done by your artillery before the attack began?'

When he heard Willie's translation of the question, the captain nodded his head and smiled. 'Yes, our artillery and your helicopters. They both did a marvelous job of preparing the target for our attack.'

When Willie had finished repeating the captain's last comments, Jan shot a look back at him. His face, impassive, was fixed on her, waiting for her response. 'Did he say *our* helicopters, Willie?'

He nodded. 'Yes, ma'am. He said ours.'

'Ask him if he means American, I mean United States Army helicopters.'

Even before the captain finished responding to this inquiry, the gleam in his eye, his head nodding, and his immediate response of 'Sí,' made Jan feel a little sick. As Willie spoke, that feeling deepened into one of depression. 'Yes, AH-64 Apaches, a flight of four. They flew in support of our attack, using rockets and 30mm cannon to hammer likely pockets of resistance just as our assault began this morning. Very effective, they were very, *very* effective.'

Busy keeping her expression in check, Jan didn't notice that they had reached the town square. It was a rather small affair, yet well defined, as most squares and market-places were in these small villages. Though there were soldiers here and there, mostly sitting about in the shade in small groups chatting, smoking, and waiting, it was the civilians that caught Jan's eye. On any other day, the center of this village would have been filled with the people of the village and the smells of fresh produce, meats, and coffee for sale. Today, however, the only villagers in the square were either dead, lined up to one side in two long rows, or languishing in an open-air aid station in front of the local church. Too wounded to join the migration west, they were being tended by two civilians in bloodstained shirts and a priest and a pair of nuns. Stopping, Jan looked around and took in a deep breath before she proceeded. This, of course, was a mistake. For the air she drew into her lungs hung heavy with the stench of death, that weird mixture of stale blood, loose bowels, charred flesh, and human sweat. Finding herself horribly close to gagging, Jan froze, her eyes bulging and her checks turning red, then white as the color ran out of her face. 'Control,' she mumbled to herself under her breath. 'Get control of yourself, girl.'

Seeing that she was experiencing a moment of distress, both JT and Willie stopped recording. Watching her, they waited, ready to dash forward to help if necessary. Closing her eyes, for the briefest of moments, she managed to regain her balance. When she was ready, Jan opened her eyes, looked at JT and Willie, nodded to them, and picked up her questioning of the captain as if nothing had happened. 'Losses seem to have been quite high, Captain?'

Canting his head to the side and looking down for a second, he nodded. 'Well, yes, of course. These type of operations are seldom undertaken without cost. As you can see, this poor village paid a heavy price.'

Not wanting to linger there in the presence of so much pain, suffering, and death, Jan ignored the captain's efforts to dehumanize the suffering around them by talking about the village as if it were an inanimate thing and quickly cut to the point. 'What price did your company pay?'

This brought a smile to the captain's face. Puffing out his chest, he beamed as he answered. 'We, my company and the rest of the battalion, were very fortunate today. We suffered no casualties. The combined weight of the artillery and helicopter attacks smashed all resistance before we entered the village.'

Incredulously, Jan asked what exactly that resistance had been.

Raising his right hand to them as a sign he wanted them to follow, the captain led Jan and her crew to a part of the square where six corpses lay stretched out under the baking sun. Three of the bodies belonged to men who had to be well over sixty. Two were mere boys. Only one, a rather heavy-set man, looked like he was of the proper age to be bearing arms in an active guerrilla unit. At their feet, neatly laid out, were a shotgun, two ancient bolt action rifles, and a pistol of questionable value. 'These men,' the captain claimed as he pointed to the bodies, 'are FARC. They kept this village terrorized and the villagers praying for deliverance.'

Though she didn't mean for her actions to be as obvious as they were, Jan looked at the six bodies before her, then turned abruptly to where the civilian dead lay, then back at the captain. Her expression betrayed her thoughts, for any traces of smile that were left on the captain's face faded. In its place there was a sneer. When he spoke, there was bitterness in his voice. Even Willie, who up to now had managed to remain aloof from all before him, found it difficult to maintain his poise. Though Willie's translation was spoken without the anger that he heard in the captain's voice, Jan understood it. 'How dare you come into our country and pass judgment on what we do to defend ourselves against our enemies. This is our war. These people, all of them, the civilians over there and the enemy at our feet, are all Colombians. Just as my soldiers are Colombians. If those people had been loyal, they would have left long ago or died resisting the enemy. But they chose to stay, and for their decision they alone are accountable. I am accountable to my commander and responsible for the soldiers in my command. When we leave here tomorrow, I will never see this village again. Its death means nothing to me. But the soldiers who follow me out of here will be with me tomorrow, the next day, and for a long time. For Colombia, and for my own sake, I dare not risk their lives foolishly. Today I had artillery and helicopters, your helicopters, to help me protect them. So I used them, just as your own Yankee officers taught us to do. This, señorita,' the captain exclaimed, sweeping his arm about the square, 'is not a Colombian invention. This is the Yankee way of war. Even the guns and the shells which we used are American, made by your countrymen, given to us by your government, to be used in the manner in which your officers trained us. So do not cast those accusing eyes on me as if you were innocent. In this war that word has no meaning.'

Too angry to continue, the captain took a deep breath, turned, and stalked off, leaving Jan, JT, and Willie standing speechless in the middle of the square. It took Jan a minute to collect her thoughts and decide that it was time to leave. There was, she reasoned, nothing more to be gained by staying there. They had in every sense worn out their welcome. So without further ado the three Americans left as quickly as they could.

It wasn't until they had put a mile or more behind them that anyone in the van spoke. Finally JT broke the silence. 'Any idea what you're going to do with this stuff, Jan?'

Though she had heard him, Jan didn't respond immediately. This one, she knew, would be a hard story to put together. It could go any of several ways, and at that moment she was just too wound up and overwhelmed by what they had just witnessed to make a sound call. That, she decided, would best be left until after they were back in

Bogotá. Perhaps, she thought, it would come to her during the long ride back. It always did. Finally Jan answered, without turning to face JT, in a manner that betrayed her uncertainty. 'I have no idea what we're going to do with this one. None whatsoever.'

For the longest time everyone in the van left it at that. Then as if to signal that she wanted to drop the subject, Jan turned her head to JT and gave him a small smile. 'JT, would you reach into the ice chest and pull out something for me to drink?'

Her request told both JT and Willie that the subject of the piece they had just shot was closed for the moment. Without another thought, JT returned Jan's smile. 'Sure thing. Your usual?'

Jan smiled. 'Yes, that would be fine, thank you.'

Steadying himself as Willie rounded a sharp turn, JT reached over, popped the lid of their cooler, and began to fish for Jan's drink.

As the van slowed to take the turn, a FARC gunner hefted the butt plate of his 7.62mm American-made M-60 machine gun onto his shoulder. Pulling the weapon back until it was snug, he sighted down the barrel as his thumb clicked the safety off. When the front-sight picture was resting dead center on the windshield of the van, he let his right index finger slowly ease itself around the trigger of the weapon. Slowly he let his breath out, then began to draw one final breath in, which he would hold before shooting.

From behind, a voice, as firm as it was low, intervened. 'No, this van is nothing. Leave it pass.'

For one final second the gunner looked down his sight into the front window of the van. Then, as carefully as he had placed it there, he removed his finger from the trigger. Letting his breath out, the gunner eased the butt of the machine gun off his shoulder and laid it gently on the ground, all the while watching his intended target finish the turn and continue its journey west to Bogotí. Though it would have been an easy mark, the gunner knew his squad leader was right. This van meant nothing. It was the Colombian Army battalion in El Frío that his local-force company, working with two regular FARC battalions, was after. Far better, he knew, to wait until darkness when everyone was set. There would be, he knew, more than enough targets fleeing their planned attack in a few hours to satisfy even his wildest dreams of revenge for the murder of his village.

And in the morning, when that lust was satisfied, he would go up the road to find his family. As so many other soldiers in his battalion had already done in other villages, he would find those of his family who were still alive. He would join their mourning, help bury their dead, and then go back to the task of cleansing his country of the corruption that had allowed such atrocities to visit them. The war for this machine gunner had become very real and very personal today, and it would never end until he was satisfied that the dead in his family were properly avenged or he himself had joined them.

Colonel Delhue didn't notice Major José Solis standing in the open door of his office until Solis softly rapped on the door. Slowly, almost absentmindedly, Delhue rotated his chair a quarter turn away from the window he had been staring out of, until he was facing the Colombian Army liaison officer. Throughout this process he made no effort to sit up or alter his deadpan expression. Only his feet moved, making the short side steps necessary to propel the chair. When he was set, facing the new direction, Delhue raised one eyebrow slightly as he looked at Solis.

For a moment Solis looked over at the division chief of staff. Even as he sat there slouched down and almost swallowed up by his overstuffed executive's chair, Delhue's tall bearlike frame presented a commanding presence. Only his face, its puffy skin dragged down about his eyes and mouth by months of stress, concerns, and unrelenting verbal and professional abuse, detracted from the image of the powerful man that Delhue's physical stature spoke of. From the moment he had set eyes on this man, Solis knew that he was a soldier, a man who would not tolerate fools or compromise either his own personal honor or that of his nation's. How fortunate for Hector Valendez, Solis thought as he suppressed a smile, that it was General Lane and not Colonel Delhue who commanded the 11th Air Assault Division. For he knew in his heart that had Delhue been running the division, the FARC would not be comfortably poised on the brink of their most ambitious effort with little to fear. Only one man in Bogotá that morning was seen as a threat by the FARC, and Hector Valendez had ordered Solis to find out all that he could about that man.

Without any introductions or pleasantries, Delhue raised his right hand from his chair's armrest and motioned toward a seat next to his desk. 'Please, Major, have a seat.'

While the Colombian major crossed the room and settled into the offered seat, Delhue sighed. Here, he thought, was another wasted soldier. A man, a native of this country and a professional soldier whose entire military career had been spent pursuing the Farcees and other guerrillas through the same jungles and over the same mountains that our people were operating in, and no one, by intent, was using his knowledge or experience. How many good soldiers, Delhue mused, had our self-righteous arrogance cost us? Seeing that Solis was settled and ready, Delhue threw his body forward with a noticeable effort, stopping it by bringing his arms up and to rest on the desktop. 'What, Major Solis, can I do for you today?'

'I would like to thank you for taking the time, Colonel

Delhue, to talk to me like this. I mean with no previous appointment.'

Solis's comment almost made Delhue laugh. It was general knowledge that Lane's manner of doing business left little for Delhue to do throughout the day. Lane's G-3, a lieutenant colonel almost as arrogant and egotistical as Lane himself, was the real center of power on the division staff. From his first day with the division, Lane had made sure that Delhue understood this and did nothing to hinder this arrangement. Though he had at first tried to do his duties, by mid-July the pain of daily confrontations and public reprimands had taken too much of a toll on Delhue's pride. So, like others in the 11th who were not favored by Lane, Delhue did what he could to avoid the division commander and busied himself doing those things that Lane and his chosen few had no interest in yet needed to be done. Since Lane's background and passion were plans and operations, Delhue worked closely with the division's support command, helping them deal with the monumental task of keeping an air assault division running.

Shaking his head, Delhue did smile, but it was a friendly, disarming smile. 'Major, you are always welcome.'

The colonel's comment struck home, for Solis knew that Colonel Delhue, like him, was an outcast. Though he understood Army politics and personality cults that often displaced professionalism, the practice still annoyed and angered him. He, unlike so many of his brother officers, had joined the Colombian Army to serve and protect his nation, not as a steppingstone to power and wealth. It was this dedication to his personal convictions and his unflinching dedication to high moral standards that made his decision to support the FARC an easy one.

Pushing aside his personal thoughts, Solis went right to the heart of the matter. 'My superiors, Colonel Delhue, are somewhat perplexed by Brigadier General Scott Dixon and his staff. You see, we are not sure what role they now play in your chain of command. When General Lane first told the Minister of Defense of General Dixon and his mission, we were very suspicious and quite alarmed.'

Delhue fought the urge to smile, since no one was more alarmed and suspicious about the introduction of Scotty Dixon and SOUTHCOM Forward than Lane himself. It had been a grim day when Lane's aide handed him the message signed by General Stratton announcing that Dixon was coming south for the express purpose of establishing a headquarters to monitor and report on American and government military operations in Colombia. Violent was too mild a word to describe Lane's reaction. Delhue, however, had no trouble finding words to define the manner in which Lane attempted to deal with this threat to his private domain. To Delhue, the orders that Lane issued to his staff, both specific and implied, crossed over the line between questionable conduct and downright unethical and unprofessional behavior. That Lane was capable of such behavior was a given. As one battalion commander stated to Delhue in private, 'Within five minutes after meeting the man, you get the urge to take one hand and cover your wallet while using the other to protect your balls.'

Personal behavior is one thing. Unethical behavior in an individual is excusable. What was not, in Delhue's mind, was Lane's demand that his subordinates conform to his moral standards or lack of them. To force another officer, especially a subordinate officer, to choose between compromising his own ethics or ruining his career was to Delhue worse than murder. Dignity and pride were in Delhue's mind the only things that a man can take to his grave. A man without dignity and pride, on the other hand, had nothing. In his view of the world, such a person was the lowest form of life imaginable, one step below an animal, since animals, unlike humans, have no choice.

When the distant look descended over Delhue's eyes like a transparent screen and the colonel withdrew into silence, Solis realized that he had hit a nerve. Unsure how to react, Solis settled back to wait for the answer that the chief of staff was obviously framing in his troubled mind. In the silence that followed, Solis began to appreciate how Hector Valendez could so easily discount the American division. Though their soldiers were, man for man, superior in training and firepower to any that Valendez could muster, the inability of their leaders to overcome their pettiness doomed their efforts. It was, Solis thought, as if the gods of war, after creating the magnificent fighting machine that the 11th Air Assault was, decided it was too perfect and therefore dangerous. So to even the playing field of war they gave the 11th leaders hamstrung with character flaws that would prevent them from leading in a manner that befit the courage and skills of their soldiers. Both Valendez and Solis realized that so long as these flawed leaders were left to their own devices, the 11th Air Assault would never become a serious threat to the FARC and their operations. And until Brigadier General Scott Dixon and his small staff came into being, this prophecy was unfolding as Valendez had foreseen.

But there was something disturbing happening that no one, including Valendez himself, understood or could explain. Despite the fact that the tempo of American operations was slowing down, those that were being conducted were bringing more pressure on the FARC. The old ratio of one operation against the FARC versus three against the drug cartel had been reversed within a matter of weeks. It was, Solis knew, a result of Dixon and his staff. How they were achieving this was not exactly clear, either to Solis or Valendez. It was, therefore, his task to find out how this new informal system worked so that the FARC could either short circuit it or if necessary destroy it.

Only after he noticed that Major Solis was still in his office and staring at him intently did Delhue realize that he had let his thoughts wander too far afield. Shaking his head as if that would clear it, he looked over to the major and smiled. 'You'll have to excuse me, Major. I seem to have deserted you there for a moment.'

Solis flashed a quick smile. 'Please, sir. There is no need for you to apologize. It is I who should apologize for bothering you with such a minor question that should be so obvious.'

This comment caused the smile to disappear from Delhue's face. He grunted. 'Nothing, I'm afraid, is obvious or simple in this division, especially the relationship between SOUTHCOM Forward and us.' While he had meant to say General Lane instead of us, Delhue's own code of ethics prevented him from being so openly disloyal to his superior, regardless of how poorly that man repaid such dedication. 'When they arrived, their sole purpose was what we told your Minister of Defense. They were to have been nothing more than a link between this head-quarters and the commander-in-chief of SOUTHCOM, General Stratton. In a nutshell, Dixon and his people were to be nothing more than a glorified message center. The FARC's offensive in Los Llanos, however, changed that. During the first few days, the superlative manner in which Dixon's small staff tracked and predicted its progress, scope, and intent made people at SOUTHCOM and the Department of the Army sit up and take notice. It didn't take long for General Stratton at SOUTHCOM to begin disregarding our intelligence summaries and basing his decisions and directives to us on General Dixon's reports and recommendations. An aside that is not too obvious was the realization that our staff was out of touch with the reality of the situation down here, which in Stratton's mind meant that he needed to give us orders that were, to say the least, very specific and could not be ignored.'

Shifting in his seat, as if he found Delhue's explanation uncomfortable, Solis thought for a moment, then responded to Delhue's revelation. 'Do you mean to say, Colonel, that your General Stratton would take the word of a junior officer with so little time in Colombia over that of a more senior commander who had been here for months?'

'If you and your Minister of Defense knew Scotty Dixon, you would understand.'

'But, Colonel, we do not. That, I imagine, is why we cannot understand what is happening in the American command system. Perhaps if you could tell me a little about General Dixon, that would help.'

'Brigadier General Scott Dixon is one of the unique individuals that come along once in a lifetime. For him and those associated with him, the normal rules do not apply. Though to the best of my knowledge he is not an ambitious man who set out to do so, it would be a great surprise to just about anyone in the Army if he didn't eventually become the Chief of Staff of the Army.'

If, Solis wondered while Delhue spoke, Dixon was not an ambitious man, how could he attain the high rank he had already achieved? Solis spoke what he was thinking. 'I do not understand, Colonel, how this can be. Officers in my Army, regrettably, simply do not make it to the rank of general just by being good soldiers. What, sir, is this officer's secret?'

'No secret, Major. Luck, pure and simple. Luck has put him into some incredible situations where he was able to demonstrate his natural talents as a soldier and unique leadership skills. I can think of a dozen other officers with as much time as Dixon has in the Army who are smarter, have more formal schooling, are better leaders, and present a sharper image than General Dixon but haven't to date achieved one tenth of what he has. If there is a key to Dixon's success, it's his ability to keep his head in unusual circumstances, use all the people he has to the best of their abilities without abusing them or wasting them, and to persevere.'

'You seem to admire him.'

Delhue grunted. 'Any soldier worth his salt has to admire Scotty Dixon and his achievements.'

'Why then,' Solis fired back without thinking, 'does General Lane hate him so and scheme to discredit him?'

The bluntness of the question rocked Delhue back in his seat. That there was an open rift between Lane and Dixon was no secret. Anyone with eyes and ears could see it and its manifestations. But to openly speak of it, that was an entirely different matter. For several seconds Delhue looked at Solis and considered ignoring his question. Then in an instant he dropped all pretenses. Taking a deep breath, Delhue let go. 'Because, Major, Lane resents Dixon. Dixon is everything that he isn't. Dixon has every chance to become what he wants. And the most disturbing thing in General Lane's mind is that while he has worked, probably from the time he was a second lieutenant to now, to reach the top, fortune and chance have catapulted Dixon into the limelight and high regard that Lane so craves. To General Lane, Dixon does not deserve what he has achieved.' Delhue paused, thought about what he was about to say, then decided to go ahead. 'General Lane has made it his mission in life to punish General Dixon.'

'Punish him for what?'

'For being the man that *he* isn't.'

Though he had known that these American officers had clay feet, like many of the senior officers in his own Army, Delhue's blunt and unabashed condemnation of General Lane in the harshest terms struck Solis with a force that he wasn't prepared for. After a minute Solis looked up at Delhue and mumbled half to himself, 'Then all of this, it is a personal matter after all, isn't it?'

Nodding, Delhue dropped his head down and looked at the blotter on his desk. 'I'm afraid so, Major. As much as I hate to admit it, we are making major decisions based on personal feelings and not military necessity.'

'But the shifting of your 3rd Brigade from the west to support our operations in the Eastern Zone, that was a sound and logical decision.'

Looking up, Delhue shook his head. 'The only reason that brigade went east was because General Dixon pointed out to General Stratton that the counteroffensive by your Army would very soon run out of steam without our support. It is his opinion that unless we keep the pressure on the FARC in the Eastern Zone, the Farcees will keep on rolling west, straight into Bogotá. The order to move the reinforced brigade east originated with General Stratton, not Lane.'

The realization that Valendez was right, as he had always proven to be, startled Solis, though it shouldn't have. Hector Valendez was always right, just like this General Dixon who so worried him. In an instant everything that had been confused was clear. The contest now was no longer one between government and rebels. It wasn't even a struggle between the opposing forces. It was all a series of bouts between individuals. It was Hector Valendez against General Scott Dixon. Everyone, Solis realized, was merely a pawn in this fight. The question now, one that Valendez would need to ponder, was how he would play the pawn that General Lane had become.

Thanking Delhue for his time and insight, Solis got up and left the office, turning this last thought over and over in his mind. Finally confident that Hector Valendez would find a way, Solis smiled. Victory, he suddenly saw, was theirs for the taking. All the pieces were there, all the cards were neatly stacked up. All that remained to be done was to tug at the right card and everything would come tumbling down. 'Yes,' Solis whispered, 'victory *is* ours.'

CHAPTER 11

November 12

Though Scott Dixon was never far from his mind, there was much that C. B. Lane had to do to shore up his sagging reputation. For while it was true that Stratton was listening to Dixon, Lane was still the senior commander on the ground. The 11th Air Assault was his. In the end, when all was said and done, it would be the achievements of the division that would be remembered by promotion boards and not the staff work of an ad hoc headquarters. All Lane had to do was to make sure that his name, and his name alone, was associated with those achievements. 'Let that little shit whisper all he wants in Stratton's ear,' he told his aide one day. 'It's my name that goes on the orders that start the battles, and after this is all over it will be my name that will go down as the man who fought and won the war in Colombia.'

Saying this and making it so were two entirely different matters. On the surface it seemed simple. All Lane needed to do was to act the role, to ensure that the people in his command and the media saw him as a fighting general.

That role, however, was not one that he wore well. From start to finish, Lane was as tied to his headquarters as a sailor lashed to the mast to weather a storm. In World War I the French referred to such commanders as château generals because of their practice of never leaving their elegant palaces and châteaus well in the rear of artillery range. In the calm, cool, clean atmosphere of their confiscated estates, the château generals of World War I and their staffs worked in comfort and almost splendid isolation. Though no one ever thought of doing so, the comparison between Lane and his World War I counterparts would have been striking.

C. B. Lane, a man who had built his reputation upon his administrative prowess and not his war-fighting abilities, knew he would be out of his element in the field. Like the French generals of the past, he had difficulty absorbing, sorting, and using the information that assailed a front-line commander like a machine gun. Lane's mind just couldn't deal with more than one or two things at a time. That was why he built around him a large staff manned by people who wouldn't rush him and would cater to his needs. In the quiet, well-appointed headquarters of the 11th Air Assault Division, hand-picked staff officers kept him from being overwhelmed with data, sorting it out and feeding it to him in digestible packages as he needed it. Safe in the cool quietness of his well-lit office, C. B. Lane worked on one problem or issue at a time in the same patient and orderly manner that a farmer plows each of his fields in its turn. Though he personally did not accomplish much, what he did produce were masterpieces. In the past, such well-crafted masterpieces delivered at the right time to an appreciative superior were enough to mark Lane for promotion. Now with events turning on him faster than he could comprehend, he realized that he needed to change his style, and neither he nor his division was ready for that.

As they walked toward Lane's command-and-control helicopter that morning, his young aide noticed his general did so with a deliberateness and stiffness that reminded him of a man approaching the electric chair. His demeanor and his expression, so unlike those that he used at staff briefings and command visits, betrayed Lane's apprehensions. While some would interpret his behavior as advance signs of cowardliness, his aide knew better. 'While the general,' he had been told by the G-3, 'was afraid of no man, embarrassment was a different matter. The old man is deathly afraid that he's going to find himself in a situation which he has no control over, and that he's going to make a dumb move. Our job,' the G-3 summed up for the aide, 'is to make sure that he doesn't get himself into a bind like that.' When the aide asked how exactly they were supposed to do that, the G-3 shrugged and patted the aide's shoulder. 'Good question.' With that, the G-3 had turned and walked away.

With all the formalities of a dress parade the crew chief of the UH-60 helicopter that Lane would ride in today greeted him and handed him his aviator's helmet. The aide, scurrying about the helicopter and entering from the other side, quickly took his place in front of the massive radio panel that controlled all the radios as well as the intercoms in the rear of the helicopter. As he settled himself in, placing the general's map where both could see it and use it, and began to check to make sure that all the radios were set properly, the aide was still wondering how he was going to keep his boss from messing all over himself.

The situation they were flying into, briefed at the 0700 hours morning briefing, had all the makings of a real circus. Even the manner in which the 11th Air Assault had become involved was in itself somewhat of a farce. It all began two days prior when a Colombian Army battalion seized a town named El Frío on the Meta

River. This effort was part of the northern arm of a government counteroffensive aimed at rolling back the spectacular gains made by the FARC. Unfortunately, the battalion that had taken El Frío was unsupported, leaving it vulnerable to attack, which the FARC promptly did. Pounced upon by an FARC force estimated to be two battalions plus, the Colombian battalion was quickly isolated and mauled. Though they had managed to hang on throughout the eleventh of November, the last remnants of the Colombian battalion had been overrun just before dawn on the twelfth.

Because the purpose of the relief effort to save the Colombian battalion that was to be mounted by two battalions of the 11th Air Assault's 3rd Brigade was no longer valid, the mission was canceled immediately by the 3rd Brigade commander. Lane was not informed of this decision until his 0700 hours briefing. Not waiting for the G-3 operations briefer to finish describing the situation, Lane stood up, walked to the front of the room, and began to speak. As this was the first time that Lane had ever done this in all their months in Colombia, no one knew what to do or what to expect. In silence they watched as he took a fighting stance, feet apart and hands on hips, before speaking. When he began to speak, he had their attention. 'There isn't a damned thing we can do to save those poor bastards in El Frío. I'm sure they did as well as they could,' he said in his finest fighting-general voice. 'But just because that battle's over doesn't mean the whole game has to be given up.' Several staff officers turned and looked quizzically at each other, each wondering where their commander was headed. Lane, either ignoring this or not seeing it, continued. 'We can still go in there and extract a pound of flesh from the Farcees before they have a chance to break up their battalions and melt away into the bush.'

While his staff gazed at him bewildered, wondering

what he was driving at, Lane took inspiration from his own speech. Looking to his aide at the back of the room, he bellowed, 'Jimmy, get me Henry R. Tell him I have a new mission for his brigade.' The assembled staff officers followed Lane as he moved to the rear of the room with a slow deliberateness that spoke of confidence and power. Except for Lane's footfalls, the only sounds being generated in the room were those made by the aide as he placed the call to Colonel Henry R. Johnson, commander of the 3rd Brigade. When Henry R. came on the line, the aide responded to him with a solemn voice. 'Colonel Johnson, please hold for General Lane.' By that time, Lane was there waiting for his aide to hand him the phone.

Grabbing the phone as he seated himself where his aide normally sat, Lane settled down and began speaking. 'Henry, I know that relief mission of yours is a bust. Seems like the Colombians in El Frío just couldn't hack it.'

This comment caused Major Solis, seated off to one side, to draw in a deep breath and glare at Lane. No one except Delhue noticed Solis's reaction. When, after the briefest of seconds, Solis saw Delhue staring at him, he knew that his face had betrayed him and quickly dropped it into a deadpan stare as he turned back to where Lane was berating the 3rd Brigade commander.

'You know, H,' Lane said with the expression of a father admonishing an errant son, 'I'm rather disappointed that you scrubbed the whole thing. Christ, we got the bastards out in the open. Now's the time to hit them, when we know where the little bastards are.'

For a moment there was silence as Lane listened. Slowly the watching staff could see Lane's facial muscles tighten up. He was becoming angry. They had all seen that look before and they knew what was coming. When he spoke this time, any hint of warmth or understanding, real or faked, was gone. Lane was angry and he wanted the commander of the 3rd Brigade to know it. 'Listen, Colonel, you just listen. I have no intention of coming down there and showing you how to run your brigade. But if I have to, I will.' The air in the room was heavy with tension. Once Lane got himself worked up like this, anything could happen, and what usually happened wasn't good. Today would be no different.

'We have been given a hell of an opportunity to smash two Farcee battalions, and I'll be damned if an unimaginative brigade commander is going to blow it.' By now Lane's face was red. As he spoke, he was jabbing his free hand forward, index finger extended, as if trying to poke the brigade commander on the other end of the line in the chest. 'I expect a maximum effort on this. The G-2 people here feel that those people are going to pull in their horns and run back east as fast as they can. If you drop one battalion well east of El Frío into a blocking position and another to the south to keep them from slipping away that way, with the Meta River to the north, we'll have them in a box. If you pull your 3rd Battalion out of whatever it's doing, drop them west of town, and have them sweep east, we'll have the Farcees between a rock and a hard place. That should be simple enough for even you to understand.'

From his seat at the front of the room, Delhue hung his head and shook it. How embarrassing, he thought, it had to be for Henry R. to be spoken to in such a manner. H. R. was an exceptional commander, a natural when it came to leadership. He had proven his mettle in every assignment and had won his current position on merit, demonstrated ability in peace and war, and plain hard work. Now, in what would ordinarily be one of the high points of any soldier's career, to have to suffer such undeserved abuse was, to Delhue, unconscionable. That he and every other officer in that room should sit there in silence and allow Lane to berate Colonel Henry R. was just as onerous. To

Delhue, the idea that Lane believed that he, by virtue of his rank and position, could do as he pleased, unchecked, and treat people in such a manner was indicative of a system gone wrong. But what, he wondered, could he do? What options did he have available? As bad as it was to turn a blind eye to such goings-on, any alternative went against everything that he and every other officer in that room had been taught. Lane was by virtue of his commission and rank their superior ranking officer. And they, every man and woman in the room, by virtue of their oath of commission, were obligated to obey his orders so long as they were legal and moral. Nothing, after all, said that you had to like your superior, only obey him.

By the time Delhue looked back up, Lane was finishing his rather one-sided conversation with the 3rd Brigade commander and preparing to hang up. As bad as the previous part of his tirade had been, the last portion bothered Delhue even more. 'You will,' Lane told the brigade commander, 'make whatever coordination and reconnaissance you need to do in the next two hours and get this operation moving. This is an air assault division. Speed and mobility are what we're about. Now get to it and start earning your pay for a change.'

Delhue was not the only person in the room that winced at Lane's last comment. It had been, several officers felt, totally uncalled for. That it was not unusual for their commanding general to degrade people in such a manner did not justify it. Finished, Lane handed the telephone back to his aide and smiled. 'Gentlemen, if all goes well, by nightfall we will have two enemy battalions in our hip pocket and another streamer to hang on the division flag.'

While Lane stood there before his assembled staff, Delhue turned away and looked into the faces of the young captains and majors beaming glowing smiles at their division commander. That Lane and his abusive manner were beyond help was a given. He would, Delhue knew, continue to ride down his subordinates until the day he left the Army. What bothered Delhue the most at the moment was the idea that there, in a room full of admiring and still impressionable young officers, a new crop of officers was being trained to carry on that perversion of leadership on officers who were yet to come forth. How sad it was, Delhue realized as Lane walked out and his entourage of loyal staff officers followed him out of the room. How sad it was for their nation and his Army.

Of course, not everyone was disappointed with the results of Lane's actions. Major Solis knew without having to be told that the hasty operation directed by Lane would be welcome news to Hector Valendez. For the trap that Lane expected to set would snare nothing. It would be the FARC rather than the Americans who would end the day with another victory. For Hector Valendez had never had any intention of turning and running back east into the hinterlands of Los Llanos. Westward, now and until final victory, had become the watchword for the FARC. The days of cautious hit-and-run operations, a sudden strike here or there followed by rapid dispersion, were over. It would be the battalion landed west of El Frío that would become the hunted, not the hunter.

Glancing down at his watch, Solis quickly calculated the time he had. Though he would have preferred to use his usual secure means of passing his information back to Valendez, that was far too slow. He therefore decided to use his emergency backup system for direct and rapid contact. Though it was risky, and there was little danger that Lane's master stroke would yield anything, the potential damage that prepared regular-force battalions could inflict on an unwary American infantry battalion was, Solis felt, well worth any chances he took.

Doing his best to mask his haste or eagerness, Solis walked out of the Ministry of Defense building and onto the busy street. After he cleared the final checkpoint. he headed toward the post office, where he would use a public phone to send his flash traffic. Freed from the prying eyes of the Ministry building, Solis could relax and smile. Two, he thought, could use speed and mobility. Besides, as one senior Colombian officer once pointed out to him after listening to a briefing given by the staff of the 11th Air Assault Division, the ability to go forward rapidly often does nothing but get you into trouble that much faster.

Within minutes, warning orders implementing Major General C. B. Lane's inspiration were en route to the units that would be involved. For the two battalions that had been slated as part of the relief operation, adjusting themselves to their new tasks was relatively simple. The companies that made up the 1st Battalion of the 417th Infantry and the 1st Battalion of the 513th Infantry were ready to go in minutes. All pre-combat checks in preparation for their previous mission had been made. All supplies, from combat rations to ammunition, were still on hand, distributed, and in the hands of the troopers of both battalions. All the staffs of those two battalions needed at that moment were line of departure time, the location where they were headed, and a mission statement that told them what was expected of them once they got there.

In the 3rd Battalion, 511th Infantry, things wouldn't be so easy. Not only would its ultimate mission be more difficult, for they had been designated as the sweep battalion in this shoestring operation, but their companies were scattered about the brigade area executing diverse missions. Company A, still under the command of their former executive officer, First Lieutenant Barbara O'Fallen, was the most available and was assigned the mission of providing security to the brigade base camp and serving as the brigade reserve. Company B, under First Lieutenant Dan Krammer, was one day out on a three-day sweep of the area around the brigade base camp. Though they were only fifteen kilometers northeast of the brigade command post when Lane was issuing his orders to the brigade commander, it would take them three hours by foot to make it back. Company C, the only line company still under the command of its original commanding officer, Captain Frank Walters, was at that moment en route back into the brigade base camp, having completed a four-day dismounted sweep to the southeast. Though they were closer than Company B, four days of patrolling during the day, ambush duty at night, and incessant marching in the late fall rains and heat had taken their toll. The time needed to pull them in and turn them around for their new mission would be equal to or greater than that for Company B.

The senior leadership of the 3rd of the 511th was just as scattered. Still anxious to escape facing the problems that the September 21 ambush had visited upon his battalion, Lieutenant Colonel Harold Cerro continued to seek refuge by going out into the field with one of his units every chance he could. Today he was with Company B, the one company that carried the least amount of animosity as a result of their perceived plight.

Major Edward J. Bond, the new battalion executive officer, was with the brigade supply officer and the 3rd of the 511th's own S-4 supply officer, paying a visit to the division support command where he hoped to learn something about the mechanics involved in keeping an infantry battalion deployed in Colombia supplied and maintained. Only Captain Nancy Kozak was at the battalion command post when the initial warning order came in over the land line from brigade alerting her that they had a mission.

That message, relayed by the brigade operations officer himself, was short and deceptively simple: '3rd of the 511th will, on order, conduct an air assault into a land zone or zones, to be designated, west of the town of El Frío. 3rd of the 511th, in cooperation with 1st of the 417th and 1st of the 513th, which will be taking up blocking positions to the east and south of El Frío respectively, will conduct offensive operations to find, fix, and destroy two FARC regular-force battalions currently operating in and around El Frío.' When Kozak asked the brigade S-3 when they could expect to receive the brigade operations order, there was a pause. When the brigade ops officer finally did speak, he told Kozak in a very guarded manner, 'Nancy, don't expect much more than what I just gave you.' With that, he terminated the conversation and left Kozak the task of pulling the scattered elements of the battalion back into the brigade base camp while preparing an order based on the sparsest of information and guidance.

Flown back to the brigade base camp in the brigade commander's own aircraft, Cerro was greeted with Kozak's estimate of the situation. In it she listed three variations or options of how she thought the battalion would execute its assigned mission. Of the three, Cerro picked the one that Kozak herself favored and had spent the most time developing. It wasn't that she had driven her commander toward it. On the contrary, after having worked with Cerro for so long, she intuitively knew how he preferred to operate and what he would have done himself if he had been left to his own devices. Good operations officers are supposed to do that, and no one who saw Kozak at work would deny that she was good.

The plan, like all plans that Cerro and Kozak developed, was simple. After landing five kilometers west of El Frío, the battalion would move forward with two companies abreast, with A under First Lieutenant O'Fallen on the right, and C, commanded by Captain Walters, on the left. B Company, led by First Lieutenant Krammer, would follow A. Krammer's job would be to react to the situation as it was developed by either one or both of the lead companies. Following far enough behind so that his company didn't get involved right off the bat in any firefight A Company might stumble into, Krammer would, on order, move forward to reinforce or attack through A, swing left to reinforce or attack through C, or go right and extend the battalion's frontage or outflank any opposition A or C ran into. This formation, two up and one back, gave Cerro sufficient flexibility to meet just about any contingency while providing the widest possible frontage they dared present.

This last item was of great importance, for the enemy situation in and around El Frío, even after the attached cavalry troop finished its recon of the area, was ambiguous as hell. Though Cerro had wanted to go with one company forward and two back, his mission required him to cover as wide an area as was prudent. 'Your battalion,' Henry R. told him during his briefing, 'will be the beaters. Your task is to drive the Farcees out of hiding and into the waiting guns of the 1st of the 417th and the 1st of the 513th. Failing that, if the enemy chooses to turn on you and fight, you must become the hammer while the other two battalions provide you with an anvil upon which to smash him.'

While all of this sounded good at the orders briefing in the safety of the brigade base camp, Cerro knew in his heart that his battalion, if called upon to play hammer, would be a very fragile one at best. The battalion, he pointed out to Henry R., was not ready and could not be ready for at least twenty-four hours for this type of operation. Even A Company, assigned to base security, was not well rested, given their need to keep 50 percent of their strength up and alert all night securing the base perimeter or lying in ambush. The other two companies were worse off, having been involved in operations at the time of the alert. 'At best,' Cerro pointed out, 'I'll have twenty, maybe thirty minutes together with my staff and all my company commanders before we have to load up on the slicks and move out. Add to that the fact that I'll never even have the opportunity to talk face-to-face with the commanders of the other two battalions involved and you have, sir, the makings of a potential disaster.'

Though Henry R. listened patiently and attentively, and the excuses that Cerro was giving were all valid, he knew that the real reason Cerro was uncomfortable with the idea of this operation was confidence. For both men knew in their hearts that after the September 21 ambush both Cerro and the soldiers under his command had lost confidence in themselves and each other. No one spoke of this openly, no one said so in so many words. They didn't need to. A trained eye could see it in the faces of the leaders and soldiers of the battalion and in the manner in which they carried themselves and performed their assigned duties. The battalion had been broken in spirit. Henry R. tried to protect Cerro and his battalion while at the same time giving his battalion small, easy missions in the hope that these would help collectively to restore their confidence. But this did not happen. As the days and weeks slipped by, Henry R. realized that what had happened during the ambush and immediately after had left a mark on Cerro and most of his officers that was beyond his ability to erase. 'They are,' he told Colonel Delhue in a confidential conversation one night, 'nothing but a shadow of their former selves. I dread the day when I'll have to put them into another hard fight.'

That day, Henry R. knew, had come when Lane had issued him his marching orders that morning. At first he tried to work out a plan in which the 3rd of the 511th would go in as one of the blocking forces. This option, however, was quickly shot down by his own operations officer. 'The blocking forces, sir, must be in place first, both to the east and south. Since the 1st of the 417th and the 1st of the 513th are on hand and ready, they have to be the blocking forces. Besides,' he added, 'since the

Farcees will be pulling back to the east, or maybe even to the south, it will be the blocking forces and not the sweep battalion that will bear the brunt of this fight. The sweep battalion's only task is to hurry them up and clean up any stragglers.'

Seeing the logic, Henry R. let the order of deployment and tasks to the battalions stand. Still, he wasn't ready to give up. As much as he hated to do so, he went back to division shortly before noon and asked that the division reserve battalion be released to his control for this operation. 'The 3rd of the 511th,' he explained to the division G-3, 'is still scattered all over hell's half acre. It will be hours before they'll be in place, and even then they will not be in any shape for a really tough stand-up fight.'

The G-3 didn't even take Henry R.'s request seriously. 'You know General Lane's feelings on the use of the division reserve, sir,' he responded in a rather uninterested voice. 'The only way we can get the old man to release it is in an emergency. Since my morning sitrep shows your brigade having three battalions available and the operation calls for only three battalions, I don't see how I can justify adding another to your troop list.' Then with a sarcastic tone in his voice the G-3 added, 'You can always call General Lane yourself, sir, and take the matter up with him.' The G-3, of course, knew that Henry R. wouldn't do that, especially after the verbal beating he had taken that morning. Having tried his best, he faced the inevitable and told Cerro as best he could that he and his battalion were going.

Cerro and his staff had never assumed otherwise. Almost to a man, everyone who had been involved in the September 21 incident went about their duties in preparation for this mission with a rather fatalistic attitude. When Nancy Kozak, in the midst of writing the brief operations order that they would use to launch the battalion into the attack directed by Lane, turned to her operations sergeant and said, 'Well, this is it,' he knew what she meant.

It was no secret, once word got out, that this mission was *it*, the test. There would be no chance for Cerro to escape his problems, which included a crippling lack of confidence in himself and the battalion. Today his skill as a battalion commander and his ability to coordinate the activities of all three line companies at once and lead soldiers in battle would be tested for the first time since September 21. His operations officer, Nancy Kozak, wouldn't be able to use her staff work and activities to busy her mind so that it wouldn't be free to dwell on the personal issues and concerns that had been eating away at her self-confidence like ravenous parasites. Though the methods of escaping coming to terms with their personal issues had been different, as different as the two people themselves, the results were the same. Issues that needed to be dealt with were ignored. Personal problems, frailties, and wounds that could have a serious impact on their performance, and hence that of the battalion, had not being tended to. Only the absence of a crisis had kept the 3rd of the 511th, and the soldiers and officers in it, from self-destructing. All that had eyes saw this, from the brigade commander on down the line. And now that afternoon, as commanders and staff officers rushed about preparing for the arrival of the helicopters, everyone realized that just such a crisis was at hand. The day of reckoning was here.

CHAPTER 12

November 12

It was late afternoon before the first lift, carrying A and C Company of the 3rd Battalion, approached the two landing zones west of El Frío. B Company, following the first two waves, was due to follow A Company fifteen minutes after that company had landed and departed the landing zone. Hal Cerro, as was his custom, was going in with the first wave. Since First Lieutenant Barbara O'Fallen was the most junior of the company commanders and Captain Frank Walters of C Company the most senior, Cerro opted to move initially with O'Fallen's unit. Kozak, having learned from the September 21 incident, would remain airborne during the initial phase of the operation. There, together with the battalion fire support officer, Captain Peter Crippen, the battalion intel officer, First Lieutenant Marion A. Dietz, and Sergeant Andy Pender of her own section, she would provide a communications link with brigade, the other two battalions involved in the operation, and the two batteries of 105mm artillery supporting the operation. If and when attack helicopters were committed to the fight, she would coordinate their activities also. By this arrangement Cerro on the ground was left free to concentrate on maneuvering the battalion while Kozak, quite literally above and away from the fight below, could call on and control whatever support was called for by the situation.

Kozak's UH-60, with extra man-portable radios lashed into vacant seats and their antennas hanging out open doors, was not alone in the skies above El Frío. Zipping about over one unit on the ground or another, like an impatient dragonfly skimming from lily pad to lily pad, Major General C. B. Lane's command-and-control helicopter fluttered about. He was there to make sure that his operation went down the way he had envisioned it. 'Sometimes, Jim,' he told his aide, 'you got to sit on these people if you want results.'

Traveling about the same circuit but at a discreet distance was Colonel Henry R. Johnson's command-and-control aircraft. He, like Lane, was moving from one place to another, landing every so often to talk with battalion commanders on the ground while waiting for Cerro's battalion to appear. Worried over the total lack of reaction from the Farcees, Henry R. spent the balance of the afternoon glancing at his watch, watching to the south for the appearance of the 3rd of the 511th, and casting every now and then a wary eye toward Lane's helicopter.

The two senior commanders and Kozak were joined on occasion by other people flying about. They were either waiting for something to happen, like the two senior commanders, or going about their duties oblivious to them. One of the aircraft waiting was a liaison helicopter from the division's attack helicopter battalion. It made its appearance just as the first of the two blocking forces went in. Cerro's request that the attack helicopters work over his landing zones before his unit went in was denied. 'It would,' he had been informed, 'serve no purpose other than to give away our intentions.' Though he argued that the Farcees would know what was afoot by the time his unit arrived, Henry R. ended the discussion by blandly stating, 'That's a call from Division, Hal.' So with nothing to do, the helicopter simply loitered about lazily, waiting for the enemy to show themselves so that it could bring to bear the devastating firepower that the attack helicopters of the battalion could deliver.

Another helicopter carrying correspondents drawn from the media pool to cover the operation also joined the traffic aloft. Like a frog jumping from one small American-controlled pond to another, this helicopter would spring up out of the bush and quickly touch down whenever a group of American soldiers were seen gathering below. Added to these and an occasional stray helicopter darting in and out of the area to deliver supplies and equipment to the 417th, 513th, and the artillery batteries already in place were other aircraft with no apparent task at hand, which only contributed to the cluttered air space. From Kozak's helicopter, Sergeant Pender watched all of this activity. Never known to hold his thoughts, he commented over the intercom to no one in particular, 'Looks like the New Jersey Turnpike on a Labor Day weekend.'

Kozak, though she heard him, ignored his comment. For no sooner had he finished his halfhearted attempt at humor than she saw two groups of dots coming in fast and low from the south. At first they looked like a swarm of insects, insignificant and distant. Those dots, she knew, were companies A and C. A quick glance at her watch told her there wasn't much time before sunset, three, maybe four hours at best. She, like everyone else in the brigade, knew that if the Farcees couldn't be brought to bay before that, then the thin line of troops that the two blocking battalions had out on the ground would never be able to keep the enemy contained. 'In the darkness,' the brigade commander had stressed to Cerro, 'the other people would go through the 417th and the 513th like water through a sieve.'

Against this deadline the soldiers of the 511th had rushed their preparations as best they could. Though nothing major was overlooked, no one felt completely comfortable. From beginning to end this was, Kozak knew, a thrown-together affair. Still, as she watched the distant dots to the south grow rapidly in size and slowly start to take the shape of transport helicopters, it was an event that would not be postponed or canceled. Rock Six, the radio call sign for the division commander, had a personal interest in this affair, and nothing short of divine intervention or a cataclysmic disaster could stop it. Ordering the pilot of her own helicopter to move off to the west, away from the battalions' approach to their landing zones, Kozak watched as the first of the helicopters carrying A Company slowed, flared out, and began to land. They were committed.

Below in that helicopter First Lieutenant O'Fallen unsnapped her seat belt, pulled herself up into the open door, and prepared to exit the aircraft as soon as she felt the wheels hit dirt. Looking back over her shoulder, she was about to yell something to the soldiers behind her when her entire body was suddenly thrown back against another soldier waiting to exit. The noise of the helicopter masked the sound of gunfire coming from the ground. Only when she flopped back onto the floor and her head flipped back, revealing lifeless eyes that were rolling back up into her head, did the troopers with her realize that she had been shot. Three days before her twenty-fifth birthday, Barbara O'Fallen, the only child of a Wisconsin couple, died, ending her parents' dream of grandchildren and a normal happy life.

Like a string of firecrackers, gunfire erupted from two

adjoining sides of the landing zone, raking the incoming helicopters that hung for a moment like suspended clay pigeons in a shooting gallery. In this sudden and unexpected hail of gunfire, the courage and skill of each helicopter pilot was laid bare. Some, with nerves that never failed them, continued to bore on, altering neither their speed nor rate of descent. Others, anxious to get out of the grueling cross fire as quickly as possible, practically did a nose dive, jerking up on their controls at the last second and thumping their aircraft onto the ground with a jarring thud. A few flinched, jerking to one side or the other so as to avoid the streams of tracers they saw racing toward them head-on. One pilot, totally unnerved by the experience, pulled up and away from the maelstrom below. That only one minor collision occurred was nothing short of a miracle. Even more miraculous was the fact that most of the soldiers survived that collision.

This fact, however, even if known, would have brought no comfort to Hal Cerro as his own helicopter came in at the tail end of A Company's wave. A disaster, he thought. He had another fucking disaster in the making, and his battalion wasn't even on the ground yet. Intently he watched, blocking as best he could all emotions and feelings as he took in as much as he could before landing. So intense had his concentration been that it was a moment or two before he noticed that not only was he not getting closer to the ground but it seemed as if he was moving away from it. Dumbfounded, he looked away from the spreading firefight below and over to the pilot. Without an aircraft crewman's helmet on, Cerro had to yell to get the pilot's attention. 'What in the hell are you doing? Land! Take this thing down, *now!*'

Cocking his head back, the pilot tried to tell Cerro something, but he didn't hear. Instead, Cerro leaped up and at the pilot, bumping their Kevlar helmets as he did so. Contorting his body around the pilot's high-backed seat so that his face was almost in the pilot's, Cerro yelled at him, spitting as he did so. 'You take this piece of shit down there now or I'll blow your fucking brains out all over the inside of your pretty fucking helicopter.'

The young aviator glanced from the firefight below, over to Cerro's face, twisted beyond recognition in anger, and then at his instrument panel. Without another word, he shoved his control stick down and over to the side, throwing Cerro off balance but bringing the helicopter around and back into the landing zone. Pulling himself away from the pilot, Cerro looked out the door, saw the ground rushing up, and prepared to jump as soon as it was close enough. This would be it. In his heart he knew it. And although the idea had never really formed itself into a clear, coherent thought in his mind, Lieutenant Colonel Hal Cerro had no intention of surviving this fight.

From their perch well above the landing zone, Kozak saw it all. Though she didn't know of the distress that her battalion commander was in, or of the death of First Lieutenant O'Fallen, the severity of the situation was immediately and brutally obvious. Keying the intercom that linked her, the fire support officer, the intel officer, and Pender, she called for immediate suppressive fires from the supporting artillery batteries. Crippen, the fire support officer, shot back without thinking, 'They won't fire them until the helicopters have cleared. We have to wait.'

Kozak, animated by what she was seeing and her own feeling of being unable to help A Company through direct action, shot back without turning her face away from the scene below. 'Call them, damn it, and get them ready. Shoot as soon as you can.' No sooner had she finished that order than a call from the brigade commander came in over the radio asking for an update. Turning her head toward Pender, she keyed the intercom. 'Tell Henry R.

that Company A is catching hell in their LZ. We're calling for fires now. Status of C Company is unknown.' With that she turned back to look out the open door of the helicopter in an effort to sort out the chaos on the ground. The thought that she and her aircraft might be in danger never crossed her mind. And even if it had, she wouldn't have done anything different. As much as she didn't like the idea of being up there, away from the fight itself, she knew she was where she belonged and had no intention of leaving, regardless of the risk, real or imagined.

From the north bank of the Meta River, Hector Valendez paced back and forth in front of a concealed 14.5mm anti-aircraft machine gun. Every few steps, he would stop, cock his head to one side, and listen as best he could to the sounds of battle. At the end of his little circuit, he would again stop and look down at his radio operator, Rafael Dario. Without having to be asked, Dario would look up and inform his commander that there still was no word that the local-force platoons covering the landing zones were withdrawing. With a huff, the only sign that he showed that he was getting angry, Valendez would turn around and start his circuit again. The plan, he knew, was unraveling, and there was nothing, nothing at all, that he could do from where he stood to pull it back together.

It had been a simple plan. It had to be. There was just not enough time for anything more ambitious. With the little time he had been given to prepare, Valendez had broken his three local-force companies down into platoon-sized elements and scattered them about, with each one covering any large open area that could accommodate an air assault force. His two main-force battalions, in the meantime, had been withdrawn to the southwest, where they would remain hidden. During the day, the scattered local-force units were to have developed the situation. At night, if and when the American units pulled into defensive perimeters, Valendez intended to throw one or both of his regular battalions at the most vulnerable of the three American battalions.

That, at any rate, had been the plan that he had briefed. He had made it clear to the commanders of each of the local-force companies that their units were to harass the Americans but avoid decisive engagements. He had carefully picked his words so that there would be no mistaking his intent. 'Units,' he had instructed each of the local-force company commanders, 'that make contact at landing zones will take the Americans under fire for no more than five minutes at the most. After that you will break contact before the Americans bring the full weight of their awesome firepower to bear. If you tarry too long, if you try to take advantage of an advantage that you have achieved, no matter how great, you and your men will pay for your delay with your lives. So don't wait. Fire, confuse them, draw some blood, then break it off.'

Someone, Valendez realized, had not listened. Instead, as he reached the anti-aircraft machine gun again, the sounds of small-arms fire, now mixed in with artillery fire, continued to drift across the river to him. Stomping his foot, he cursed. He cursed at whoever it was that had chosen to disobey him. He cursed at the Americans flying so arrogantly above the town of El Frío in their helicopters. Finally he cursed at the pair of 14.5mm anti-aircraft guns he had deployed north of the river. Though his choice had been a good one when he had made it, they were unable now under present conditions to do anything of value. Though the gunners continued to track any aircraft that appeared to be headed their way, they didn't fire. To do so, unless the aircraft drifted out over the river itself, would be useless. So, like Valendez, who stood there and mumbled beneath his breath, the anti-aircraft machine gunners watched and waited for things to work themselves out.

*   *   *

It was the fighters of the Number 2 Platoon, 27th Local Defense Company, recruited from the town of El Frío and its surrounding area, that had added the unexpected friction to Valendez's plan. Local men, every one, they had no intention of giving ground when they had the enemy to their front. They were tired of watching. They were tired of waiting. They had watched three days before as the Colombian battalion moved forward and brought devastation down on their families and homes. Their discipline had held. And the next day, when they supported the attack of the two main-force battalions against the government troops, they had held themselves in check, providing a base of fire while the better-trained regular-force fighters closed with and broke the back of the enemy's forces. Even after walking through the streets asking stunned survivors about the fate of their loved ones, the men of the 27th Company refrained from killing the government soldiers who had gone over to the FARC at the last moment rather than die.

But now with their blood lust unquenched, with revenge burning in the mind of every man in Number 2 Platoon, neither the orders from their own platoon leader, himself the father of three who had once been a shopkeeper in El Frío, nor Valendez's plan could keep them from meting out the vengeance that they so much needed to purge from their souls. To a man, without a word having to be spoken, the fighters of Number 2 Platoon had resolved to stand where they were and bring the bastard Yankees to their knees. It wasn't that any of them were fanatics. It wasn't that they had a death wish. On the contrary, they were all simple men, each and every one. They were men who had answered Valendez's call to arms and had come forth to defend their homes. Now, however, many of those homes and the families that they had tried to defend had been wiped away by the army of a corrupt government that ruled from a strange, distant capital. All that mattered now to these men was that they extract what they believed was justice, simple, brutal, biblical justice. So, against Valendez's wishes and plans, Number 2 Platoon stood its ground, pouring volley after volley of fire into the confused and shattered ranks of A Company, 3rd Battalion of the 511th Infantry, as fast as they could.

Out on the fireswept clearing, the soldiers of A Company, now under the command of the only surviving officer in the company, Second Lieutenant Tyler Wiezman, were flooded with images of the September 21 debacle. For the second time in as many months they found themselves in a desperate situation, pinned by heavy enemy fire and taking casualties at a prodigious rate. The memory of the previous encounter, the brutal heat, the devastating small-arms fire, and the ever-present specter of death all about them had a numbing effect. Even the best efforts of the sergeants and Lieutenant Wiezman couldn't shake the sixty-odd men and women who were still alive and unwounded from their inactivity. Singly and in small groups of two and three, the sky troopers of A Company hugged the ground with all their might and prayed for darkness or deliverance.

Only two things kept those soldiers from breaking and running, despite the tremendous volume of automatic weapons fire that was being thrown at them. The first was immediate and effective artillery fire, called for and directed by Nancy Kozak and Peter Crippen from above. Heeding Kozak's order, Crippen brought down volley after volley of 105mm howitzer fire as soon as the last helicopter had dropped the troopers of A Company off and cleared the landing zone. Firing ICM, or improved conventional ammunitions, at first, Kozak quickly realized that the Farcees were well dug in, and she requested that the supporting batteries switch to high-explosive rounds with delayed action fuses. This, she reasoned, would allow the artillery rounds to burrow into the ground first before detonating and hopefully dig the enemy out like a gardener rips into the earth to pull out a bothersome weed by its roots. Once that was having an effect, Kozak worked with Crippen to adjust the artillery batteries' pattern of fire so that all the rounds impacted evenly along those enemy positions that they could identify from the air.

The other factor that saved A Company, for the moment, was Hal Cerro's conduct. Once on the ground and in the thick of the firefight, Cerro gave up all pretense of caution and moved about the kill zone in a rather cavalier manner. While he didn't totally throw caution to the winds by walking about as if nothing was happening, neither did he take any extraordinary measures to conceal himself or take cover. With the calmness of a man who looked forward to his own imminent death, Cerro moved about from one group of soldiers to the next, encouraging them to fire and directing that fire against the nearest or most dangerous positions. Some of his troopers, wrapped up in the depths of their own fear, were startled to see Cerro crouched next to them looking about the field as if he were searching for wild game and not the enemy. When the flash of an enemy weapon firing revealed a Farcee position, Cerro would point to it and tell the soldier he was next to, 'There, trooper. The enemy is over there. Start putting some fire on him for a change.' Looking up at Cerro, most reacted partly out of habit and partly out of shame. Only after he had succeeded in getting the soldiers he was with up and returning fire would Cerro leave. Afterwards, when the survivors were able to compare their impressions of the battle, the one thing that all would agree on was the manner in which Cerro conducted himself. 'He was,' one sergeant commented for the record, 'going about as if he were on the rifle range giving us a block of instruction on small-arms marksmanship. All the time he was with me, he wore a strange sort of half smile on his face. You know, the kind that an officer gets when he sees a training exercise going well. I've never seen anything like it. If it wasn't for him, I think we'd all still be there, dead or eating dirt.'

What most of his people did not appreciate was that the smile Cerro was wearing was not because he was satisfied with what was going on. Cerro, unbeknownst to them, was oblivious to what was happening around him. He, like the soldiers he was directing and encouraging, was merely reacting, doing what came naturally to him because of training and practice. The smile that the sergeant would speak of was there because he knew that any second now an enemy bullet would bring his moral pain and suffering to an end. He would in the twinkling of an eye be relieved of all his worldly concerns and problems. In the back of his mind, over and over again as he moved about the landing zone, the ancient Japanese saying swirled about: 'Duty is heavy. Death lighter than a feather.'

Above the drama being played out between the Number 2 Platoon of the 27th Local Defense Company and A Company, Nancy Kozak was working at full speed. On one hand she was keeping the artillery coming in where it was needed, coordinating it with rocket and gun runs being made by attack helicopters. On the other hand she was trying to get Frank Walters, who had managed to overcome the enemy resistance at his landing zone, to move over to A Company's landing zone. Crippen sat next to her, radio handset pressed to one ear and air crewman's helmet pulled down on the other. Sergeant Pender, across from Kozak, bounced back and forth from the battalion radio net to the brigade command net, relaying situation and spot reports to Colonel Henry R. as they became available and requesting additional attack helicopter support from the brigade operations officer every time Kozak told him to do so.

In the midst of this confusion and activity, neither Walters nor Kozak realized that the Number 3 Platoon

of the 27th Company had broken contact, not because of
pressure put on them by C Company but because it had
been planned that way. They had been ordered to. Nor
did anyone realize, American or rebel, that in the course
of this withdrawal away from the Americans, the platoon
leader of Number 3 Platoon did as he had been trained
to do. Based on his assessment of the situation as he perceived it, on his own initiative he altered the direction of
his retreat. The ongoing firefight at A Company's landing
zone, clearly audible after his breaking contact with C
Company, drew him in that direction. By moving that
way, he was unknowingly applying the old military axiom
that advised commanders to march to the sound of the
guns. Though his sole motivation was to go to the aid of his
fellow platoon leader, the effect would be the same. The
FARC fighters of Number 2 platoon, and not the troopers
of A Company, would receive reinforcements first.

The idea of reinforcing the battle in progress was also on
the mind of Henry R. Within minutes it was obvious that
the plan that he had based his operation on was no longer
valid. Rather than being the hammer, the 3rd of the 511th,
for whatever reason, had now become the anvil. Without
hesitation, Henry R. contacted the commander of the 1st
of the 417th in the east and ordered him to conduct a
movement to contact toward the 3rd of the 511th's current
positions. The 1st of the 513th, in the south, would be
prepared to support either the 417th or, on order, to
reinforce the 3rd of the 511th once they had stabilized
their situation.

After the commander of the 417th acknowledged the
order, Henry R. contacted Kozak. Sergeant Pender,
answering at first, tugged on Kozak's pant leg and yelled,
without bothering to key the intercom, 'Captain, Henry R.
on the horn. Needs to talk to you now.' Kozak, who was
busy consulting with Crippen concerning the use of white

phosphorus and smoke rounds to cover the withdrawal of
A Company, told Crippen to hold his thought and switched
radios. As Kozak gave Henry R. a quick update, explaining
that C Company would be moving out in the next minute
or two to relieve A Company, Henry R. listened, then
explained to her what he was in the process of doing.

It was at this moment that the situation was exacerbated
by the appearance of the battalion executive officer, Major
Edward Bond. Frank Walters and his company had been
delayed by the enemy from responding immediately to
Kozak's order to rush over and relieve A Company.
This and the need to re-form his company into attack
formation headed south rather than east took Walters
several minutes. Walters was about to move out when
Major Bond's voice came over the battalion command net.
Having been informed that no one could contact Cerro and
that A Company was in dire straits, Bond assumed control
of the fight from Kozak. Next he directed that the flight
carrying B Company land in C Company's landing zone,
not A Company's as originally planned. His intention was
to form both C and B companies up before moving out.
Over the radio, before he landed, he told Walters, 'We
can't go off half cocked into the middle of a firefight.
Hold Charlie Company until Bravo arrives.' Reluctantly
Walters acknowledged the order and signaled his platoon
leaders to spread their units back out while they waited
for the arrival of his new commander.

In his aircraft, with the door open and the rush of air
coming in at him, Bond was beside himself with excitement. Originally he had come along on this operation
for no other purpose than to observe and learn. He was
fresh from the Command and General Staff College at
Fort Leavenworth and an abbreviated Spanish language
course in Monterey, California, and this assignment was
not only his first troop assignment in over seven years, it
was his very first time in combat. Even the low morale

and sullen mood he found in the 3rd of the 511th did little to diminish the thrill of finally being in an infantry unit in an active theater of operations. This thrill, as was normal for most Americans approaching their first battle, was tempered ever so slightly by a host of concerns and apprehensions.

Whatever concerns he had about his own abilities were washed away by the sudden rush of adrenaline when he heard, as the aircraft drew near the landing zone, that the battalion operations officer was unable to contact the battalion commander and was running the operation. Though Captain Kozak's response that she was too busy to give him an update had irritated Bond, for he had perceived it as a rebuff by a subordinate, he let it drop for now. There would be plenty of time later to discuss the chain of command with young Captain Kozak.

Having finished her discussion with Henry R. and Crippen, who was now busy coordinating the shifting of fires to cover the withdrawal of A Company, Kozak called Walters and asked if he was moving yet. Walters, a little confused, responded that he wasn't. This both surprised and upset Kozak. Mashing down on the radio transmit button, Kozak yelled into the boom mike hanging in front of her mouth. 'Charlie Six, this is Sky Rider Three, why in the hell aren't you moving? Over.'

Before Walters could answer, Bond cut in. 'Sky Rider Three, this is Sky Rider Five, I ordered him to stand fast until Bravo Six and his element landed and linked up with them. If you had been monitoring this net like you should have, you'd know what in the hell was going on. Over.'

From where he sat, Sergeant Pender could see Kozak's face turn red with anger. Only with the greatest of effort did she keep herself from shouting back at the new major. Not that he gave her much of a chance to respond. Before she could compose herself, Bond was back on the air. 'Sky Rider Three, this is Sky Rider Five. Until we find out what happened to Sky Rider Six, I am assuming command of this battalion. Do you acknowledge? Over.'

Taking a deep breath, Kozak looked straight ahead with a deadpan stare, depressed the transmit button, and acknowledged with a perfunctory 'Roger.'

Satisfied in his mind that all was in hand, Bond looked out the open door of his helicopter as it made the final run into the landing zone. Despite the fact that he was more anxious to get out and on the ground than anyone in B Company, by the time he undid his seat belt and pulled himself up and out of the nylon seat, he was alone in the cargo bay of the aircraft. All of the troopers he had been traveling with were a long time gone and already scattered in the prone position on the landing zone. Though this startled him a bit, he recovered his composure, made a mental note that he would have to be faster than this in the future, and climbed out of the aircraft.

Once on the ground, he paused for a moment and looked about as the last of the aircraft in his lift pulled pitch and flew off. Satisfied that all was in order, he scanned the landing zone, half expecting the C company commander to run up and report to him. After several seconds of searching the surrounding brush and tree line, he saw two soldiers, whom he took to be Walters and his company command group. Remembering that this was war and not a peacetime maneuver, Bond shook his head at his own foolishness, made another mental note, and began to walk over to where he had seen the two troopers.

Out beyond the tree line, from a small covered spider hole, a fighter left by the commander of the Number 3 Platoon to delay the advance saw the lone American standing out in the middle of the open field before him. He watched him for a moment, wondering why this man was behaving like he was. Only when the enemy soldier, wearing what looked like a new crisp, clean uniform, stepped out with deliberate, unhurried pace, did the fighter conclude that this man was an officer. Though he had been told to wait until the enemy column had started to move before firing, the FARC fighter decided that the impudence of this Yankee officer needed to be punished. With great care he raised his rifle, took careful aim, and fired.

From where he sat waiting with Dan Krammer of B Company, Frank Walters watched Major Edward Bond start to walk toward them like he was strolling across the Plain at West Point on a Sunday afternoon. Walters no sooner shook his head in disbelief than a burst from somewhere out beyond the perimeter of the landing zone cut loose. Without having to look, Walters knew that it was from an AK-74, a Russian-made assault rifle. He also knew what the target was. When he saw Bond spin about like a top, he didn't rush out or get excited. Instead he stuck his right hand over his right shoulder. Seeing Walters's hand, his radiotelephone operator slapped the hand mike of the radio on the battalion net into it without having to be told. While he continued to watch where he had seen Bond go down, Walters keyed the hand mike. 'Sky Rider Three, this is Charlie Six. Sky Rider Five is down. I say again, Sky Rider Five is down. You have the helm again. Any change in orders? Over.'

From somewhere above him Kozak's voice came down and through the radio. It answered his question in a matter-of-fact manner. 'Charlie Six, you will assume command of both your element and Bravo. Move out as quickly as possible and link up with Alpha as soon as you can. Those people are in deep trouble and need your help now. Over.'

Looking over at Dan Krammer, commander of B Company, Walters called out, 'You hear that, Dan?'

Krammer nodded and waved. 'Okay by me. Let's get moving.'

Turning to the platoon leader of his lead platoon, Walters waved his free hand over his head and then brought it down, pointing in the direction of A Company's landing zone. Without a word, the young lieutenant stood up, waved his right hand over his head, and stepped off headed south toward the sound of the guns. Satisfied, Walters called Kozak. 'Sky Rider Three, this is Charlie Six. Bravo Six acknowledges your last. We're moving now. Over.'

Finished, he handed the hand mike back to his radiotelephone operator and prepared to follow the lead platoon. Before he did, he took one last glance back to where he had seen Bond go down. A medic from a B Company platoon was out there in the knee-high grass tending to Bond. As his company moved by him, Walters shouted out, asking the medic if the major was alive. The medic, looking up at Walters for a moment, smiled. 'He took one in the left lung and two in the shoulder. This here officer's lucky. He's earned himself the combat infantryman's badge, the right to wear the 11th Air Assault patch on his right sleeve, a Purple Heart, access to all them VA benefits, and a free trip home, all with less than sixty seconds of combat time. Now ain't that some lucky shit.'

Walters grinned back at the medic, waved, and turned to march off with his company. If that was luck, he decided, he didn't want any part of it.

Above all this confusion, listening over the radio to the orders and counterorders of the 3rd Brigade, the 3rd of the 511th, and other units involved, C. B. Lane hung in the sky like an impatient vulture. Things were not going as he had envisioned them. Someone, he realized, had screwed up. Though he couldn't tell for sure yet who that someone was, he swore to himself that as soon as he knew, he'd nail the son of a bitch to the front door of division headquarters as an example. With no one else but his aide to talk to, Lane turned to him and threw his hands out in disgust. 'Listen to that garbage. In all my years in uniform, I've never heard such amateurish behavior.'

The aide, Captain James William Adderly III, looked at Lane, as was his habit, and nodded without thought. Only his eyes, if Lane had cared to look, would have betrayed Adderly's true thoughts. Responsible for operating the sophisticated radio system found in all true command-and-control aircraft, Adderly heard everything that Lane did. In the course of the battle so far that afternoon, he had heard or seen nothing really wrong, not like Lane was trying to make out. All battles, he knew from his own experiences in the Persian Gulf as a second lieutenant and every training exercise he had ever been on, took on a life of their own and seldom evolved in the manner that commanders on either side had envisioned. Having been a platoon leader, a company commander, an assistant brigade operations officer, and a watch officer in the 11th Air Assault Division's operations center, Adderly had enough of a background to judge what was happening on the ground and between the various commanders of the 3rd Brigade. In his opinion, an opinion he didn't share with Lane, everything was going about as well as could be expected.

Looking over at Lane, Adderly shook his head. The idea that this man was not the great warrior that he made himself out to be had been slow to sink in. From a distance and in small doses, as he had viewed the man when he had been assigned to the division operations section, Adderly had been fooled, like so many before him. Lane, as he would breeze into and out of briefings, training inspections, and short visits to the field, talked the talk, as the saying went. It was only when he had been assigned as Lane's aide-de-camp that Adderly found out that Lane couldn't walk the walk. 'The man,' he wrote his wife, the only person whom he could confide in and pour his heart out to, 'is a paper soldier. In a pinch, I fear he could cost us lives. Were I not at odds with my obligation to adhere to the stringent code of honor that depends on unflinching loyalty and adherence to orders that binds the officer corps into such a tight-knit professional group, I would have spoken to someone about what I saw a long time ago. But I fear, my love, that I, like many around me, am morally bankrupt and a coward hiding behind the words Duty, Honor, Country.'

Across from Adderly, Lane was beside himself. Peering through the windows of the closed doors of his aircraft, Lane tried to pick out which cluster of men on the ground were A Company, 3rd of the 511th. Every now and then, when he caught a glimpse of something he thought he understood, he'd say something, more to himself than to Adderly. On one pass, just as Frank Walters was finally getting his and Dan Krammer's company moving to where A Company was pinned, Lane mumbled, 'Too slow, too slow. Everyone is moving too damned slow down there.' Then to the pilot he yelled out, 'Take it around again, lower this time.'

As he had done for the past twenty minutes, the command pilot of Lane's aircraft banked to the right, swinging wide and away from the 3rd of the 511th's fight for a moment. Leveling out just this side of the river, the pilot headed east for a minute or two, then brought his aircraft around to the right until he had completed a 180-degree turn. Slowing, he dropped some and began another low, slow pass over the 3rd of the 511th, watching as he did so for the other aircraft that hovered over the area or darted this way and that in all directions. If he had any concern about enemy anti-aircraft fire, he didn't show it.

Of course, had he been aware of the pair of gunners smoothly tracking his helicopter with their 14.5mm machine guns every time he made an eastbound pass along the south side of the river, Lane's pilot would have been a little more attentive about what was going on down there. But since no one had been fired on all day, and he was there to serve Lane's needs come hell or high water, the command pilot concentrated on his flying and left all the thinking and ground watching to Lane. He was, after all, the division commander.

Had anyone bothered to ask the soldiers of A Company how long they had been out there in the middle of the landing zone under fire, none could have answered. It was without exception an eternity for each and every one of them. Only Cerro, still up and wandering about, seemed unfazed by their terrible predicament. It wasn't until he came across Second Lieutenant Tyler Wiezman, now wounded for the second time that day but still in command, that he begin to consider their overall situation. 'Colonel,' Wiezman yelled as Cerro approached, 'we've got smoke and willie pete coming in to cover our withdrawal.'

To Cerro, a man who had not considered the possibilities of surviving the day, the idea of leaving the landing zone was a revelation that he had to pause and think about. 'Where are you going to go, Tyler?'

Struck by Cerro's question, Wiezman looked at his commander and wondered if he had heard right. Blinking, he shook his head and pointed toward the northeast corner of the landing zone. 'Over there, away from the enemy and closer to C Company.'

Squatting between Wiezman and his radioman, Cerro studied the area that the young officer had pointed to, then looked back down at Wiezman. 'Yeah, that's probably a good idea. When are you going to move?'

Suddenly it dawned upon young Wiezman that his commander was out of it. Somehow, in all of the confusion, Lieutenant Colonel Cerro had lost track of the situation. Although he still appeared to be functioning after a fashion, Wiezman decided to take matters in his own hands. Over on the edge of the landing zone, where the enemy positions were, he saw that the smoke and white phosphorus were finally having the desired effect. Though tongues of small-arms fire still lashed out of the billowing white smoke, it was wild and very much diminished. Struggling to stand up, Wiezman looked up and down the ragged line of riflemen that represented A Company. From where he stood he could clearly tell which of the prone figures were still fighting and which were dead, dying, or severely wounded. What he couldn't tell in the confusion of the moment was which of his sergeants were still with him. Deciding to wait until they were under some sort of cover to sort that out and reorganize, he shouted, first to his left, and then to his right while he pointed, 'Everyone up and to the rear over there. Re-form in the tree line. Everyone up and to the rear. Re-form in the tree line.'

Slowly, in ones and twos, the survivors got to their feet and began to drift back in the direction that Wiezman was motioning them toward. Most, mindful of their stricken comrades, attempted to help those who couldn't respond. Grabbing the nearest wounded trooper, they dragged or threw him over their shoulder as best they could. Though there was no guarantee that all of the wounded were being policed up, Wiezman was grateful that there was still enough discipline left in the soldiers of his company to think about someone other than themselves.

Wiezman's actions and the response of the survivors of his company finally began to bring Cerro out of his despondency. Standing next to Wiezman, he noticed for the first time that his radioman wasn't with him. Somewhere, without realizing it, he had lost him to enemy fire. Knowing that this was no time to go around and look for him, he turned to Wiezman. 'Lieutenant, I've lost my radioman. I need to borrow one of yours. Can you manage things without a company radio net for a while?'

Looking at Cerro, Wiezman tried to hide the anger he felt. 'Sir, there isn't enough of a company left to make a radio net worthwhile.' Seeing the surprised look in Cerro's eyes, Wiezman realized that he had come on too strong. Not that he cared, it was true. A Company was now down to little more than two platoons. Still . . . Reaching behind him, he grabbed the first radioman his hand fell on. 'Smitty, put your radio on the battalion command net and go with the colonel. Now.'

Smitty looked at Wiezman. 'But, sir, it's already on the battalion push.'

'Okay, then just go now.'

When Smitty moved over next to Cerro, Cerro nodded. 'Great! I appreciate the loan. We're going to double-time over to the tree line and set up a battalion CP just inside the tree line, where the north and east side of the field come to a point. I'll get a hold of Frank Walters and we'll meet you there.'

With a nod, Wiezman acknowledged and Cerro turned to head off for the spot he'd designated. Glad to be rid of his commander, Wiezman got back to matters at hand. With a quick scan he checked out the area where the company had been pinned. Satisfied that everyone that was able to was up and headed back to the rear, he turned his back on the enemy positions and followed his radioman. As he limped along, he kept shouting to the ragged line ahead of him, 'Come on, get a move on. Keep it going over there. We don't have all day. Keep it moving.'

It wasn't until Hal Cerro and Smitty, running now ahead of the rest of the people clearing off the landing zone, reached the cover of the tree line and bounded in, without looking, that they realized that they were in trouble. Suddenly, without so much as a warning, a lone fighter of Number 3 Platoon, 27th Local Defense Company, jumped up off the ground right in front of Cerro and Smitty. Leveling his AK-74, he let fly, hitting Smitty in the stomach with a long burst that sent him sprawling backwards. Seeing that the first American was finished, the FARC fighter turned and prepared to fire on Cerro, now less than three feet away from him and closing fast.

CHAPTER 13

November 12

The shifting of A Company from the open toward the northeast corner of the landing zone caught just about everyone off guard. Involved in dealing with other concerns at that moment, no one besides Wiezman's soldiers and the fighters in Number 3 Platoon took notice of the vicious little firefight that had broken out at point-blank range at the edge of the tree line. Even the platoon commander of Number 3 Platoon, who had been waiting for the fleeing Americans to close, was taken aback when one of his people opened fire without waiting for his order.

He didn't know, of course, that the young fighter, a tenant farmer from birth, had seen that he had no real choice. Cerro and his radioman were only a second away from stepping on him. In the split second before he fired at the radioman, the fighter knew he was violating his platoon commander's order to wait until he gave the command. But there was no way he could comply with such an order. Like much of what had happened to him in the last forty-eight hours, the rebel fighter was reacting to the situation as best he could. That his action had initiated the engagement and cost the Number 3 Platoon its surprise was not his immediate concern. He hadn't made an error. It hadn't been a mistake, at least from his standpoint. For him it had been necessary, a simple matter of life and death. But that individual's decision and action gave the troopers of A Company several vital seconds in which to drop to the ground and spray the tree line they now faced with a wild but very intimidating volley of fire.

Hovering to the north of A Company's landing zone, Kozak was busy looking for the lead element of Frank Walters's combined command when the fight between A Company and Number 3 Platoon broke out. Caught up in her thoughts and concerned that Walters was taking too long, she was wondering if it would do any good to call to hurry him along when Pender, looking out the other side of the aircraft, called across to her. 'Captain, A Company's stepped in some shit. There's another enemy unit down there taking them under fire.'

Shifting herself in the nylon seat, Kozak looked out the right door of the helicopter. From where she was she could make out a ragged line of soldiers fifty meters or so short of the northeast corner of the A Company landing zone, shooting in the direction of that corner. At first she looked around the helicopter, then at the horizon, wondering if they had become disoriented and were south of the A Company LZ and not north, as she had assumed. That such a thing in the heat of battle could occur was not unheard of. But the river, the village, and the lingering smoke from fire caused by the barrage of smoke and white phosphorus rounds against A Company's first assailants told her that they were where they should have been.

That didn't make any difference, however, at that moment. Something new and unexpected had been added to the tactical equation and was at that moment threatening to finish the destruction of A Company. Once she was satisfied that she was seeing the true situation, Kozak blurted out a rare expression of surprise. 'Damn! Where did they come from?' Then, without hesitation, she pointed to Crippen. In a voice that betrayed no excitement, no confusion, Kozak began to issue instructions to her battle staff. 'Have one battery repeat the fire mission of smoke and white phosphorus and the other stand by for an immediate suppression of the new enemy positions. But tell them not to fire until I give the word. We don't have a good handle on the location of B and C companies.' Without waiting for an acknowledgment, Kozak turned to Pender. 'Contact Walters. Tell him what's going on and that we're preparing to fire artillery on the northeast corner of the landing zone. We need a solid fix on his lead element now. If necessary, have him pop smoke.' Finished with Pender, she looked over to Lieutenant Dietz. 'Marion, get on the radio with the attack helo liaison. Find out if they have anyone on station and ready to go in.' Though he was the intel officer, Dietz didn't hesitate. He did what needed to be done. With a nod that Kozak didn't see, since she was already looking back out the open door, he keyed the mike attached to the radio set on the attack helo liaison frequency and began to call.

With everyone in the cargo bay of the helicopter busy relaying information or requesting it, Kozak keyed the intercom to the pilot and pointed in the direction of the firefight. 'George, get me over there fast.' Then, with nothing further to do until Crippen, Walters, and the pilot responded to her flurry of orders, Kozak turned and leaned out the door as far as she could, trying hard to catch a glimpse of what was happening on the ground and wondering what she would do when she got there.

To the southeast, the brigade commander was on the ground talking to the commander of the 1st Battalion,

417th Infantry. Out of the loop for only several minutes, he would miss the crisis that was building as C. B. Lane's helicopter, now finishing its eastward run over the 3rd of the 511th's fight, prepared to make its turn. Adderly, Lane's aide-de-camp, saw the new firefight at the same moment that Pender did. Pointing, he keyed the intercom. 'General, looks like there's a new firefight erupting over in the 3rd of the 511th's area.'

Lane, who had been busying himself studying his map, looked up and in the wrong direction at first. Realizing his error, he leaned over to look where Adderly was pointing. Too late to see what his aide was talking about, Lane called out to his pilot, 'Take this thing around fast. I want to see what Jim is talking about.'

Jerking his collective over hard, the pilot threw both Lane and Adderly off balance as he began a banking turn that took them over the Meta River and its north bank.

On the north bank of the river, Hector Valendez, now standing next to one of the two 14.5mm anti-aircraft guns, heard the chatter of rifle and machine-gun fire to the southwest. The momentary silence that had followed the barrage of smoke and white phosphorus rounds on the Number 2 Platoon's position had been a good sign. Finally, he thought, they were disengaging. His plan was salvageable. That illusion, however, was shattered with the renewal of firing and the sudden and violent maneuvering of the helicopters over the area occupied by the 27th Company. Standing there listening to the last glimmer of hope for his hastily laid battle plans fade, Valendez became angry. Angry at the local-force commanders for ignoring his orders. Angry at being faced with his first military failure. Angry at his inability to reach out and do anything about it. But most of all, as he stood there and listened, he realized his greatest anger was aimed at the American helicopters, machines that gave their

commanders the mobility to flit about from one crisis
to the next, reacting and adjusting their plans with the
greatest of ease while he stood there rooted to the ground
like a tree. Hector Valendez was barely managing to hold
back his anger, clutching his fists until his knuckles turned
white as he did so, when the shadow of a helicopter passing
overhead fell upon him. He looked up and saw the under-
belly of the aircraft only yards away, and he lost whatever
control he had held on to up to that moment. Turning to
the gunner of the anti aircraft gun, Valendez thrust his arm
skyward and yelled, 'SHOOT THE BASTARD, DAMN
IT! SHOOT! KILL HIM. KILL THEM ALL.'

Hearing the order to fire, the anti-aircraft gunner
ignored Valendez's red, contorted face and his wild ges-
turing. Continuing his smooth and steady tracking of the
helicopter overhead, the gunner leaned into his sight,
made a minor adjustment, and squeezed the trigger until
his weapon began to buck, spewing out a stream of ball
and tracer rounds at C. B. Lane's helicopter.

Everyone on Lane's helicopter noticed the sudden series
of small jerks and muffled thuds but didn't pay any heed to
them until the co-pilot saw a stream of tracers go racing up
past his windshield. With understanding came a moment
of panic. 'Jesus Christ, we're under fire.'

The pilot, only a second behind in his partner's discovery, stiffened in his seat, then began to twist his head to
the left, to the right, then to the left again. He thought
for a split second about jerking his aircraft further into
its turn, but then decided against that. Unless he knew
for sure where he was taking fire from, that wouldn't be
a smart move. For all he knew, he could be maneuvering
himself and his crew into the enemy fire and not away
from it. Still frantically scanning the cockeyed horizon
while he held his aircraft in its tight bank, he yelled over
the intercom. 'Where? Where are we taking fire – '

The crew chief's shout drowned out the pilot's harried question. 'Christ! We're hit! We're being hit! Jesus H. Christ!'

The pilot, knowing this, jerked his head around to admonish his crew chief and tell him to stick his head out the damned window and see where the fire was coming from, but he cut himself short when he saw the crew chief jumping out of his seat, shifting his body wildly from one side to the other in an effort to avoid the shower of sparks and fragments that were filling the rear of the aircraft. The enemy had their range. Without hesitation, the pilot began to jerk the stick in the direction opposite to the sharp bank he was already executing, but not before he felt a sharp rap at the base of his spine as a round struck the bottom of his armored seat. Without realizing it, he shut his eyes and began to mutter repeatedly, 'Hail Mary, full of grace. Hail Mary, full of grace.'

The aircraft was just beginning to respond to the pilot's radical maneuver when he felt his joy stick go slack. At the same instant the earphones in his crewman's helmet came alive with the shrill voice of the co-pilot and the buzz of the malfunction warning alarms. Excited, he started to yell over and over, 'We're losing it! We're losing it!'

Popping his eyes open, he looked down at the bank of warning lights, now a crazy quilt of orange flashes. In his worst nightmare, during his most demanding simulation, he had never beheld such a sight. Again he closed his eyes and whispered a silent prayer as he leaned as far to his left as he could with the joy stick.

Behind him, C. B. Lane sat frozen. Even the warm stream of urine running down his pant legs failed to shake him from the paralysis that locked his mind and body in place. Across from him his aide, Captain Jim Adderly, was caught up in the confusion of the moment. Like the crew chief, he was turning this way and that, trying hard to take everything in while looking for some way of helping, for he too had been witness to the accuracy and effectiveness of the enemy anti-aircraft fire. Unlike the crew chief, he knew without having to think that jumping up and dancing from one side to the other would do no good. Unable to predict the pattern of the impacting rounds, a shift to the right could be the kiss of death rather than salvation. Only the pilot and co-pilot had any armor protection from ground fire. Everyone else, including the general, had to rely on luck and the skill of the pilot.

It was then, in a sudden flicker of thought, that Adderly turned to Lane. Ceasing his rapid but measured scanning of the aircraft's interior, Adderly looked straight at Lane. When his eyes focused on his superior, he was taken aback. Across from him the man he had so looked up to, the man who had a reputation as a severe and harsh master, brutal and uncompromising to anyone he felt was a lesser man, sat riveted in his seat, ashen-faced with unblinking eyes that bulged like an excited blowfish's. In an instant he took it all in, even the spreading darkness running down the general's leg. 'Oh, God,' Adderly shouted as he realized that Lane had been hit.

In a flash he unhooked his seat belt and pushed himself up from where he sat. The wild gyrations of the pilot didn't make this easy, causing Adderly to lurch forward. Losing his footing, Adderly had to alter his effort from one of trying to reach Lane to that of trying to keep from smashing into his wounded commander. Throwing his hands up and out to either side of Lane's head, Adderly barely managed to grab the side of the seat and stop himself from colliding with him. Hanging on to the sides of the seat, Adderly steadied himself, took a deep breath, then froze as his nostrils filled with the pungent odor of loose bowels and urine. Without thinking, he glanced down at Lane's crotch just as Lane, shaken out of his coma by Adderly's advance, looked up at his aide's face as it contorted itself in disgust.

Embarrassment quickly followed by anger were the first conscious feelings that Lane had as he stared into Adderly's eyes. 'What the fuck are you looking at, Captain?'

Shaken as he had never been shaken before, Adderly pushed himself away from Lane's face, now screwed up in rage and turning beet red. 'I – I thought – '

'For Christ's sake, don't think, Captain. Do something!'

'I thought you were hit. I was trying to see if I could – '

'I'm not hit. But I will be if you don't do something.'

Recovering his mental balance, yet now totally thrown by this experience, Adderly shot back without thinking. 'What? What in the hell do you want me to do, sir?'

It was the snide slur that Adderly used when he pronounced the word 'sir' that hit Lane the hardest. As much as Adderly's discovery of his momentary panic bothered him, Adderly's outburst and sneering rocked him more. Here was a subordinate, a mere captain, talking to him, a major general, like he was a rank second lieutenant. Without thinking, Lane lashed out at him. 'Call for artillery fire, you asshole. Get on the radio and get some suppressive fires on the enemy triple-A positions.'

In the heat of the moment, Adderly let his own anger get the better of him. He knew he didn't have any idea where the enemy fire was coming from. And he damn sure knew that Lane didn't either. With a sharpness that he didn't intend, Adderly shot back to Lane, 'Okay, General, where do you want me to put this fire?'

Though the question was a sound one, Adderly's response stoked Lane's growing anger. Intending to take Adderly to task, Lane glanced out the right side of the aircraft just in time to catch a glimpse of 14.5mm tracer rounds from the last volley of anti-aircraft fire arching back and down to earth toward the village of El Frío.

At that moment, as if a snapshot had been made in his mind, Lane took an association between the anti-aircraft fire and the village of El Frío.

Without hesitation, he thrust his arm in the direction of El Frío. 'There, the enemy anti-aircraft fire is coming from that village. I want every gun in range to blow that dump off the face of the earth.'

Looking over toward the village, then back at Lane, Adderly realized that his boss was regaining his equilibrium. Still the stern look on his face and the tough words couldn't hide the smell of piss and shit that filled the rear of the command-and-control aircraft. Though he still wore the stars, Adderly knew that from that moment on he would never be able to look at Lane as he had before.

Watching and waiting for his aide to respond, Lane could see the disdain well up in Adderly's eyes. He knew what it was about. He knew what Adderly was thinking. Though he couldn't do anything to change that, Lane was bound and determined to make sure that the pissant little captain across from him did what he was told. Leaning forward, Lane thrust his face at Adderly. 'Mister, I gave you a goddamned order. Now you do what I told you or you turn over your bars. Is that clear?'

For the longest of seconds Adderly paused and returned Lane's stare.

Above the chaos and confusion that A Company's firefight had degenerated into, Kozak and her tiny battle staff were racing to get the artillery fire that Wiezman and his shattered command so desperately needed. When Crippen was finished and he had a response from the fire support center controlling the two 105mm howitzer batteries, he tapped Kozak on her shoulder and shouted, 'Okay, Nancy, we got both batteries up and ready to fire nonstop, danger close.'

Kozak was still half hanging out the open door watching

the flashes of small-arms fire stabbing out from the tree line and the return fire from the ragged circle that A Company had formed in the open. Though greatly diminished, fire was now coming from the southern and western edge of the landing zone again, indicating that the enemy who had originally initiated the ambush had shaken off the effects of the last volleys of artillery. For a moment she wondered if this was what the Little Big Horn looked like at its climax. After shaking off the shudder which that thought sent down her spine, she lifted her left hand over her right shoulder, gave Crippen a thumbs-up, and yelled, 'Send it, now!' without bothering to take her eyes off the drama being played out below.

Though she didn't see it, and Crippen didn't bother to look up at her, he returned Kozak's thumbs up, keyed his radio hand mike, and ordered the batteries to fire at will. The response he was given to his last message, however, was not what he expected. Instead of saying 'On the way,' the radiotelephone operator at the fire support center gave Crippen a 'Wait. Out.'

Pulling the hand mike away from his ear for a moment, Crippen looked at it as if he didn't believe what he had just heard. Tucking it back up under the rim of his helmet, he keyed the hand mike and shot back. 'Wait. Out? What in the hell do you mean. Wait. Out? We got a whole bunch of people down there on the ground with their ass in a wringer that are going to die unless you shoot now! Do you copy? Over.'

There was no hesitation when the voice on the hand mike responded. 'Roger, Sky Rider Nine, I understand your situation. We have a priority mission that we have to fire before we shoot yours. How copy? Over.'

Crippen flushed. Though technically a member of the artillery battalion that was providing the fire support, he, like most fire support officers, trained with, lived with, and identified more with the infantry battalion to which he was assigned. Providing them the best fire support was his assigned duty. Taking care of the men and women of the 3rd of the 511th, people who had become his family since deploying to Colombia, was his passion. With all his might, Crippen mashed the push-to-talk button on his hand mike and shot back, 'PRIORITY? PRIORITY? What in the hell is more important than saving an entire company from getting wiped out?'

Bothered that he was being badgered like this, the radio operator's voice at the fire direction center was noticeably sharp when he replied, 'Eagle Six has a mission that overrides yours. Do you copy? Over.'

Crippen didn't know which angered him the most, the detached and unmistakably arrogant tone of the radio operator sitting some distance away in the safety of the artillery fire direction center or the division commander whose radio call sign was Eagle Six. Not that it mattered, for Crippen shot back, raising his voice noticeably as he dropped all efforts to hide his anger, 'What in the hell could Eagle Six have that is more important than saving the lives of his own men?' Then, before the radio operator could respond, Crippen managed to seize control of his anger. 'Listen, trooper, before you say another word, put Red Sky Six or Red Sky Three on. I want to talk to them.'

Looking about him, the radio operator saw the artillery battalion commander who used the call sign Red Sky Six sitting in front of the situation board being briefed by the duty officer. He paused for a moment, considering if he should bother his battalion commander or not, then decided to. Maybe the battalion commander would be able to get Captain Crippen, who was obviously quite hyper at the moment, to calm down or at least back off some. 'Colonel Day, Captain Crippen needs to talk to you, sir. He's pissed off about the CG's fire mission.'

There was a pause as Day, the artillery battalion commander, hesitated. He knew when the duty officer told him of the two missions that it wouldn't be long before the infantry battalion in contact would come up on the net and bitch about losing their fire support. For a moment Day even considered ignoring the call. He was a battalion commander, after all, and was under no real obligation to respond to Crippen's request. Ignoring Crippen by falling back on the prerogative of his rank, however, was a poor answer to his dilemma, and Day knew it. A subordinate was in a bind and wanted an answer, needed an answer, a real answer, right now. Twisting in his seat, Day picked up the radiotelephone hand mike that was attached to the remote set sitting on the duty officer's table, turned the volume on the speaker up, and keyed the push to talk button. 'Sky Rider Nine, this is Red Sky Six. Send your traffic. Over.'

Crippen, though somewhat calmed down when he heard Day, jumped right in, his voice betraying the pressure, stress, and excitement he felt as Kozak's helicopter continued to orbit about the desperate struggle that continued below them unabated. 'This is Sky Rider Nine. We need fires and we need them now. The Farcees have one whole company stuck in the open between two forces and are chewing them up. Without those fires a lot of good soldiers are going to die.'

Day felt his stomach begin to knot up. He knew that. He had known that when he had heard Crippen's initial call for fires come in not more than a minute or two before, followed immediately by Lane's order, relayed by his aide, to concentrate all fires on El Frío. Yet he had said nothing. Even when the duty officer looked over at him with a questioning look on his face that asked him what to do without having to speak, Day had done nothing. In the back of his mind he had hoped that he wouldn't need to do anything. That perhaps they could fire the mission on the village, satisfy the division commander, and then return to supporting the 3rd of the 511th. That was what he had hoped, for he, like every other battalion commander in the division, feared Lane. They feared the repercussions of crossing him. They feared having him drop in out of nowhere and degrade them in their own command post, in the presence of their own soldiers and staff. They feared having him and his staff turn on their commands and ride them into the ground, just as they had done to the 3rd of the 511th and other battalions that had in Lane's opinion screwed up. And secretly, hidden way back behind these other fears, there lurked another, the fear that Lane, whose star was still on the ascendant in the Army, would one day sit in judgment of their professional career.

None of this, of course, had anything to do with duty. Not really. It was all personal feelings, all perceptions and fears. Still, people cannot escape those fears and feelings. They can stuff them, deny them, even mask them, but they are always there waiting to crop up when circumstances permit. Even in a situation as clear-cut as this one, all of Day's thoughts and decisions were being tainted by such personal fears and apprehensions, for the circumstances laid bare every aspect of his soul, good and bad. Only a man with blind dedication to duty and moral courage can overcome, in a situation like the one Day found himself in at that moment, his own shortfalls, real and imagined.

Crippen was still waiting for a response from Day when Kozak, noticing that they weren't receiving the fires she had requested, turned to face Crippen. 'Pete, what's taking so damned long? Are we going to get the fires or not?'

Embarrassed by the perceived ineptitude of his own parent artillery battalion and confused by what was going on between Lane and Day, Crippen moved the radio hand mike away from his mouth as he shrugged. 'Don't know for sure. I think they're debating who gets priority of fires.'

Not knowing about Lane's priority mission or who 'they' were, Kozak's eyes flew open as her face dropped in surprise. 'Trying to decide? Why in the hell do they need to decide anything? We're the only people in contact, aren't we?'

The last part of her comment was directed at Pender. Listening to the conversation, Pender shouted out, 'That's right, Captain. Except for some anti-aircraft fire directed at a helicopter over there, north of the river, we're the only people being shot at.'

Though Pender was pointing out his door, to the north, Kozak ignored him after he had confirmed her suspicions. Moving in from the door, she leaned closer to Crippen. 'Here, give me that hand mike.'

Peter Crippen could see the anger in her eyes. He had no doubt that if she got on the artillery fire support net and started talking to Day, she would say something that everyone would regret. Though he himself was angry and ready to dump on Day for what he believed was indecision and moral cowardice, Crippen knew that in these circumstances it was better if he handled the artillery battalion commander. Raising his hand to wave her off, he was about to tell her that he could deal with it when he heard Day's response. Looking down at the floor of the helicopter, Crippen shoved the index finger of his left hand into his exposed ear and squeezed the receiver end of the radio hand mike tight against his right ear.

Without asking, Kozak and everyone else in the cargo bay of the helicopter knew that Crippen was listening to someone on the radio. Silently they waited. Finally Crippen pulled his finger out of his ear and with his free hand gave Kozak a thumbs-up. After acknowledging the call he had been listening to so intently, he looked up at Kozak and smiled. 'Okay. We're in business. Colonel Day says you got both batteries as long as you need them.'

Still not understanding everything that had gone on

between Crippen and the fire direction center, or Lane's priority mission, Kozak was unimpressed with Crippen's minor victory. With hardly a change in expression, she shot back at him, 'Good, now get those fucking guns shooting, *now*.' With that, she slid over to the open door again, pausing only long enough to grab the door gunner's arm and shout to him. 'Shoot, damn it. Use that gun and draw some fire.'

The door gunner, a young kid not more than twenty, looked at Kozak. What did she mean, draw fire? he thought. Did she mean she wanted him to shoot at the enemy so that they would shoot at them? That was crazy, crazy. But as he watched the female captain continue to slide over to the open door, stopping only when the loose seat belt about her waist snapped taut, he realized that everybody was getting a little crazy, everyone in this helicopter. The pilots were whipping the bird about like mad, flying lower and faster than he had ever seen them do. The officers and sergeants on the radios were chattering a mile a minute, cursing and screaming at each other and other officers and sergeants over the radio. And the enemy, they seemed to be everywhere down there, chewing up those poor bastards on the ground. It was crazy. But maybe it all made sense? Maybe these officers knew what they were doing?

What the hell, the door gunner thought. Everyone else was going nuts. He might as well join in. Leaning into his gun, he scanned the landscape flashing below him looking for targets. When he saw movement in the bush along the tree line, he braced his arms, squeezed the trigger, and let loose a long burst from his gun.

Just inside the edge of the tree line in the northeast corner Harold Cerro opened his eyes. It took him a moment to realize that he was lying on his back. It took him even longer to realize that he had been shot. But when he finally did, the spasms of pain that swept though his body were horrific. Where he had been hit, how bad it was, how long he had been there, and many other questions were all mysteries to Cerro that would have to wait until the waves of pain that assaulted his brain subsided.

At first Cerro did nothing, did not even think. He simply lay there looking up at trees, waiting. Only after the passing of the dark underside of a helicopter clipping treetops and spraying machine-gun fire out of both sides as it flashed overhead, did Cerro begin to wonder what was going on. Slowly, painfully slowly, he asked himself what it was he was waiting for. When that thought finally managed to take root, he began to listen and look about. He was not alone. From every direction came the crack, chatter, and pop of small-arms fire, rifle and light machine guns. There were many different caliber weapons being fired, some of which Cerro didn't recognize offhand. While this bothered him, the idea that the reports of weapons that were strange to his ears were drowning out the familiar pop-pop-pop of the American-made rifles began to bother him. He was closer, he figured, to the enemy than to his own people. But how far? And why?

Slowly he rolled his head to one side, then the other. Though there was pain, it wasn't as bad as he had feared. To his right there was nothing, at least nothing that he could see, since there was a thick tree root less than a foot from his head that blocked his view. When he twisted his head around in the opposite direction, his eyes fell upon the soles of a pair of shoes two feet from his face. He knew right away that whoever wore those shoes wasn't an American. The soles lacked the intricate stamped pattern common to combat boots. Intrigued, Cerro thought for a moment, then with an effort lifted his head up off the ground and peered over the toes of the shoes.

Surprisingly, he was able to keep his head up and look about. Though it was painful, the pain now had receded to a numb throbbing that stayed in the background, sufficient to remind him that he had been shot but not enough to stop him from continuing his slow investigation of the area around him. The man or, more correctly, Cerro thought, boy he was looking at was definitely a Farcee. Letting his head drop back down to the ground, Cerro thought about this for a moment. Images of the last few seconds before he lost consciousness began to tumble about in his mind. During this, he remembered that he had run into the woods accompanied by a radioman. Hoisting his head up again, he turned to the right and looked over the tree root.

He was there, lying face down, unmoving. Both arms were tucked in tight to his sides and his hands were hidden under his body, as if he had been clutching something close to his chest. His wound, Cerro figured. He was clutching his wound. What he was doing, however, soon became academic for the moment as the earth beneath Cerro heaved up and quivered. The shattering blast of artillery impacting near at hand startled Cerro for a moment, but then he relaxed when he concluded that it was a good fifty or more meters away. Again he let his head drop back to the ground. He was safe, he thought. There was no danger for now. Though surrounded by the chatter of enemy small-arms fire, none of the rebel fighters seemed to be interested in him or the other bodies on either side. And the artillery was far enough away that he didn't need to worry about it.

That thought, however, triggered a new chain of thoughts. Cerro's mind, still racked with an occasional spasm of pain, was far from being fully functional. So each idea had to queue up behind another and wait to be dealt with in its turn. In this way Cerro was able to piece together as clear a picture of his plight as was possible. He and his radioman had made it to the tree line in the northeast corner of the landing zone. They had run into a

Farcee fighter. The Farcee had shot the radioman. Cerro had shot the Farcee, but not before the Farcee had turned his gun on him. And now he was still there in the middle of the Farcee position, wounded, listening to the firefight. It was these last two thoughts that stuck in Cerro's mind. If he was in the middle of their position, he thought, and the artillery wasn't hitting here, it was missing the enemy.

Without any need to consider his situation, Cerro lifted his head again and looked over to the radioman. The radio on his back, little more than an arm's reach away, looked like it had survived the ordeal unscathed. For the first time since regaining his consciousness, Cerro began to move. And although his efforts were rewarded with pain, Cerro had a purpose in life now, a quest. Focusing all of his attention on the radio, Cerro began to inch his way toward it.

Straining against her seat belt, Nancy Kozak was for the moment helpless to do anything more than she was doing. It was now up to the artillery fire and Frank Walters to save A Company. That, however, would take five minutes, maybe more, according to Walters. In the meantime, A Company continued to lie out in the open with nowhere to hide, suffering punishing fire from two directions.

Kozak was about to key the intercom to ask Sergeant Pender if the attack helicopters were finished rearming yet when a familiar yet unexpected voice came up on the battalion net. 'Sky Rider Three, this is Sky Rider Six. Adjust Fire. Over.'

The shock of hearing Cerro's voice, the first time she had heard him since A Company went in, caused Kozak to bolt upright in her seat. Jamming the push-to-talk button on the long cord that connected her air crewman's helmet to the radio, Kozak responded. 'Sky Rider Six, this is Sky Rider Three. Where are you? What's your status? Over.'

Ignoring her question, Cerro started to give her directions. 'This is Six. Your fire mission is missing the enemy's main body. From the gun-target line, drop five zero, left five zero, and fire for effect. How copy? Over.'

Puzzled, Kozak looked down over to the tree line and thought for a moment about where that correction would put the strike of the rounds. When she had a mental picture in her mind, she rekeyed the push-to-talk button. 'Six, this is Three. We are already firing danger close. If we bring it in closer, A Company might be hit.'

There was no pause as Cerro responded. 'They're already being hit. Your fires are missing the enemy main body. They are right on the edge of the tree line, in the open and exposed. Either make that correction or stop firing. The artillery isn't hitting a damned thing, and the Farcees aren't bothered by it. That's an order, Captain.'

Though she paused, concerned about what Cerro was telling her to do, Kozak dropped it and turned to Crippen. 'Pete, have the battery that's firing on the northeast corner of the tree line adjust fire. From the gun target line, drop five zero, left five zero.'

Without hesitation, Crippen looked at his map, then out the door of the helicopter, then up at Kozak. 'No way. You'll hit A Company.'

Kozak, not wanting to argue, leaned closer to Crippen. 'I know what the hell I'm doing. Make the correction and fire for effect, now.'

Things, Crippen knew, were desperate. But he wondered if they were that desperate. Maybe they were, he thought. He wasn't on the battalion radio net, so he wasn't sure what was going on down there. With little more than a shrug, he turned his attention to calling in the adjustment of the fires and prayed that Kozak knew what she was doing.

*   *   *

When Lane saw the impacts of artillery over in the 3rd of the 511th's area and not on El Frío, he threw a fit. The full force of that rage, of course, was directed at Adderly, the person who had made the call for fire. 'What in the hell is going on, Captain? Didn't I tell you to have the artillery take out that town?'

From where he sat, Adderly looked at Lane. At that moment he wasn't sure what he felt. Was it anger? Was it loathing? Was it disgust? Odds were it was a combination of all of them and more. Regardless of what was driving him, Adderly felt like taking his helmet off and throwing it at Lane, telling him to call his own stupid and pointless fire mission in. For even though he, like everyone else in the command-and-control bird had been shaken by being hit by ground fire, Adderly knew that the 3rd of the 511th was in deep trouble and they needed the fire support.

Still Adderly held his temper and he held his tongue. Though he was a little afraid to unclench his teeth, he managed to respond to Lane's outburst with a controlled and very tempered answer. 'The mission was called in, sir, as you directed.' He thought about adding on that perhaps there was a more important mission that needed to be fired, but didn't. Hell, Adderly thought, that's got to be obvious, even to Lane.

That, of course, was an assumption, just as Lane assumed that the fire had come from a town no longer occupied by the enemy. Adderly's assumption that the tracers he had seen had been arching up instead of streaking away reinforced this collective assumption, and without anyone from the helicopter's crew able to confirm or verify, even had they been asked, Adderly deferred to both Lane's judgment and orders. So circumstances continued to run their own misguided course.

Lane, shaken by what was his first near-death experience, was too excited to leave things stand as they were.

He had given an order and it was going to be carried out. 'Get me the artillery fire direction center.'

Knowing what Lane was about to do, Adderly said nothing. It wouldn't make any difference if he did. In the past Lane had taken great joy in berating battalion commanders over the radio, and this, he figured, was going to be just another one of those whipping sessions. When he had switched Lane over to the fire direction radio net, Adderly keyed the intercom between him and Lane. 'Your radio is set, sir. The call sign for the artillery is Red Sky.'

The only response Lane gave Adderly was a glare before he mashed the push-to-talk button. 'Red Sky Six, this is Eagle Six. Over.'

During the pause that followed Lane's call, Adderly looked away from his boss and tried to imagine the scene in the fire direction center. There would be a silence for the briefest of moments while the radiotelephone operator sat upright in his seat, turned to find his battalion commander, and then in a sonorous monotone announced that the division commander wanted to speak to him. With a slow yet deliberate pace, the battalion commander would walk over to the radio like a condemned man walking the last mile. How many of them, Adderly wondered, were tempted to have the radiotelephone operator make an excuse for them, to tell Lane that they weren't there or were unavailable? Probably all of them, he thought. Yet they always answered. They had to. Postponing the event would only make things worse. Besides, Lane's lack of professionalism and compassion in his dealings with subordinates didn't mean that they could in turn ignore protocol and etiquette. So they always answered, just as Lieutenant Colonel Day did. Still Adderly noted that he didn't, or wouldn't, use Lane's call sign. Instead Day simply keyed the radio and announced, 'This is Red Sky Six. Over.'

When Lane spoke, he dropped all call signs, all radio-telephone procedures. 'Did you or did you not receive the fire mission I sent you?'

'This is Red Sky, affirmative. Over.'

'Then why in the hell did you choose to ignore it?'

For a second, a very brief second, Day pondered his answer. He even considered not answering at all such a patently absurd question. Christ, he thought as he stood in his own fire direction center, didn't that man know what was going on?

The pause was too long for Lane. He jumped back on the radio. 'I asked you a question. Either answer me or put the next man in your chain of command on the radio.'

Tilting his head back, Day took a deep breath and responded. 'This is Red Sky Six. We acknowledged your mission and will fire it as soon as we complete the missions going in to support Sky Rider. Over.'

'To hell with Sky Rider. They have nothing to do with my fire mission. I am giving you an order, Colonel, and I expect you to carry it out. Do you understand?'

Day was now becoming angry. Little by little he was losing his ability to contain himself. 'This is Red Sky. I say again, we *will* fire your mission as soon as we complete those fire missions in progress. Sky Rider is in serious trouble. I must complete those missions before I can – '

'Mister, you ain't going to be able to finish anything. You put your next in command on – '

Without another word, Day leaned over, turned the radio off, and walked away, leaving his staff where they stood or sat stunned into silence.

Confusion was fast becoming total. Though the artillery fire and corrections requested were coming in, Crippen yelled to Kozak that he had lost contact with the fire direction center. Switching over to the batteries' internal net, he prepared to make any additional corrections that might be called for. Pender added to Kozak's concerns, announcing that the attack helicopters were still several minutes out and that he had been unable to raise either the brigade commander or his operations officer. They were, he told her, in some kind of meeting somewhere in the 417th's area.

Turning her back to her battle staff, Kozak looked down at the ground, grasping the intercom-radio transmit button in her right hand. With her left hand balled up in a tight fist, she absentmindedly pounded her left thigh again and again. Though it hurt, and eventually would leave a deep dark bruise, she didn't notice it. She was, like everyone else in the cargo bay of her helicopter, in a high state of excitement.

Below her she could see the soldiers of A Company. At that moment that was all that mattered to her, all that mattered to anyone in the helicopter. Though she was doing all that she could, Kozak felt the urge to undo her seat belt and leap out onto the ground just meters below them and rush forth into a fight that was just as chaotic and confusing as the one she and her staff were waging on the radio nets.

In the midst of this, Second Lieutenant Wiezman finally came up on the battalion radio net. 'Sky Rider Three, this is Alpha One Six. The enemy in the northeastern corner has broken contact. Request you shift fires to cover our rear. Over.'

Though she was glad to hear that, Kozak delayed responding to Wiezman's request at first. 'Alpha, this is Sky Rider. Are in contact with or near Sky Rider Six? Over.'

'Negative, Sky Rider. He took off with one of my radiomen before we were hit the second time. Over.'

'Where did he go? Can you reach him? Over.'

'He went over to the northeast corner of the woods,

where I was taking the company. I think he's down. Over.'

Wiezman's last transmission sent a shiver down Kozak's spine. 'Dear God in heaven.'

Crippen, hearing her yell,' reached out and tapped her on the shoulder. 'What happened? What's wrong?'

Turning to face him, she yelled, 'Have the battery firing on the northeast corner cease fire immediately.'

'What about the other mission, should we keep – '

'Yes, Pete, yes, keep firing it. Just lift fires on the northeast corner. Now.'

She was about to rekey the radio when a strange voice came in over the net. 'Sky Rider Six, this is Eagle Six. What in the hell are you doing down there?'

Kozak didn't make the connection. She had no idea who this Eagle Six was and had no intention of finding out. Cramming the push-to-talk button down as hard as she could with her right thumb, she shouted at the radio boom mike hanging in front of her lips, 'Unknown station, this is Sky Rider Three. Get off this net. *Now*!'

There was no pause. As soon as Kozak let up on the push-to-talk button, Lane jumped back on. 'This is General Lane. Who the hell am I talking to?'

Just as she was about to respond, Crippen yelled from behind her. 'That's the last volley going in on the northeast corner now.'

Keying her radio, Kozak yelled out over the net to Wiezman. 'Alpha Six, go, go, go. That's the last of the artillery fire to your front. Move out now.'

'Sky Rider Three, we're – '

Wiezman's transmission, made over a lower-powered man-portable radio, was drowned out by Lane's transmission, which was made using powerful helicopter-mounted radios. 'Listen, soldier, I don't know who in the hell you are, but I want to speak to your battalion commander right now.'

Enraged by these senseless interruptions by someone whose call sign or voice she didn't recognize, Kozak shot back without pausing to think, 'I don't give a shit who in the hell you are. Get off my net and stay the hell off it. Out.'

Raising her left hand level with her shoulder, Kozak brought it down onto her thigh with all the force she could muster, screaming out the door, 'GO! GO! GO!' as she watched A Company's ragged line of riflemen rise off the ground and cover the short distance between them and the northeast corner of the woods.

Alone in his thoughts, Lane considered having his pilot take them over to where the 3rd of the 511th was and ripping Sky Rider Three a new asshole right then and there. But he couldn't do that. The dampness in his crotch and the smell of loose bowels told him that he wouldn't be able to leave his helicopter even if he could safely land over there. He was pondering what to do when Adderly broke the silence. 'General, the pilot says we've taken too much damage to hang around here. We need to leave now or we won't be able to make it back to Bogotá.'

He was about to object, but decided that it would be pointless. There wasn't anything to be gained by staying here and watching this screwed-up operation any longer. No, he thought, someone's going to pay for trashing my plan, and they're going to pay big. Lane keyed his intercom button. 'Fine, let's go back. And while we're headed back, contact Division. I want Colonel Webb to meet me at the airport the moment we touch down.'

Adderly looked into Lane's eyes. In those eyes he saw anger and rage. There was no need for him to ask or even to wonder why Lieutenant Colonel Frederick Webb, the division's staff judge advocate, was being summoned. Lane, Adderly knew, was going to have a public hanging. Some poor schmuck, he thought, was going to get screwed, blued, and tattooed simply because they did their job and Lane was an asshole. Though he didn't like it, Adderly knew that this was the way things were, and that there wasn't a damned thing he could do about it. All he could do was the same thing everyone who hated Lane did, put in your time, do what you had to do, and endure. After acknowledging Lane's order and telling the pilot to head on back, Adderly turned away from him and watched the battle west of El Frío as it faded in the distance. Yeah, he thought, someone is going to hang.

CHAPTER 14

November 15

It was fitting that the day was heavily overcast with an occasional spasm of drizzle when the advance elements of the 3rd Battalion, 511th Infantry, assembled on the military airfield outside Bogotá. Any anticipated joy or relief in having finally been rotated to that city as the divisional reserve had been crushed by the weight of the circumstances that put them there. For most, it was exhaustion and the delayed stress of battle just beginning to assert itself. It was a strange sensation, one that was as much mental as it was physical. Others, too many, in the words of one first sergeant, were finally allowing themselves to mourn the loss of a close friend or a well-loved sergeant or officer.

Foremost among this last category was Lieutenant Colonel Harold Cerro, killed by an artillery barrage that he had called in on top of himself. As Jan Fields-Dixon went from company to company, soldier to soldier, within the battalion, she found that the feelings over the circumstances surrounding the death of Cerro varied. Company A, which

benefited directly from his sacrifice, was especially torn up.
Second Lieutenant Wiezman, who had thought that Cerro
had lost it during the chaotic rush from the landing zone,
had harbored a great deal of anger at the time Cerro had
taken one of his radiomen away from him. Though he
told no one of this, the remorse and guilt he felt at having
doubted such a man and defiled his name, if only in his
mind, troubled Wiezman greatly, leaving him withdrawn,
sullen, and badly shaken. The sergeants in A Company
were less troubled by such considerations, though they
still mourned Cerro in a practical sort of way. 'If there
had been any other way of it,' one sergeant told Jan, 'I
would be really upset. But we were at the end of our
rope. He made all the difference, Ms. Fields. Out in the
LZ walking around in the middle of the firefight, getting
people to hang in there and return fire, in the end he did
what he had to do. As hard as it may be for some people
to understand, he had no choice. Not really. He picked
dying so the rest of us could live. It ain't fair. And it ain't
right. But hell, lady, what is anymore?'

That wasn't necessarily the view taken by others within
the battalion. Many felt that Cerro was forced to take
such a radical step because of A Company's ineptness.
Few spoke about it, at least not publicly. One trooper in
C Company, who had landed north of A Company at the
same time, felt very keenly about this, however, and didn't
care who he told about it. When Jan shoved a mike in
the young soldier's face, he just started to talk, becoming
more and more angry as he did so. 'We landed in a hot
LZ, just like them, and didn't have half the problems they
had. Neither did we leave the colonel in such a bind that
he got himself killed. I'm not calling those people over
there in A Company a bunch of losers. Hell, I'm even
friendly with a couple of guys there. But they got the
colonel killed because they screwed up. And that pisses
me off, big time.'

Regardless of their opinion, all were united in the collective heartfelt feeling of personal loss. Though there would be another battalion commander, the men and women in the battalion knew there would never be another Harold Cerro. His passing more than anything marked the loss of innocence. For if he, a soldier of his drive and reputation, could be killed, then all of them could. Even the youngest troopers in the ranks now realized that they were all mortal, and unless things changed, few if any would come out of this war alive.

Against this somber background, Major General C. B. Lane delivered what many felt was the coup de grâce to what little confidence and self-respect the soldiers in the battalion had when it was announced that Captain Nancy Kozak would be charged with disobedience of a direct order, conduct unbecoming an officer, and disrespect to a superior officer.

Even the manner in which she had been notified of the charges infuriated the soldiers of the battalion. Few had little doubt that the occasion had been intentionally staged that way, for the Judge Advocate General, or JAG, officer arrived at the airfield just as Kozak was assembling the battalion. Refusing to be delayed from the execution of his duties, the JAG officer walked up to Kozak, standing in front of the survivors of the 3rd of the 511th, and presented himself with little fanfare, no warning, and a voice that even troopers in the rear rank could hear. 'Captain Nancy Kozak, by order of the commanding general of the 11th Air Assault Division, it is my duty to inform you of the following charges that have been brought against you.' Taking great care, the JAG officer then read them one by one as Kozak stood before him ashen-faced and too stunned to react.

Only a growing murmur from the ranks of combat veterans behind broke the reading of the charges. From the rear of the battalion, the command sergeant major was shaken from his shock when he heard the voices of the soldiers become louder and their cries of astonishment begin to slowly turn into sharp comments of rage sprinkled with muted threats. Though his soldiers' response mirrored his sentiments, he kept his feelings and reactions in check. He had heard of such humiliations being played out in the '70s and '80s but never, in his wildest dreams, did he expect to be a witness to such a spectacle. Responding in the same professional manner that Cerro had taught the officers and noncommissioned officers to react when faced with a crisis, the command sergeant major called out in the best parade-ground voice he could manage, 'Silence in the ranks. Silence in the ranks. First sergeants, get control of your people and keep them quiet.'

Watching this spectacle from one side, Jan Fields-Dixon neither understood what was going on nor how exactly to deal with it. Only JT had the presence of mind to keep the tape running, catching as best he could the battalion's response to this spectacle and Kozak's reactions. They were, JT thought as he watched through the eye of the camera, surprisingly subdued. Kozak's only comment to the JAG officer when he finished was a question. 'Am I under arrest?'

Showing no sign that what he had just done had any effect on him, the JAG officer shook his head. 'No, you are not under arrest. You will continue with your assigned duties until further notice. Do you have any questions at this time concerning the charges being preferred against you?'

Whether she meant it as an insult, or whether she reacted in an effort to keep from saying something she would later regret, Kozak turned away from the JAG officer and faced the battalion, still being held in check by threats from the senior noncommissioned officers. Slowly she scanned the battalion from left to the right, taking deep breaths as she struggled to contain the anger and tears that welled up inside of her. Finally, when she was ready, she held her head up and, looking into the vacant sky above the heads of her soldiers, she shouted her last order. 'Company commanders, take charge of your units.' As they saluted, she stepped off to her right and marched briskly away. Only her training and discipline kept her from fleeing the scene of the single greatest humiliation she had ever experienced or imagined.

Later, off camera, the battalion command sergeant major summed it up best when he told Jan Fields-Dixon that Lane's decision to prosecute Kozak was 'the dumbest thing that he could have done. Hell, he might as well put a gun to every trooper's head in this outfit now and pull the trigger, 'cause no matter how this comes out, he's lost himself a battalion.' In the process of talking to the leaders and soldiers of the 3rd of the 511th, Jan began to see what the command sergeant major meant.

While there was a great difference between how the soldiers felt about the death of their battalion commander and the circumstances that led up to it, to a man they knew that what Lane was trying to do to Kozak was wrong. That he was doing it, and that no one seemed to be stopping it, shattered what little morale and stability the troopers individually and collectively had managed to hang on to up to that point. So strongly did they feel about what Lane was doing to Kozak and them, few had any qualms about expressing their opinions before Jan's camera. 'It makes no sense,' Captain Frank Walters told Jan. 'He was wrong. Dead wrong. His treatment of this battalion after the big ambush in September was wrong, his handling of the artillery over El Frío was wrong, and his decision to bring charges against Nancy was wrong. That he doesn't realize it and that no one above him is doing anything to stop this insanity is, is . . .' Unable to find the right word to express himself, Walters stopped. He looked down at the ground, shook his head once, shrugged, then turned and walked away from Jan and her camera crew without another word.

And that was the way it stood that morning as helicopter after helicopter brought the soldiers of the 3rd of the 511th in from the field, shattered in spirit and body.

Sitting alone in her darkened office that night, Jan didn't quite know how she was going to approach Scotty on the matter of Nancy Kozak. In all the years she had been with Scotty, first as a lover, then as his wife, Jan had always made sure that neither one took advantage of the other. How easy, Jan knew, it would have been on numerous occasions to dig for or pry information from Scotty. What an advantage she would have had, being married to a living legend who knew just about everyone worth knowing in the Army and who was privy to information few had access to. The cost, though, to her pride as well as their relationship, would have been far too heavy. Both of these, not to mention her career, meant a great deal to Jan. When asked by a young female just entering the field of television news which was more important to her, Jan looked at the bright young face set in an expression that showed how deadly earnest she was and smiled. 'Please don't ever ask me to answer that question, for I really don't think I could, not honestly.' Tonight, however, as she looked at the phone and waited, Jan began to fear that she was going to have to answer that question soon. How much better, she thought, this would be if Scotty were here in Colombia instead of in Washington going ten rounds with the bureaucrats, which was how he described his frequent trips north.

When the phone finally did ring, it startled her. Jolted from her deep, troublesome thoughts, Jan shot forward and reached for the phone. Though she had no doubt that it was Scotty returning her call, she answered it as she answered all calls, in the office or at home. 'Jan Fields speaking. How may I help you?'

When Scott spoke, his voice betrayed his exhaustion. 'Sorry, Jan, about calling so late. I was called back by the chief for another round of discussions with the Secretary of Defense. People are starting to get really worried up here about what's going on down there.' It was not only the way he sounded, harried and worried that caught her off guard. He was often worried as of late. It was the fact that he had blurted out, without any prodding on her part, who he had met with and their concerns that really took Jan aback. Things had to be bad if he was getting that careless, Jan thought. In the next instant, as Scott continued to recount some of the people he had briefed that day, Jan began to wonder if this was a good time to approach Scotty. Turning this thought over in her head while Scott continued to rattle on, Jan didn't hear much until he was about finished. 'I just got into the hotel and saw the message light on the phone flashing. The front desk screwed up the message, naturally, and it took my tired old brain a few minutes to make sense of it. But I'm sure you didn't have me call back just so that you could listen to the pre-senility rantings and ravings of a broken-down old tanker. What do you have for me, babe?'

Jan hated it when he called her babe, hated it with a passion. Ignoring it, since she saw no point in putting him on the defensive before it was necessary, Jan prepared to respond, but paused. She was still unsure how to broach the subject. Though she could be as devious as the best of her co-workers in twisting and turning a conversation until she eased gently into the heart of the matter at hand, Jan didn't feel up to such manipulations. Nor was this a matter that she felt comfortable playing with. Instead, she opted to launch into it with all the grace of a cavalry charge. 'You've heard about Nancy Kozak.'

Not sure what she was talking about, Scott waited before feeling his way into the discussion. 'You mean about what happened to her battalion outside of El Frío? Yes, Jeff

Worsham has been keeping me well posted on operations down there.'

'That's not exactly what I'm talking about, although the issue at hand is a direct result of that fight.'

Now Jan could hear an audible drawing in of breath before Scott answered. With a voice that was more authoritarian than conversational, he began to inch his way forward into a position. 'Jan, I have been informed that there may be charges brought against Captain – '

'No, Scotty, there's no maybe about it. They have been dropped on her today. In fact, she no sooner stepped off the helicopter, bringing the survivors of her battalion in from the field, than wham, she gets informed by the division staff judge advocate himself, in front of her entire command, that she's under investigation for a laundry list of stupid charges.'

'Jan,' Scott cut in, 'disobeying a direct order from a superior ranking officer in battle is not a stupid charge. The Army takes obedience and chain of command rather seriously, especially in the middle of a fight.'

Scott's tone and what she perceived as his efforts to lecture her angered Jan. It was a natural reaction, for Jan hated it when a man, any man, got on his high horse and spoke to her like that. Forgetting in her moment of blind anger that Scott was her husband, and not some nondescript information officer who was giving her a bad time, Jan shot back. 'I talked to those soldiers in Nancy's battalion, and what she did was right. The company on the landing zone, A Company, I think, was pinned down and badly cut up, facing annihilation. If she hadn't hung tough and told Lane where to get off, how many of those soldiers would still be alive today? Can you tell me that, mister?'

'Can you tell me, Ms. Fields, with any degree of certainty, that what Lane was trying to do was wrong? Have you spoken to Lane? Have you spoken to the brigade commander? Were you there?'

'I didn't have to be there. I don't have to be shown every day that Major General C. B. Lane is a moron who doesn't know his ass from a hole in the ground.'

'Jan, Jan, wait a minute, just hold on here. Listen to what you're saying. You've already passed judgment on Lane when it's not him on trial. It's going to be Captain Nancy Kozak and her actions in relation to Lane over El Frío, and not Lane's personality or his past record that will be brought to question. Kozak's actions, and only her actions, will be judged in a court of law.'

'So you have no intention of doing anything, do you?'

Half angry, half frustrated, Scott tried pleading with her. 'Jan, what do you expect from me? I have no authority in this matter. I'm not in the chain of command. Anything that I do would be inappropriate and unethical. You know that.'

Though she heard the tone of his voice, Jan didn't back off. She was angry and to a large extent disappointed. 'Scott Dixon, don't talk to me about ethics. What you and Big Al Malin did in Mexico was unethical as hell and you know it. Besides, speaking of Mexico, how can you stand to turn your back on Nancy Kozak? She saved my life while – ' She was about to say 'while you sat on your ass' but managed to check herself.

During that pause Scott jumped in. 'Jan, please stop before you say something you and I will both regret. And for God's sake, listen to what you're saying.'

'And what's that supposed to mean, Dixon?'

'Jan Fields, you're acting like a woman.'

Though rather oafish, Scott's last comment had its desired effect as Jan took a moment to think about what she was saying. After giving her that moment, Scott continued. 'You've lost your objectivity in this whole affair. I've forgotten nothing, not a damned thing about what Nancy Kozak did for you in Mexico. But she did exactly what she was ordered to do. She did her duty, just like any other officer in her place would have done. That you are grateful to her for it is natural. That you have become great friends, because you are both independent and professional women, is also natural. But you can't deal with Kozak as you would anyone else. Nancy Kozak is an officer in the Army, bound and obligated to a system that requires strict and unquestionable loyalty.'

'Even,' Jan jumped in, 'if that loyalty is to a man more responsible for the death of his own soldiers than the enemy?'

Jan's refusal to give ground on this issue and her last comment finally broke Scott's restraint. With a roar he thundered back, '*YES*, damn it. Even to Major General, By-God C. B. Lane. So long as Kozak wears the uniform and draws the pay, she lives and dies by the rules she willingly and freely obligated herself to, just like Hal Cerro.'

It wasn't Scott's tone or his argument that finally checked Jan's fury. It was the simple mention of Cerro's name that caused her to halt. Though there was no appreciable break in the conversation, when Jan came back her tone had changed from that of an angry lioness to one of quiet and concern. 'Did you . . . were you able to talk to . . .'

Sensing the change in his wife, Scott didn't wait for her to continue. Like her, when he spoke again, his voice was subdued, almost hushed. 'Yes, I spoke to Kay today.' He was about to say more but couldn't think of anything appropriate to say.

Kay, the wife of Hal Cerro and mother of his three children, had also become a close friend of the Dixons. Hal had, while in Germany, served as the operations officer on Scott's brigade staff and, even earlier still, as the training officer for Scott when he had been the division operations officer before and during the American incursion into Mexico. In truth it had been Cerro and not Nancy Kozak who had led the raid that had saved Jan, along with other hostages being held by a group of mercenaries that were employed by a Mexican criminal. 'I suppose this sounds dumb, but how is she doing?'

'I don't think it's really hit home yet. These things never really seem to hit the wives until the funeral. I don't know what it is, whether it's the twenty-one-gun salute, or the playing of Taps, or when the officer in charge hands the widow the folded flag that breaks wives. Whatever it is, that's when Kay will need you the most.'

'I know.'

'You do intend to be there as a friend, don't you?'

'Yes, Scott, I will be there. But you don't intend to be here for Nancy, do you?'

There was an audible sigh before Scott answered. 'Jan, please. If I did anything, even hinted at being interested in this matter, I'd be in the wrong, and it just might make things worse for Nancy.'

'How much worse can they be? My God, her career is in jeopardy. Do you realize how much her career means to her?'

'Jan, I know how much her career means to her. But I've got to be honest with you. Her career is over. Regardless of how favorable the decision is, her future as an Army officer was sealed the instant the division staff judge advocate issued those charges against her. Even if she is totally exonerated and Lane is proven to be the ass that he is, the stigma of this affair will follow her about as long as she wears the uniform.'

'Then you've already tried and sentenced her, haven't you?'

Sensing the renewal of Jan's anger, Scott decided that he wasn't up for another round with his wife. 'Look, Jan. It's late. I'm tired and frustrated and I think you are too. Could we please drop this now before one of us says something that we'll regret as soon as we hang up?'

Though she was reluctant to end this argument here, Jan knew that Scott was right. If either one of them went on much more, something would be said and both of them would suffer. No, she thought, this was something best done face-to-face, after he returned to Colombia and had been given some time to think things over. For now Jan decided that she had made her position clear and hoped that it would be sufficient to motivate her husband into some kind of action. With a hint of reconciliation in her voice, Jan agreed. 'Yes, Scott, we're both tired. It's been a rough five or six days down here, and I don't think things are going to get much better. If half of the reports filtering out of the bush are true, the FARC have no intention of letting up their pressure on the Bogotá government or its army.'

'They smell blood, Jan, and they're going for the throat.'

Picking up Scott's meaning, Jan perked up. 'You think the Farcees are preparing for the kill?'

'Jan, don't you dare quote me or come out in any of your stories stating that an unnamed high-ranking official said this or that, but – ' Scott paused and drew a deep breath – 'if the government of Colombia doesn't do something in the near future, and I mean near, nothing these pencil-necked geeks in Washington or the noble troopers of the 11th Air Assault do will make a difference.'

'That bad, huh?'

He was about to say that it was worse than that, but didn't. In his frustration, he had already said too much to Jan, his wife and bureau chief for World News Network. Instead he changed topics without warning. 'Listen, Jan. I think I'm going to order some room service, turn on some mindless TV program, and veg out for a while.'

'I understand. I'd do the same, but I'm not impressed with Colombian sitcoms. Do you think they'll get better after the revolution?'

'I doubt it. The Farcees don't strike me as having much of a sense of humor.'

'No, I didn't think so. Well, honey, take care of yourself, for me, and hurry back.'

'Oh, you don't need to worry about that. As soon as the chief says "That'll be all, General Dixon," I'm outta here.'

'Okay, that's good. Love you.'

'Love you too, Jan. Night.'

Reaching out, Jan rested the receiver back on the phone's cradle slowly. Holding her hand on it for a moment, she stared at it. He had no intention, she thought, of doing anything to help Nancy. As far as he was concerned, she was on her own. Though that didn't set well with Jan, in a twisted sort of way she understood why Scotty took the stance he was taking.

Letting go of the receiver, Jan threw herself back into her seat and folded her arms. 'Well, *mister* General Dixon,' she said to herself out loud, 'that's all well and good for you. But I can't stand by and watch that bastard take Nancy down like this. It's not right, it's not fair, and it's not going to stand, not so long as I can do something about this whole stinking mess.' Without knowing exactly what she was going to do or how she was going to help Nancy Kozak, Jan was determined that Nancy wasn't going to face the lions alone. Not as long as she had something to say about it.

On the other end of the phone line, Dixon sat propped up against the headboard of his hotel room bed and stared blankly at the opposite wall for a moment. Though Jan's call had bothered him, the reaction of the Army Chief of Staff upon hearing the particulars of El Frío and the charges against Kozak shook him even more. 'Scotty,' he said, 'Lane's beginning to really worry me.'

Dixon had felt like asking incredulously, 'Beginning?' but held himself in check.

'Everything you said about the situation down there,' General Fulk continued, 'has been right on the money or too damned close for me. What's more, from what we're seeing now, I don't think Lane can handle it. The El Frío affair, if everything I'm being told about what led up to it is true, is only a case in point.'

Watching the chief as he took deep puffs of the cigarette he nervously handled as he paced to and fro in front of his desk, Dixon felt like asking what he intended to do about Lane. That, however, would have been inappropriate. Besides, after this buildup, he suspected Fulk was going to tell him anyway. Though he wasn't disappointed in this regard, Fulk's comments that followed served only to deepen the gloom Dixon felt over the news of Cerro's death.

'Scotty, Lane isn't doing well at all, not at all. But he hasn't really screwed up yet, not enough to justify his relief. Hell, if every commander got relieved for making a bad tactical call, no one would be left to command.'

Unable to hold back, Dixon finally chimed in. 'Major General Lane, sir, is making a habit of making bad tactical calls.'

Rather than being angry, Fulk paused in front of Dixon and nodded in agreement. 'Yes, true, true. But we still can't relieve him.'

'What does that man have to do, sir, to convince you he's unfit for command?'

Fulk took a deep drag on his cigarette, squinting his eyes as he did so. 'That, General Dixon, is my concern. Yours, I'm afraid, is to go back down there and do what you've been doing and be ready to pick up the pieces if this thing becomes unglued.'

Dixon had been ready to counter with '*when* it becomes unglued' but again held himself in check. Instead he gave Fulk a firm 'Yes, sir,' and left, knowing that he had pushed Fulk as far as he dared at that moment and knowing that in the end what had to be done now would eventually be done.

What bothered Dixon at that moment and now as he sat on his bed staring at the wall was that more good men and women would die before that day came. In the meantime he was stuck in a moral and ethical dilemma unlike any he had ever faced before. For while the Chief of Staff of the Army could shrug off the Lane-Kozak affair with no more than a wave of a hand, Dixon could not. Just as he could not forget his duties and obligations as a soldier, Scott Dixon could not forget those he called friends.

PART FOUR

A QUESTION
OF DUTY

CHAPTER 15

November 16

After spending the better part of two hours tracking down the person he was supposed to defend, Captain Samuel Ulrich was beginning to think that she either didn't want to be defended or didn't exist. Arriving at the battalion headquarters of the 3rd of the 511th shortly after nine in the morning, Ulrich was directed to the battalion adjutant by a sullen soldier on guard. Entering the adjutant's crowded office, he introduced himself to the harried female first lieutenant who bordered on just this side of being chunky. When asked if he could see Captain Nancy Kozak, the lieutenant informed Ulrich in a rather offhand manner and without looking up from the paper she was holding in front of her that Captain Kozak was taking the newly arrived battalion commander on a tour of the battalion area. Though she had a sweet, round face, the female lieutenant conducted herself as if Ulrich were nothing more than a nuisance that she wanted to shed as quickly as possible. After reluctantly taking the time to give him some rudimentary directions on where in the battalion area the captain might be, the lieutenant went back to shuffling papers from one side of her desk to the next, leaving Ulrich to begin his chase.

As crowded as the battalion headquarters was, with squads of soldiers busily generating paperwork for the companies or responding to paperwork dumped upon them from higher headquarters, the barracks area was deserted. Alone, Ulrich blundered his way through one set of cinder-block barracks buildings to another. Were it not for the neatly packed and rolled gear of soldiers, Ulrich would have sworn no one had been in those buildings in days. It wasn't until he was roaming about in the fourth barracks building that he was challenged by a nasty little first sergeant.

Coming up quietly behind Ulrich, the first sergeant made his presence known only when he was two feet away from Ulrich. '*YOU*! Is there something I can help you with?' The ferocity of the first sergeant's words was matched only by the suddenness with which they were delivered. After jumping what seemed like a foot, Ulrich spun around and found himself looking at the top of a neatly blocked camouflage cap. Glancing down, he saw heavy jowls set in a stern and defiant posture, just like the rest of the first sergeant's squat but muscular body. Looking Ulrich up and down as if he were inspecting him, the first sergeant noted that the intruder he had accosted was an officer, causing him to add a 'sir,' reluctantly.

Recovering his composure, Ulrich unconsciously tugged at the bottom of his camouflage shirt and took a deep breath. Though he was quite pissed at the first sergeant for what he had just done to him, not to mention the disdain that he showed for his rank, spitting out the delayed sir as if the word had left a nasty taste in his mouth, he knew the first sergeant had achieved his desired effect. Ulrich was off balance for the moment and on the defensive. 'I was, I am looking for Captain Nancy Kozak. Your adjutant said that I would find Captain Kozak somewhere around here. Have you seen her, First Sergeant?' Squaring back his shoulders, the stocky first sergeant put his hands on his hips and barked out his answer as if it were an order being given on the drill field. 'You missed them by ten, maybe five minutes, *sir*.'

Ulrich waited for several seconds for the first sergeant to continue before he realized that this little obnoxious man had no intention of surrendering any additional information unless he was forced to. Finally Ulrich, becoming annoyed at the first sergeant's attitude, not to mention his tone, tried again. 'Well, you wouldn't happen to know where exactly they went to, would you?'

Folding his arms across his chest and squeezing them together, the first sergeant cocked his head slightly, almost as if he was pondering whether or not he should give such valuable information to this stranger. Finally, just as Ulrich began to part his lips to ask once more, the first sergeant spoke. 'The captain is taking the colonel on an inspection of the perimeter, *sir*.'

Again, as before, there was a pause as the first sergeant waited for Ulrich to ask what perimeter he was talking about. For a fleeting moment Ulrich considered not asking and playing the first sergeant's waiting game. But he didn't have time for that. More correctly, Captain Nancy Kozak didn't have a lot of time. The charges filed against her had received the personal attention of the division staff judge advocate. The appointment of an Article 32 officer, responsible for conducting a preliminary investigation into the incident, had been accomplished the same day as the incident, and the officer selected for this task left no doubt in anyone's mind that the outcome of those proceedings would be the one most desired by C. B. Lane, the man initiating the charges.

As fast as the prosecution had worked, the defense, which was what Ulrich was responsible for, had lagged behind. Part of this delay was to be expected. The 3rd Battalion, 511th Infantry, had remained in place west of El Frío after the fighting around the landing zones had died down. It wasn't until late the following day, after sweeping the area to ensure that the region was secure, not to mention tending to the collection of its dead and accounting for all personnel and equipment, that Kozak's battalion was relieved.

Speaking of the 3rd of the 511th as Kozak's battalion was not an idle thought. The discovery of the battalion commander's body at twilight on the evening of the twelfth of November, and the wounding and evacuation of the battalion executive officer earlier that day left Kozak as the senior ranking officer within the battalion. Only two other captains were still with the battalion, and both of them, Frank Walters of C Company and Dale Pulaski, the battalion S-4, were considered too junior to take over the shattered battalion. So, despite the charges leveled against her, the brigade commander kept Nancy Kozak with the battalion and persuaded the division chief of staff not to attempt a change of command until the battalion was out of the field and in Bogotá.

Though he was already tired of doing so, Sam Ulrich continued to pry information out of the rude and taciturn first sergeant, who in turn yielded every kernel of information with great reluctance. 'You'll have to excuse me, First Sergeant, but I'm not familiar with this area. Where exactly is this perimeter you're talking about?'

For the first time, Ulrich detected the traces of a grin. The bastard, he thought, was mocking him. Looking down at his boots, then back up at Ulrich's face, the first sergeant broke out into a broad grin. 'Well, *sir*, that doesn't surprise me. *The* perimeter is a network of defensive bunkers and fighting positions that surround the division's main support area and helicopter park here at the airfield. The reserve battalion has certain responsibilities along that perimeter.

Captain Kozak, who assigned the companies to their sectors of responsibility, is walking the new battalion commander around *the* perimeter in preparation for his assumption of command, *sir*.'

'Well, yes, of course. Now if you would be so kind, *Sergeant*, as to tell me where exactly your battalion's area of responsibility is, I'll be on my way.'

Noting that Ulrich was starting to become visibly upset, the first sergeant changed his approach, but only marginally. 'Well, it would be my pleasure, *sir*.'

For the next forty-five minutes Sam Ulrich went from one post to the next along the wire entanglements and barriers that surrounded the sprawling military installation. Colonel Christopher Delhue, the division chief of staff, often referred to the main support area as the heart of the division, since practically everything, from men to material, used by the 11th Air Assault arrived and was distributed from here. It was in itself the size of a small Midwestern town, complete with its own streets neatly laid out and a police force, an MP platoon, to be exact, to patrol them. On any other day Ulrich would have enjoyed this time away from the madhouse that the 11th Air Assault's division headquarters had become. The chance to get out, around real soldiers and the equipment that made this division the fearsome weapon that it was, served to renew Ulrich's conviction that what he was doing made a difference. Unfortunately, the need to get his case together quickly, coupled with the piss-poor attitude of the soldiers of Kozak's battalion, wasn't letting Ulrich enjoy this outing. The fact was, he was about to reach the end of his patience when he finally caught sight of two people that he assumed were Kozak and her new commanding officer.

Relieved, Ulrich picked up his pace, being careful to make sure that he didn't run, since that would be undignified. He managed to reach the pair just as they finished inspecting a pair of bunkers guarding an entrance into the aircraft park. Deep in conversation, neither Kozak nor the lieutenant colonel noticed Ulrich's approach until he called out, 'Captain Kozak?'

Turning, both Kozak and the lieutenant colonel looked over at Ulrich as he slowed his pace. Saluting as he neared the two infantry officers, Ulrich stopped and faced the colonel. 'Sorry to disturb you, sir, but I'm Captain Samuel Ulrich from the staff judge advocate's office. I need to speak to Captain Kozak.'

The look on the colonel's face told Ulrich that he was not happy with this interruption, nor the reminder that Kozak was up on charges. Without returning Ulrich's salute or even acknowledging his presence, except for a cold, sharp once-over, the colonel looked at his watch, then over to Kozak. 'I have seen enough for now, Captain. Your dispositions appear to be impeccable and the soldiers are some of the best I've seen. Tend to this officer's business and meet me in my office at sixteen hundred hours. I want to go over our contingency operations as soon as possible.'

When Kozak raised her right arm to salute the colonel, she did so slowly and without a word. She held her salute for several seconds, watching her colonel as he returned her salute, turned, and walked away. Only when he was out of earshot did she slowly let her right arm fall to her side, whispering, 'Bloody pissant,' under her breath loud enough that Ulrich heard.

Taken aback by her obvious disrespect, Ulrich's eyes widened as he looked at the colonel, then back at Kozak. 'Excuse me, Captain Kozak.'

Turning toward him, Kozak showed no sign of repentance for what she had just said. Instead she launched into a tirade. 'He's a jerk, an idiot. What in the hell does he know about fighting positions, let alone what soldiers are supposed to look like? He hasn't seen a real combat infantry-man in six years, maybe seven. Christ, I'd like to have five minutes alone with the moron who pulled him out of the Pentagon and sent him down here to take command of this battalion.'

Pausing only long enough to catch her breath and bring her temper under control, Kozak eyed Ulrich before she spoke again. 'I suppose you wouldn't understand what I'm talking about, would you?'

Barely able to hold back the anger that had been building up inside of him as a result of the frustrating morning he had spent going from one angry and rude soldier to the next, Ulrich kept at Kozak, though now there was a pronounced edge in his voice. 'Listen, I don't pretend to know what's going on here, but I do know that every soldier in this battalion I've come into contact with so far has a chip on his or her shoulder the size of the state of Montana. I know that you've taken your sweet time about tending to the charges that have been preferred against you, ignoring my calls and refusing to furnish me or anyone else with a statement concerning the incidents at El Frío.' Preparing for his summary as if he were in a courtroom, Ulrich raised his right hand and pointed his index finger up toward the pale blue sky. 'And I know that if you and the people in this battalion don't start giving me and my office some cooperation, you'll have to find some other dumb bastard who is willing to put up with your deplorable attitude and high-handed arrogance.'

'What,' Kozak countered nonchalantly, 'do you expect?'

Taken aback by her question, Ulrich shook his head. 'Excuse me?'

'I asked you, Captain, what do you expect?'

'I'm sorry, Captain Kozak, I don't understand.'

This caused Kozak to smirk. 'I wouldn't expect you to.'

Though his anger at her manner continued to push him

closer to the breaking point, he kept his temper in check. 'I'm sorry, but I simply don't understand what you're talking about, just like I don't understand why you've been avoiding me.'

Kozak squared off in front of Ulrich with her feet placed shoulder-width apart and her hands on her hips. 'It's easy, Captain Ulrich. You're from Division. Nothing good comes from Division. Not to this battalion, not to anyone who is out here on the line.'

'If, Captain Kozak, you feel that way about me, why didn't you ask for another defense council from outside the division?'

Folding her arms across her chest, she threw her head back. 'Who? I don't know any JAG officers, at least none worth mentioning.'

Her attitude and this last comment in particular were insufferable to Ulrich. Still he persisted in as even and unemotional tone of voice as he could manage. 'You could have asked for a civilian attorney, you know.'

'Listen, Captain, both you and I know how everyone in uniform feels about civilian attorneys. Only the guiltiest bastard would turn to a blood-sucking shyster lawyer. If I were to go into that courtroom with a civilian pleading my case, that would be my third strike.'

'What are your first two?'

'First, and most obvious, is the fact that the commanding general himself is involved in this case. That in itself, is – '

'Is what, Captain Kozak?' Ulrich shouted as he cut her off. 'Enough to make this wimpy JAG officer quake in his boots and piss all over himself? Listen, I don't care who is involved in this case or who preferred the charges, my duty is to defend you, and I intend to do that, in spite of yourself. Is that clear?'

Now it was Kozak's turn to be rocked back on her heels. Even as he spoke, the bitterness in her eyes began to fade away. During the tense and uncomfortable pause that followed his outburst, Ulrich noticed for the first time how tired she looked. It was more than the dark circles under her eyes and the droops on either side of her mouth. It was her eyes, sad, lusterless eyes that he finally took the time to look at, that spoke of her exhaustion and weariness. When she did break the silence, she tried to speak with an even, unemotional tone but couldn't. Her exhaustion, made more pronounced by a faint note of personal grief, came through. 'They're starting to call themselves the Orphan Battalion. To a man, they feel that they and every officer that has stood up for them have been betrayed, berated, or screwed. It's no wonder that you, sporting that nice new shiny uniform, all clean and crisp, and sporting the wreath and quills of the JAG corps on your collar, got the treatment that you did. No one in the battalion area, I'm sure, took the time to find out if you were a good guy or a bad guy. All they saw was an outsider. And right now,' Kozak continued as she looked over in the direction in which her new battalion commander had disappeared, 'anyone who's an outsider is a bad guy.'

'And you? What do you think?'

Ulrich's direct and simple question caused Kozak to look back and study the JAG officer standing in front of her. Though she knew he had to be in his mid-twenties, he looked older in a mature sort of way. His sandy blond hair, too long for regulation by better than half an inch and cut in a box cut instead of being tapered like the infantrymen of her battalion preferred, lay against the side of his head in soft, easy waves. The most striking feature, six-foot-one-inch slim frame notwithstanding, was his china blue eyes. Rather than being piercing, as that color is in some people, Ulrich's eyes were gentle, comforting. As she looked into them, they seemed to draw her into them. For a moment Kozak forgot what she had been talking about as she stared at him and searched for words that would describe the eyes that were staring back at her.

This silence made Ulrich feel uncomfortable. Averting his eyes, he reached over and began to fumble with the thin briefcase he had been carrying. Finding the paper he was looking for, he pulled it out and offered it to her. 'I have been appointed to represent you. Do you have any objections to that, Captain Kozak?'

Realizing the embarrassment that she had caused Ulrich, and somewhat startled by her own indiscretion, Kozak looked away from the JAG officer as she answered quickly, 'No, not at all. You're as good as anyone else, I suppose.' Then, thinking about what she had just said, Kozak looked back up at Ulrich and added quickly, 'I didn't mean that to come out the way it did.'

Ulrich, still flustered by the momentary confusion and not paying attention, looked up at Kozak. 'Excuse me, Captain Kozak?'

Not understanding that he was as off balance as she, Kozak blushed and began to explain away her comment as quickly as the words came to her. 'Well, what I mean is that we, I mean I, really don't know any lawyers, not personally, like I said before. There isn't anyone I'd rather have . . .' Catching herself, Kozak paused, a pause that only served to accentuate her last few words. When Ulrich's eyes registered his surprise at that comment, Kozak became totally flustered, something that was truly rare.

In an effort to save her from further embarrassment, Ulrich tried to make a joke. 'Well, don't worry. I know exactly how you feel, Captain Kozak. Until two minutes ago I didn't know any female infantry captains, not personally.'

Without thinking, Kozak stuck her right hand out. 'It's Nancy, Captain Ulrich.'

Taking the hand offered to him as a sign of her efforts

to make amends, he grasped it firmly and smiled. 'Sam. Just plain old Sam.'

Though reprieved from her own awkwardness, Kozak still wanted to make sure that what she was trying to say was understood. 'What I meant, Sam, was that I had no intention of looking for a lawyer other than the one appointed to me. To have made a big fuss over the lawyer, especially a civilian lawyer, will leave a bad taste in some of the jury's mouths.'

'Wait a minute, Nancy. Who said anything about a jury? There's always the possibility of lesser charges, plea bargaining, and – '

The easiness that had crept into their conversation suddenly evaporated as Kozak pulled her hand away from Ulrich. 'There will be no plea bargaining, no acceptance of lesser charges. I want a general court-martial, with jury.'

The transformation that swept over Nancy Kozak amazed and bewildered Ulrich. Her eyes, eyes that had a moment before been wide and on the verge of smiling, were narrowing down to mere slits as furrow after furrow cut deep into her brow. Even her nose perceptibly changed shape, crunching up to conform to the wild and uncontrollable contortions of her face. For a moment he was almost afraid to speak, unsure of what her response would be. Finally recovering his nerve, he began cautiously. 'You know, of course, this may never come to a court-martial. You may be offered an Article 15, or even a simple reprimand.'

'No. I want a general court-martial.' There was no hesitation, no give. Kozak's response was as firm and uncompromising as the stance she took, clenched fists on her hips and jaw jutting. 'That bastard is going to atone for what he did to Harold Cerro and this battalion. His ineptness and callousness are going to be laid bare for all to see.'

Though he suspected that he knew who she was talking

about, Ulrich wanted to be sure. 'Nancy, exactly who is it you're after?'

'Lane.'

'The division commander?'

'Is there another Lane in this division that anyone gives a damn about?'

Ulrich looked down at the ground between his feet as he shook his head and folded his arms across his chest. 'No, not that I'm aware of.' Looking up, he saw that Kozak was still standing before him defiant and angry. 'Look,' he started, 'as your defense counsel, provided you still want me, I have to make sure that you understand that it is you and not General Lane that is up on charges.'

Shaking her head as she followed suit and folded her arms, Kozak straightened up slightly. 'That, sir, is where you are wrong. It was his ineptitude that bled this battalion white. It was his stupidity that put us asshole deep into the shit four days ago. And it was his blind arrogance that damned near cost us an entire company. Imagine trying to take all the fire support away from a unit in contact, just because someone shot at him and caused him to mess his pants.'

Ulrich's jaw dropped. 'You know about that?'

This caused Kozak to laugh. 'Hell, Sam, everyone in the division knows about Crap in his Breeches Lane. Lane's own pilot was griping to everyone over on the flight line this morning that he still hasn't been able to get the smell out of his aircraft.'

Like everyone else involved in this case, Ulrich had been told officially to keep to the facts at hand and make sure that nothing, absolutely nothing, concerning the commanding general was mentioned unless it pertained directly to the matter at hand. Unofficially he had been told to do whatever he could to downplay Lane's role and performance. Nancy Kozak, in the first five minutes of his initial interview, had made it painfully clear that she had every intention of doing just the opposite, leaving Ulrich with a real dilemma. Regaining his balance, Ulrich decided to push the fact that they needed to be discreet about what was said before and after this case came to trial, if it made it that far. 'Nancy, please. I know that you are upset and anxious to find a target for your anger and frustration. It's only natural in a case like this to seek to excuse one's actions by making someone else the scapegoat. The fact is – '

'The fact is,' Kozak shouted before Ulrich could finish, 'that Lane was out of line. While he had every right to be where he was, playing Cowboy Bob or John Wayne, or whatever the hell he was trying to do, he screwed up when he started interfering with a military operation that was reaching a critical juncture. He jumped the chain of command and threatened to unhinge the whole operation. If it weren't for the fortitude of Lieutenant Colonel Chris Day, the battalion commander of the artillery unit supporting us, we would have lost our fire support just when we needed it the most. And since we're looking into this whole sordid mess, why is it just me who has been brought up on charges and not Colonel Day, who also refused a direct order from Lane?'

The issue of Colonel Day's role in this case had been discussed, but briefly. Like many other things, though, that discussion had been short, inconclusive, and summarily dismissed by Colonel Webb, the division staff judge advocate. 'The only matter, gentlemen, we need to concern ourselves with at this time,' he had told Mark Moretti, the prosecuting attorney, and Ulrich, 'is the case of the United States versus Captain N. Kozak, period. Anything else, any other issues, will be dealt with in their time and by other means.' Ulrich, of course, knew that Webb's comment meant that Kozak, and Kozak alone, would be charged, regardless of what was fair or appropriate. He had come out to the military airfield with the full intention of making sure that his client understood the official and unofficial rules of engagement for this case.

But any thought of doing so was, to say the least, history. Everything about Nancy Kozak, from her piercing stare, to the uncompromising and defiant stance she was holding, told Ulrich that she would not be denied. 'You understand, Nancy, that if we go to a court-martial, your career is shot.'

'Sam, my career ended the moment I keyed the radio net to tell Old Crap in his Breeches where he could go. You know as well as I do that in today's Army even the hint of any adverse action, whether it makes its way into your records or not, is the kiss of death. Besides, C. B. Lane must be made to atone.'

As she spoke, Ulrich could feel his heart sink lower and lower. By the time she finished this last pronouncement, accentuated by a thrust of her right index finger down toward the ground, Ulrich felt as if his heart had struck rock bottom. It wasn't justice she was interested in, he thought. This woman was seeking vengeance. For a moment he considered shoving his papers into his brief-case, thanking Kozak for her time, and heading straight back to division headquarters to tell Colonel Webb that his client was crazy and needed a shrink instead of a lawyer. Then it struck him. Like so many others in the 11th Air Assault, he had seen and been subjected to, directly and indirectly, C. B. Lane's tyranny and arrogance. He had personally watched Lane on numerous occasions belittle field grade officers and senior sergeants whose only crime had been being too close to him when he lost his temper or, even worse, when he felt like demonstrating his power over other people. Such antics from a junior officer would have been to Ulrich intolerable. Coming from a general officer, a man who was the closest thing to a god on earth, they were beyond contempt. Suddenly, like a light-bulb being turned on in his mind, Ulrich saw what he could do, what he had to do. For here in the person of Captain Nancy Kozak and the defense he was charged to deliver on her behalf he was being offered the perfect opportunity to make Lane pay for all those little crimes against human decency that he had committed for as long as Ulrich could remember against the officers and soldiers of the division.

To Kozak's surprise, Ulrich flashed a smile. 'Okay, you got yourself a lawyer. But from here on in you play the game by my rules. If anyone, and that includes your closest friend, gets wind of your Avenging Angel routine, we're both screwed. Is that clear?'

Now it was Kozak's turn to be thrown off guard. Up to that very moment she had thought him to be nothing more than a useless division staff today. His last comment, however, set her to thinking. Maybe, she thought, there's a man hiding somewhere in those clean, well-pressed fatigues. If there was, and Kozak hoped there was, perhaps she could do what she had set out to do, consequences be damned.

Standing there facing each other, the two officers began anew to consider what it was each would need to do in the coming weeks to achieve what was required of them by fate, duty, and design. In their thoughts, neither was troubled by issues of professional ethics or morality. Such concerns, much ballyhooed in the pristine environs of the Command and General Staff College at Fort Leavenworth or the Army War College in Carlisle, had long since become meaningless to the officers and troops in Colombia. Not that anyone who cared to look seriously into the matter could have blamed the two young captains. How could they, after all, be expected to live up to high professional and moral standards when in the middle of a war the very people who should have been enforcing those standards were themselves incapable of living by them.

So the two of them, joined together by circumstances,

made their way past the men and women of the division support command busily going about the task of keeping the heart of the division pumping and working hard to survive one more day in a hell not of their making. None of the young troops, each tied up in his own struggle, bothered the two captains as they passed by, headed toward a fight that they knew would be more vicious and brutal than anything the FARC could ever hope to wage.

From across the busy Bogotá street, Major José Solis could see the man he had been instructed to meet. Nervously he glanced first to his right, then to his left. He hoped that to anyone watching him he was checking the stream of cars and trucks that whizzed by him. While this was true and very necessary, given the way people in Bogotá drove, the traffic before him was at this moment the least of his worries. It was the National Police, or Terrorist Police, a branch of the National Police that specialized in anti-terror operations. They, and not the steady stream of vehicles, were foremost on his mind at that moment.

He had tried to convince himself that there was no need to worry or be so cautious. After all, worrying about being picked up by the police at this point made no sense, for he knew that if he had been followed by counterintelligence people, any precautions he took now would be pointless. Other officers, after all, had been arrested for less than simply being in proximity to a FARC officer. No one, Solis knew, was above suspicion anymore, not since the aborted coup of last spring.

Still his training as well as his natural instincts caused him to look back. It was foolish, he thought, to go tromping about in broad daylight in the middle of the capital, meeting rebels like this. Even wearing the clothing of a day laborer, clothes that did not fit his stature and carriage at all, did nothing to ease his discomfort. Since leaving his apartment, Solis had felt like every eye was on him. This is mad, he kept telling himself, foolish and mad.

Yet despite his better judgment, he stepped out into the street and began to cross, headed for the sidewalk cafe, walking as a condemned man marches to his death. Almost as if to confirm this image that clouded his mind, the sudden screeching of a truck's brakes behind him just after he reached the middle of the street caused his heart to skip a beat. Without looking, he could see in his mind's eye hordes of national policemen pouring out of an unmarked car, racing up behind as they prepared to wrestle him down onto the pavement like a common criminal. Freezing where he stood in the middle of the street, Solis cringed before reluctantly looking over his shoulder. Only after he had located the source of the noise, an old truck overburdened with produce, did he relax as best he could. Recovering, he felt himself flush as he pulled himself together and, hurried on by the honking of impatient drivers angered at his unexplained delay in clearing the road, continued across the street. Once on the sidewalk, Solis moved quickly over to the cafe and slipped into the chair across from the man he had been told to meet.

The man, amused by Solis's antics, grinned. 'It is fortunate that you have not attempted to make a living by being a member of the Terrorist Police, for I fear that your family would starve to death.'

Solis's cheeks flushed with anger. 'Not everyone, Señor Valendez, takes the dangers about them as you do.'

Hector Valendez's grin broadened. 'My friend, I do not take anything lightly. If I did, do you think our movement could have gone as far as it has?'

Though Solis in theory worked for Valendez, he would not let this man make light of his concerns. Nor did he like anyone telling him that he was part of the insurgency sponsored and controlled by the FARC. He was a Colombian soldier, an officer sworn to defend his country against its enemies. It just so happened that at this moment the greatest enemy, in his eyes and those of many of his fellow officers, was the government itself. His choice to provide the FARC with information at the direction of a very senior officer on the general staff was, he had been told, a political necessity, nothing more. Solis held no love for the man across from him. He didn't understand his ideology or the cause for which he was fighting. To Solis, Hector Valendez and all members of the FARC were tools, instruments to be used to achieve his goals and those of the Colombian Army. In an effort to ensure that Valendez understood that he was a man and not a mere pawn, Solis stared into Valendez's eyes with a firm and defiant gaze. 'There are those who feel your movement would do better if you exercised a little more caution.'

Rather than wipe the smile from his face or cause him to reconsider his comment, Valendez's smile only grew larger. 'And if I listened to those people, men who huddle in the corner like frightened old women in the night, we would still be out there hidden away high in the mountains gathering moss, no nearer to pulling down this corrupt and inept government than we were last spring.' Suddenly he dropped his smile. Leaning forward, Valendez took his fist and softly yet firmly brought it to rest on the table before Solis. 'No, this is not the time to give in to groundless fears and apparitions. We must stand up like men and go forward. And we must do it now, while we have the upper hand and the government itself is still reeling from the blows it has received both from us and from within.' Having made it clear that he was serious, Valendez sat upright, throwing his left hand out with a flippant gesture as he continued his argument. 'Why, even the vaunted American Army is beginning to tear at itself from within. The trial of a mere captain, as you have pointed out, has the entire officer corps of the division in an uproar and has captured the attention of the American media.'

Whether Valendez's comments were meant to be a slur on the timidity he had just shown when crossing the street or not, Solis took it as such. Feeling the need to defend his actions and honor, he leaned forward and faced Valendez almost nose to nose. 'It would not be wise, my friend, to make too much of the affair between the general of the American division and the female captain he has brought charges against. She, like any other soldier, is only a small piece of the whole, and to judge the workings of the machine by studying just one piece would be a terrible mistake.'

Sensing Solis's mood, Valendez chose to defuse the confrontation. Leaning back into his seat, he signaled the waiter. Without having to be told, the waiter brought two beers over. Watching the performance, Solis suddenly realized that he had in part been right about being watched. The only thing that he had gotten wrong was the who. Rather than members of the Terrorist Police, the people watching him had been FARC. Glancing around, he wondered how many of the men lounging around in this small nondescript cafe, busily chatting with one another or lazily reading the daily paper, were armed and on guard.

'You are correct.' Valendez countered, 'to a point. While it would be foolish to consider the events at El Frío that brought the American general and the captain into conflict as cataclysmic in themselves, the incident is symptomatic of a rot in spirit and morale that is infecting everyone charged with defending this government. And if this one tiny piece of the American division does manage to destroy herself, it will not mean an end to the division's effectiveness. But if we help matters along, perhaps we can cause other little pieces to malfunction. How long, Major, can that fine watch of yours continue to work if half the little wheels and gears one by one stop working?'

The openness with which he spoke of the American division and even the casualness with which he used his title convinced Solis that this cafe was a safe haven, if only temporarily. Relaxing, Solis took a sip of his beer, eyeing Valendez as he did so. Following the bottle down with his eyes as he set it on the table, Solis spoke without looking up. 'You obviously have something in mind, my friend. Some way of sprinkling grains of sand into the workings of the American division.'

Slowly the smile returned to Valendez's face. The confrontation was over. Major Solis was now in the frame of mind necessary to discuss the matter for which he had been summoned. 'While the initial phases of the battles around El Frío yielded the results we had hoped for, the final operations, those we had not planned, the ones involving the Americans, did not live up to my expectations. The Yankees were simply too strong, too well supported, too quick, and our own local forces too unpredictable.' Reaching out with his right hand, Valendez took his beer, sipping it as he reflected on what he was about to say. Only when he was ready did he continue. 'Still, what happened there on the twelfth cannot be considered a total defeat. On the contrary, after looking at the fallout from that affair, there is much we can use to our advantage.'

Solis nodded his head in agreement. 'Yes, all of that is very true. There was much dissatisfaction over how the operation was carried out and what happened. There are still howls of recrimination echoing through the halls on our side of the Ministry of Defense as one general blames the other for the massacre of the infantry battalion during the initial fight. The report filed by the American correspondent, the woman who is now making the court-martial of the female captain such an issue, has done nothing to calm the anger of the general or the government. Everyone, from the President on down' – Solis started to make wild gestures as he twisted his face in a mock look of confusion – 'is running around like a frightened chicken, squawking. In front of the entire general staff, the Minister of Defense stood up and shouted in the face of the chief of staff, "Who is responsible for all of this? Who? Is anyone in charge of anything anymore?" ' For a moment he joined Valendez, who was already chuckling. Then, on a more serious note, he continued. 'Not even the Americans came away from the fight satisfied.' Then as an afterthought Solis corrected himself. 'Especially the Americans. Even though their 3rd Brigade was left in control of the battlefield and they annihilated two local-force platoons, the American media have made El Frío look like a thoroughly bungled affair. I saw this morning on the news channel that the Americans monitor in their headquarters a congressman complaining that their Army was using sledge-hammers to kill ants.'

'Ah, yes,' Valendez cut in, 'the American media.' His smile broadened again. 'It was this powerful tool of democracy that gave me the idea which I want to discuss with you.'

'I had hoped, Señor Valendez, that there was a reason, other than making me nervous and treating me to a beer, that you called me here.'

Delighted that Solis was now comfortable enough to make light of his own fears, Valendez lifted his beer toward him for a toast. After the two men clinked their bottles together and took a long, hard pull at them, Valendez launched right into the matter at hand. 'In terms of combat power, resources available, control of land and population, the position of the FARC is very, very shaky compared to the government, its military, and the Americans. That is a fact. But it is a fact that means very little these days. We have achieved, through operations that have been anything but militarily decisive, psychological and moral ascendancy over our enemies.'

Though he did his best to maintain his impassive air as he

listened, the frankness and accuracy with which Valendez summed up the FARC's military effort impressed Solis. He found himself intrigued by the man whom the Colombian Army's intelligence bureau referred to as nothing more than 'a gifted amateur.' 'It is true,' Solis interjected. 'We, the Colombian Army, have failed to bring our full might to bear at any point. The loss of a few battalions and companies,' Solis said as he waved his hand as if he were shooing a fly, 'can be made good. But the loss of our reputation and confidence in our ability to deal with you,' emphasizing the last point by pointing his index finger at Valendez, 'that is an entirely different matter. As you have said, what you have gained, my friend, in these small battles far exceeds your investment of manpower or blood.'

'Yes,' Valendez agreed after hearing Solis out. 'Now we have a new problem.'

Before he could continue, Solis sat back in his seat, took his beer, and pointed the long neck of the bottle at Valendez. 'Exploiting your success and maintaining the pressure.'

'Exactly, Major Solis. Exactly. Unfortunately, we do not have the military strength to do so. Though I have tried hard to maintain a reserve, the tempo of our operations and the vast area over which we have been stretching ourselves in an effort to create the illusion that we are more powerful than we are have worn my main-force battalions thin. Now, when a couple of fresh battalions could make a real difference, I do not have them. While we do have local forces that have yet to be committed, the incident outside of El Frío proves that they, the local force units, are a poor substitute for well-trained and -led regulars. Besides, in concentrating our efforts in preparing the nine battalions of regular forces, I have through necessity been forced to postpone providing the local forces with battalion-level staffs and training. Now,'

Valendez concluded with a frown on his face, 'when I need such battalions, I do not have them.'

'So what is your solution to this problem, señor? You obviously have something in mind, otherwise you would have not risked your neck in a casual visit to the capital.'

Valendez smiled. 'You make too much of the risks you or I take. The fact is, I am safer here in the capital than I am out there in Los Llanos. Many members of the central committee, you know, think that I am too modest, that I should not shy away from the publicity that they themselves crave so much. But in their efforts to inflate their egos they forget that they are only setting themselves up as targets. You can, no doubt, close your eyes and see the face of each of the principal members of the central committee, thanks to the interviews they so freely granted to our friends the media. I, on the other hand, have been able to retain my anonymity, and thus I am free to come and go pretty much as I please.' Looking around the cafe and then out into the crowded street, Valendez shook his head. 'I can do what no other member of the central committee can. I can hide in plain sight.'

While all of this was to Solis very interesting, it did nothing to explain why he had been summoned. His look of impatience, he realized, must have shown through, for Valendez quickly went back to the matter at hand with very little fanfare. 'In lieu of reserve battalions, which we do not have, I intend to use the media and well-aimed and directed terrorism to keep up the pressure while the regular battalions rest and refit.'

'That is dangerous. If you commence such acts of violence you will lose the support of those in the military who hate the government as much as you do and have to date worked more or less in concert with you.'

'Does that,' Valendez asked pointedly, 'include you?'

Without any hesitation or effort to hide his convictions,

Solis nodded. 'Yes! Most definitely. For I am still a soldier dedicated to the defense of my people.'

This answer seemed to satisfy Valendez, for he smiled. 'And so I suspected, which is why you, my friend, will be so important to us during this next phase of our little war. You see, I intend to sever the shield arm that has been defending the government.'

'I am sorry, señor, but your analogy escapes me.'

'The Americans. They have been protecting this government from us, from your Army, from its own people ever since the spring coup. Using the Americans like a shield, the government has hidden, free to continue the purge of the Army and delay the social and economic reforms so necessary to the people. By concentrating our attacks against the Americans now, when their own media are laying them bare to criticism, perhaps we can make this war too uncomfortable for them. Perhaps we can encourage their people and Congress to do what we ourselves cannot do – get them to leave.'

Relieved that Valendez was not creating a moral dilemma for him by striking at his own Army, Solis saw the plan's merit. 'It is well known,' he stated, 'that American staying power is quite fragile. We discuss that among ourselves in private frequently. If you can through your efforts make this war politically uncomfortable and costly to the American politicians who put their troops here, then you are correct, they will leave.'

'Besides,' Valendez added, 'such attacks would serve as a warning to the Army.'

Though he thought he knew the answer, Solis looked over at Valendez. 'Oh? And how?'

Realizing that he had in his enthusiasm threatened the Army that Solis was so dedicated to, Valendez quickly explained. 'We are going to do that which we have refrained from to date. We are going to embarrass the Americans right here in Bogotá where all the eyes of

Colombia and the world can see. We are going to kill so many senior American officers and soldiers in the streets of this city that they themselves will be begging their government to pull them out. And in the process, as each American officer goes down in a hail of gunfire, every senior Colombian officer will have to ask himself, Am I next? We, of course, will make it clear in a quiet, gentlemanly way that such a thing will not happen, provided . . .'

'Provided what?'

'Provided the Army, your Army, steps aside and leaves us a clear path to the presidential palace once the Yankees are gone.'

In the silence that followed, Solis thought about Valendez's comments and about the feelings that he and many of his fellow officers shared concerning their role in the current struggle. He knew that there already was a great deal of sabotage from within the Army itself aimed at doing exactly what Valendez was proposing. He knew that the units being deployed to fight the FARC in Los Llanos were not the best and those that were being committed to that fight were being fed into it in a piecemeal manner. Even the dispatch of one of the battalions of the Presidential Guard brigade and its subsequent massacre had been a setup, an effort to weaken those forces that were unshakably loyal to the government. No, Solis thought, what Valendez was plotting was no mere dream. It was as cold and ruthless as it would be effective. In fact it was the very ruthlessness of their acts to date and what Valendez was proposing that made everything he did so effective. It left those who survived with the thought planted firmly in their mind that they were fighting a heartless killing machine that had no remorse, that held to no constraints. Satisfied, in his own mind, that he understood what Valendez intended to do and that he could with a clear conscience support it, Solis peered into the rebel's waiting eyes. 'Your strategy has merit. What, señor, do you require from me?'

CHAPTER 16

November 19

Of all the concerns and unresolved issues that Scott Dixon brought back from his extended visit to the Pentagon and SOUTHCOM headquarters, the one that he had the least desire to deal with was Jan's anger. She was, he knew, upset with him because he had done nothing to help Nancy Kozak and had, as he had told her in so many words, no intention of helping.

It wasn't the fact that she said anything, for Jan never said a word about Kozak and the trial from the moment she picked him up at the gate of the military airfield, through supper, and into the evening. On the contrary, it was precisely her avoidance of the subject that cued Scott to the severity of her anger. Scotty knew, from dealing with other lesser matters in the past, that the longer she held back the worse it would be. 'It was,' he told a friend once, half in jest and half in earnest, 'like watching a uranium atom becoming excited, pinging about madly in its own little orbit until, POW, it reached critical mass.'

'Well,' his friend asked, smirking, 'what does a well-trained professional soldier like you do when faced with that kind of peril?'

'I do,' he responded as he continued to grin, cocking one eyebrow, 'what the pioneers did when faced by a savage attack; I circle my wagons and keep my eyes open.'

'For a chance to attack?'

'Attack? Don't be foolish. I wouldn't last a minute. Don't forget, this woman is a trained correspondent. Her specialty is dismembering notable public figures, particularly men, before the all-seeing eye of the TV camera. No, when faced with Jan's fury, your only chance of surviving with your dignity and sanity is to turn into the wind and weather the storm. Then, when she has spent her anger, you seek an honorable surrender at the earliest opportunity under the best conditions possible.'

This caused his friend to break out in a broad smile. 'So you don't say anything. You just sort of let her run her course, tire herself out, and then apologize.'

'That, good buddy, is about the size of it.'

The 'storm' struck home that night in the hotel room they were sharing, just after they had turned in on what normally was neutral ground. Scott, finished first in the bathroom, moved about the room like a cat. As Jan rose from her chair, he slipped around her and hopped into bed, leaning back on two pillows to do some reading while he waited for her to reappear. Unlike most nights, when she insisted in keeping up her conversation with him from the bathroom, despite the fact that he couldn't hear her over the noise of running water and he was trying to concentrate on the book he was reading, Jan said nothing. This Scott took as a bad sign, a sort of calm before the storm.

With this thought running through his head, he was unable to concentrate on the book he held propped up on this chest. Instead he watched her move about the room from one place to another, picking her outfit for the next morning. She's very much like me, he thought, down to her habit of laying everything out the night before, allowing her to lie in bed until the last possible moment, snuggled up to her pillow or me, when I'm here. Even her habit of going against the odds, standing on principles that few in her line of work could understand or appreciate, becoming the champion of causes that others shy away from, is no different than my habit of accepting what others consider preposterous missions with nothing more than a hand salute, a well-trained poker face, and a hearty 'Can do, sir.' Watching her move about in front of him clad in a white linen dressing gown that only came down to her mid-thighs, flipping her head to the side every so often to shake her long brunette hair from her face, Scott wondered if she did it all as much for the excitement that such challenges presented as for the high ideals that were often used to justify such fights.

Finished, Jan turned to Scott, flashed her famous smile, and cocked her head in a very charming manner. 'Ready for bed, or would you like to read for a while longer, dear?'

Dropping his chin on his chest, he looked up at her over the reading glasses that he needed so badly but seldom used in public. 'Well, I don't know. Why? Do you have something else in mind?'

'Well,' she said, averting her eyes slightly, 'we could talk, couldn't we?'

Like a soldier hearing the blare of the enemy's bugle sounding the charge, Scott winced slightly and prepared for the attack that was about to be delivered. Closing his book, he laid it on the night table and slowly removed his glasses, setting them on top of the book before turning to face Jan, arms folded across his chest. 'My failure to do anything to help Nancy,' he stated without fanfare or prelude, 'has been bugging you since this whole thing hit the street, hasn't it?'

Seeing that he had opted to take a defiant and combative stance right off the bat, Jan dropped all pretense and drove right to the heart of the matter. 'I'm sorry, Scott. I simply cannot understand how you can so casually turn away from a person who has been a friend, not just a good little loyal minion, all these years. Like I told you the other night, what she did in Mexico, in my opinion, ranks somewhere above and beyond the call of duty.'

Jan's last comment angered Scott. With all the effort he could muster, he clenched his teeth lest he yell or say something that he would immediately regret. From the foot of the bed, Jan watched him, satisfied in part that she had struck a nerve while at the same time a little afraid that she had just pushed the wrong button too soon in this discussion. It would be terrible, she realized, to let this degenerate into an angry shouting match before she had made her point. Slow down, she told herself. Make your case. There's too much at stake here to lose it all in a fit of rage. In an effort to retrieve the situation, Jan dropped the accusatory tone in her voice and instead switched to one that was more conciliatory. 'Scottie, dear, I understand that there are things that regulations and custom prevent you from doing. I'm not asking you to do anything that's illegal.'

Though he was tempted to come back and accuse her of not understanding diddly about military law or regulations, her change in approach kept him in check. Though he too tried to change the tone of his voice to one that was more conciliatory, it came out instead as if he were delivering a lecture to a confused student. 'Jan, darling, I'm afraid that you don't quite understand my position. Even the mere appearance of my trying to use my rank or influence in this matter would go against just about every principle – '

'Principle?' Jan shot back as she hastily brought her hands up to her hips and leaned forward at the waist toward Scott, chin jutting and eyes ablaze with passion.

'You can lie there in your bed and talk to me about principle? Are they the same principles that his highness Major General C. B. Lane has been using to run this division? The ones that permit him and his staff to generate erroneous reports and information designed to further their own personal careers? Are they the same principles that allow young men and women to be sent out day after day on poorly planned and ill-advised missions, to die in this shithole of a country for political reasons that our own government can't explain? And why, sir, do you feel so obligated to live by some holy principles that no one else understands or even cares about?'

When Scott responded, there was no anger in his voice. 'For the same reason, Jan, that you feel obligated to stand by Nancy even when common sense and your duty as a correspondent dictate that you step back and hide behind your camera.'

Having expected a violent reaction, Jan pulled her head back, as if Scott's words had hit her square in the face. The manner in which he had delivered his last comment and the need for her to think drew the vehemence from her tone and argument. Standing upright, she gave Scott a quizzical look that slowly softened to one that bordered on being embarrassment. Since she had learned of Hal Cerro's death, she had become so drawn into fixing the blame on C. B. Lane that she lost her objectivity. She was out to prove a point, using her reports, and didn't give a damn anymore about balance, objectivity, or relevance. Now that she appeared to be more rational and receptive, Scott began to make his case. Pulling the sheet back, he swung his legs out of bed and pulled himself up till he sat at the edge of the bed. Thus seated, he covered his lap with the sheet and turned to face Jan, still standing at the foot of the bed.

'If there was something, anything, that I could do that

was within my power to help Nancy Kozak, that was both legal and within bounds, I would.'

'Couldn't you,' Jan shot back, 'at least come forward as a character witness?'

'Even if Nancy or her attorney asked, which they haven't, my vouching for her past character would do nothing to change the facts of this case. By her own admission, she did tell Lane over an open radio net where to get off while he was exercising his command prerogatives. She was wrong.'

'But so was he. He had no right to interfere with Nancy's conduct of the battle. She was in the middle of an engagement, a fight in which a good part of her battalion was in danger of being wiped out. Lane was going to take away her artillery support.'

'And,' Scott interrupted, 'he was well within his bounds to do so. Those guns belong to him, just like every soldier, weapon, and piece of equipment in that division. He is not only the division commander, he is the senior U.S. commander in country, charged by the President of the United States in executing policy. He had every right to divert those guns to a new target.'

'But it was wrong, Scott. The official statement from his pilot indicates that Lane's aircraft was out of danger when he had his aide call for the artillery. He didn't need those guns anymore. Kozak did.'

Caught off guard by what she had just said, Scott hesitated for a moment. 'How, Jan, do you know so much about this case, including what the pilot's statement said? They haven't even convened the Article 32 investigation yet.'

Throwing her head back, she thought about his question before giving him an answer that was somewhat aloof and snooty. 'I have my sources.'

Raising his right index finger, Scott shook it at her. 'For your sake and your source's sake, you'd best be careful.

You can get your pompous little behind thrown out of this country if you're not careful. Don't forget, the President of this country has declared himself and his nation at war, and both he and Lane have the right to invoke any part of the martial law restrictions they deem fit. Interfering with an official investigation would be more than enough justification for Lane to get rid of you.'

He was right. Jan knew it. Moving over to a chair facing the bed, she plopped down and let her arms fall to her sides. Scott could see a hint of moisture in the corner of both her eyes. 'He killed Hal, Scotty. As sure as I sit here, he killed him. And he's out to ruin Kozak simply because she called him a name while she was doing her duty. That, by anyone's measure, is not right.'

Lowering his head, Scott pondered Jan's comments. Yes, he thought, Lane was responsible for ordering the operation that had resulted in Cerro's death. And yes, his insistence on bringing Kozak up on charges for ill-chosen words spoken in a burst of passion was, in Dixon's mind, inappropriate. To do so, however, was well within his right and, some could argue, his duty. War, whether it was a small one-division sideshow being waged in a remote corner of a minor third-world country or on the plains of northern Europe, demanded disciplined and professional armies. Breaches of the discipline that held units together were dangerous and left unchecked could lead to future breaches of that delicate and necessary commodity. While it was not unusual for subordinates deeply involved in a fight to become frustrated and lash back at superiors they felt were interfering too much or were out of touch with the situation as they saw it, such incidents were nonetheless wrong and contrary to the maintenance of discipline. Equally common, Scott knew, was the practice of making an example of one soldier, officer or enlisted, who had erred, regardless of the circumstances which prompted them to do so.

Scott looked at Jan and stared at her for the longest moment. He was familiar with every aspect of the fight at El Frío. His chief of staff, Jeff Worsham, while Dixon was in Washington, had looked into the matter, assuming correctly that he would want to know. As much as he wanted to find fault with what Lane had done during the battle and immediately after, all his actions were, as best he could determine, well within regulations and policy. Yet, he wondered, how could he explain this to Jan? How could he make her understand that on any given day he would do the same. The fact was, as he thought about this, that the image of the radioman, back on the twenty-first of September, flashed across his mind. He had on that day come within a hair's breadth of bringing that trooper up on charges. That he didn't do so didn't make him a better man. In fact, by failing to do so, Scott realized that he had allowed a serious transgression of his secret discipline to go unpunished. Voltaire said it best when he claimed that an admiral had to be put to death every now and then to encourage the others.

That witty saying, however, wouldn't do him much good at the moment. Dropping his head, he sighed. How, he wondered, could he explain that to her? How could he explain it to anyone who hadn't lived with this kind of thing their entire adult life? You couldn't, Scott thought. You simply couldn't put such ideas into words that could be understood by someone who had been hurt by war. Sitting there, he couldn't even explain it to himself. Like many others before him, he had long ago given up any hope of applying rationality to a human pursuit that defied rational explanation. War, as William T. Sherman told a Union Nashville matron who was hosting a dinner in his honor, was hell. It was that simple, period. The real sadness in this whole affair, Scott realized, was that no matter what anyone did, the cost of all this insanity was lives, lives of good people. On the twelfth it had cost Hal

Cerro his life, and in the next week or so, unless she was damned lucky, it would cost Nancy Kozak her career.

He looked back at Jan, who continued to sit in her chair staring at him. 'I'm sorry, Jan, but Hal Cerro died in the line of duty. If I had been given the same information that Lane had that morning, I would have done the same. Lane seized a fleeting opportunity to destroy two FARC battalions using the units available and the mobility of his division. To have allowed that opportunity to pass without doing anything would have been negligence on his part. It just so happened that one of those units was Hal's. On another day it would have been someone else's. And if that had been the case, the death of that battalion commander would have gone unnoticed by you, and because you had no association with the individual involved, the entire American public would not have noticed.'

Though she doubted that Scotty would let Hal's death pass in such a casual manner, Jan let that point slip by. Instead she continued to hammer at the incident that resulted in Kozak's pending trial. 'That still does not make right what Lane's doing now. Besides, I doubt that you would choose to crucify a subordinate just because he or she got a little excited and let words pass between you. I've heard more than enough stories bantered about concerning your indiscretions with higher ranking-officers when you got yourself excited.'

Scott leaned back some as he dropped his arms down to his lap and shook his head. 'Just because I did it and got away with it doesn't make such behavior right or even justifiable. The only reason I didn't get drawn and quartered was because the officer involved chose to ignore the incident or handle it in a different manner. In that regard, I was lucky. Nancy Kozak wasn't. And don't be so quick, Jan, to pass judgment.'

Slowly she shook her head as she spoke through the tears that she fought to hold back. 'Scott, he hurt me. He hurt me by hurting people who mean something to me. I can't let that go by simply by saying that it was nothing more than the luck of the draw. If it had been some other poor bastard instead of Hal, would that have made it any more right? Less painful for me, yes. Right, no. And now he's going after Nancy.'

She paused, wiping away a stray tear that had escaped her efforts to keep it in check and ran down her cheek. In her mind the issues at hand, avenging Hal Cerro's death and saving her friend Nancy Kozak, were flip-flopping about and merging together. For the first time, Jan began to fear that she wasn't making any sense. Finished, she caught her breath and continued. 'I know I don't understand everything the military did. I never have pretended to do so. And I know that at times I let my emotions get the best of me, causing me to react before I think. But I, Scott Dixon, am able to live with that and with myself. There's nothing I can do to help poor Hal. He's gone in all but memory. Though I wish there was something that I could do to help some other poor devil from going through what he did and sharing his fate, that is as important right now as doing something for Nancy. She is still here and very much in need of help and, more importantly right now, a friend.'

Scott listened, watching Jan's face as she spoke. While he could mask his fears and emotions behind an impenetrable poker face, Jan's face, especially her eyes, spoke legions. What he saw now in that face and those eyes was blind determination. She was, he knew, hell-bent on doing something, consequences be damned. Though he had never in his heart disagreed with that assessment, his stubborn adherence to the code of honor and the regulations that were so much a part of his life and his personality held him in check like twin anchors holding a ship. But Jan was not bound by those principles. She, unlike he, could do something. But what, he wondered, could she accomplish on her own? 'And what, Jan, do you propose to do? What in God's name can you accomplish by giving this story more attention than it deserves?'

The anger that she felt helped her draw back her tears. From one of forlorn sorrow, her face slowly transformed itself into a mask of angry resolve. 'I intend to make sure that the American public sees Lane for what he is. I'm going to give him the type of coverage that he should have had months ago, before his ineptitude and his campaign of personal gratification cost lives. I intend to be there, camera in tow, ready to catch him each and every time he trips or stumbles.' Fired up by her resolve, Jan jutted her chin and drove her index finger into the arm of the chair she was seated in. 'I can't bring back Hal, but maybe I can save Nancy and others from paying for Lane's climb to the stars with their blood.'

From the bed, Scott studied her. Her poise and tone left no doubt that she was determined. Perhaps she was right. Perhaps Scott thought, she could even accomplish something. Though the odds were against her, since many a reporter had set out on just such a crusade, perhaps Jan, with her camera, charm, reputation, and incredible luck, could do what he himself was unable to do.

Then it struck him. At first he felt ashamed that he even considered the idea. But he did. He was, after all, a human being possessing all the emotions and drives that everyone else had. That included anger, disgust, and the need to seek retribution or revenge on those who deserved to be punished. Though he himself couldn't be the agent of that retribution, because of his obligation to his office and position, perhaps he could help someone like Jan who was both willing and eager to bring Lane down, if only a peg or two. Even a simple humiliation in public would satisfy Scott's lust for revenge, for he was wise enough to hope for little more.

Putting aside any last-minute qualms or doubts, Scott

locked eyes with Jan. 'What you're proposing isn't going to be easy. If you have any hope of doing what you claim you want to do, you're going to need help, and a lot of it.'

There was a brief moment before Jan realized what Scott was saying. When finally she did, her eyes opened wide, for in all the years that they had known each other, as lovers and husband and wife, he had never, even as a joke, hinted at giving her information or assistance that would be harmful to the Army or anyone connected with the Army. That he was willing to violate this self-imposed code of ethics, a code she thought no one else in the Army bothered to live by, was nothing less than a shock. Lowering her head slightly, but keeping eye-to-eye contact with her husband, Jan carefully picked her words as she spoke. 'Are you proposing to help me bring Lane down?'

It was Scott who broke the eye-to-eye contact, but only for a second. When he looked back at her, his face was relaxed, as if he had made a great decision and it had brought him physical as well as mental relief. 'Just now, Jan, it dawned upon me that when all the old soldiers said that there were no rules in war, they meant just that, there are no rules. To do what is right for you or me as an individual does not always mean doing what is deemed proper by others living by their code. Lane, because he has chosen to violate the paper-thin code of honor that he as an officer is obliged to live by and enforce, has left me no choice. I either turn my back, as I have done for so long, and let him continue to drag his division down, or I do what I can to put an end to it.' He paused, dropping his eyes to his lap. 'I don't like doing this. Not one bit. But' – shaking his head, he continued – 'there's no other way.' He looked up and repeated in deadly earnest, 'There's simply no other way.'

'Then you really intend to help me?'

Reaching behind him, he grabbed a handful of sheets on her side of the bed and lifted them. 'Jan, I have no real idea what I or anyone else in the Army can do to help. But that doesn't mean I can't try. Come on over and let's discuss this together. After all,' he said with a slight smile, 'some things that must remain in the dark are best discussed in the dark.'

Without another word, Jan rose from her seat, switched off the light, and slipped quietly into bed next to Scott. There in the darkness the two of them discussed in hushed voices how best to achieve their mutual goal.

Downstairs in the lobby bar of the same hotel the object of their concern, young Captain Kozak, was sitting across from Sam Ulrich discussing the exact same thing. More correctly, Ulrich was telling Nancy what he intended to do in her defense. 'We have to remember,' he repeated at measured intervals, 'that the charges in isolation are quite justified. While even I can understand how someone like yourself can do what you did in the heat of battle, this fight will not be waged in the same pressure-filled, kill-or-be-killed environment that the incident took place.'

While he was well meaning and quite serious about what he was doing, Kozak all but laughed every time he used his colorful terms to refer to the battlefield, especially when he came out with 'kill-or-be-killed environment.' Only the severity of the charges against her and her burning desire, made sharper with each day of reflection, kept her focused and listening. He might be somewhat of a wuss, she thought, but he seems to know what he's talking about. But even more important to Kozak, he appeared to be as determined, for some reason, to thump Lane as she was.

'Throughout the trial, Nancy, we have to work hard to re-create the image of that battlefield in the minds of the jury. When we finish, they need to understand everything that was going on, not only between you and Lane, but between the enemy on the ground and the forces you were commanding.'

'In other words, you need to make Lane look like a bungling fool tactically.'

Kozak's interjection caused Ulrich to visibly recoil. He thought about what she had said, shook his head, then corrected her. 'No, we don't. In fact, the last thing we want to do is give the appearance that we are trying to make the commanding general look bad.'

'We,' Kozak cut in, 'don't have to do much to make him look bad. He does a great job of that on his own.'

Drawing in a deep breath, Ulrich leaned forward and threw out his open hands. 'Nancy, damn it, we've been over this again and again. You, and not Lane, are on trial. If we vary from our course – '

'Your course, Sam. Don't forget this grand plan is yours.'

'It's yours too. I am your defense counsel. I'm not doing this just for shits and grins, you know.'

'That's right, you are my defense attorney, and as such, you're . . .'

Across the room, in a group of strangers, a familiar face flashed into Kozak's view, causing her to seize up in midsentence. For the first time since early September she looked upon the face of Captain Aaron J. Pierce, a man she had once thought she was in love with. That she still had deep, unchecked emotions for this man became painfully obvious as her eyes locked on him and every thought in her head faded into obscurity.

Noticing the sudden midstride change in Kozak, Ulrich looked at her eyes. Seeing that she was staring at something or someone intently, he turned his head in an effort to see what she was staring at. Noticing a group of aviators of the division, he assumed that one of them was the object of Kozak's attention. Facing back to her, he quipped, 'Old boyfriend?'

She ignored his comment. In fact for several seconds she ignored everyone and everything about her as she focused on sorting out her feelings toward AJ. In the process of doing so, memories both good and bad flashed through her mind. She knew she hadn't been fair to AJ when she had, without fully explaining herself to him, broken off their relationship in the emotionally charged aftermath of the September ambush. Nor had she answered his calls or responded to his messages, leaving him wondering what he had done wrong.

He had, she knew, done nothing wrong, not really. The root cause of their breakup, Kozak knew, was her own inability to deal with the crisis that the ambush and Lane's actions afterwards had plunged the battalion into. That, and the unreasonable blame she leveled against AJ simply because he was an aviator and the aviators had on the day of the ambush failed to support her battalion as she thought they should have, led to their estrangement.

But how, Kozak thought as she watched him and his friends as they began to move toward the bar, do I explain all of that to him? And at that moment she suddenly thought, Do I want to bother doing so?

As if her thoughts drew his attention to her, AJ turned and looked right into Kozak's eyes. His reaction, like hers, was one of surprise and momentary confusion. Stopping in midstride, AJ caused a minor pile-up in the center of the lobby as two of his friends behind him bumped into him. 'Hey, hot shot!' one of them kidded him. 'How 'bout using your brake lights next time?'

Mumbling a muddled apology, AJ broke away from the knot of aviators and made his way over to Kozak, who slowly began to stand as he approached. Pausing several feet away from her, he stopped, looked her in the face, and slowly began to speak. 'Nancy, I heard your unit was in Bogotá. I was meaning to – '

Embarrassed, Kozak spoke, her words coming out in a hesitant, faltering manner. 'I was too. I mean, I was going to contact you as soon as I took care of some things. I've been quite busy these past few days.'

Without thinking, and looking for something to say, AJ blurted out, 'Yeah, I've heard. Do you think you can beat the charges Lane's brought against you?'

Kozak was upset that AJ had broken the magic of the moment by reminding her of her problems. She was searching for some way of steering the conversation away from that subject and back onto the one that she really wanted to talk about, which was their relationship, when Ulrich stood up and cut in. 'Well, her chances will improve immeasurably if she listens to me.'

Annoyed by the interruption, AJ turned and looked at Ulrich. With a sneer that betrayed the contempt he felt for JAG officers, AJ commented dryly, 'You must be her lawyer.'

Miffed that he had all but said 'scum-sucking lawyer,' Ulrich put his hands on his hips. 'Yeah, I'm her lawyer.'

In horror, Kozak watched the two men as they squared off against each other. 'God!' she called out in a sudden burst of anger, shouting out the first thing that popped into her head. 'Why do men always feel this compelling need to hack away at each other before they shake hands?'

Stung by her comment, AJ turned and faced Kozak. 'Oh, I'm sorry, Nancy, for bothering you. I just thought I'd come over and say hi.' He looked down at the floor, thinking for a moment, as if he was trying to find a word to smooth things out. He was still doing so when one of his buddies called out, 'Hey, AJ, you coming?'

Turning to where his friends were waiting, he looked over at them, then faced Kozak again. 'Well, I see that you're real busy, and my friends are waiting. So I'll just leave you two here alone. It was nice seeing you again, Nancy, and good luck.'

Without waiting for a response, AJ turned and walked away, leaving Kozak glaring at Ulrich and for the moment caught between two burning desires. The first was to burst out and call for AJ, which was something that her pride wouldn't allow her to do. The second, equally compelling desire that she suppressed was to turn and rip out Ulrich's heart for screwing up the one chance she had of making amends with AJ. That she didn't do so would for days amaze her and, as the trial began, cause her grief.

CHAPTER 17

November 21

Had they not been so wrapped up in their own concerns, the sudden shifts in Major José Solis's attitude would have been obvious to the dullest member of Lane's oversized division staff. That, however, would have required both parties, Solis as well as the American officers, to change their habits. Nothing, however, could shake the division staff of the 11th Air Assault from its myopic view of the world. Not even the steady stream of grim news from the east seemed to deter the division staff of the 11th Air Assault from its precious routine as it labored ponderously forward. Like a great, mesmerized bull elephant, the officers of the division staff continued to stumble about with no apparent goal, no purpose in life other than to keep themselves fed and busy.

Not even Colonel Christopher Delhue, normally the only person on the 11th's staff who, in Scott Dixon's words, bothered to pull his head above the daily mire, did so anymore. He, like everyone else on the division staff, was beginning to miss what was happening in the real world outside the walls that housed them, and certainly didn't notice the change in a person few bothered with during the best of times, Major José Solis. If Delhue or anyone else had bothered to do so, they would have seen a new man, one who was possessed, a person with a mission in life and anxious to get on with it.

Today, less than two weeks before a scheduled commander's conference, was no different. As the captains, majors, and lieutenant colonels from the various staff sections in the division headquarters ran about, much to the amusement of their sergeants, who were content to stand aside and watch the spectacle of officers running around in smaller and smaller circles, Solis moved about the floors of the Colombian Ministry of Defense building occupied by the division staff. Unnoticed, except by an occasional harried staff officer in a rush to get by him in a crowded corridor, Solis moved slowly, thoughtfully, from one room to the next, up the stairwells and through the corridors. While he allowed his American counterparts to charge forward, eyes fixed straight ahead, Solis took his time, looking at everything and everyone he met during the course of his solitary journeys. During frequent halts he would make a note or two in the little green notebook he kept in his left breast pocket, closest to his heart. Had an unbiased observer been present to compare Solis's comings and goings with those of the American officers, they would have without doubt claimed that Solis and not the Americans was nonproductive.

To have understood the truth, however, would have required closer observation and a mind uncluttered by the trivial pursuits that Lane's headquarters passed off as staff work. José Solis, being as unintrusive as possible, was refamiliarizing himself with the building, learning all he could about this part of it. Though he had been through every room before and knew what staff occupied what section of the American wing of the building, he was looking at that same structure now through different eyes. Now, as he walked into a room looking about and taking in what he saw, he did not concern himself with desks or the people who occupied them. Instead, as his eyes danced about the room, he saw entrances and windows, supports and pillars, any opening or obstruction that would dissipate or block an explosion. He also looked for and noted as he glanced about where boxes and containers were kept, making careful note of their size, shape, and composition as well as how often, if at all, they were used. Such observations, he knew, would be important when it came time to smuggle the large quantities of explosives that he envisioned.

In his endeavors, Solis was not alone. After thinking about the task given to him by Hector Valendez, Solis had rushed back to the revolutionary with his idea. 'Though they have been in the same place since they arrived here months ago,' he told Valendez, 'the Yankees insist upon being able to pack up and move out at a moment's notice.' Leaning over the table of their cafe rendezvous, Solis's eyes danced with delight as he explained to the puzzled FARC military man. 'To accommodate this, they keep hundreds of boxes and special containers stacked up along walls and in corners in practically every room in the building. They even have blocked off stairways, partially for security reasons, using containers used to ship computers, copying machines, and other such devices.'

Understanding immediately what Solis was driving at and infected by his excitement, Valendez immediately dedicated his best men to the mission. To handle the explosives, two of his best demolition experts, one of whom was famous throughout South America for his creative use of explosives, were put in charge of a sapper platoon and smuggled into Bogotá with all the high-grade explosives they could lay their hands on. To assist these men, Valendez had, through his former associates at the university, assembled a team of engineers and architects, including men who had worked on the Ministry of Defense building from its inception through its completion. Armed with his notes and observations gathered during his daily wanderings, Solis met each night with Valendez's team of experts. He would give each in turn the information that they had requested or that Solis felt they could use. Finished with that, the team members would give Solis a new list of information requirements and questions that he would need to answer the next day. In this way the FARC team by now knew more about the internal organization and layout of the 11th Division's headquarter than the headquarters' commandant himself. They, of course, had to, for each man involved knew without having to be told that they would only have one chance to strike at the heart of the Yankees' headquarters. For once they had made the effort and experienced success or failure, the shock value and potential for a cheap, decisive strike would never be available to them again.

Reaching the end of his tour for that day, Solis found himself standing outside the door of the main division conference room. A military policeman standing at parade rest was posted outside the door. Not remembering seeing any briefings or special meetings scheduled for that day, Solis stopped and looked at the MP. 'Excuse me, but who is using this room today?'

The MPs, like most troopers in the 11th, were normally not impressed with the Colombian Army officers and tried hard to pretend that they didn't exist, but Solis delivered his inquiry in such a manner that the MP could not ignore him. Though he didn't come to attention, he responded quickly, 'The division staff judge advocate is using the room to conduct an Article 32 investigation.'

Though he noted that the Yankee didn't add the customary 'sir' that his rank demanded, Solis made no comment. Instead he looked at the MP and then the door. Forever curious about how and why the American military did what it did, Solis moved past the MP and began to enter the room. The MP, caught off guard, wasn't sure what to do. He had been posted at the door to ensure that no one accidentally entered the room in the middle of the proceedings. His first inclination, as it was with everyone in the division headquarters, was to challenge the Colombian. But then he caught himself. This investigation, to the best of his knowledge, wasn't a classified or a closed session. If it had been, he would have been told and been given an access roster listing all those who were authorized to attend. Unable to justify keeping Solis out based on his skimpy instructions, the MP allowed Solis to pass through the door. Closing it behind him, the MP shrugged his shoulders. Oh, well, he thought, shuffling his feet and looking up and down the hall for a moment, maybe no one will notice. Resuming his relaxed stance, he shifted himself slightly to the right. This allowed him to get a better view into the office across the way. Fixing his gaze straight ahead, the MP hoped that the five-foot-three brassy blond female sergeant with a bosom so ample that even her loose camouflage uniform couldn't hide it would return to her desk, which faced out into the hall where he stood.

Inside the conference room, Solis hesitated at the door before taking a seat. Though he had acted with authority and confidence in front of the MP, he wasn't sure if the Yankees wanted an outsider here watching what must be for them an embarrassing affair. Such a proceeding, he knew, in the Colombian Army would have been conducted in secret, far from the prying eyes of uninvolved outsiders. After looking about the room and noticing that no one, except for a lone sergeant standing at the back of the room, took note of him, Solis quickly and quietly moved over to the first open seat he saw near the rear of the room, sat down, and began to watch.

The tables at the front of the room were arranged in a horseshoe with the open end pointed at the rear of the room, where Solis sat in one of several rows of chairs set up for spectators. Seated at the head table in the center was a major whom Solis recognized as belonging to the division's operations section, and a captain of the division's staff judge advocate corps, which they referred to as JAG. The major appeared to be running the investigation while the JAG officer sat there in silence, scribbling an occasional note on a pad set before him. Though Solis couldn't remember the JAG officer's name, he knew the major, having dealt with him on several occasions. He was, Solis knew, a dedicated if somewhat dull-witted man. He did exactly what he was told to do to the best of his ability. No brilliance there, he thought, and no backbone. Familiar with the charges brought against the female infantry captain seated at the table that made up the left side of the horseshoe, Solis understood why the major at the head table had been selected to conduct this preliminary investigation. He would do as he was told and, as he did with everything else, deliver the results his commander desired without question, without protest.

The female captain, a woman allegedly with a reputation and combat record that put every officer on the division staff to shame, sat quietly next to another JAG officer. The two of them, sitting as if they were uninterested in the proceedings taking place before them, said nothing either to each other or to other people involved in the investigation. Even when the major conducting the investigation turned to them and asked if they had any questions for the current witness seated in the center of the horseshoe after the prosecuting attorney finished, the female captain's attorney merely glanced up from his notes, shook his head, and murmured, 'No, sir, not at this time.' It was as if, Solis thought, after watching witness after witness come up, be questioned by the prosecution, and then be dismissed by the defense without a counterquestion being leveled at him, the female captain and her attorney had given up. Perhaps, he thought, they had. Or maybe, he thought, this was a sham trial, a mere formality that had to be acted out in order to satisfy the judicial niceties that the Americans seemed to be so fond of.

That this proceeding was of interest was obvious based on the people he saw in the audience. Almost directly in front of Solis sat the division commander, Major General C. B. Lane. He was positioned, Solis noticed, so that the investigation officer had to look at him. There is, Solis thought, no subtlety in the intimidation that the Yankee division commander was using this day. Even a blind man, Solis thought, would be able to see that this whole affair was set up to deliver only one result. The charges against the female captain would be found proper and a court-martial would be convened. Unless he had missed something earlier, that was the only way that he could see this.

Glancing over to his left, Solis looked toward the female television correspondent, Jan Fields, who was seated in the rear of the room, like him. How, he wondered, would she report this affair? Her mounting criticism against the manner in which the commander of the 11th Division was conducting operations was becoming a bother, an irritant, and an embarrassment to everyone in this headquarters. Even more than the female infantry captain under investigation, Jan Fields was a puzzle to him. How, he wondered, could she, the wife of an Army general, be allowed to openly stalk and criticize a senior Army field commander? That she had been allowed to remain in Colombia, especially in light of the bitter tone that her reports had taken after the disasters at El Frío, was a wonderment not only to Solis but to every officer in the Colombian Army, not to mention the FARC. 'Were it not so amusing to watch her make that jackass general who struts about like a peacock squirm so,' one Colombian colonel told Solis in confidence, 'we would have arranged a fatal accident for her.' That the Americans hadn't done so, and probably never would, only lowered Solis's opinion of them a bit further.

He was lost in this last thought when something that was said by the witness then being questioned caught Solis's attention. Turning his head away from the female reporter, he looked up and saw Captain James Adderly, Lane's aide-de-camp, sitting in the witness chair. The prosecuting attorney, seated at his table, was reading off a list of questions. 'Then the enemy anti-aircraft fire from the village was effective?'

Looking over at the attorney, Adderly nodded. 'Yes, that's right. We were taking effective fire.'

'From the village?' the investigating officer added.

There was a pause as Adderly looked down at the floor, lost in thought. When he finally did look up and answer, he spoke in a hushed, almost hesitant manner. 'Yes, I believe that's correct.'

In the rear of the room, Solis shook his head. No, he thought. No, that's not correct at all. Based on all the reports he had seen, both Colombian and unofficial FARC accounts Hector Valendez had shown him, there were no FARC fighters in El Frío. And the only anti-aircraft guns on the field had been north of the river, well away from the village. Valendez himself had confirmed this. At one of their meetings he recounted how in a moment of utter frustration he'd ordered a pair of guns he was standing by to fire on the helicopter he thought was a command-and-control aircraft. Either the general's aide did not know for sure what had happened, or . . .

Like a brilliant flash of lightning streaking across his mind, Solis twisted his head over to where Jan Fields sat, then back at Adderly. If, Solis thought, Adderly was lying and this whole investigation was a sham being conducted

under the watchful eye of the division commander, revelation of the truth to the American public would be an
embarrassment that could create a furor that could not
be ignored. Though he did not know how it would be
done, Solis was confident that Hector Valendez, once
convinced of the value of such a propaganda stunt, would
find a way.

Not needing to hear more, Solis got out of his seat and
moved quickly to the door, attracting no more than a
casual glance from Nancy Kozak as she sat there trying
hard to ignore what was going on around her.

Nancy Kozak wasn't ignoring everything. Her time, she
knew, to speak out would come. But not here, not in
this kangaroo court. All this was, she thought, was a
rubber stamp, a ticket punched by Lane's legal staff as
they went about carrying out his desires. When her eyes
swept away from the departing Colombian officer, they
fell on Lane sitting in the front row, watching intently
as his personal aide answered the prosecuting attorney's
questions. Instinctively her eyes narrowed as her face
screwed itself up in a tight expression of determination.
As God is my witness, she swore to herself, you're going
to pay for Hal Cerro's murder. You're going to pay.

Ulrich was too busy paying attention to his friend
and counterpart, Captain Mark Moretti, the prosecuting
attorney, to notice what Kozak was doing. Moretti, Ulrich
knew, was enjoying this, for he realized from the beginning
that Ulrich was not going to make much of a contest here
during the Article 32 proceedings. Ulrich had as much
told him that, not to mention the whole world, when he
informed Lieutenant Colonel Webb that there would be
no witness for the defense today. 'Are you sure?' Webb
probed.

'Sir,' Ulrich responded, trying hard to hide the anguish
he felt over Kozak's decision, 'the witness and I have

discussed this matter in great detail. *She* knows of no one at this time who can materially assist her in her defense.' The manner in which Ulrich stressed *she* every time he mentioned the word left little doubt in Webb's mind that Ulrich was against such a course of action. But, other than asking, he did nothing to change anything. The sooner this case was disposed of with a favorable verdict, the happier Webb would be.

A favorable verdict, of course, meant one that suited Lane.

As Sam Ulrich had predicted, given Nancy Kozak's desire to air her case during a general court-martial, the Article 32 investigation was turning out to be little more than a formality. Everything was going quickly, with the prosecution presenting its witnesses and the defense none. Even when the few witnesses called forth did step up to the stand, they to a man deferred to the written statements already in the hands of the major appointed to conduct the Article 32. No doubt, Ulrich thought as Lane stepped up to the witness chair, Lane will do the same.

The unannounced appearance of Major General C. B. Lane, as well as his agreement, or rather insistence, that he be questioned by the investigating officer, did little to shake his or Kozak's resolve or stance, although he wished she would have allowed him to start what he called his preparation of the battlefield. In the confines of the clean, well-lit conference room being used for the proceedings, each of the witnesses called by the major serving as the investigating officer recounted his version of the incident, delivering each word with well-practiced precision and no apparent malice or emotion. This is all too clean, too neat, too comfortable, Ulrich thought. We're going to have to work real hard to make the members of the jury feel what Kozak felt. For now, however, Sam Ulrich had to content himself with watching Mark Moretti do his thing with Lane.

Standing up after Lane had taken his oath, Moretti walked to a spot six paces before Lane. Holding a manila folder up in his right hand, he began to question Lane. 'Sir, I have here in my hand a copy of the statement concerning the incident in question that you prepared immediately after that affair. Is there in this statement anything you wish to change or add at this time?'

Dropping his voice so that it sounded more commanding, more manly, Lane shook his head as he responded. 'No, there's nothing that I need to add that isn't already part of the record. As far as I'm concerned, that statement and those of the other witnesses you've had up here today pretty well speak for themselves.'

Though he wasn't sure if Lane's last comment was a warning or a summary designed to bring these proceedings to a close, the major conducting the investigation had no doubt in his mind what Lane was saying. With a nervous twitch in his eye, he looked at Moretti. 'Captain, if you would please continue with your questions, if you have any?'

For a moment Moretti looked into Lane's eyes. Even from where he was seated, Ulrich could notice them as they narrowed slightly. That action reminded him of a cat narrowing her eyes as she focuses on her prey before pouncing. Moretti, no doubt, saw Lane's action in the same light, for he turned his gaze away from Lane and faced the major. 'No, sir, I have no further questions at this time.'

Nodding as Moretti turned to make for his seat, the major looked over to Ulrich. 'Does the defense have any questions for the witness at this time?' To everyone's surprise and discomfort, Ulrich stood up as if he were going to walk out before Lane and ask him something. He was tempted, very tempted, to have a crack at Lane then and there. But then, just as he was about to go forth, he held back. Looking over to the major conducting the investigation, Ulrich allowed him to quiver a few seconds longer before he finally announced, 'No, sir. Not at this time.' Taking his seat, he allowed his division commander, against his better judgment, to leave the witness chair unmolested by cross-examination.

Shaken by Ulrich's last action, the investigating officer looked first at Ulrich, and then over to where Lane had taken his seat. 'Does either the attorney for the defense or the prosecution have any further witnesses they wish to call on?'

Moretti and Ulrich, both men unsettled somewhat by the manner in which this whole affair had been handled to date, merely shook their heads. Not waiting for anyone to change their minds or giving anyone time to spring a surprise on him, the major began to bring the session to a close. 'Let the record show that both attorneys indicated that neither had any further witnesses to call on. I therefore declare these proceedings at an end and thank everyone for their cooperation.' With the closing of his notebook, the major ended the hearing.

Kozak, in a hurry to escape the accusing eyes of Lane's division staff, left as soon as people began to get up and leave the room. Ulrich, knowing that she was uncomfortable with what was going on, let her go without comment. There was, after all, he thought, no need to discuss anything further. He had played his hand the way she wanted it. Unless something dramatic happened between now and then, Kozak would get her court-martial just as she had wanted. Maybe, he wondered as he took his time and gathered up his notes and papers, Nancy was hoping that the stories her friend the TV news correspondent was running on Lane and his performance would do her some good. Though he didn't see how they could, and Kozak had never mentioned anything about

Jan Fields's efforts, Ulrich began to wonder if somehow those two weren't up to something.

Ulrich was still pondering this when he walked out of the room into the crowded corridor. It was there in the corridor that the real shock of the day came. Just outside the door Lane stood talking to the investigation officer who stood with his back against the wall. When Lane saw Ulrich emerge, he promptly turned away from the major and faced him, flashing a smile that unnerved Ulrich. Reaching out, Lane placed his right hand on Ulrich's shoulder and gave it a firm, almost playful squeeze. 'You did a fine job in there, Sam. As much as this incident is regrettable, I am glad to see that we' – he paused as he looked at the investigating officer, then back at Sam – 'are all working together to get this affair out of the way so we can get back to some serious war fighting. It will do us no good to squander our time or the reputation of this fine division in a protracted and possibly bitter courtroom slugfest.' Then, as his grasp tightened on Ulrich's shoulder, Lane leaned forward and stared into Sam's eyes, dropping any hint of a smile and replacing it with what could only be described as a menacing glare. 'You understand that, don't you, *Captain*?'

The tone of Lane's voice and the manner in which he emphasized the word *captain*, coupled with the painful digging of his fingers into his shoulder, left no doubt in Ulrich's mind that this was not a question. Rather, Sam realized, it was a warning. Lane was serving him notice, more directly and bluntly than he had imagined even Lane, for all the gall and arrogance that he had displayed in the past, would dare. The impact of what was happening in full view of the officers who had taken part in the just convened investigation stunned Sam. After all, Sam thought, here he was, the man appointed to defend another officer, to the best of his ability, being told by the most senior officer in the country that he was expected to do his part, just as the hand-picked investigation major was doing, to find Kozak guilty and ensure that the trial was conducted with as little fanfare or theatrics as possible.

Stunned by what he took to be Lane's meaning, reinforced by his close physical presence and Lane's grasping hand on his shoulder, Sam was speechless for several seconds. After several long, almost intolerable seconds, the smile returned to Lane's face as he let Sam go. Finished with Sam and the major he turned and without another word walked away. Sam, for his part, was so thoroughly shaken that he didn't even bother looking back at the investigation officer before he too turned and walked away, or more correctly, fled. That he should have stayed a little longer and questioned the investigation officer about whether he too had understood Lane's meaning as Sam did didn't occur to Sam until he reached his office, an office that he shared with two other JAG officers assigned to the division as defending attorneys.

In a daze, he wandered about the empty office for a moment, pondering what to do. Both of the officers with whom he shared the office and the duty of defending personnel in the division were gone at the moment. One, the most senior of the three, was working another case. Detached by Major Oberson, the Regional Defense Counsel and their superior, to the brigade operating to the southwest in the mountains, he had been gone for several days and would not be back for another week, maybe two. He was assisting in an investigation concerning an alleged case of willful negligence by a mechanic that had led to the crash of a helicopter. The investigating officer needed, according to Oberson, to take his time in putting his case in order, since there was the chance that the mechanic might be brought up on charges of murder. Though both Sam and his office mate seriously doubted that such charges could be supported, the other defense attorney left for the field without a protest. 'Any chance to get away from the flagpole, Sam,' he had said with glee, 'is too damned good to pass up.' The second JAG officer who worked out of the office, also senior to Sam and by all rights a better choice to defend Kozak's case, was back in the States. He was on leave, a leave, Sam suddenly realized, that was granted the day after the incident involving Lane and Kozak had occurred, and before Kozak's attorney had been appointed.

Stopping in midstride, Sam shook his head, looked up blankly at the ceiling, and uttered a mournful 'Oh my God!' as it dawned upon him that not only Kozak but he had been set up by Lane. At a time when he was in the greatest need of his colleagues, when their collective wisdom, advice, and support were needed the most, he had been systematically stripped of them. He, like Kozak, had been isolated and left on his own.

Still recovering from this latest shock, Sam refused to believe that a senior Army officer, a general commanding a division in battle, could stoop to such blatantly unethical behavior. Looking down at the floor, he twisted his head first to his right and then to his left, mumbling to himself, 'No, no,' each time his head turned. It was as if he were arguing with an invisible opponent.

When a voice from behind interrupted his disturbing internal debate, the surprise caused him to jump literally off the floor. Spinning about as quickly as his feet hit the floor and he regained his balance, he turned to see his friend and fellow JAG officer Captain Mark Moretti leaning against the frame of the doorway, arms folded across his chest, with a smirk on his face. 'Can't do any better in court, so you decided to come back here and argue against yourself?'

His fright turning to embarrassment, then anger, Sam managed to calm himself before he responded. 'Mark, I've got to talk to someone about this case, another JAG officer.'

Moretti threw his arms up. 'Woo, buddy, I'm the pros-ecution, the enemy. Don't think it would be too swift an idea for you to talk to me about anything concerning Miss Nancy Kozak or this affair. You've got enough problems already.'

Undeterred by his friend's attempt at keeping him from discussing the case, Ulrich shot back, 'You ain't kidding there, partner. Fact is, I think we all have a problem.'

'Who,' Moretti asked, 'do you mean by "we"?'

'Anyone involved in the Kozak case. I think that there are some serious breaches of ethics, not to mention the illegal use of command influence, going on here.'

Though he kept his arms folded, the smile disappeared from Moretti's face as he arched one eyebrow up. 'Oh? And by whom?'

'The division commander, for starters. Colonel Webb and Major Oberson too, I think, might be involved.'

Looking behind him into the corridor, Moretti finally left his position in the doorway, careful to close the door as he came into the office. Pulling out a chair from behind Ulrich's absent officer mate's desk, he spun the armless chair around, straddled the seat, and sat down, resting his arms on the chair's backrest. 'Okay, you've got my attention. What brought you to this conclusion?'

Walking over to his own desk, Sam pulled his chair out and plopped down before he spoke. When he told Moretti of the confrontation he and the investigation officer had just had with Lane, Moretti could tell that Sam was both shaken and concerned. 'My God,' Sam exclaimed when he finished, 'if that isn't abuse of rank and command influence to throw a case under investigation, then I don't know what is.'

'Is that,' Moretti responded in a rather casual tone, 'what you think? Do you really believe that Lane's interest in ending this case is an effort to sway either you or me from doing our duty?' Then, he chuckled. 'Sam, you're overreacting to this command influence thing. Best you forget about looking for something that you can't control and start concentrating on Miss Nancy Kozak's defense.'

Not catching the significance at first of Moretti's inclusion of 'or me' in his statement, Sam looked his friend squarely in the eyes. 'Listen, I've been around long enough to know when someone is playing their macho-bullshit games of intimidation and browbeating with me. Lane wants me to roll over like a good boy and watch the judge and jury hang Kozak out to dry for what amounts to nothing more than a moment of indiscretion in the heat of battle.'

'You said the investigation officer was there. How did he view Lane's comments? What did he think?'

There was a pause before Sam responded sheepishly that he had not asked the investigation officer about the incident. 'I was too stunned,' he explained, 'to think straight. I mean, my God, I never in all my years expected to have a major general come up to me and all but order me to screw a client by not doing my duty.'

To Sam's surprise. Moretti smiled. 'Hey, buddy, don't feel like the Lone Ranger.'

'What do you mean?'

'I mean,' Moretti said as he stood, 'that you're not the only person involved in this mess to feel the strongarm tactics of Conan the Bureaucrat. At least he was nice to you.'

'You mean Lane's approached you?'

'Summoned is more like it. Before I even knew who the hell Captain Nancy Kozak was, let alone what she had done to offend his imperial personage, Lane had me in his office. He explained to me in no uncertain terms that my career in this man's Army depended upon my ability to bring Miss Captain Nancy to justice. "We need," he said as he spread his arms out before him like a TV evangelist preaching to the gathered masses, "to make an example of that officer. We need to ensure that this flagrant violation of orders, breaches of discipline, and unwarranted disrespect for rank be punished quickly and severely, if for no other reason than to serve as an example to other officers in this division." Hell, standing there in his presence, unaware of what exactly he was talking to me about, damned near scared the daylights out of me. I thought we had another My Lai massacre on our hands.'

With his alarm growing by the moment, Sam cut short Moretti's description of Lane's rantings and ravings. 'What,' he all but shouted, 'did Webb say when you told him about this?'

Pausing, Moretti looked at Sam as if he were an idiot. 'What do you mean, told Webb? There was no need to tell Webb anything. He was sitting there the whole time Lane was giving me my marching orders, listening to all of this. Webb, I guess, had already received his fire-and-brimstone speech.' Then cocking his head to the side, Moretti chuckled. 'The only surprise, I guess, is that Lane waited as long as he did before he collared you.'

With a feeling like a great ball of bile was rising slowly from the pit of his stomach, Sam felt himself become sick. It must have shown in his face, for Moretti stopped smiling. 'What, are you surprised by all of this?'

'Shocked,' Sam responded as he fought down the growing sense of nausea that was slowly spreading throughout his body.

'Jesus, you are naive, aren't you? I mean, what in the hell do you expect? A captain, a runny-nose little runt of a captain told Lane off, told him in front of God and country, over a radio set on a battalion command net, to go fuck himself.'

Angered by his friend's attitude, Sam forgot his nausea and fired back. 'Mark, she did so in the heat of battle! My God, a company was in the middle of being decimated and

Lane was taking away their only hope of survival just to save his own precious lily-white ass.'

Indignant that Sam would talk to him in that manner, Moretti pressed the chair forward and jabbed his index finger on the desk before him. 'Major General C. B. Lane was the senior tactical commander present. He was well within his rights to divert whatever assets he deemed necessary to deal with a new and unexpected threat to his entire command. In his judgment, at that moment the safety of the entire brigade, and not just a lone infantry company, was in jeopardy.'

'Do you, Mark, for one moment, believe that Lane was thinking about the security of his brigade, let alone one company, when he ordered the artillery to fire on that village?'

'It doesn't make any difference what I believe. Nor does it really make any difference what the tactical situation was. The facts are that your client challenged a valid order issued by a duly appointed superior officer, in the face of the enemy, and conducted herself, when challenged by that superior officer, in a manner that was prejudicial to the maintenance of discipline and morale of the units and personnel present.' Finished, Moretti stood up and shoved the chair he had been sitting on back against the desk. Turning, he started to storm out of the office but stopped. Spinning around, he glared at Sam. 'My advice to you is that you forget about improprieties on Lane's part, a man who is not on trial, and start worrying about putting a case together for your client, or Miss Nancy Kozak is going to be in Leavenworth well in advance of her year group and long after they've all finished with their staff college course.'

Though he didn't appreciate Moretti's attempt at humor or his advice to him, Sam said nothing as he watched Moretti leave. Though he hated to admit it, what Moretti said was right. Though Lane and everyone else who allowed him to get away with what he was doing might be wrong, such concerns were at the moment academic. There was no chance of getting Kozak to change her mind and appeal for a trial somewhere else. She was bound and determined to have it out right here and as soon as possible. With his hands tied, all Sam could do now was to save her from herself and C. B. Lane, a goal, Sam began to think, that was beyond his grasp.

So deep in thought was Sam over the gloomy prospects of Kozak's chances that he hardly noticed Major José Solis as he stuck his head through the open door. Remembering that he had, in his excitement to discuss his plan with Hector Valendez, forgotten to finish his inspection of this floor, Solis had all but run back to do so. Mumbling a brief apology to Sam, Solis looked around the room quickly, noted the windows and a stack of three computer shipping crates in the corner, and then disappeared without another word.

CHAPTER 18

November 24

Finishing the last bit of paperwork he intended to deal with before taking a break for lunch, Scotty Dixon closed the manila folder before him. Picking up the neat, clean file, he gave it a backhanded toss into his out box, murmuring to himself, 'Take that!' With a shove at the edge of his desk, he pushed himself away from it, stood up, and prepared to leave when Jeff Worsham stuck his head through the open doorway.

'Jeff, just the man I wanted to see. I'm done with the morning dump of drivel and trivia and ready to flee this place for a quiet lunch with my bride.'

Worsham managed a smile. He was glad to see his boss, who had been brooding since his return from Washington, in such an obvious good mood. Never the friendliest man, Dixon's view of the situation in Colombia over the past week had made him grumpier than usual. 'It's as if,' said Major Herman M. Hagstrom, Dixon's intelligence officer, in a private moment with Worsham, 'General Dixon, after running around screaming that the sky was falling, suddenly realized it was true.' Worsham, who agreed with Dixon's glum assessment of the situation in Colombia, nevertheless had attempted to do all in his power to keep Dixon's morale up. Which was why as he entered Dixon's office he was upset. Sensing his chief of staff's mood, Dixon stopped what he was doing. 'Why so down in the mouth, trooper?'

'Well, sir, it's about your luncheon date with your wife.'

There was no need to say more. Like a puppet that had just had its strings cut, Dixon's shoulders slumped down. 'Don't tell me, Madam Media called and had to cancel.'

Worsham nodded. 'Yes, sir, she did. Not more than five minutes ago.'

Cocking his head to the side, Dixon sighed. 'Jeff, war may be hell, but being married to the media is a bitch. Thank God we never decided to have children. Jan would never be able to keep a due date, and the poor kid would spend half its life penned up in her belly waiting to be born.' Though meant to be funny, his tone betrayed both his disappointment and irritation. Looking back at his desk, then over to Worsham, Dixon mused, 'Oh, well, Jeff, me boy, looks like I've got enough time to finish going through all that crap the staff keeps piling on my desk before Colonel Agustin arrives.'

'Well, sir, that's the other thing I need to tell you. Colonel Agustin is already here. He has been for ten minutes.'

Surprised, Dixon looked at Worsham. 'Here already? Was the office call he asked for set for – '

'Yes, sir, it was scheduled later this afternoon. But he showed up here and asked if he could wait.'

'Why in the hell,' Dixon demanded with a decided note of anger in his voice, 'didn't you tell me he was here? Colonel Agustin is the new commander of the Presidential Brigade, an important assignment in their Army. Whose brilliant idea was it to let him . . .'

Worsham threw his hands up and diverted his face as if he were trying to protect himself from Dixon's verbal blast. 'I told him I would announce him to you, sir, twice. But he declined both times, insisting, no, demanding, that he wait.'

Understanding Worsham's gestures and puzzled by Agustin's insistence that he not be disturbed, Dixon calmed down. 'Please, Jeff, do me a favor and show him in.'

Without another word, Worsham left. When he reappeared, a tall, well-turned-out Colombian officer followed him into the room. Stepping aside, Worsham motioned to Agustin with his right hand. 'General Dixon, Colonel Marco Agustin, commanding officer of the Presidential Brigade.'

Walking over to the colonel, Dixon smiled and offered his right hand. Rather than take his hand, Agustin saluted stiffly. Caught short by his action, Dixon stopped and returned the salute. Only then did Agustin drop his hand and reach out for Dixon's. When they finally did shake hands, the Colombian gave two quick shakes that were as formal as his salute and then pulled his hand away. 'It is, sir, a pleasure to meet a soldier with your reputation and background.' Even his words were delivered with a rigidity that gave no hint of emotion or even sincerity. It was, Dixon thought, as if someone were holding a knife in this man's back and dictating his every word and action. That, of course, didn't mean that he had to respond in the same cold manner. Nodding in acknowledgment of Agustin's compliment, he smiled. 'Your reputation is quite legendary itself. The leadership you displayed during the withdrawal of the garrison at Puerto Carreño and your trek through enemy-held territory is in itself quite extraordinary.'

If Dixon had meant mention of his retreat from Puerto Carreño as a compliment, it had failed, and he quickly realized it when Agustin's face went flush with anger and not embarrassment. Agustin, realizing that his reaction had shown through his frigid exterior, quickly tried to change the subject. 'General Dixon, I am in your debt for allowing me to interrupt your busy schedule on such short notice.'

Sensing that Agustin wanted to get down to business, Dixon motioned to Worsham, who quietly withdrew, closing the door behind him as he left the room. 'Please, Colonel, sit down.' Moving over to the overstuffed chairs that his sergeant major had managed to liberate from the embassy staff, Dixon sat, crossed his legs, and then leaned over on his left arm which was perched on the chair's arm. Agustin followed, seated himself, but did not relax, not at first. 'I assume, Colonel, that this is more than a social call.'

With those words, Agustin allowed his rigid frame to slump over, letting his back ease itself into the chair, his knees coming apart, and his arms going limp. It seemed to take a long time and a great deal of effort to arrest his change from his exaggerated formality to near total collapse. When he looked up, the face Dixon saw was not the same one Agustin had worn during the introductions. Dixon could now see the haggard face of a man who was both exhausted and worried. There was much more to this meeting, he realized at that moment, than a simple social office call. Only when the Colombian colonel appeared to have finally come to rest, did Dixon speak. 'Though I have just met you, Colonel, it is obvious that you are troubled and that you are hesitant to speak. If for whatever reason you wish to leave without going any further, please do so. I will forget this entire incident, and we can both go about our duties as if this meeting never took place.'

There was no immediate response. Instead, Agustin looked into Dixon's eyes and studied them for a moment. Whether he was looking into them in the hope that he could see past the exterior and get a measure of the man before him or whether Agustin was merely searching in his own weary mind for the right words with which to answer him, Dixon could not tell. Though the suspense was beginning to irk him, Dixon chose not to rush the colonel. He would, Dixon knew, either tell him all in his own time or get up in another moment and leave.

'Have you ever, General Dixon, committed treason?'

Totally taken aback by the question, Dixon let his jaw drop. 'Excuse me, Colonel?'

Agustin narrowed his eyes and spoke slowly, more distinctly as he repeated his question. 'Have you ever committed treason?'

Dixon thought about that. In Mexico, both he and then Major General Al Malin had exceeded their authority in launching a raid that freed several hostages including his wife, Jan. And in Germany during the Ukrainian nuclear weapons crisis he had helped Malin lay out an operation that gave the illusion of being treasonous. But the outright committing of treason, the act of aiding or assisting in the compromise of his nation's security, no, he hadn't. With his face frozen in a well-controlled stare, Dixon shook his head. 'No, I have never done so.'

Averting his eyes, Agustin sighed. 'It is not, señor, an easy thing to do. I have until recently never even imagined that I could bring myself to do so. But circumstances, well, as they teach in your command and general staff school at Fort Leavenworth, extreme situations sometimes call for extreme measures.'

Though he was anxious to get to the heart of the matter, Dixon realized that he dare not rush the colonel. Instead he simply nodded. 'Yes, that is very true. Sometimes we are presented with situations that are beyond the scope of our training and past experience.'

'I have, General Dixon, dedicated my life to the military with the understanding that by doing so I would be serving the people of my country. I have always in the past trusted my superiors and performed my duties without question and demanded that those under me do likewise, for I believed in the Army, my Army.' As he spoke, he began to become animated as the anger inside of him began to build. 'I was always taught, from my cadet days on, to do what is right and have trust in your superiors. Yet now,' he said, throwing out his arms to emphasize his point, 'now I find out that it is impossible to do both. What I believe is right no longer appears to be in concert with what my superiors are doing.'

Pausing to catch his breath, Agustin looked down at the floor, spoke without looking up. 'How could I be so blind? How could I be so naive? I have been a fool, a fool for a very long time. And yet now when I realize it, I do not know what to do about it.' Looking up at Dixon, he said, 'I am like a junior lieutenant lost in the jungle with no map and no one to guide me. I am, señor, worse than useless. I have become a traitor.'

Unable to restrain himself, despite his realization that Agustin seemed to be pushing himself to the verge of a mental collapse, Dixon began to prod him. 'I realize, Colonel Agustin, that there is something troubling you. That I have gathered. But what, sir, causes you to discount your loyalty to your government? And why discuss this issue with me?'

'Because, General, I am not the only traitor to my nation. You see, I can no longer willingly follow my superiors, because they have taken it upon themselves to deal with the enemy. While your division was roaming the mountains to the west and my garrison was being wiped out in the east, those officers who had sent us out there were busy preparing for another coup. And even worse, since the disasters of the past two months have made it clear that the FARC is a force to be reckoned with, regardless of who controlled the seat of government

here in Bogotá, the General Staff of the Colombian Army
has been holding preliminary discussions with the FARC's
central committee. They are, as we speak and our soldiers
fight, seeking to strike a deal with them.'

Though he had been told by both Colonel Chester
Thomas, the military attaché, and his own intelligence
officer, that there existed a strong possibility that the
Colombian Army might be considering another coup,
to have it confirmed by one of their own officers, the
commander of a key unit that would play a major role
in just such an effort, was a bit shocking and unsettling.
It took Dixon a moment to recover his balance. When he
did, he wasn't quite sure where to start. Stalling for time,
so that he could sort out the implications that Agustin's
pronouncement gave rise to, Dixon changed the course of
the conversation for the moment. 'Why, Colonel, have you
chosen me, a foreigner whom you have never met before,
to discuss this matter with?'

There was a hint of resignation in Agustin's voice when
he answered. 'To start with, señor, there is really not
much to discuss. I fear that what will happen will happen
regardless of what you or I do. You see, my superiors
have taken care to correct all those deficiencies that the
last coup revealed. Even if my President were to be
told today that another coup was coming, any efforts
he made to round up the ringleaders or to rally units
he might believe are loyal to him, would fail. One by
one the units that the General Staff felt uncomfortable
with have been scattered to the far reaches of our country
or fed into the FARC's meat grinder. Underequipped
and sent in piecemeal, the officers and men who would
have stood by the President have been eliminated. As
your own report submitted months ago suggested, the
modern equipment that your government has given us
has not gone to the units most likely to be used against
the rebels. It has gone without exception to those units

which the General Staff deemed loyal to them and not to the government.'

The mention of his report, a highly classified project that was not meant for distribution outside the U.S. Army, troubled Dixon. Though who and why someone had released it to the Colombians troubled Dixon, he didn't pursue the matter. That he knew was academic at the moment. What was important was ascertaining, if at all possible, whether this Colombian colonel sitting before him was reliable and how true his story of gloom and doom was. Agustin, for his part, was watching Dixon during the uneasy silence, and answered as best he could the unspoken question, the one that Dixon was trying to find words for. 'It is difficult, I am sure, for a soldier from your Army to believe the word of an officer who appears to be betraying his nation.'

Not quite sure how to react, Dixon simply sat and stared at the Colombian colonel. In his silence, he confirmed what Agustin had just stated. Well, Agustin thought, it is his privilege to believe what he will. It is my duty to do what I must. Leaning forward, he rested his elbows on his knees and clasped his hands together. When he spoke, the whining softness of his voice was gone. In its place there was a firm, almost accusatory tone. 'There are many ways a man can betray his country, General Dixon. Some men do it out of a misplaced sense of loyalty. Others, more vile creatures, do so for personal gain. Regardless of why they do it, the results are the same. Solemn oaths and pledges are forgotten as the traitor begins to create his own standards of conduct, ethics, and morality so that he can justify his actions. In the process, those under him suffer, sometimes physically but always in their hearts, as they watch their ideals and principles being surrendered one by one by those they are pledged to follow and obey. That death, Señor General, the death of the spirit and the heart, is the more painful of the two.' Sitting up, Agustin puffed out his chest. 'I know, for my heart has bled itself white. I am, like you, still a soldier.' Then, he let himself go limp and shook his head. 'But I am no longer a man. This war and the politicians, both in and out of uniform, rebel and loyal, have killed my pride and my faith.'

Of this last part, Dixon heard little. The first thought that popped into his head was that Agustin was talking about him. Then without any conscious effort he asked himself if he was talking about Lane. Or was he talking about both him and Lane? It was this last thought, the idea that he could no longer tell the difference between himself and a man whom he despised, that finally shook Dixon to the point that all displays of outward control were lost. Without a word, he jumped to his feet and turned away from Agustin. He stormed across the room several feet, then checked himself.

By the time he turned, Agustin was on his feet, standing erect and watching him. 'Perhaps, General Dixon, this was a mistake. I apologize for disturbing you.' The colonel's voice was anxious and worried. Dixon tried to say something to calm him, to keep him from leaving, but no words came. Like a fish stung into senselessness by a man-of-war, Dixon stood in the center of his office and watched Agustin pivot about and flee as quickly as he could.

With Agustin gone, Dixon was left on his own, left to sort out and account for his sins, both real and imagined.

En route to the cafe where she and Willie Freeman were scheduled to meet with someone alleged to be a member of the FARC, all Jan could think about was her missed luncheon appointment with Scott. It was becoming harder, she realized, to put her career and work before her relationship with him. It should be getting easier, she thought. By now their need to demonstrate their love and devotion to each other should be less, not more. Instead it was becoming demanding, more demanding than anything that she had ever known before. Is there always, she wondered, the need to reaffirm one's love and devotion over the years? Is there a break-even point where both parties settle into a comfortable routine? Or would there always be the need to recommit herself emotionally and physically to a person whom she was already legally and morally bound to? Looking out the window of the taxi as it bumped and ground its way through the busy, narrow streets, Jan pondered these questions, all but forgetting their meeting.

Big Willie, however, hadn't. Sitting next to her, he interrupted Jan's train of random thoughts again and again. 'How do we know, Jan, that we can trust these people? For all we know, this could be a setup by the Colombian government. You know they're anxious to get rid of anyone who doesn't toe the party line. The way you've been hammering away at them isn't exactly winning you friends in this town.'

When she bothered to answer, those answers were quick and short. 'It's not a setup. Trust me.'

Jan's confidence, however, didn't put Willie off. 'I trust you. No need to worry about that. I just don't trust the people who set this whole thing up. I mean, if they are real rebels, what happens if they try to grab you, you know, for propaganda reasons? Or they could be setting you up for a hit. I can see it all now. "Famous Yankee newswoman and trusting sidekick killed in bold broad-daylight terrorist attack in the heart of the Colombian capital. More on this story and others at eleven."'

Turning to face him, there was anger in Jan's eyes. His nagging and persistent interruptions were getting to her. 'If you're so worried, stay in the taxi while I handle this.'

Willie shook his head. 'No way, Jan. Someone needs to save you from yourself.'

'Oh, and you're elected? You got the duty today, I suppose?'

Quite literally he did, but he could not say so. When Jan had been approached that morning by a woman claiming to be connected with the FARC, to arrange the meeting they were headed for, both Willie Freeman, Jan's soundman, and JT Evens, the cameraman, agreed between themselves that one of them had to go with her. Since Willie knew Spanish, and his size and bearing were more imposing than JT's, both men decided that Willie was the natural choice. Neither Willie nor JT, of course, told Jan how they came to their decision. That, however, was not necessary, since both men, as Genny Conners liked to say, were always tripping over themselves in an effort to outmacho the other and save 'poor little Jan' from the imaginary big bad wolf.

As reassuring as this attitude could be, there were times, like now, that it grated on her nerves. She was about to turn and snap at Willie when the taxi slowed, then pulled over to the curb. In Spanish the driver announced that they had arrived. Glancing out the window, then back at Willie, Jan decided to postpone her talk with her self-appointed guardian. Without a word, she was out of the cab, leaving Willie to pay. Might as well let him be of some use, she thought.

Used to meeting people under such circumstances, Jan stood there on the sidewalk waiting until someone approached or showed an interest in her. That did not take long. From behind a man came up and took her arm. 'This way please, Ms. Fields.' Though his grasp was light, it was firm enough to direct her to a table where a man somewhat short in stature sat watching their approach. With dark hair and a pinched face that accentuated his lean, almost skeletal frame, the man reminded Jan of a professor, not a revolutionary. When he stood and extended his hand across the table by way of greeting,

Jan could see that she was an inch, maybe two inches, taller than he. 'Señorita Fields, I am so glad that you were able to come on such short notice.'

Taking the hand offered, Jan allowed him to take hers and shake it. South American men, she knew, didn't take kindly to having a woman challenging them, even symbolically, as many people did in the United States when shaking hands. No need, she thought, to get this guy bent out of shape unless she needed to. With a smile, the tone of her voice was both light and cheery. 'It is, señor, a pleasure.'

Standing, the Colombian eyed as much of Jan as he could see of her. 'Your beauty, señorita, is surpassed only by your reputation.' The words, Jan thought, were spoken with the same obvious glee in his voice that a child uses when describing a bowl of chocolate ice cream covered with chocolate spills and chocolate syrup. Though she often was accused by Scott of being overly sensitive to such things, Jan could tell from the way this man was looking at her and talking that he saw woman first, correspondent second.

Easing into the chair being held by the man who had escorted her to the table, Jan folded her legs and began. 'Your kind invitation, señor, was too good to pass up.' Jan made a slight nod of her head toward Willie, who had finally come up and joined them at the table. 'Though some of my staff feel that accepting your invitation is neither prudent nor wise, I believe that if you meant to do me or anyone on my staff harm, you could have done so without going through all of the trouble of arranging a meeting such as this.'

Hector Valendez smiled. They had been right. Everyone who spoke of this woman said that she was as straightforward and as blunt as she was beautiful. There would be no room, he realized, for dancing in the shadows with this one. Directness and openness, these were what she respected and insisted upon. Well, he thought as he nodded, then let us drop the chase and get on with this. 'We have no intention of bringing any harm to you or your staff. Though I do not mean to denigrate your status, there are many, many targets that better deserve our attentions and efforts. And besides, we are revolutionaries, not murderers. Though the government makes no distinction between its own people and those who are fighting against its corrupt rule, we have no such problem.' Leaning forward, Valendez's eyes narrowed as his voice softened to a hiss. 'We know who our enemies are and how to deal with them.'

Jan realized that the Colombian's statements were meant to both reassure her and to threaten her. By agreeing to this meeting and coming this far, she knew that she had already made a pact with the devil, a pact that he would insist be fulfilled.

From her silence and expression, Valendez knew that Jan Fields had taken his meaning. Easing back into his seat, he let his face go calm, and raised his right hand to signal a waiter who had been hovering nearby. 'Would you care for something, señorita?'

Jan nodded. 'Coffee, please.' Though she was dying for an ice-cold Diet Coke, she knew it would be impolite and in bad form to order one. Keep the natives happy, she thought, as long as you can. After the order had been placed and the waiter disappeared, Jan decided to regain the initiative if possible. 'You went through a great deal of effort and have placed yourself in some risk asking us here. There is a reason, I trust, for doing so.'

'There has been recently a great deal being made by the Colombian military and your own about how our operations are placing innocent civilians at risk. Stories, such as the one recently published in the government-controlled press, about us using small children to carry messages and explosives through their lines, are patent lies, poor attempts to make us, and not them, appear to be the evil ones.'

With as little expression as possible, Jan agreed with a slight nod, knowing that this Colombian and his masters were as guilty of lying to the media as was the government he spoke and fought against. Though the abuses were not as widespread as the government claimed, this rebel group, like all those before it, used civilians when it suited them. Even as they spoke, though she didn't realize it, a group of women employed by the Colombian Ministry of Defense to clean their building nightly were being trained in the fine art of smuggling, emplacing, and setting explosives.

Ignoring Jan's less than enthusiastic endorsement of his denial, Hector Valendez continued. 'Another fine example of the government and the American military trying desperately to smear my cause with innocent blood is being played out here in the capital by your own senior military commander. In a court of law he has lied. He fabricated a fantasy, and you supported him.'

Thrown and confused by this last comment, Jan cocked her head. 'What fantasy are you talking about? If you are talking about the case against Captain Kozak, I was there during the proceedings. Nothing that came out then, to the best of my knowledge, was a lie. What exactly did General Lane say that was incorrect?'

He had hit a chord. Though Jan tried to keep her expression in check, he could tell by a slight flutter of her eyes and the pace with which she now spoke that he had been right. 'Your general,' he continued, 'during that hearing claimed that he was fired on from the village of El Frío, a village which had already been brutalized by government forces. No one, however, was defending El Frío at that time. In fact it was all but deserted. After the government force raped it, an event that you so courageously recorded and publicized, the FARC retook the town but did not reoccupy it. There was, as you know, little left to occupy. The few survivors who were left among dead, having suffered enough, were left alone by our fighters.'

'Then why,' Jan injected, 'the second battle? Why did the FARC choose to fight for a worthless objective? And where were the guns that fired on General Lane's helicopter? He was fired on, you know. That part of the story is too well documented.'

Though he wanted to smile now that he had Jan snarled in his trap, Valendez forced a frown. 'No land, no village in my country is worthless, Ms. Fields. Though El Frío may not measure up to your ideas of an ideal community, it is for my countrymen a home.'

Not sure if the indignation was feigned or real, Jan apologized. She did not want to lose this lead, a lead that could be important to Nancy Kozak's defense. 'I did not mean to imply that El Frío was useless. I just don't understand why three battles in as many days were fought over it.'

Propping his elbow on the table, Valendez raised three fingers. 'The first was waged by the government against its own people. It punished El Frío in the manner that it did in order to discourage its own people in other villages from joining us and fighting for their own rights and freedom.' He dropped a finger. 'We, the FARC, went back into El Frío for revenge. It would have been wrong to allow the government to commit such a crime and go unpunished. Though it was their soldiers and not the corrupt politicians who ordered the attack who paid, the message we left was clear.'

That, of course, was a lie. The FARC counterattack, ordered and directed by Valendez himself, had been well planned and prepared for. El Frío had been the bait that the government had readily taken, just as Jan Fields was now taking the bait that he was dangling before her. Letting the scowl on his face grow, Valendez dropped his third finger. 'The final battle, initiated by your Army, only had one purpose in mind, to kill Colombians. And as your General Lane admitted during an interview with another news correspondent after the operation, he didn't much care whether the people they killed were civilian or military.'

The Colombian's accusation angered Jan. Most of the Army officers she had come to know, over the years, would never do such a thing. In all the operations her own husband, Scott, had been involved in, he had been scrupulous in avoiding any unnecessary suffering or harm to the civilian populace. But then she realized that Scotty hadn't been in charge of this operation. In fact, since he had arrived in Colombia, he had been uneasy and at times upset over the manner in which Lane was doing things. Maybe this, she mused, was why he had been so willing to offer her advice the other night, advice that could only be damaging to a fellow officer. Like his self-imposed silence on discussing any current military matters with her, he had never spoken badly of a senior officer in her presence. Perhaps, Jan thought, there is some truth to what this Colombian was saying. Like many of the reporters covering this war, she had read up on Vietnam, especially after her own husband began to openly draw that parallel. In that war, cases of killing civilians in order to inflate body counts, while exaggerated, were too numerous to ignore or deny. Had, Jan wondered, the American Army here in Colombia reverted to that brutal practice? Pushing that thought aside for the moment, she restated her third question. 'If the guns that fired on General Lane's helicopter were not in the village, then where were they?'

'North of the river, a good three kilometers away from the village. In the pre-trial proceedings held the other day, the pilot of General Lane's helicopter stated that they were flying at three thousand feet, just north of the river, when they were fired upon. From the village, it is impossible to see an object, even one as large as a helicopter, flying at that height while moving along the north bank of the Meta River.'

'How do you know this for sure?'

Valendez leaned back in his chair, throwing out his chest in a show of pride. 'Because, Ms. Fields, I was there. I was beside the guns and I gave the order for them to fire on General Lane's helicopter.'

This announcement was enough to even solicit a response from Willie, a man known for his ability to remain unflappable under the most harrowing circumstances. Jan and Willie looked at each other for a moment, then at the Colombian. 'Can you prove this? I mean the part about the guns being north of the river and not in the village?'

'I am willing, Ms. Fields, to have your team escorted to the site of the battle, both where the guns were and in the village, where your general claimed that they were. You will be free to roam about as you please, interviewing the gun crews, the villagers, and anyone you like. I will even arrange for a helicopter to fly at the same altitude and on the same course that Lane's pilot claims to have flown when they were taken under fire. You and your camera will be able to see clearly that no one in El Frío could have fired on your general while his aircraft was flying over the river as his pilot testified.'

It was only then that Jan realized that she had no idea who this man was. It was clear from the manner in which he was now talking that he was no lackey, no mere messenger boy. 'Can I interview you on tape?'

Valendez shook his head. 'No, I am afraid not. You see, I am a modest man, and in reality what I have to say would add little to this that isn't best answered by the people who actually did the shooting and the villagers who saw it all.'

Jan looked over at Willie again. He gave her a blank stare in return. Facing back to Valendez, Jan asked how soon he needed her answer. 'Tonight, Ms. Fields. I will need to know by then so that I can make sure the arrangements are taken care of and you can be back in time for the upcoming trial.'

The fact that the Colombian seemed to know a great deal about Nancy Kozak's trial didn't strike Jan as strange. Nor was she bothered by the possibility that this could, as Willie pointed out, turn out to be nothing more than a propaganda event staged for her benefit by the rebels. What was important, as she and Willie stood up and prepared to leave, was that she was going to be able to do something, perhaps something really big, to help Nancy Kozak. That, and only that, at this moment was her chief concern. All others, including her personal safety, were forgotten.

When the two North Americans had gone, the waiter who had served Valendez and Jan their coffee came over and sat next to Valendez. 'I will be glad,' he stated, 'when we are finished here and can go back to the jungles and mountains. I will never again, Commander, complain about carrying your radio.'

Rafael Dario's comment made Valendez laugh. 'You never complained before. In fact, the only time you are a nuisance to me is when you get this crazy idea in your young head that carrying a gun and pulling a trigger is more important than what you do for me.'

'Important, perhaps, in your eyes. But I have never given up the hope that you will someday show mercy on my humble soul and let me once, just once, stand up and fight for my country like a man.'

'We all must do our duties, my friend, regardless of how mundane or unglamorous.'

Looking around at the street, Dario grunted. 'Well, I do hope that our duties will soon take us away from this city. It is without doubt the filthiest and unfriendliest place I have ever seen on earth.'

'But it is the heart, my young friend. It is the heart of this country and of our enemy. And one well-aimed stroke delivered here, held true to its mark, is worth a dozen great victories out there. No, we still have much to do here, and if we are patient we might be able to bring all of our efforts together soon.'

'But how soon?'

Valendez ignored his radioman's impatience. Instead he too looked around, sipping his coffee as he did so. Slowly returning his cup to the saucer, Valendez smiled. 'Soon. Very, very soon, my young friend.'

CHAPTER 19

November 28

The morning had progressed as anticipated. One by one the witnesses for the prosecution were called forward by Captain Mark Moretti. Each in turn recounted his version of the incidents surrounding the insubordination and disrespect that Captain Nancy Kozak had allegedly committed against Major General C. B. Lane on November 12 over El Frío. Prompted by Moretti's questions, the witnesses without exception repeated their stories almost word for word as they had recorded them on their written statements some two weeks prior. Everything, Lane thought as he watched from the front row of seats provided for the spectators, was going well. He liked things that not only went well but did so in a neat, orderly, and predictable manner, like a train running on schedule.

First came the crewmen of Lane's helicopter, in ascending order of rank, starting with the door gunner. As he had during the Article 32 investigation hearing, Mark Moretti started his questioning by holding up each of the witnesses' statements and asking, 'To the best of your knowledge, is this statement of yours a true and accurate description of the events of November twelfth?'

Without hesitation, each man in turn nodded, responding with a firm and unflinching 'Yes, sir, that statement is correct.'

'Would you please, for the benefit of the jury,' Moretti would continue, 'summarize what you saw and heard that day, while operating over El Frío?' Each man did, of course, respond to Moretti's request, using the same firm and steady voice that they had used when answering Moretti's first question. Jan Fields-Dixon, seated in the rear of the temporary courtroom between J. T. Evens and Big Willie, groaned every time Moretti started his routine. 'You know, he could have saved the government a fortune if he had recorded his witnesses' statements at the Article 32 and simply replayed them here.'

'Yeah,' JT responded. 'But then your friend General Lane and mine wouldn't have had another chance to tromp Captain Kozak's face into the mud again.'

Mention of Lane's name caused Jan to glance over to where he sat like a fat cat watching mice at play in his snare. 'You're probably right. Though I don't understand it, he's no doubt enjoying this.'

'Not for long,' Willie intoned in his deep, solemn voice.

When Ulrich would wipe the smirk off Lane's face, however, remained a good question. When Jan had approached him with the videotape that Hector Valendez had been so instrumental in orchestrating, Sam Ulrich had initially rejected it out of hand. 'I can't use that! That's the enemy you were dealing with.'

But Jan would not be denied. 'What in the hell do you think Lane is, Santa Claus? He's out to get Nancy Kozak, and since you're the attorney for the defense, that makes him the enemy.'

Reluctantly he accepted the film pledging that he would

use it during his cross-examination of Lane's helicopter crew. 'If I can show that they were so badly confused that they couldn't tell where the enemy fire was coming from,' he told Jan as he began to see the possibilities the video offered, 'then perhaps I can start setting the stage for when I call Nancy's people to tell how difficult things really were that day. And even if the judge throws it out on some pretext or another, at least the jury will have seen some of it, and a shadow of a doubt concerning the prosecution's statements will start to muck up his case.'

Jan, of course, had little confidence in Ulrich. 'He reminds me,' she told Willie after her meeting with him, 'too much of an office boy I had when I was covering the war in Egypt years ago. Nice kid, but a little short on common sense and decidedly lacking in the backbone area.' This, and a chronic cynicism that had settled down over everyone who was trying to do something to save a deteriorating situation in Colombia, left Jan, Willie, and JT worried as they watched the morning's proceedings go on like a dress parade. Even the defense seemed to be on line with the program. When offered the opportunity to cross-examine the witnesses called forth by Mark Moretti, Sam Ulrich cross-examined them in a subdued, almost hesitant manner. One by one Mark Moretti walked them through their stories, just as the investigating officer had during the Article 32. And one by one Sam followed the prosecution, asking no brilliant questions, making no startling revelations, only asking each witness to clarify a point or rephrase a comment he had made before. One, two, three, the witnesses came and the witnesses left, like batters facing an ace pitcher.

Sitting next to Sam, Nancy Kozak watched with a face that was as set and expressionless as a young art student's first sculpture. No words were passed between her and her attorney while he waited for his opportunity to cross-examine the current witness, no sidewise glances,

either from him or Kozak, were cast while he was doing
so. It was, one spectator noted, as if the two were
strangers sharing a bus ride, each absorbed in his or
her own thoughts and not interested in the person seated
next to them.

Jan, however, more than made up for Nancy's lack of
emotions as her squirming increased as the morning and
Sam Ulrich's uninspired performance wore on. Though
she knew that Kozak's attorney had an ace in the hole,
an ace that only she, her crew, and Nancy Kozak knew
of, she was becoming angry at the young JAG officer. 'He
can do better than that,' she would comment to no one in
particular. Or she would whisper to Willie, 'He needs to
be a little more aggressive, more probing.' While Willie
ignored her, Jan was beginning to wonder if, rather than
to shock the jury, Ulrich's strategy was to lull them to sleep
or bore them to the point that they gave in and demanded
the trial be brought to a close. Hoping for a short recess,
Jan, despite her pledge to remain in the background, told
JT, 'I swear I'm going to give Sam Ulrich a swift kick if he
doesn't start acting like a defense attorney soon.'

It wasn't until he got to First Lieutenant Clarence G.
Kelly, C. B. Lane's pilot, that Sam started to come alive.
Starting as he did with all those who had gone before, Sam
approached the witness, statement in hand, and asked
questions that were meant to emphasize certain points
at issue, points which until now seemed totally unrelated.
'Lieutenant Kelly,' Sam said in a rather casual manner,
'you stated that at the time you began receiving fire from
the ground you were over the river.'

Quick to point out the JAG officer's error, Kelly cut in.
'North of the river, sir. We had drifted over the north bank
of the Meta River.'

Looking down at the sheet of paper, Sam pretended to
look for the passage that Kelly was talking about, then
exclaimed, even though he had not found it. 'Oh, yes,

so you did.' Looking at Kelly, Sam's face dropped into a pronounced inquisitive stare. 'Are you sure, Lieutenant?'

Bothered by being brought to task for such a trivial matter, Kelly's answer was sharp, almost to the point of being rude. 'Yes, Captain, I am positive. As the aircraft commander, I am responsible for keeping track of where we are at all times.'

Sam thought about that for a moment, shaking his head before he continued. 'Why, Lieutenant, were you there?'

'We were executing a sharp, steep bank in order to turn around quickly.'

'And this bank, it was to the left?'

Again displaying the same impatience as he had before, Kelly responded quickly and pointedly, 'No, to the right, just as I wrote in my statement and stated for Captain Moretti.'

'And while you were making this bank, where were you looking?'

'To the right, naturally.'

'I'm sorry, I'm not an aviator. You'll have to explain that to me,' Sam blurted as he reached out behind him and tossed the pilot's statement onto the table where Kozak sat. Only Kozak, who leaned back slightly as the statement came flying toward her, and Jan caught the significance of Sam's gesture. He had symbolically thrown down the red flag.

'In such a steep bank, I have to use the ground as a reference to make sure that I don't bank too far.'

'Why not use your instruments? Aren't your instruments more accurate than your eyesight and judgment?'

'Sir, I am an experienced pilot. Though I do use my instruments, I have more than enough experience to make such an elementary banking turn I was executing when we were taken under fire.'

Sam noted the hint of arrogance that was slipping into

the pilot's voice. 'Back to the point. You said you were looking to the right, correct?'

'Yes, sir, that is correct.'

'What, Lieutenant, did you see?'

Kelly paused for a moment, in part because he needed to search his memory in order to recall the images of that day and time, and in part because he was confused. This, he thought, had nothing to do with the incident. Nor had anyone made such a fuss over these details before. It was, he knew, not part of the prepared script that his superior and Captain Moretti had drilled him on. Still it was a simple, harmless question, and he prepared to answer it as best he could, making sure that he didn't surrender any more information than he needed to, just as Captain Moretti had instructed him. 'I saw the river, which was just at the bottom of my view. In the center was the area where the village should have been. And above that the southern horizon. Here and there along that horizon, there were several helicopters, a couple of scouts and several UH-60s.'

'You said, Lieutenant, where the village should have been. Didn't you see the village?'

'I saw the church steeple. It was a great terrain reference point, the only really reliable one, as a matter of fact, other than the river, that we had.'

'And,' Sam continued as he turned away to face Kozak, 'what happened while you were making your turn and watching this church steeple?'

'We were taken under fire.'

'How did you become aware of this?'

'That we were under fire?'

Sam glanced over his shoulder and nodded. 'Yes, that you were under fire.'

'Well, sir, the whole aircraft suddenly started to jerk and buck, as if someone was underneath it rapping it with a hammer.'

One member of the jury and a couple of spectators who had not yet been lulled into a near state of inattention realized the significance of Kelly's last statement. One of them, an aviator, shot upright in his seat, his eyes opening wide. This sudden reaction acted as a cue, alerting those around and behind him, that something had just happened. What it was they didn't know. But there had been a change, and now they were attentive to what was happening in the front of the room.

'What, Lieutenant Kelly, was your first reaction?'

'To look around, first at my instruments, then to the warning lights on the control panel, and finally about the cabin.'

Turning to face Kelly again, Sam eased himself back so that he rested half sitting on the table. Folding his arms, he narrowed his eyes. 'Before you turned away, away from a village that was obscured by so much vegetation that only its church steeple was visible, what did you see?'

As before, he paused. Cocking his head, Kelly looked down as if he were scanning the inside of his mind in an effort to review the images of that scene he had stored there. When he was ready, he looked up at Sam, his confusion now obvious. 'Just the church steeple, the far horizon, and the other helicopters. That's all.'

'You didn't see any tracers?'

'No, sir, I didn't see any tracers.'

'None, none at all? You saw no indication of ground fire directed at you before your aircraft was hit?'

'No, sir. As I said, the first clue I had that we were under fire was when we started getting hit, from underneath.'

Over where the jury sat, an aviation captain who was one of the jury bolted upright as he kept his eyes fixed on Kelly and muttered an abrupt exclamation. In the silence of the conference room, his soft 'Oh, shit!' caught off guard those who were still unaware that something significant had happened. Even Moretti, who had been listening intently, took several seconds to catch on to the fact that the pilot of Lane's aircraft had just stated in so many words that the fire they had received could not possibly have come from the village. Slowly, as that revelation began to sink in, Moretti's mouth dropped as he shook his head.

In the rear, Jan, watching intently, broke into a broad smile and turned to smack JT on the shoulder with a clenched fist. 'Yes!' she whispered. JT recoiled from the unexpected blow, and Willie looked over at her in surprise. 'Yes! He did it. The wimp did it. He's going to do it.'

While a wave of hushed conversations and murmurs broke out throughout the conference room, Sam turned to face the spectators. Spinning his briefcase around on the table, he opened it, reached in with his right hand for the videocassette that sat in the center of the case, laid his fingers on it, and paused. Looking down at the cassette, he thought for a moment. Then, pulling his hand away as if he had just been burned, Sam slammed the briefcase shut and pivoted about to face the judge. 'Your Honor, I have no further questions for this witness.'

Lieutenant Colonel Edward Cole, serving as the judge in this case, was, like everyone else in the room, caught completely off guard. This, Cole thought, was not expected. Not expected at all. As he considered what Sam had just done, Cole looked over at Lane. Lane, visibly shaken by the last few minutes, locked eyes with Cole. There would be hell to pay, Cole knew.

In the rear, Jan's exuberance suddenly turned into a stunned silence. Not caring who heard her, she exclaimed out loud, 'What in the hell is he doing?'

Willie, glancing about him, leaned over and whispered to her to calm down, that she was drawing attention to them.

Jan, however, would not be put off by Willie. 'The idiot had him by the throat. He had his knife right there, ready to drive it home, and he flinched! The little rat bastard flinched!'

As forcefully as he could, Willie told Jan to keep quiet. Looking past her at JT, Willie nodded his head. Together, each man grabbed an arm. Standing up, they all but lifted her out of her seat and escorted her out of the room while Cole slammed down his gavel, calling for the audience to be quiet. Giving in to Willie and JT's efforts, Jan allowed herself to be led away, though she continued to protest.

Once in the hall, JT and Willie let her go. Jan, spinning around to face her camera team, threw her hands up in the air. 'Doesn't he realize that we're going to run the full video tonight on the prime-time news program? He's going to lose the shock value of our efforts.'

Glancing about in order to see who was watching them, Willie in a calm but firm voice tried to settle Jan. 'He knows what he's doing. He's in charge of this case, Jan, not you. Maybe he's going to show it later.'

Growing angry at Willie's attempts to mollify her, Jan pulled away from him as soon as they were in the corridor. Turning to face him, she hissed as she spoke. 'He doesn't know his ass from a hole in the ground. He's as limp-wristed as the rat bastards on this division staff. By delaying his defense, he's giving Lane a chance to recover and work him and Cole over.'

In a calm, slow voice Willie spoke. 'What happens in there, Jan, is out of our hands. We did what we could and now, well, it's up to Ulrich. We've got to trust him.' Jan's angry glance told Willie that she didn't like that part. 'Besides, Jan,' Willie continued, 'we've got enough to worry about.'

'Yeah,' J. T. added. 'Like getting hung out to dry by the Colombian government as soon as that video hits the evening news.'

Though she hated to admit it, Jan knew they were right. What would happen to Nancy was, and probably had always been, beyond her control. And they were probably also right about the reaction that the FARC El Frío tape would create as soon as it was aired. Jan was already on the outs with most officials, both American and Colombian, for the harshness of her criticism since September, and the El Frío tape would in all probability be her swan song in Bogotá.

Without a word, Jan dropped her head, turned, and began to head out of the building. There would be hell to pay that night, and she needed to get ready for it.

Back in the courtroom, Mark Moretti had already called the next witness, Captain James William Adderly III, Lane's aide-de-camp. Cole, on the verge of calling a recess, remembered that Adderly was up next. Reasoning that there could be no harm in letting Lane's aide testify, Cole leaned back in his seat and allowed the proceedings to continue.

Adderly approached the stand with a tight, expressionless face. There was nothing unusual about that. Most everyone who worked around Lane for a long period of time wore that look, one that showed no feeling or emotion. If you looked close enough, you could see that the bearer was holding on to his or her feelings and thoughts tightly, as if afraid to let go. In many ways that was exactly how Adderly felt that morning, especially after the revelation that Lieutenant Kelly had just made. Taking the oath, he reminded himself over and over that he would have to be careful about not only what he said but how he said it.

Confident that he was on firm ground with Adderly, Moretti cut the preliminaries and got right to the heart of the matter. 'Captain Adderly, could you tell the court what you saw and heard that day over El Frío?'

He didn't respond at first. Rather, he looked beyond Moretti, as if his gaze was fixed on a distant object at the rear of the room. Everyone assumed that he was reviewing in his mind the events of the day and trying to form them into a coherent answer. If it had been as simple as that, Adderly would have responded instantly. But it wasn't. For the image that came to Adderly's mind first and sharpest was that of a frightened old man, panicked and unable to control himself, let alone a division. Even as he sat there in the cool quiet of the courtroom, Adderly imagined that he could smell the pungent odor of Lane's loose bowels. He could see, as clearly as if it were happening then, the growing darkness about Lane's crotch and pants leg as urine and shit flowed as freely from Lane's body as the fear his face betrayed.

Jerking his head to the right, he looked over to where Kozak sat. Like him, she wore a mask that hid all emotions. All signs that she had any feelings one way or another over what was transpiring in that room at that moment were safely hidden behind her expressionless face. Still, as bland as she tried to make it, Adderly could see a strong, determined look. Everything about her face, the manner in which she held her head, the set of her jaw, the steady stare she gave him in return, spoke of pride. It wasn't the flashy assumed pride that Lane and his staff wore on their sleeves like a badge. Rather Adderly saw that Kozak's pride was born from her skills and achievements as a soldier.

That, Adderly suddenly realized, was the difference. With a slight cocking of the head, he looked over to Lane, who was becoming annoyed over his delay. Kozak, he thought, was a soldier. Despite the fact that she was a female and had never made any pretenses to the contrary, she was something that Lane wasn't and could never be. And Lane hated her just as he hated anyone who was smarter than he was. And just as he degraded, belittled, and crushed anyone who showed any sign of success or intelligence that he could not lay claim to, Lane was determined to crush Kozak. For months, from his desk outside of Lane's office, Adderly realized that he had watched a parade of good men and women, soldiers each and every one, go in and be brutalized by a man who didn't deserve to wear the title. And now today he was going to participate at the direction of his boss in the destruction of another good trooper, all to satisfy some unfathomable personal need of Major General C. B. Lane.

'Captain Adderly,' Moretti finally asked, 'is there a problem?'

Adderly wanted to say yes there was, but he didn't. Instead he shook his head. 'No, sorry. I was just making sure I understood what was going on here.'

The perplexed look on Moretti's face didn't bother Adderly as he began to speak. 'We were, as I stated in my affidavit, operating near El Frío.'

After waiting several seconds for Adderly to continue, Moretti realized that Adderly had no intention of doing so. Not understanding what was going on, Moretti began to prod Adderly. 'What, Captain, were you doing there.'

'We were observing operations of the 3rd Brigade.'

Again after waiting for an expansion on that theme, or any other for that matter, Moretti realized that Adderly wasn't coming forward with one. Deciding to lead Adderly through his questioning piece by piece if necessary, Moretti began again. 'What occurred that day, at El Frío, Captain Adderly?'

In a manner that was as cold and detached as he could manage, Adderly responded, 'The 3rd Brigade conducted an air assault operation in the vicinity of El Frío.'

Cocking his head to one side, Moretti looked at Adderly with a puzzled expression on his face. What in the hell, Moretti wondered, was going on here? He felt like asking Adderly why he was being such an ass, but he managed to maintain his composure. Whatever the reason, Moretti figured, I have no patience right now to deal with this man.

Determined to get him off the stand as quickly as possible, Moretti continued, deciding to be as direct and exact with his questions as possible. Moretti's tactic, and Adderly's short, precise responses resulted in a quick, almost comical series of exchanges. 'What happened when the commanding general's helicopter was taken under fire.'

'The pilot took evasive actions.'

'What did the commanding general do.'

'He had me call for a fire mission against the village of El Frío.'

'Did the artillery respond to this call for fire?'

'Yes.'

'I mean, did they fire the mission requested.'

'No.'

'Why not.'

'They were firing another mission.'

'What other mission.'

'One in support of the 3rd Battalion, 511th Infantry.'

'Why didn't they respond immediately to the commanding general's request.'

'I don't know.'

'Could you venture a guess.'

'No.'

By now it was obvious to everyone that Adderly, for whatever reason, had no intention of volunteering information other than that which he had to by the rules of the court. And those answers given were, to Moretti's growing frustration, not coming out the way he wanted them. Still he was determined to finish up what he had started, even if it were only for appearance sake. 'When the artillery unit in question refused to fire the commanding general's fire mission, what did the commanding general do?'

'He called the artillery unit.'

'And?'

'And what?'

Moretti drew in a deep breath as he held his growing

anger in check. 'And what happened when the commanding general called the artillery unit?'

'I believe they told him that they were firing another mission.'

Unable to hold back, Moretti turned to Cole. 'Your Honor, permission to consult with the witness in private?'

Before Cole could respond, Ulrich jumped to his feet. 'Your Honor, I object. This would not be in the best interest of my client.' Though he had no idea what Adderly was up to, it was obvious that he was not cooperating with the prosecution. Though that didn't necessarily mean that he would cooperate with the defense, Ulrich was ready to grab at any opportunity that presented itself.

Without thinking, also rattled by Adderly's performance, Cole shouted out, 'Objection sustained.'

Stymied, Moretti called out while Ulrich was bending over to speak to Kozak as he took his seat, 'Your Honor, I would like to call for a recess until tomorrow.'

Caught off guard, Ulrich turned and stood up again, prepared to ask that he be allowed to cross-examine Adderly before the recess, but he was too slow. Seeing an opportunity to bring this distressing and confusing session to a close, Cole slammed down his gavel. 'This court is in recess until zero nine hundred hours tomorrow morning.'

Pushing their way past a group of Colombian cleaning women who had been waiting patiently to go into the conference room to prepare it for the big meeting of all the primary commanders and staff officers the next morning, Adderly followed Lane to his office. He ignored his boss's mutterings as he kept turning over and over in his mind what he had overheard between Kelly and the defense attorney as he waited to go in and testify himself. He had been there. He had experienced the same sensations that Kelly described as the helicopter had been hit, the hammering sensation on the bottom of the aircraft. And he had seen the tracers. He had looked out the door toward the village and seen the tracers. He knew that. Adderly had no doubts about that. Even now in his mind's eye he could see the tracers.

When he stopped, as if he had smacked into an invisible wall, a major who had been following Adderly ran into him. Jarred out of his deep thoughts by the commotion behind him, Lane looked at his aide and the major for a brief moment before he growled, 'Captain, quit screwing around. We've got a lot to do between now and tomorrow.'

Dazed more by his sudden revelation than by the collision, Adderly apologized to the major and then stumbled a few steps behind Lane, making no effort to catch up. He had lied. That thought, swimming about in his head, couldn't be casually pushed aside. He had lied in his statement concerning the incident over El Frío. At the Article 32 investigation he had reconfirmed that lie. And now, because of it, the career of a fellow officer was on the line. But what, he wondered, should he do now? If he went back, if he tried to change his statement to read that the tracers he saw were falling toward and not rising from the village, what would they do to him? He had made a sworn statement, a statement that had already been introduced in an official investigation as evidence and which he had reaffirmed under oath during the Article 32 investigation. Would changing his statement, he wondered, constitute the admission of perjury?

Reaching Lane's office, Adderly drifted in as Lane bellowed out to the sergeant who served as secretary, 'Get me Colonel Cole on the phone. No.' Lane paused, thrusting his index finger out at the sergeant. 'Have Cole see me in my office immediately.' Without waiting for an acknowledgment, Lane stormed into his office, slamming the door as he went.

Easing over to his desk across from the sergeant, Adderly plopped down into his seat and stared at the wall over the sergeant's head absentmindedly for several minutes. The sergeant, while dialing Cole's number, looked over at him. Though he was dying to ask what had happened, he knew better than to ask. After working in this office as long as he had, the sergeant knew that it was best to keep his head down and mind his own business, especially when the head bull was on a rampage.

Adderly was still staring at the wall, his expression as blank as the wall itself, when Cole came into the office. Without bothering to stop, Cole went to Lane's door, knocked once, and then entered after Lane screamed a stream of indistinguishable curses through the closed door by way of acknowledgment. Shaken out of his deep and troubled thoughts, and unable to sort out how his sudden revelation concerning the incident at El Frío would affect him, let alone what to do about it, Adderly leaned forward and over the desk and opened a large planning calendar. Picking up a mechanical pencil, he clicked it a few times to draw the lead point out and prepared to write in the time when the court would reconvene. It was then that he noticed that the commander's conference, the one that everyone had been preparing for, was scheduled to start the next morning at nine.

'Damn,' Adderly moaned when he realized the court-martial now conflicted with the division commander's conference. With Kozak's trial going awry, Lane would insist upon being there the whole time. Yet he needed to be at the commander's conference. Every primary staff officer, his deputy, and all special staff officers on the division staff, not to mention brigade commanders and key members of their staffs, were scheduled to be there. Arrangements and preparations for this all-day round of briefings and discussions had been in the works for almost a month. It was a cinch that Lane wouldn't be able to skip

it just for a court-martial. He would have to be told of the
scheduling conflict so that the trial could be delayed.

Yet Adderly, listening to Lane as he paced back and
forth across his office, yelling and screaming at Cole, knew
Lane would become even more unglued when he was told
of this. When he got himself going, Adderly knew, and
pinging off the walls, he came down on any target, even
an innocent bystander, to vent his wrath upon. Looking up
at the sergeant, Adderly considered for a moment having
him tell Lane of the problem. That, however, would be
cowardliness of the first order, something that Adderly
despised in an officer. No, he thought, I'll have to do it
myself.

But not right now. Even though it would be the perfect
time, with both Cole and Lane together, the last thing
Adderly wanted to do was to stick his head into the center
of the hellfire and damnation Lane was raining down on
the shaken staff judge advocate. He'd wait, he figured, till
later in the day, hoping to find a time when he could pop
the bad news on his boss. Maybe after Lane'd reviewed the
G-3's pre-brief on the commander's conference he'd be in
a better frame of mind. That at least was what Adderly
hoped. Pushing the calendar away, and all thoughts of
the trial aside, Adderly turned his attention to the in box
holding all the actions and messages that had found their
way onto his desk en route to Lane's office. After wading
into the heap of files and papers sitting in front of him,
he began to forget the conflict entirely.

Major José Solis felt no trepidation today as he approached
the cafe for his daily meeting with members of the special
team that Hector Valendez had assembled for the operation against the headquarters of the 11th Air Assault. He
hoped that Valendez himself would be there, for he had
some reservations concerning the timing of the attack.
Though there was little that anyone could do, since so

many of the explosives had already been emplaced and their timers set, Solis hoped that the least he could do was to get Valendez to agree to have the charges that were placed in the main conference room changed so that their detonation would coincide with the opening of the division commander's conference.

Crossing the street with care, for the late-afternoon traffic was quite heavy, Solis walked into the cafe. Spying Valendez seated with two leaders of the special team, he headed over toward them. As he did so, he caught the eye of Rafael Dario, who stood attentively near the entrance of the building. With a motion of his hand, held as if he were drinking from a cup, Solis let Dario know that he wanted coffee. A young and serious man, Dario nodded before he disappeared into the building, and half a dozen other FARC men, scattered about the busy cafe for security, went back to whatever they were doing before Solis had entered.

Standing up to greet Solis, Valendez reached across the table and offered his hand. 'We have, Major, come to the end of our little project.' As they shook hands, Solis noticed that Valendez wore a broad and unabashed smile on his face. He was pleased, Solis thought. Satisfied and pleased with how things had turned out. Not that Solis wasn't. On the contrary, he too was quite content with the way things had gone so far. Accepting Valendez's warm hand and shaking it once vigorously, Solis took his seat across from the rebel leader.

Dropping his friendly smile after exchanging greetings with the other two men, Solis launched right into the business he felt compelled to discuss with Valendez. 'As you know, I am not completely satisfied with the time selected for the attack. I still feel that nine o'clock, and not nine ten, would be more appropriate.'

Picking up his cup of coffee, Valendez nodded, the smile still on his face. 'Yes, I know that you are not happy with ten minutes past the hour. Neither were these gentlemen,' he added, pointing his cup at the two leaders of his special team. 'Too difficult to set the timepiece, this one complains. It adds another opportunity for error, the other said. But' – he paused as hc took a sip – 'I added the extra ten minutes just to avoid any errors. Few meetings, even those of our vaunted central committee, start on time. I want to make sure that we have a margin built into our plan to cover any and every contingency imaginable.'

Solis shook his head in disagreement. 'These people are not Colombians. Especially not that jackass who calls himself a division commander. He insists that every meeting start on time and holds his staff to that requirement. In all the months that I have had to endure working with them, they have yet to start any later than the time announced.'

Waiting for Dario to finish serving Solis, Valendez nodded, still smiling. 'Yes, yes, I know that one's habits and history. But I also know about human nature. And if there is one thing that I have learned, both as an educator and as a military leader, it is that there is a first time for everything. Mistakes and miscalculations often crop up at the most inconvenient times. So we plan as best we can to ensure that such errors, which are out of our control, do not hinder our efforts.'

'So,' Solis sighed, putting his cup of coffee down, 'you have no intention of making the change.'

'No. We will go as planned.'

'Well, then it is settled. We go forth as planned.'

'What?' Valendez exclaimed. 'You are not going to protest our plan to fire on the Yankee supply and support center at the military airfield with some of our captured artillery?'

Now it was Solis's turn to smile. 'No, not at all. Though I am still, as a professional soldier, appalled that you would so casually throw away four good 105mm howitzers, I understand the overall propaganda value of such an attack. I think that doing so will be a nice touch. Executed in conjunction with the attack on the headquarters, the artillery attack will magnify the shock of the other. Such a strike by conventional artillery will show that the raid on the Ministry of Defense is not simply an isolated terrorist attack. Since the government is responsible for the defense of the capital, the attack by large-caliber artillery will demonstrate how ineffective our security measures are. The retribution from the Yankees, I expect, will be most violent.'

'Ha!' Valendez shouted as he looked at one and then the other of the special team leaders. 'See, I told you we would make a revolutionary out of this young man, didn't I?'

The four men laughed, sipped their coffee, and chatted for several minutes. In the course of the casual, almost idle talk, Solis mentioned the trial, and how the lawyer for the defense had failed to show the video that Valendez had arranged to be made. Shrugging, Valendez showed that he was not overly concerned. 'As I said before, we cannot plan for everything. Besides, the video will be seen. The lady correspondent, who thinks like me, made arrangements to run a modified version of it on the news show her network runs. There will be howls, I am sure, from our dear General Lane once he gets wind of that.'

Solis chuckled. 'He is already howling. All the planning and preparations that he personally put into rigging the trial of the female captain were beginning to come unglued today just before the attorney for the prosecution asked for a recess. Rumors are that he spent the rest of the day calling in each and every person involved in those proceedings in an effort to ensure that there would be no more mistakes.'

'Isn't that,' one of the other men asked, 'according to their system, illegal?'

'Yes,' Solis responded. 'Quite. But General Lane, the

senior commander here in Colombia, has been doing what he pleases for so long that he now believes that he can do anything. And his staff, isolated here, as it were, from the rest of their Army, is for the most part hand-picked and intensely loyal to him. Those who are not are kept in line by those who are through peer pressure, inertia, or simple despondency. One officer whom I heard the other day complaining passed off his failure to do anything about Lane's abuses simply by saying that dealing with such things was not in his job description.' Solis paused, took a sip of coffee, and then chuckled again. 'Have you thought, Señor Valendez, that we might be making a mistake in killing off General Lane and his staff? After all, they are already a known commodity. You have for months been taking advantage of their ineptitude. They, every one of them, will be replaced quickly. We have no guarantee that their replacements will repeat their errors.'

'Major,' Valendez chided Solis, 'remember who our target really is. I am not interested in killing Yankees. We have, after all, proven that we can do so quite effectively for months. The corpses we add to that pile tomorrow will be just that, additional corpses. Our target, Major, for tomorrow is the psyche of the Colombian staff and the collective will of the American politicians. If we wanted a quick, cheap propaganda victory, we could have struck at the American embassy, just as the Viet Cong did in 1968 during their Tet offensive. But we would have lost the impact on the Colombian Army's general staff that our attack tomorrow will have. Think of it, Major. Every day after tomorrow the senior officers of your general staff will walk into a building partially destroyed by us, knowing that we can at any time destroy the rest of it along with them. Their lives, and not some foreigners', will be in jeopardy, and the ruins of the building, not to mention the smell of burnt wood and flesh, will be there in their faces to remind them of it. In the end,' Valendez claimed with all the confidence of a man who saw the future, 'they will come to their senses and see that their future lies in a coalition with us and not defending the government that has since the spring so ruthlessly decimated its ranks.'

Lifting his cup in a salute, Solis smiled. 'I hope, for all of us and our people, you are right. If not . . .'

Valendez threw out his right hand and shrugged. 'And if I am mistaken, we will meet here again, or somewhere else, and come up with a new plan next week.' Then without any further ado, he stood up and looked at the faces of the three men he had been sharing coffee with. 'In the meantime, I have work to do, as we all do. Tonight I return to the field.' Looking at his watch, he thought for a moment, then looked up again. 'Tomorrow night at this time four regular-force battalions, supported by two dozen howitzers provided to us compliments of the Army, will open their attack on Villavicencio. Just in case the Colombian Army doesn't understand the message we will be delivering at nine-ten tomorrow morning, the fall of Villavicencio will suffice.'

Reaching down, he took his coffee cup and raised it over his head. 'Gentlemen, to the New Violence.'

In response, the two special team leaders stood up, raised their cups, and shouted as loudly as they dared, 'To the revolution.'

Solis, witnessing this ritual for the first time, didn't quite know what to do. Then, when he saw all eyes in the cafe were fixed on him after Valendez and his captains had finished their toast, he rose slowly. With a determined look in his eyes, he lifted his cup just as Valendez had done. When he spoke, his words were firm and sure. 'Gentlemen, to Colombia.'

Though they were spoken with a hushed dignity, every man in the cafe heard them. One by one they rose, lifting their cups above their heads. Valendez, seeing this, smiled broadly as he puffed out his chest, before he, and every man present, repeated Solis's toast. 'To Colombia!'

Led by a Marine guard to the overcrowded offices where Scotty's small staff worked, Jan skipped the usual light-hearted conversation that she often shared with Marines of the embassy staff. Though by training they were quite formal and dedicated, most of the tall young Marines who escorted her through the building were eager to talk to a celebrity who was both a female and good-looking, once of course they were out of earshot of the commander of their relief. 'Woe be it,' Scott explained to her one night, 'to the poor jarhead who lets down his guard while on duty. A Marine,' he told her, 'has no friends when he's on guard.' Jan, always anxious to disprove Scott's pet theories, didn't need to try very hard to prove him wrong. One young Marine told her one night as they wandered through the corridors how much of a treat it was to talk to a real American girl who wasn't connected with the government or the military. 'We get,' he told her, 'mighty lonely for real female company, even if it's just for a short chat.' Flattered at what she took to be a compliment, Jan had made it a point to be friendly from that point on with all the Marines.

Tonight, however, the disappointments of the day, plus her pending expulsion from Colombia, were just too heavy a burden for her to shove aside. As she walked behind the Marine, her shoulders were slumped forward and her eyes were glued to the floor in front of her. To those few people still working at that hour who saw them go by, Jan and her Marine escort looked like a guard taking a prisoner to her execution. Though no one said so to her, Jan would have been inclined to agree.

Reaching the area occupied by SOUTHCOM Forward, the Marine took her through the maze of offices, now almost vacant except for the skeleton crew that pulled night duty. Reaching Scott's office, the Marine was about to enter when Scott's aide-de-camp, First Lieutenant Wally Frazier, came popping out. Bumping into each other, both men took a step back. Though each mumbled an apology, Jan could tell that the Marine's was forced and rather short, almost as if he had to cut himself off before he added 'idiot.'

Frazier, noticing Jan behind the Marine, called out to her. 'The general's still in, ma'am. Just go inside and take a seat.'

He was about to go past them headed down the hall when the Marine objected. 'Sir, we cannot leave a civilian who lacks a security clearance unescorted in this section of the building.'

With a look of distress on his face from some kind of physical discomfort, Frazier stopped and looked at the Marine. 'Look, Private, I'll take responsibility for Ms. Fields. You can go.'

With a wary look in his eyes, the Marine saluted and walked away. When he was out of sight, Frazier turned to Jan. 'Ma'am, the general's on the phone with General Stratton at SOUTHCOM. I gotta go real bad and can't stay here with you. So please, go in and take a seat in my office. He shouldn't be too much longer.'

Without waiting for her to even say hello, Frazier turned and fled down the hall toward the latrine. Left alone, Jan shook her head and walked into the office where Frazier and a sergeant usually sat outside Scott's tiny office. Noticing that the door to his office was ajar, she walked over to it and peered in.

With the exception of a small desk lamp, all the lights in the office were out. Sitting sideways to his desk, with his back to the door and his feet propped up over an open desk drawer, Scott held the phone with his right hand while his left hung listlessly over the arm of his chair. Though she knew that she shouldn't, Jan leaned against the door frame and listened.

In a voice that betrayed an exhaustion that was accentuated by frustration, Scott responded to his commander on the other end of the secure telephone. 'No, sir, I don't like it any more than you do. But I am still convinced that everything out there in Los Llanos has been nothing more than a preliminary operation. The Farcees are getting ready to dump the big one on us and when they do I think the Colombian Army is going to buckle regardless of what we do.'

There was a pause as Scott listened to Stratton. In the course of that part of the conversation, Scott lifted his left hand up to his forehead. With his thumb and pinkie he rubbed his temples. He's tired, Jan thought. Worried and tired. Suddenly all her troubles were by comparison trivial. Though they could be far-reaching for her and Nancy Kozak, none of her failures today, she thought, would result in anyone's death.

Clearing his throat, Scott responded again. 'Yes, sir, I know that neither the CIA, DIA, nor any other intelligence agency has come across any hint that the Colombian Army is now dealing directly with the FARC or preparing for another coup. But neither can they deny it.' A pause. 'Yes, sir, I know General Fulk isn't thrilled with the idea of revising and preparing to implement our contingency plans for a hasty withdrawal. But neither was Churchill in May of 1940 when Gort told him the battle on the continent was lost and it was time to leave.'

Making a mental note to ask Scott who Gort was, Jan shuffled her feet and folded her arms across her chest while Scott listened to Stratton speak. 'The revised contingency plans my staff submitted to you three weeks ago remain fundamentally unchanged. All we need to do is to present them to Lane's staff.' Taking his hand away from his temple, Scotty twisted the phone receiver so that the receiver end stayed over his ear but the lower half was away from his mouth. Covering his mouth with his hand, he coughed, then lowered the phone back to his mouth. 'No, sir, I don't think that it will be necessary to issue those plans from your end, though I would appreciate it if you would give General Lane a call and let him know what we're up to. He's not going to like having to listen to me or anyone else on my staff, but he will.'

Dropping his left hand down on the desktop, he began to slowly drum it with his fingers. 'Tomorrow, sir, I've been invited to the 11th's commander's conference at zero nine hundred. I'll take my planning staff with me, and when Lane starts talking about future operations, we'll brief those contingency plans to him.'

Tired of drumming the desktop with his fingers, Scott lifted his left hand up to the top of his head and ran his fingers through his thinning hair while he listened. 'No, sir. There will be no Saigons, not here. Whatever happens, I will do my best to make sure that the American government isn't seen escaping from the rooftop of its own embassy by the skin of its teeth.'

This last statement hit Jan like a hammer. Though there had been a great deal of loose talk about this being another Vietnam, to hear Scott talk about the final evacuation of Saigon in 1975 like that to his superior was frightening. Suddenly the severity of the whole situation came crashing down upon her, and for the first time in a long time Jan felt herself shudder with fear.

She was still pondering the dark images that Scott's conversation was conjuring up in her mind when she heard him mention her name. 'I haven't spoken to Jan all day, sir. I was informed by a member of the embassy staff that the Colombian government had asked that she be out of the country by tomorrow. Not that I can't blame them. I saw her televised report on the El Frío incident, and it was, well, quite a piece of propaganda. But other than seeing it on the evening news like everyone else. I know nothing.' Suddenly he dropped his hand and chuckled. 'Yes, sir, she certainly does know how to keep a secret. I'm afraid that once again I'm literally the last to know.'

As quickly as the sudden laughter in his voice came, it was gone. Now he was deadly earnest again. 'Other than rumors, I have no proof that there have been irregularities in the manner in which the Kozak affair has been handled. I do not have a JAG officer on my staff and haven't been able to spare anyone to keep an eye on those proceedings.'

Slowly he craned his neck back and stared up at the dark ceiling. 'As much as I hate to, sir, I have to agree with you. For me or any member of my staff to go over there and poke our nose into that trial at this time could be counterproductive. It's going to be hard enough to get Lane and his people to sit down and listen to my people without my sticking my nose into an affair that he is so personally involved in, regardless of how wrong it is.' There was a sigh, then a pause as he held his breath for a second. 'I will keep my ears open, and if anything solid does come my way I'll give your inspector general a call. Till then I do agree with you, we have to keep our eye on the ball.'

Lifting his legs, Scott reached out, shoved in the desk drawer that his legs had been resting on, and then let his feet fall to the floor. 'Thank you, sir. I appreciate your confidence. I only wish I could give you better news, but I'm afraid we've not yet seen the worst. Good night, sir.'

Leaning forward, Scott eased the receiver into the cradle of the desktop unit. But rather than letting it go, he stopped, frozen in midmovement, with his hand still holding the phone as he stared at it. Figuring that he was finished and that he could use a little cheer and a hug, Jan pushed her concerns aside and softly knocked on the partially opened door.

Without looking up, Scott grunted, 'Yes?'

'Hey, sailor, looking for a good time?'

Caught off guard by Jan's favorite little ditty, Scott spun his head around to where she stood. 'How long have you been here?'

'Oh, I just got here.'

Noticing the wicked smile on her face, Scott let go of the phone, eased back into his seat, and twisted it around. 'Ah-huh, sure.'

Pushing the door open just wide enough for her to enter, Jan reached in, turned on the overhead lights, and entered the office. 'Are you practicing to be a mushroom or do you miss being in the Pentagon?'

'No one, Jan, in their right mind, misses working in that puzzle palace. Now back to the question. How much, my dear, did you hear?'

'Not much, just the end. And who, dear, is Gort?'

Scott rolled his eyes, realizing that she had heard more than just the end. Knowing, however, that there was no point in saying anything about that now and making a note to find out where his aide had been while Jan had been eavesdropping, he answered her question. 'Lord Gort was the commander of the British Expeditionary Force in France and Belgium in 1940 when the Germans invaded the Low Countries. When he realized that his army was in danger and that there was no way they were going to be able to stop the Germans, he began positioning his forces so that they could be evacuated from the continent despite his government's insistence that they stand and fight a battle that was already lost. When, belatedly, Churchill realized that Gort was right and ordered the evacuation, units of the BEF were in the proper positions. Had Gort not done so, the miracle at Dunkirk would never have taken place.'

'Are we,' Jan asked hesitantly, 'preparing to stage a miracle at Cartagena?'

With his eyes closed, Scott nodded. 'Something like that.'

'How soon?'

Standing, Scott stretched out his full length and yawned. 'God, Jan, I wish I knew. I really wish I knew.'

Jan moved next to him, wrapping her arms around his waist when she was close enough, and laid her head on his chest, and sighed. 'Well, if it does come to that, do me a favor?'

Dropping his arms down to her sides, he encircled her with them and gave her a gentle squeeze. 'Name it.'

She returned his squeeze. 'Don't be a bloody hero. You're getting too old for that kind of thing.'

'What kind of thing?'

She pushed away from him so that she could look him in the eyes, and her face clouded. 'Scott Dixon, you know what I'm talking about. You and your motto, "First in, last out," that's what.'

'Oh, and that from a woman who spends her day tromping about in the jungle with armed revolutionaries shooting stories about evil generals who eat their own dead.'

Letting her face go blank, Jan looked down for a moment, then she looked back into Scott's eyes. 'How much do you know about that?'

He smiled. There was, he realized, no point in being upset over something that had been done. Besides, by now he had become used to her unpredictability. 'I know everything that's worth knowing. The only thing I don't know is when you have to leave.'

Laying her head back against his chest, she squeezed his midsection tight. 'Tomorrow morning at eight-thirty.'

At first he said nothing as they held each other close. Finally he kissed the top of her head. 'I'll run you down to the airport, if you don't mind.'

Slowly rocking back and forth, Jan responded with a

quiet, almost mournful tone. 'No, I don't mind.' Then she added as an afterthought, 'But won't you be late for your nine o'clock meeting with Lane?'

'Nah. I should make it in plenty of time. And even if I'm a few minutes late, no one will notice. And if they do,' he said as he pulled away and looked down at her with a big grin, 'fuck 'em! I'm a general. Who's going to yell at me?'

Jan was going to say his highness Emperor Lane, but didn't. She didn't want the mention of his name to ruin this moment. Instead she smiled. 'Have you eaten yet?'

Scott lifted his arm up behind her back and, sticking his head over her shoulder, looked at it. This caused Jan to laugh. 'Since when does knowing the time have anything to do with whether or not you've eaten?'

Dropping his arm, he looked at her with a serious expression. 'Jan, you just don't understand, do you? It's an Army thing.'

'Yeah, right. Well, I'm hungry and I don't need to look at a watch to know that. How about we go back to the hotel, get a bite to eat, and then go up to our room.'

'I got a better idea. Let's go back to the hotel, go to our room, and have room service. I got a feeling it's going to be a long time before I have the pleasure of eating dinner in the buff with a lovely woman.'

Jan's face went into a scowl. 'Well, Mr. God Almighty General Dixon Himself, unless you're planning a trip to Washington, D.C., in the near future, let's hope that's the case. Otherwise, Colombian revolutionaries and maverick division commanders are going to be the least of your concerns.'

Without another word, Scott reached out and snapped off the overhead light, leaned over, and began to kiss Jan passionately. They were just getting into it when the outer door of the office flew open and Lieutenant Frazier came bursting into the office and looked around. Not seeing anyone in the outer office and the lights in Scott's office off, he went barging in there. In doing so, he managed to smack Jan's tilted head with the door and scrape Scott's forearm with the edge of the door, thus bringing their romantic interlude to an abrupt and painful end that only a young lieutenant could manage to engineer.

PART FIVE

OLD SOLDIERS
NEVER DIE

CHAPTER 20

November 29

When he walked into the room that would serve as court that morning, Sam Ulrich had no more delusions, no doubt about what today would be like. He knew he had screwed up. The moment that Cole had slammed down his gavel yesterday, he knew he had lost his only chance to derail Lane's drive to crucify Captain Nancy Kozak. What he would do today was still very much in question, especially since the person he had been charged to defend had managed to avoid him, his calls, and every effort by his office to contact her. Not that he could blame her. Nancy Kozak did not appear to be the type of person who tolerated weakness and indecisiveness well, especially in a man.

Swinging his briefcase up onto the table that had been set up for the defense, Sam looked around the room. Behind him at the prosecution's table Mark Moretti sat alone, pretending to be busy. Sam could tell by the look on his face that he too had been keelhauled by Lane yesterday, either in person or through the good offices of their superior, Lieutenant Colonel Cole. Cole, already seated at the table set up for the judge, sat staring at the door at the rear of the room, glancing down at his watch every few seconds, then back at the door. He, like everyone else, was waiting to see if Lane would show up today or attend the division commander's conference.

Sam had heard that morning about the lively debate throughout the previous evening, accompanied by a good deal of betting, on where Lane would show up. Smart money, he had been told, was on the trial. Though Sam doubted that even Lane would forsake his duties in such a manner, he knew in his heart that Lane would be there. Lane had by now clearly demonstrated to anyone who cared to see that his interest in this affair was more than one would expect from a commander interested in punishing a violation of the Uniform Code of Military Justice. No, Lane had been wronged, in front of God and country, and he was determined to inflict his vengeance on the wrongdoer.

Besides that, Sam had never had the kind of luck that would have had it otherwise. As a kid, he had never managed to get away with anything. If he had broken something at home, his mom had always found it no matter how well he had covered up the evidence. If he had been involved in trouble at school or had failed a test, his mom was always waiting for him, ready to question him concerning the offense as soon as he got home. Maybe this was the reason he had never been able to stand up effectively to a strong-willed woman.

Sitting down, Sam reached into his briefcase, pulled out a file, and set it down before him. Perhaps there was something Freudian about all of this. Maybe his acceptance of the plan hatched by Nancy Kozak and Jan Fields was nothing more than buckling under, as he had done with his mother when she confronted him as a child. They had approached him concerning the video.

When told of its existence and content, Sam had refused to even discuss the matter. 'How can we possibly show this in a military court?' he had shrieked. 'Jesus, Nancy, those people are the enemy!' But Jan Fields, an older woman, and one even more determined and practiced in the fine art of persuasion, took over and, against his better judgment, persuaded him to use it. That he hadn't used the video, Sam was convinced, was as much a fault of the system as it was a personal failing. For he, like so many other people involved in this sordid affair, found it impossible to violate the code of honor that had been pounded into him since the day he had accepted his commission. The film was to him first and foremost enemy propaganda. To have used it would have been aiding the enemy. Of course, not using it aided Lane's efforts to punish Kozak. Stuck between these extremes, Ulrich had chosen the easiest, safest way out, thus allowing an important piece of his strategy to defend Kozak to fall and shatter on the floor, like his mother's crystal vase.

He was pondering this analogy as he fiddled with the file when the door at the rear of the room opened. Like everyone else in the room, he turned to see if it was Lane. When Nancy Kozak, and not 'The Man' himself, came through the door, all but Sam turned back to whatever they had been doing. Anxious to talk to her outside, in the hall away from prying eyes and curious ears, Sam jumped up and began to head toward her.

When they met midway in the aisle left open in the space opened to spectators, Nancy Kozak avoided his eyes and all but shoved him out of the way. Embarrassed, Sam looked about and noticed that several people, including Cole and Mark Moretti, were watching. Taking a deep breath, he regained his composure and returned to his table where Nancy Kozak was already seated with her arms folded across her chest and her stare fixed straight ahead. 'Nancy, I tried to contact you last – '

Turning to face him, her eyes were reduced to narrow slits, like a cat's that was about to pounce on its prey. 'That's Captain Kozak to you, Mister Ulrich.'

The contempt in her voice was as sharp as it was loud. He lowered his voice. 'Listen, for better or for worse, I'm still your defense attorney and I have a job to do. Now I tried to get hold of you last night so I could explain why – '

'Save your breath, mister, because in five minutes you're going to be out of a job.'

Stunned, Sam blinked and pulled away. 'Do you mean you want to postpone this, or ask for a change in location for the trial?'

Leaning forward to close the space between them, Nancy continued to stare at him with the hard, cold look in her eyes that told him that she was offering no quarter this morning. 'Listen, you spineless excuse of a soldier. You threw away my best chance of a win yesterday. Not yours, not anyone else's. Mine. You had your chance. Now I'm taking over my own defense.'

Blinking, Sam shook his head. 'You can't do that. You're not a school-trained attorney.'

'But I am an officer in the United States Army, schooled in military law, and entitled to defend myself. If you don't have the – ' She was about to say balls, but for the first time she pulled her punches. 'If you can't stand up to Lane and this mockery of a court of law, then I will.'

Looking about in an effort to see who had heard or was listening, Sam raised his hand and tried to calm Kozak down. This effort, especially his absentminded 'Shush,' infuriated her. She lifted her finger and pointed it at his nose, just like his mother had done to him. 'Don't you shush me, mister. I listened to you. I trusted you. Even Jan Fields trusted you, despite her misgivings.'

Taken aback by this last part, Sam wondered why Jan Fields had felt uneasy about trusting him. Though he

would have liked to know, Nancy didn't give him a chance
to ask. Instead she continued to lecture. 'Now Jan's gone,
thrown out of the country in disgrace, and I'm sitting here
with a noose around my neck waiting for you and the rest
of this vigilante gang to kick the chair out from under me.
Well, if I'm going to go, it will be by my own hand, just
like Hal Cerro.'

The seriousness of her commitment, as evidenced by
her reference to her former battalion commander, escaped
Sam for the moment as he continued his efforts to dissuade
her. In a calm, steady voice, he spoke slowly so that
Nancy heard every word and there was no chance that she
wouldn't understand. 'Nancy, if you go up there and try
to defend yourself, they will tear you apart limb by limb.
This trial, already a shambles, will become a massacre.'

Straightening up, she took a deep breath. 'Good!'

Again unable to comprehend Nancy's frame of mind,
Sam shook his head and looked at her in surprise. 'Good?
What in the hell do you mean good? Don't you under-
stand? They are going to nail you to the wall.'

'They may, mister, but not before I get my licks in. Yes,
there's going to be blood on this floor today, but not all of
it is going to be mine.'

Turning away from her, Sam looked down at the
file in front of him, his mind going a mile a minute.
Somehow, between now and when Cole reopened the
trial, he had to come up with something, some way
of stalling. Looking down at his watch, he saw that it
was eight fifty-nine. Convinced that talking to Kozak
was useless, he was about to stand up and go forward
to have a word with Cole when the door of the room
opened. As before, everyone turned to see who entered.
When Captain Adderly, Lane's aide, came through the
door, a sudden and perceptible tension swept over the
room. Then, when he did not announce Lane but instead
walked to the front of the room alone and took his seat,

there was a moment of confusion, followed by a collective sigh of relief.

Sam, on the other hand, couldn't relax. He needed time to organize his thoughts. He needed to come up with some way of saving Nancy Kozak from herself, not to mention what little dignity and self-respect for himself that he could still muster. Most of all, he needed a break.

Looking down at his watch, Colonel Cole asked the MP standing near his table to call the court to order at precisely nine o'clock. Seeing what could be an opportunity to question Adderly without Lane present, Sam Ulrich decided to seize it. Jumping up before the bailiff finished, he called out, 'Your Honor, I would like to call Captain James Adderly back in order that I may cross-examine him.'

Hoping that they were finished with Adderly, Moretti looked up to Cole with a pleading look on his face. Cole, however, said or did nothing, at least in response to Moretti. Instead he nodded his approval. Over at the table where Kozak and Ulrich were, Kozak glared up at her attorney. 'I told you I was going to – ' Now Sam leaned over and whispered, 'Listen, you'll be given more than enough opportunities today to slit your own throat. At least let me get a crack at Adderly. After that you can do as you damned well please.' Without waiting for a response, Sam stood erect and called over to Adderly. 'The defense calls on Captain James Adderly to take the stand.'

Standing bolt upright, Adderly marched up to the witness chair. He held his head rigid, looking neither left nor right, as if he were on parade. Though neither Moretti nor Sam had any idea how Adderly would go, Sam was willing to play his hunch that Adderly had finally reached the breaking point and was about to tell the truth.

In the conference room where the gaggle of officers from the division had gathered, they were pondering the same question that the people in the courtroom were agonizing over: Where would Lane fly his standard today? Near the front of the room the assistant division commander for logistics, Brigadier General Ken Overten, was speaking with the division G-4 and the commander of the division's support command. Together they formed one of many little knots of officers scattered about the room that were discussing that issue. Overten had no sooner stated that even Lane would not let something like Kozak's court-martial keep him from a conference as critical as this, given the changing situation they faced, when Lane entered the room alone and unannounced. A major from the division operations staff posted at the door to cover just such a contingency called out, 'Gentlemen, the division commander.'

Stopping in midsentence or where they were, everyone in the room came to attention. Lane, a bit edgy that morning, didn't give the order 'At ease' right away. Rather, he made his way to the front of the room, going by the little groups without paying them or any of the senior officers in the room any attention. His mind was preoccupied with other matters. Only after reaching the front of the conference room, well decorated with the crests and the flags of the division and various subordinate commands, did Lane stop, turn, and order the gathered commanders and staff officers to take their seats. In silence the participants made their way to their places, took their seats, and prepared for the opening of the conference. A few already seated took note that it was three minutes past nine, making this the first time in division history that a meeting Lane had called and attended was starting late. Not that this fact brought them any satisfaction. On the contrary, it was ominous. 'Only death, or an act of God,' Lane often stated, would serve to excuse a late start. Since neither was in evidence, that meant that Major General C. B. Lane, scornfully known as Conan the Bureaucrat, was going to have to eat his own words. And when Lane was made to look bad, even if by his own hand, everyone suffered.

But as he stood there in front of the assembled leadership and key staff members of the division, Lane shuffled his feet for a moment, looking down at the floor as if he were lost in thought. In the quietness of the room, silence broken by an occasional nervous cough, everyone watched and waited. Finally, as if he suddenly woke up to the realization of where he was, Lane looked up and scanned the room. Placing his hands on his hips, he threw his head back. Looking about the room for Colonel Delhue, it took Lane a second to realize that he wasn't there. Delhue was, Lane suddenly remembered, at a meeting called at the last minute that morning by someone in the office of the Colombian Army chief. Major Solis, informing them of this meeting, suggested that he and Colonel Delhue represent the division. Glad to be rid of Delhue, who always managed to irritate him during conferences like this with his questions, Lane had agreed and sent the two of them packing. Looking down at his watch, Lane noted the time and began to speak. 'We, ah, need to get on with this, I'm sure.'

The total lack of emotion or anger, accentuated by the absentminded manner in which Lane's words came out, threw everyone in the room. The old man, Overten thought, does not have his stuff together today. Though he had seen Lane rattled before, on occasion in private when something unexpected suddenly happened to him, he had never seen his boss so unstrung in the presence of subordinate officers. He knew that Lane, like many of the senior officers in the Army, had perfected his ability to portray his presentation as the man in charge to the point where he could kick into action without thinking. Leaning over, Overten whispered to the commander of the division support command, 'Well, at least he knows where he belongs.'

As disrespectful as that comment was, it was appropriate, and the commander of the support command nodded. Lane, in the past month rattled by the changing situation and the growing role of Dixon's SOUTHCOM Forward, had been making a lot of bad calls, almost on a daily basis. Now, before the commander of every major subordinate command and key staff officers from throughout the division, Lane made another one. 'I am sorry for the delay in opening this conference, but, ah, there is a conflict between this meeting and another affair that demands my immediate attention. Though I expect to be back for the open discussions this afternoon with the brigade commanders, I am afraid that the ADC for maneuver will have to hold the fort during this morning's round of briefings.' Then, without another word, Lane briskly walked to the rear of the room, not looking back and totally unaware that no one, in the stunned silence that followed, had bothered to call the room to attention to mark his departure. Only after a moment or two passed did the commander of the division support command lean over to Overten and announce in a rather matter-of-fact manner, 'Well, sir, you owe me five bucks.'

Down on the street level, Scott Dixon's sedan pulled up in front of the entrance used by the staff of the 11th Air Assault. Glancing down at his watch before getting out, he noted that it was now seven past the hour. Though he had been rather casual about being late last night while he had been talking to Jan, Scott was rushed and anxious. Already on Lane's shit list just by being in Colombia, coming in late for his commander's conference wasn't going to make the plans that he and his staff were about to force-feed him any more palatable. Hurrying up the steps to the building, he was about to go through the door when he heard Jeff Worsham call out to him, 'General Dixon, sir.'

Stopping, he looked around to see where Worsham was. 'Over here, sir, behind you.'

Turning his head, he saw Worsham come trotting from under a tree across the street toward him. Behind him, Dixon could see the other officers, Major Don Saventinni and Major Herman Hagstrom, sitting under a tree in a small plaza across the way. Coming about completely, Dixon slowly began to descend the steps, headed for Worsham. Confused as much as he was surprised, Dixon raised his hand in a gesture to stop Worsham. 'No, you wait over there,' he called out. 'Let me come to you. Maybe, just maybe, by the time I reach you, I'll have figured out why you and Tweedledum and Tweedledee are over there lounging about in the shade and not in there mixing it up with the lions.'

Stopping at the curb, Worsham went limp, letting his shoulders drop forward and his head hang down a bit. The general was mad. Though he often joked with his staff, and usually used humor to make a bad situation a little more tolerable, Worsham could tell by Dixon's voice that this was not one of those times. While Dixon was waiting for a car to pass, Worsham started talking. 'Sir, I can explain.'

Dixon shook his head. 'God, I hope so.'

'There was a screw-up on the access roster. The division G-2 security officer put a new access roster into effect today because of the commander's conference. Added security, the guard at the door said.'

Without another word, Dixon knew what had happened. 'Wait, let me guess. We're not on it.'

'Well, sir. You are, but we,' Worsham said as he pointed over his shoulder at Saventinni and Hagstrom, now on their feet, 'aren't.'

Dixon slowly twisted his head around. Looking up at the wing of the Ministry of Defense that housed the headquarters of the 11th Air Assault Division, he muttered a silent curse. Facing Worsham again, he raised his right hand. 'You and your trusty companions stay there. I'll go in there and get this thing squared away. This should only take a minute.'

'Captain Adderly,' Ulrich started, 'you were an assistant operations officer in an infantry battalion, weren't you?'

'Yes, back at Campbell.'

'And you served as an infantry company commander during the Second Gulf War?'

Adderly nodded. 'Yes. I was with an airborne unit in that one.'

'I submit,' Ulrich called out as he turned to Cole, 'Your Honor, that his experience, as well as his formal military education at Fort Benning and Fort Leavenworth, makes Captain Adderly a competent judge of infantry company and battalion combat operations. I therefore intend to question him, using his expertise, to establish the situation as it existed on the ground that day as well as the responses of Captain Kozak, both to the situation and General Lane's actions.'

Moretti stood up. 'Objection.'

Cole didn't bother looking over at him. 'Overruled. Captain Ulrich, proceed.'

In contrast to the short, blunt responses that he had given the day before, Adderly spoke quickly yet clearly in response to Ulrich's questions. With great detail he described the situation as he saw it, taking great pains to emphasize that they, he and Lane, were only catching glimpses of the fight. When he got to the part where Lane started to call for the artillery mission against the village, Ulrich raised his hand. 'If you please, Captain Adderly, allow me to sum up, for my sake and the jury's, the situation as it stood at this moment. And please correct me if I'm wrong. The lead companies of the 3rd of the 511th are dropped into two hot LZs and are pinned.'

'That – ' Adderly nodded – 'is correct.'

'The commander of one of those companies, a First Lieutenant Barbara O'Fallen, is killed in the first few minutes of that fight and the battalion commander accompanying O'Fallen's company loses touch with the rest of his company.'

'Yes, that is correct. I was able to gather that by listening to their battalion command net.'

'So Captain Kozak then assumed command.'

'As soon as she was convinced that her commander was not in a position to command or control the fight, yes, she assumed tactical control of the fight.'

Ulrich shook his head. 'Then from the rear, the battalion executive officer, a new man to the unit and this theater of operations, comes in, disrupts the flow of operations as he assumes command without first consulting with Kozak, and then promptly gets himself wounded.'

'Again, correct.'

'Was it wise in your opinion, Captain Adderly, for the new major to come into a situation that he was unfamiliar with, one which was being controlled by a competent officer already, and start changing things without consulting with the officer in charge?'

Adderly smirked. 'Well, while it was totally within his prerogative as the next officer in the chain of succession, no, it was a dumb move on his part. His insistence on exercising that prerogative cost the unit valuable time and created unnecessary confusion.'

Nodding, Ulrich turned away, looked at the jury. 'I don't think there is any officer, at least not one who had been in combat, who would dispute that.' Turning, he stared at Adderly intently for a moment. Then slowly he continued. 'Using that same measure, that same subjective call, how do you, as a veteran combat commander and a subject-matter expert in infantry operations, judge General Lane's efforts to deny Captain Kozak use of the artillery at a critical point in time, when he had no idea what her battalion's situation was and he and his aircraft were out of danger from the enemy?'

Adderly was about to answer Ulrich's question when the door of the temporary courtroom swung open and Lane entered the room. There was silence pause as every eye in the room turned to look first at Lane then back at Adderly.

Adderly, standing up, was about to call out 'Attention' when the detonation of dozens of explosives scattered throughout the American wing merged into one ear-splitting roar. Though everyone, surprised by the sudden rocking of the building and the flicking of the lights caused by the explosions, braced themselves as best they could, Lane pulled back against the wall and crouched. His expression as he did so caught Adderly's eye. It was, Adderly thought, the same wide-eyed fear that he had seen when their helicopter had been fired on over El Frío.

Heedless of the commotion breaking out about him, Adderly stood there and watched as Lane's head, tucked down in his shoulders, turned this way, then that, looking up at the ceiling as if he were waiting for it to fall on him. The bastard. Adderly thought, had no more idea where the enemy fire had come from than anyone else in the helicopter had. He had, like Adderly himself, assumed that it was coming from the village, a place that all the intelligence reports up till then had indicated was occupied and heavily defended. The tape made by the Colombian rebels was right on the money.

Turning his head, Adderly caught sight of Nancy Kozak standing at the front of the room. Around her the officers and noncommissioned officers of her battalion, brought into the court today in anticipation of their use by the defense, rallied around her. Alternately they turned to her for guidance while scanning about the room, watching for either an escape route or danger. Though Kozak herself was unsure of what to do, Adderly could see her eyes darting about, checking out every exit and all of the actions of the others in the room. She was thinking, preparing to give orders to those around her, and jump one way or the other as soon as she figured out which way was the best. No, he thought, she didn't deserve to be screwed over by –

Turning back to face Lane, Adderly shook his head. Though he didn't know what had happened and, like everyone else at that moment, wondered if this could be their last, Adderly knew for sure what he would do as soon as he got the chance. Consequences be damned.

Jeff Worsham would later describe the scene on the street that he and the rest of the SOUTHCOM Forward staff had witnessed like a scene from the movies. 'One moment we were all standing there watching General Dixon reaching for the door of the building, the next, chaos. A low rumble from deep inside the building, then bang, every window and pane of glass is blown out along with body parts, paper, scraps of furniture, and huge yellow flames. Before we realize what's happening, the whole one wing of the building comes tumbling down around General Dixon, just like a house of cards. When we saw that, we all took off, to a man, at a dead run to where we last saw the general, each of us praying that we'd find him in one piece and alive but knowing in our hearts that he was . . . Well, not alive.'

CHAPTER 21

November 29

Except for the shuffling of chairs or a hushed apology when someone accidentally bumped into another person as the staff of SOUTHCOM Forward made their way into the semicircle about the wall where the maps of Colombia were displayed, there was silence. It was, Colonel Christopher Delhue thought as he sat near the front next to Colonel Chester A. Thomas, like sitting in a funeral parlor waiting for the bereaved family to enter. Not knowing what to say or how to act, no one did or said anything unless they had to. He was about to turn and make a comment to Thomas when someone in the rear of the room that served the SOUTHCOM staff as a combination operations center and briefing room shouted a crisp, sharp 'Attention.'

Coming to their feet like everyone else, Delhue and Thomas looked toward the center of the gathered SOUTH-COM Forward staff officers as they parted to make room for the assistant commanding general of the 11th Air Assault Division. Slowly, dragging his left foot slightly, he made his way forward. Looking at his face, Thomas could tell that Scott Dixon was still suffering from shock and the loss of blood. At least, he thought, Dixon had the good sense to keep the medics from shooting him up with all sorts of painkillers. The last thing they needed, he knew, was a commander with a foggy brain. Though he had no doubt that Dixon was in pain, as evidenced by the slight wince he made every time he put some weight on his left leg, Thomas knew that Dixon was an old warhorse, like him, and could handle a little discomfort.

Taking his place in a seat between Delhue and Thomas, Dixon eased himself down into the chair. After pausing to catch his breath, he spun the gray steel office chair about and looked into the faces of the staff officers before him. Being careful not to lean back into the seat lest he put pressure on the freshly stitched wound that ran almost the length of his back, Dixon managed a smile. 'Why so glum?'

There was a heavy silence until Jeff Worsham, looking to either side of him, finally spoke. 'We were . . . well, concerned, sir.'

Dixon chuckled. 'Jeeze,' he responded, rolling his eyes and doing his best to smile, 'I thought by now you guys would have figured out that I'm a tanker, an old one at that. There isn't a damned thing the Farcees have that can penetrate this hide.'

Picking up on the fact that Dixon was trying the best he could to shake his staff out of the shock they felt over the string of disasters that had befallen the 11th Division and the sudden change in their mission, Thomas chimed in. 'Ah, General Dixon, they were under the impression that your skull was the only impenetrable part of your anatomy.' While this comment caused everyone in the room to break into spontaneous laughter, Christopher Delhue looked about. No one, he thought, would have dared make such a comment in the presence of C. B.

Lane, let alone about him. This staff, he realized, from Dixon on down, was an entirely different creature.

Gathered about, sitting in a chair or on the floor, standing, or leaning against a wall or piece of office furniture, there was no rhyme or reason to them. Sergeants, both those on and off duty, were mixed in with the officers. Each and every man and woman, eyes riveted to Dixon, had broken out into a broad and uninhibited smile or laugh after Thomas's comment. They were younger, fewer in number, and lower in rank than the division staff they had just been ordered to replace. But Delhue suddenly realized that they were more than ready for the challenge. If Dixon, battered and knocked about as badly as he was, could generate this kind of response with just a few well-chosen words, then the people gathered in this room could do just about anything.

Raising his hand to signal an end to the chatter and laughter, Dixon hung his head in thought for a moment. When he raised it, the smile was gone. So was the mask of pain that he had worn when he first came in. His expression was now one of deep resolve. When he spoke, his words were clear and firm. 'Each of us in his own way feels a great sense of shock and grief over the loss of so many of our comrades and fellow soldiers. It is right and proper that we should mourn their deaths and honor their memory as best we can. But,' Dixon stated, accentuating this with a sweep of the room, taking the time to look into the eyes of every officer he could while he did so, 'we are at war. Those people over in the Colombian Ministry of Defense fell while performing their duties. It has now been left to us, by order of the commanding general, Southern Command, to fall into the ranks left vacant by today's attack and continue to press forward. As cruel and as cold as this may sound, the senior officers and the staff of the 11th Air Assault Division killed this morning are beyond feeling, beyond help. Behind them they have left over fifteen thousand men and women scattered about this country who are no doubt as badly shaken by today's events as you are. We, each and every one of us, must show them that we are in control and have confidence not only in them but in our own abilities to carry on with the division's assigned duties.' Waiting a moment for his words to take root, Dixon added, 'Is that clear?'

While everyone else was nodding, Herman Hagstrom slowly raised his hand. Dixon could always depend on Herman to ask the question that everyone else was thinking about but afraid to ask. Looking directly at Hagstrom, Dixon nodded. 'Yes, Herman?'

'Then, sir, it is official. General Lane has been relieved and you have assumed command of the 11th?'

Looking over to Thomas and then Delhue, who in turn looked at Dixon, Scott took a deep breath. The official order announcing that SOUTHCOM Forward would assume all duties and responsibilities of the now decimated 11th Air Assault Division staff had not been specific on that point. Only after a round of phone conversations between General Jerry Stratton, the SOUTHCOM commander-in-chief, and Dixon, Delhue, and Lane was the matter clarified, to a degree. Leaning over, Thomas whispered in Dixon's ear. 'Best you get this over with now, General.'

Nodding that he agreed, Scott squirmed in his seat, making himself as comfortable as possible before speaking. When he did, he picked his words carefully, in order not to open his superior, General Stratton, to later criticism. 'Major General C. B. Lane has not been relieved of command. And my title, pending approval by the Chief of Staff of the Army, is assistant division commander for maneuver. As the ADCM, I am the second in command of the division, responsible for operations and command of the division in the absence of the division commander. General Lane has been ordered to report to the commander-in-chief, SOUTHCOM, immediately. At this time I am not privy to the reason why he has been so ordered or how long he will be absent.' Delhue, leaning back in his seat, glanced over to Thomas, who in turn faced Delhue. That, they both knew, was not true. It was Stratton's intent to take Lane out of the picture and give Dixon as much time as possible to pull the division back together as best he could. Though neither man, professional to the core, liked the way this matter was being handled, the two colonels had agreed in a private conversation that, given the current situation, this was the best solution. To leave Lane, already badly shaken by the day's events, in Colombia would be tantamount to exposing the division to total disaster.

Turning back to the front, the two colonels continued to listen in silence as Dixon went on. 'While we will integrate those members of the 11th Division's staff that were not on duty at the time, none of the principals or even their deputies escaped death or serious injuries. We, this staff, will therefore assume those duties.'

Dixon lifted his right hand and pointed his thumb at Delhue. 'Colonel Delhue will, of course, continue to serve as the chief of staff. Listen to him and listen to him good. He knows the division and will serve as the chief engineer and unifying element throughout this transition. Jeff Worsham, our old chief, is now the division operations officer. Everyone else falls into their appropriate staff position. Herman the Horrible is now the division intel officer, God help us.' There was a slight interruption as a muted chuckle rippled through the gathered staff and Hagstrom blushed. 'Mary Anderson is the division G-4, Pete Northrup the division G-1, and everyone else per the assignments listed on the sheet Jeff posted earlier this afternoon. One appointment that I just managed to confirm before this meeting started was Colonel Thomas's.' Turning to face the military attaché,

Dixon smiled. 'Chris here has agreed to pull his retirement papers and accept the position as the assistant division commander for logistics. Given his knowledge of this country, the people, and his contacts, I didn't have too much trouble convincing General Stratton he was the right man for the job.' While some of the gathered staff officers simply nodded their approval, others clapped, causing Thomas, a man who had always been well liked by Dixon's staff, to blush, as Hagstrom had.

'A liaison officer from the Colombian Army,' Dixon continued, 'will be provided by Colonel Marco Agustin.'

'Is there any reason,' Delhue asked, 'why we can't simply use Major José Solis? He's already familiar with the division.'

'While that would be a good move, we have a problem here in the embassy that you didn't have over at the ministry. The CIA insists on clearing everyone, and their procedures take a long, long, time. Colonel Agustin's man is almost finished with that. To start that nut roll again, with everything else going on, wouldn't be a good idea.'

Though he would have liked to keep José Solis, Delhue was unable to find a good reason for challenging Dixon's decision. Letting that issue pass, he decided to get on with the evening briefing. 'Sir, we have a great deal to cover. Are you ready to start?'

Carefully shifting in his seat, Dixon nodded.

Signing Worsham with a wave of his hand, Delhue turned to Dixon. 'I thought we'd start with a quick overview on the status of the division and where we stand concerning today's events before we launch into the full evening briefing, sir.'

Dixon nodded. 'Proceed.'

Moving into the center of the semicircle, Jeff Worsham opened his notebook, found where the notes he needed started, looked up at Dixon, and began. 'I spoke to the commander, headquarters and headquarters company,

just before you arrived, sir. Recovery operations at the
Ministry of Defense are being delayed due to the discovery
of unexploded devices scattered throughout the American
wing. While he couldn't say if the devices were intentionally set to go off at a later time or they had simply failed
to function properly, they are slowing the search and the
rescue teams.'

'Have there been any more wounded and injured
found?'

'No, sir,' Worsham responded in a solemn voice. 'No
change since the last report I gave you.'

Closing his eyes, Dixon nodded for him to continue.

'Thanks to the efforts of the division signal battalion,
we now have data as well as voice contact with all major
subordinate commands as well as backup. This has allowed
us to transmit the warning orders for the redeployment of
the division with full graphics.'

'How long ago did those orders go out?' Dixon asked.

Glancing up at the clock on the side wall, Worsham made
a quick calculation in his head. 'Two hours and thirty-five
minutes ago. All commands acknowledged receipt.'

Satisfied with the answer, Dixon motioned to Worsham
to proceed.

'Though we are still short computers, each staff section
does have access to at least one tactical computer and is
able to access their appropriate computer network. Division support command operations out at the military airfield have returned to normal. Colonel Thomas and Major
Anderson were out there a short while ago and talked to
all the officers in charge of all the principal organizations
and sections out there. Mary will cover what they saw and
were told, in detail, during her portion of the briefing.'

Dixon now leaned over toward Thomas. 'What exactly
were the Farcees aiming at?'

Thomas threw out his right hand and shrugged. 'Nothing, sir, in particular. It was a nuisance raid. If their aim

hadn't been so good, I would have said they were firing at random. But they hit too much for beginners' luck.'

From his perch on the edge of a desk, Herman Hagstrom chimed in. 'Amazing what they can do with guns they don't have.' This caused a somewhat embarrassed pause as everyone looked at him for a moment. For weeks he had been warning anyone who would listen to him that the artillery pieces being lost by government forces would turn up, sooner or later and be used against them. The CIA chief at the embassy and the G-2 of the 11th Air Assault had both come on line and stated that the FARC lacked both the training and the know-how to use the guns, if indeed they still had them.

Ignoring Hagstrom's snide remark, Thomas took up where Worsham had left off. 'Though they did manage to score a direct hit on a C-17 that was unloading and damage two other Air Force planes, most of our helicopters were in revetments and escaped damage. The fuel dump took a few hits and they had a devil of a time controlling those fires, but that was about it. By the time they turned their attention to the support command headquarters, everyone was pretty much under cover and a pair of attack helicopters were in the air sniffing out the locations of the guns.'

'Seems a waste,' Delhue mused, 'of four good howitzers.'

'Not really, sir,' Hagstrom added. 'The shots the news cameras got of the fuel depot blazing away, added to the devastation of the American wing of the Ministry of Defense, were quite impressive. If they were only after a propaganda coup, then they achieved what they were after, in spades.'

While Dixon shook his head, Thomas continued. 'Herman's right. The people back home are already being told that the American military hasn't suffered this kind of setback since Tet, 1968.'

Not wanting to dwell on an analogy that he himself had been instrumental in starting, Dixon pointed to Worsham. 'Continue, if you please.'

Jeff Worsham was about to open his mouth to go on when the door at the rear of the room swung open, banging against the wall behind it, and a hurried, surprised 'Attention' followed. Everyone except Dixon, who took his time, jumped to their feet. Like the parting of the Red Sea, the officers and sergeants standing or seated between the door and the front of the room separated, making way for C. B. Lane.

Reaching the front edge of the semicircle, Lane faced Dixon. There was anger in his eyes, an anger and contempt that distorted his face. Looking first at Delhue, then at Thomas, Lane scanned the faces of the newly designated division staff. Finished, he looked at Dixon, square in the eye. 'I want a word with you, mister, in private.'

Though he felt awkward and quite uncomfortable, Dixon didn't show it. Focusing on the pain that shot through his leg and up his spine, rather than on his feelings, Dixon managed to return Lane's cold, angry stare without flinching. Only when he turned to Delhue, instructing him to continue, did he take his eyes off him.

Delhue's manner and matter-of-fact response to Dixon infuriated Lane. But he held himself in check. He was saving himself for his showdown with Dixon. Delhue, he thought, could be dealt with later.

Moving toward his private office, Dixon made no effort to keep from brushing Lane's sleeve as he passed him in the crowded semicircle. Breathing deeply and quickly, like a teakettle about to boil over, Lane followed him, slamming the door closed once he was in Dixon's office.

From the door of the main office, Captain James Adderly watched the two generals disappear into the smaller office. When the door was closed, he looked over to the front of the room and managed to catch

Delhue's eye. 'Colonel Delhue, could I have word with you in private?'

Not knowing what Adderly wanted, but sure that he wasn't going to like it, since Lane often left his aide to pass on messages that he didn't want to convey, Delhue turned to Thomas, excused himself, and walked to the rear of the room to where Adderly stood. When he spoke, there was no mistaking the contempt he felt for Adderly. 'Yes, Captain?'

'Sir, I need to talk to you about . . .' He paused.

'I'm in the middle of a meeting, *Captain*. Now if you don't mind.'

'Sir, it's about the incident over El Frío.'

Delhue's ears perked up. 'What about that incident?'

Committed, Adderly blurted his words. 'I lied, sir. I lied about the whole incident, on my statement and at the Article 32 investigation. And General Lane knew I lied.'

Alone with Lane in his office, Dixon hadn't even managed to get himself turned around and leaning up against the front edge of his desk before Lane started hammering away at him. With his index finger held up and inches away from Dixon's head, he went to it.

'Did you issue a warning order to my brigades alerting them to a redeployment that will pull them out of the western mountains and the eastern plain, away from the battle?'

Dixon nodded. 'Yes, sir, I did. The 2nd Brigade will be flown north by the Air Force from Cali to Cartagena within forty-eight hours. The 3rd Brigade will move, starting tomorrow, to a new base of operations just north of here. And 1st Brigade – '

'I know what the order said. I want to know what gave you the idea that you could just go around on your own and issue such an order?'

'It is,' Dixon corrected him, 'just a warning order. General Stratton and I discussed – '

Without waiting for him to finish, Lane cut Dixon off again. 'We'll get to him in a minute. As if that wasn't bad enough, just before I walked out the door, I got informed that you have instructed Lieutenant Colonel Cole to postpone indefinitely Kozak's court-martial. Then, to make matters worse, you go and return her to duty, as if nothing had happened. Do you realize how foolish that makes me look?'

Dixon was speechless, appalled that Lane would bring up the Kozak matter at all, let alone discuss it in the manner he did. My God, Dixon thought, you've just lost, for all practical purposes, every senior commander in your division and most of your staff. And the biggest concern you have is how you look. This is the Caine Mutiny in living color, strawberry ice cream and all.

Lane didn't wait for Dixon to recover his balance before he continued his tirade. 'I don't know what in the hell you think you're trying to pull here, but whatever it is, you and that motley crew out there are going to pay.'

Finally Lane had gone too far. Folding his arms across his chest slowly, so as not to pull at the tape holding the bandage on his back, Scott stared at Lane with cold, emotionless eyes. Seeing that he was not succeeding at riling Dixon up, Lane continued. 'I don't know what Stratton told you, but make no doubt about it, I am still the division commander, and you and your staff work for me, not him.'

'Neither I nor my staff believe otherwise.' That, of course, was only half true. Scott had already made it clear to both Delhue and Thomas that as soon as the plane carrying Lane lifted off that evening, he was to be kept out of the loop. Any orders from Lane, given verbally or in writing while he was out of country, were to be acknowledged but not acted upon, by order of General

Stratton. Though Dixon didn't much care for playing that kind of game, and fully realizing that it could blow up in his and Stratton's face, he also realized that if they were to have any hope of holding things together, Lane had to be out of the way. 'We'll pay the piper, Scotty,' Stratton had told him, 'when the bill comes due. Until then I want you to sort out that mess down there and minimize our losses. Hopefully, by the time I run out of excuses for keeping Lane up here, the people in Washington will realize the wisdom of our efforts.'

'And if they don't?' Dixon asked.

'Then, Scotty, we'll both be out on our butts, selling insurance or real estate.'

Realizing that Dixon was deep in thought and not paying attention to him, Lane stopped his monologue. 'You haven't heard a word I said, have you? Who the hell do you think you are, mister?'

Shaking his head as if he had just woken up, Dixon let a slight smile crease his lips. 'Oh, I've heard every word you said, sir. Something about your still being in command.'

Had he been a violent man, Lane would have punched Dixon in the face right then and there. Instead he just glared at him. As he pushed himself away from the desk, a spasm of pain raced up Dixon's leg, easing his smile for a minute. Looking down as he carefully rubbed his upper thigh, Dixon mused, 'Second Purple Heart, you know. Or is it my third?' He looked up at Lane. 'Hard to keep track of those things after a while, isn't it?'

The slur on Lane's combat record, which was nonexistent until he had arrived in Colombia with the 11th Air Assault, was too much for him. Clenching his left hand, Lane raised the index finger of his right hand up again and pointed it at Dixon's nose.

For a moment the anger in Lane's face left no doubt in Dixon's mind that the two men were about to come to blows. But then, just as suddenly as he had leaped toward

Dixon, Lane pulled away and pivoted. Facing the door, he allowed his head to drop down between his shoulders, his arms going limp to his side. With Lane standing there like that for several moments, Dixon was unsure what to do. The only motion Dixon could see was the heaving of Lane's shoulders as he took in deep breaths in an effort to calm himself.

Finally cocking his head over his right shoulder, Lane spoke. When he did, Dixon was for the first time that night taken aback. For the bitterness and anger in Lane's voice were gone. Instead it betrayed a hint of sorrow and reflectiveness. His words were no less compelling. 'You know, General Dixon, I was about to curse your medals and ribbons like I have cursed those of so many other officers who, due to the luck of their assignments, were given the chance at a young age to test themselves in battle. I never had that opportunity. I never was, as they say, in the right place at the right time.' He dropped his head and shook it, his voice dropping to an almost inaudible mumble. 'God knows, I tried. I tried. But . . .' When his voice trailed off, the two men, Lane still with his back to Dixon, stood there, alone in the heavy silence of the room, lost in their own thoughts.

Standing there looking at Lane, Dixon began to wonder if he had been too hard on him. Perhaps this man was after all just a simple soul like so many others he had come across in the Army, doing the best he could. Perhaps had he himself not been afforded the opportunities, through incredible luck for him and all too often misfortune for others, he would be standing there across the room in Lane's shoes. Perhaps. But then like a mist rising from the recesses of his mind, the memory of Hal Cerro served to remind Dixon of what Lane had done to Hal. This, of course, led to what he was trying to do to Nancy Kozak, a person who was more than a good soldier and a friend to Dixon. She had in many ways become a sister, a peer, if not in rank then in achievements and spirit. Realizing that if left unchecked by someone, Lane would be free to do her damage, Dixon began to draw himself together, stomping out any thoughts of mercy or sympathy in his mind like a man beating out a grass fire. No, Dixon thought. Might-have-beens are not part of my job description. I must, he reminded himself, stay the course and follow through now while the bastard is vulnerable. He would, as Stonewall Jackson always implored his men to do when things were tough, 'give the enemy the bayonet.'

Dixon had renewed his resolve just as Lane was drawing in a final deep breath. Turning to face Dixon, Lane looked at him. Any doubt or confusion that had been there in Lane's face a moment before was gone. In its place was a steady resolve. 'I did my time, serving in one hole after another, going from one thankless assignment to the next, just like every other officer. I may not have been as bright as some, nor did I ever possess the brave, dashing figure that so many expect of a combat arms officer. Like you and everyone else I did the best I could with those skills and talents I have. And do you know what, General Dixon? I succeeded. I made my way to the top, and I am not about to let a bunch of frightened politicians or desk generals in Washington pull the rug out from under me now. I'm leaving here within the hour, headed for Washington. By the time I get back, you and your goddamned medals won't be worth the scrap iron they're made from.'

For the second time tonight Lane's words elicited a response from Dixon. Not believing what he had heard, he gaped slightly before he caught himself. Was Lane, Dixon wondered, intending to go over Stratton's head? Not even Lane, noted throughout the Army for his arrogance and disregard for protocol, was that foolish. Or was he? Though tempted to ask the obvious, Dixon didn't. If he's willing to slit his own throat, I'm willing to let him.

Still not satisfied that he had made an impression, Lane was about to launch into a new round of threats when there was a knock on the door. Before Dixon could respond, the door opened and Jeff Worsham stuck his head around the corner. 'Sorry to disturb you, sir, but I think you need to come out here for a minute.'

Lane turned toward Worsham and snapped, 'You're interrupting us, Colonel.'

He's gone too far, Scott thought. Raising his hand as Worsham started to back away, Dixon called out. 'Hold on. What do you have, Jeff?'

Worsham cast a sideways glance at Lane before facing Dixon. 'We've just got several reports in that the Farcees have launched a major attack on Villavicencio, artillery and all. There's even a rumor that the garrison commander has capitulated.'

Knowing a saving throw when he saw it, Dixon nodded. 'I'll be right out.' Noticing that Worsham left the door open, he turned back to Lane. 'Is there something else we need to cover before you leave, General?'

Unable to think of anything appropriate, Lane took one more hard look at Dixon, then turned and walked out, leaving the door to Dixon's office wide open. While he had wished that they could have avoided that scene completely, Scott was glad it was over. Moving around to the back of his desk, he pulled the center drawer out and started rummaging about in search of a bottle of aspirin.

With his head down, absorbed in his search, he didn't see or hear Delhue enter through the open door. Only when he heard the door close did he look up. 'Yes?'

'General, we need to talk.'

'About?'

'General Lane. I just had an interesting talk with Captain Adderly, his aide. I think it's time we sat down and placed a conference call to General Stratton and his inspector general.'

'What about the reports concerning Villavicencio?'

'Sir, Villavicencio can wait.'

There was something in Delhue's tone that told him that as bad as things might be down south for the Colombian Army, they were at this moment far worse for his own little piece of the American Army. Easing himself into his seat, Dixon called out to his aide. Lieutenant Frazier opened the door and stuck his head into the room. 'Wally, would you be so kind as to pass the word to the rest of the staff that the evening briefing will reconvene in thirty minutes. And when you're finished doing that, put a call through to General Stratton. I need to speak to him.'

When Frazier was gone, Dixon leaned forward and folded his hands in front of him on the desk. 'Lane?'

Delhue nodded. 'Yes, sir, it's about General Lane.'

'Well now, Chris, now's as good a time as any, I guess, to compare notes. Shoot.'

Some seventy miles to the south of Bogotá, what should have been a joyous and exciting moment for Hector Valendez was turning out to be something of a letdown. Sitting in the front seat of an open jeep at the head of a column of trucks filled with his fighters, Valendez rode through the streets of Villavicencio. Though he was without a doubt the most realistic man who belonged to the FARC's central committee, he was still disappointed at the lack of enthusiasm the populace of Villavicencio showed as his convoy wound its way to the city center. There were no cheering crowds, no reception committee. Only a smattering of pedestrians going about their daily business moved about the streets, paying little heed to him or anyone else. Despite the strong sense of realism that kept him on track, Valendez was genuinely upset that somehow someone had cheated him of his storybook entry and triumphant march. Folding his arms across his chest, he tried hard not to let his disappointment show as they reached the city's main plaza.

Pulling out from the narrow streets into the open plaza, Valendez was stunned by the sight that greeted him. On one side of the plaza, he saw the garrison commander, a Colombian Army colonel, waiting in front of the town hall with his staff. Across from him, separated by an open space of no more than ten meters was the commander of the lead FARC regular-force battalion, Commander Julio Nariño, and his staff. Milling about a short distance behind their respective commanders were armed soldiers and rebels, eyeing each other like rival packs of dogs waiting for the word to pitch into each other.

Since he had been under the impression that the Colombian Army garrison had surrendered, Valendez was both shocked and momentarily excited. 'Stop, stop the jeep,' he yelled as he pulled his crossed arms apart and fumbled some while grabbing for the rifle on his lap. Hearing the squeal of the jeep's brakes, Nariño turned and saw his superior, whom he had always called El Jefe. Not understanding why he was reacting in such a manner, Nariño turned away from the Colombian Army colonel and calmly walked over to where Valendez's jeep finally came to a halt. Only when Valendez shouted, 'What in God's name is going on here?' did Nariño finally realize that his commander didn't understand the situation.

Seeing the troops in the trucks that had followed Valendez into the plaza begin to spill out onto the street, weapons at the ready, Nariño raised his hands, palms down and signaled them to lower their guns. 'Jefe, please call off your men before someone gets hurt.'

Confusion replaced Valendez's excitement. Throwing his legs out of the jeep, he eased himself out of it and slowly laid his rifle on his seat. 'I assume, my friend, that you can explain this?' he asked as he waved his right arm about the plaza filled with armed men from both sides.

'I was, Jefe, hoping that you could help.'

Valendez's eyes grew large. 'Oh? I come into the center of a town, one in which its garrison is supposed to have been subdued. But instead of a vanquished foe and a triumphant command, I find one of my battalion commanders all but chatting and drinking coffee with the enemy, who, by the way, is still armed. And when I ask him to explain, my veteran field commander, a man known throughout all of Colombia for his skill as a fighter, asks *me* to help him explain what's going on. How interesting.'

The expression on Nariño's face showed his frustration. 'Fighting is easy. Politics and diplomacy aren't.'

'I sent you in here to attack the place,' Valendez countered. 'How is it you managed to convert yourself into a diplomat?'

'As ordered, we followed the initial barrage in as closely as possible. But no sooner had my lead element penetrated the first row of buildings than the firing stopped. When I came forward to find out why, I found myself face to face with a group of Colombian officers standing in the street with a white flag of truce. They led me here, with my troops following, where I met the commander of the brigade responsible for this city and region.'

'And?' There was a distinctive hint of impatience in Valendez's question.

'It seems, Jefe, that Colonel Guillén Montes wants to declare his command neutral in the fight between us and the Bogotá government.'

Valendez turned his head sideways and gave his lieutenant a look that left little doubt that he thought him crazy. The battalion commander, however, maintained his gaze without flinching. Looking over Nariño's shoulder at the Colombian army colonel, Valendez thought about the situation for a moment, then let the expression of doubt leave his face. Reaching out, he placed his hand on Nariño's shoulder, spun him about, and came up next to him. Pulling Nariño as close to him as possible, Valendez spoke to him in hushed tones. 'This, my friend, is a test.'

Now it was Narinō's turn to stare incredulously at his commander. Seeing the doubt in his eyes, Valendez explained. 'Whether our friend the colonel over there knows it or not, he is testing us. We both know that the Colombian Army is only waiting for a chance to try its hand again at bringing down the same government we are trying to throw out. Maybe, just maybe, this is the Colombian Army's way of telling us that they are willing to let us do it for them.'

Nariño's face showed his disbelief. 'Do you think they will stand aside and let us march on Bogotá?'

'Why not? Even a blind man can see the writing on the wall. They know they are losing this war despite the American presence. They have watched week by week while our strength and skills grow and theirs diminish. Slowly their officer corps is being reduced day after day from the attrition they suffer fighting a losing war. In the meantime the government they are supposed to be defending continues to purge their ranks one by one of officers they don't trust. They are surrounded, with us to their front and their own President in the rear. Don't you think that they would want to do something before we kill all the soldiers that they depend upon for their own power?'

'If this is true, if they are willing to treat with their enemy and betray the government they are pledged to defend, then how can we trust them? Won't they, as soon as *we* finish pulling down the government, turn on us?'

Pulling away, Valendez smiled. 'Yes they will, my friend. In time, I agree, they will. But for now,' he said with a glance over to the Colombian Army colonel, who stood with legs shoulder-width apart and hands behind his back impatiently rocking back and forth on his heels, 'we must see what we can do to turn them and this situation to our advantage. If we handle this right, then perhaps other garrisons may be encouraged, either on their own or on order from the general staff of the Colombian Army itself, to follow suit. With their shield lowered, and the Americans preoccupied with sorting out the mess we made of their command structure, we will be free to cut directly into the malignancy that has been slowly killing our country for years.'

Nariño shook his head. 'This, Jefe, is quite risky.'

'War, my friend, is a risk. It always has been and always will be. And victory has more often than not gone to the side that has been willing to take the biggest risks.' Valendez smiled. 'Come, let us speak with the colonel and see if we can't come to some sort of understanding. We both claim, after all, to be fighting for the people of Colombia. Perhaps it is time that we sit down and see if we can work with each other, for a while.'

Though uncomfortable with the whole idea of dealing with government forces while they were still capable of resisting, Nariño nodded. When Valendez dropped his arm and turned away to walk over to where the Colombian officers waited, Nariño followed, just as he and every FARC fighter had for many hard and bitter months.

Several hours later, just before midnight, a different convoy, an American convoy, wound its way through the dark and deserted streets of Bogotá. When the lead vehicle reached the gate of the American embassy, the Marine guards, arrayed in full battle gear and protected by newly reinforced sandbag bunkers, challenged it. Ordering the driver to turn out the humvee's headlights and stop, Captain Nancy Kozak dismounted from her vehicle and approached the barrier set up in the middle of the gate. The corporal of the guard, a six-foot-plus

Marine, came out from behind the sandbags and met her.

When he was close enough, Kozak called out. 'I'm Captain Kozak, the operations officer for the 3rd Battalion, 511th Parachute Infantry. I've got Company B with me. We're here by order of Brigadier General Dixon to augment the embassy security force.'

Upon hearing Kozak's voice, the Marine felt like telling her 'No thanks, lady,' but kept his tongue in check. They had been told before going out for their tour of duty to expect a company from the Army units out at the airfield. This, in light of the events earlier that day, had brought jeers from the assembled rifle squad. 'How in the hell are they going to protect the embassy,' one lance corporal moaned, 'when they can't even protect their own division headquarters?' Though privately he agreed with his men, the captain commanding the security detachment at the embassy squelched all such talk and set about preparing for their arrival.

Now as the corporal stood facing Kozak waiting for his gunny to come up and verify her identity, he laughed to himself. The skipper, a Marine through and through, wasn't going to much like working side by side with a female infantry captain, especially one, he figured, that might outrank him, if only by date of rank. Life, he mused to himself, was about to get interesting around here.

CHAPTER 22

December 6

When the end came, it came with the rapidity of a house of cards tumbling down, with the fall of Villavicencio, without a fight, being the card that started the collapse. But it was not only the rapidity that rattled all the parties involved in the struggle. Everything about it was unexpected. 'Even Herman,' Scott Dixon commented one night in private to Colonel Chris Delhue, 'in his wildest fantasy could never have dreamed this one up.' Delhue's only comment, as he gazed at the map showing the disposition of both the FARC units and the government units reported to have 'gone neutral,' was to correct Dixon's choice of words, substituting nightmare for fantasy.

For the Colombian government, the nightmare began the first day of December. On that date, during a meeting between the American ambassador and the Colombian President to discuss the possibility of additional military commitments by the United States, the President was handed a note by an aide. From where he sat, the American ambassador watched as the blood drained from the Colombian's face. When he asked what the problem was, the Colombian President stood up, excused himself, and walked out of the room. Only after he returned to his own embassy did the ambassador find out that the Colombian Minister of Defense had committed suicide in his own office. Neither Dixon nor Thomas believed that the Minister of Defense had died by his own hand, especially since the minister's successor by default was the chief of staff of the Colombian armed forces. That this man was related to Colonel Guillén Montes, the man who had started this current crisis by stepping aside and opening Villavicencio to occupation by the FARC, escaped no one's attention. 'If you had any doubts,' Dixon warned the ambassador, 'about the seriousness of this whole affair, I hope this latest move by our dear friends has changed your mind.'

Unfortunately, from Dixon's standpoint, it didn't. Obligated by the foreign policy dictated from Washington, D.C., the ambassador continued to work with the Colombian government as they tried to stem the collapse that gained momentum as garrison after garrison followed Colonel Montes's example. By the simple act of tying a red strip of cloth about their left arm, the soldiers of the Colombian Army went from supporting the government in Bogotá to a state of armed neutrality.

This deteriorating state of affairs placed Scott in an awkward position. On the one hand, everyone in the military chain of command concurred with his analysis and decisions, encouraging him to expedite his shifting of forces from their widely scattered outposts to locations that would facilitate their extraction from Colombia. On the other, the ambassador, still hoping to salvage the unsalveagable, had Dixon review the military situation and come up with a list of military recommendations that he could forward to both the American and Colombian presidents.

As November gave way to December, Dixon began to feel more and more like Lord Gort, the commander of the British Expeditionary Force in Belgium in 1940. While he did as the ambassador directed, dedicating several officers to the development of plans he knew would never see the light of day, the bulk of his energy and that of his small ad hoc staff was bent toward salvaging all they could while they could. Though this contradiction led to confusion, not to mention frustration on the part of Dixon's staff, Chris Delhue managed to keep the staff's attention focused, leaving Dixon free to deal with the ambassador, General Stratton, and the Army staff back in Washington. Only once during this time of confusion did Lane's name come up. As he was explaining on the phone to the ambassador that the 11th's redeployment was nothing more than an effort to prepare for future operations, which was the truth, Dixon was informed that Stratton was on another line asking why it was taking so long to shift units north. Covering the receiver's mouthpiece, Dixon turned to Delhue. 'Where's Lane when you need him?'

Lane, of course, was in Washington, pending an official inquiry into his conduct of the Kozak trial. So was Jan, stranded and unable to return to what she called the 'cockpit of the war,' because the Colombian government, branding her El Frío videotape leftist propaganda and Jan an undesirable, refused to grant her a visa. Jan being the type of woman she was, however, wasn't idle. Using her time, her proximity to the seats of power, and her connections, she worked tirelessly to complete the undoing of Major General C. B. Lane that she had started in Colombia.

These machinations, though resented by some in the military, served her purpose well, ensuring that the Army could neither ignore nor postpone the investigation of charges that Lane had used his influence as a commander in a manner that was both unethical and in violation of regulations. Not that General Fulk, Chief of Staff of the Army, cared to do otherwise. In a private conversation with General Stratton, Fulk mused. 'You know, Jerry,' he said the day after the President of the United States ordered Lane relieved of his command and Dixon named as interim commander of the 11th Air Assault Division, 'last night was the first night in months that I was able to turn out the lights in the office and go home to a sound sleep.'

Stratton, equally pleased to have Dixon's status and position secured in such a manner, agreed. Only Dixon at that moment would have taken issue with this momentary euphoria. For while one problem was solved, a whole new crop awaited Dixon's attention.

Capitalizing on his success of November 29, and anxious to test his theory, Hector Valendez pushed his victorious regular-force battalions north in the direction of Bogotá. The Colombian Army promptly sent a small brigade, taken from the command charged to defend Bogotá, south to meet this threat. Officially it was the capitulation of this brigade to Valendez, without even making any pretense at a show of resistance, that caused the Colombian Minister of Defense to commit suicide. Rumors, of course, circulated that the minister had been assassinated by a military aide. These rumors could neither be proved nor disproved, since the incident took place in his office and the people finding the dead man were all members of the Colombian general staff.

Failure of the Colombian Army to stem the northward march of the FARC led the Colombian government to appeal to the American Army for assistance. 'If you can but buy us a little time, a few days,' the Colombian President pleaded with the American ambassador, 'we will be able to muster troops still loyal to me and deal with this threat in our own way.' Accepting the call,

the ambassador put pressure on Scott to provide the
Colombian President the time he needed. Though neither
he nor anyone else who understood the true political and
military situation believed that such an effort would do
anything other than lengthen casualty lists already too
long for a cause that was hopeless, Dixon complied. On
the second of December a battalion of the 3rd Brigade,
redeploying from the east, was dropped astride the main
road leading from Villavicencio to Bogotá.

Not wholly unexpectedly, Valendez and his battalion commanders simply bypassed the roadblock that the
American infantry battalion established. Leaving local-
force companies, reinforced with two heavy mortar batteries, to deal with the American roadblock, the main-
force units continued their march north. Even steady
day-and-night patrols of attack helicopters and armed
aeroscouts throughout the area made little difference. 'It's
like turning on the light in a room full of cockroaches,' one
disgruntled attack helicopter pilot complained to Dixon
after returning from a mission. 'You may get one or two
if you're quick, but that's all. The rest disappear like magic
into the woodwork and hide until after we leave.'

The woodwork that the pilot was talking about was the
villages, homes, farms, and towns that lined Valendez's
path to the capital. While Dixon had been told by the
Colombian President that the stringent rules of engagement that had so restricted American operations in the
past had been suspended, Scott knew better than to
turn his division's firepower loose in the densely populated areas where the FARC sought shelter. When the
ambassador took him to task on this issue, telling him that
he had no choice, Dixon stood his ground. 'You seem to
forget,' he pointed out to the ambassador, 'what happened
when we did that in Saigon and Hué in 1968. In the process
of winning the battle, we leveled the country we were
supposed to be saving and lost a war, not to mention our

pride and self-respect.' When Dixon's chain of command backed this stand all the way back to the President, the battalion dropped across the FARC's advance, chewed up after proving to be nothing more than a speed bump, was withdrawn. Though no one knew it at the time, this effort was to be the last one conducted by the United States with the aim of supporting the Colombian government. From that point on, everything the 11th Air Assault did had but one purpose: 'to cut our losses,' Dixon told his staff, 'and salvage what little pride we can still carry out with us.'

The last night in Bogotá started as all the others had with an unrealistic, artificial silence settling over the sprawling city. Within the compound of the American embassy, the combined Army and Marine security force went about their tasks of buttoning down and preparing for another long night's vigilance. In the operations center of the security force, located to one side of the main lobby of the embassy, Captain Nancy Kozak received the reports from the outposts scattered about the perimeter of the embassy compound. Absorbed in this effort, neither she nor the skeleton staff that worked for her noticed Scott Dixon when he came up behind her.

Taking a break from his own efforts, and not wanting to interfere with hers, Scott stood a short distance away from the cluster of tables, chairs, map boards, and desks as he watched. Like any well-drilled team, they went about their tasks with a minimum of effort. Scott enjoyed watching good people working together. It gave him a sense of accomplishment and pride. This was especially true when he had in some way had a hand in molding and training the people involved, and felt the pride of knowing that he was part of something bigger than himself and that their combined efforts made a difference.

As quickly as these thoughts raced through his mind, a sadness clouded them. How terrible, he thought, that all of our efforts, all of our sacrifices in the past months, will come to nought. Rather than being portrayed in the light that they deserved, the people and their efforts would be pushed aside like all failed ventures and forgotten as quickly as possible. 'Until someone has the courage to tell the truth of what really happened down here,' Chris Delhue mused in a moment of deep reflection, 'we'll be viewed as losers.' As heavy as that burden seemed to Dixon, the people that he felt for the most at that moment were the families who had lost sons and daughters, husbands and wives in Colombia. Jan said it best one night after getting over Cerro's loss. 'To lose a loved one is hard, the hardest thing I can imagine. But to lose them for no good reason, that's cruel, bitter and cruel.'

Lost in his own melancholy thoughts, Scott wasn't paying attention when Kozak, finished with her duties for now, stood up and walked over next to him. 'Is there something, sir, that I can do for you?'

Shaking his head as if to clear away his dark thoughts, Dixon managed a slight smile. 'No, nothing right now. Just thought I'd take a break from pondering the imponderables and wander about. I've been penned up in that little cubbyhole of mine too long and need to get some exercise.'

Reaching up and stretching her arms above her head, Nancy looked back at her people as they went about their duties. 'That, sir, sounds like a great idea. Care to join me while I walk the perimeter?'

After telling his aide, Wally Frazier, to head back up to the office and inform Colonel Delhue that he was going to take a short walk about the grounds of the embassy, Dixon looked back at Kozak. 'Sounds like a winner. Lead off, Captain.'

Walking out onto the steps of the embassy, the two officers stopped and stared at the night sky of Bogotá.

They stood there for several minutes in silence, each lost in their own thoughts. Finally Nancy mused almost to herself after watching the lights of the city wink on one at a time, 'It's strange. Out there just beyond the wall and barbed wire people are going about life as if nothing out of the ordinary was going on.'

Scott sighed. 'For them nothing is. Political upheaval and violence are as much a part of the social fabric of this country as the birth and death of its citizens. Those people out there, the ones turning on all those lights, they really don't much care who is in charge. Their lives, they realize, will change very little. Only the name of their President and maybe the ruling party will change. Within a month after we're gone, it will be as if we were never here.'

Raising her eyebrows, Kozak looked at Dixon. 'You certainly are in a cheery mood tonight, sir. What's the matter, did your dog die upstairs or is Jan in the middle of running one of her notorious crusader rabbit series on TV?'

Standing in front of the embassy out of earshot of the Marine guards at the door, Scott said nothing. Instead he just hung his head, looked over at Kozak, and started to walk. For the longest time neither said anything, each retreating into their own private thoughts. Though they were both thankful to have someone there next to them, each was thankful that the other made no demands on them or cluttered this peaceful moment with idle conversation. Only when they came to the rear of the main building did Dixon finally come to a halt and say something. Even then he was in no rush. Rather he stood motionless in the shadows with Kozak watching truck drivers and assistant truck drivers go about checking their vehicles. When he finally did speak, he spoke in soft, almost hushed, tones. 'Are they ready?'

'They' referred to the trucks gathered in the embassy

compound for the purpose of whisking away any Americans, including the security force, that still remained in Bogotá. With scattered reports of FARC units probing the suburbs, both Dixon and Kozak knew that such an evacuation could come at any time. Kozak, responsible for developing and implementing the evacuation plan, nodded. 'If we decide to go by land, we can be on the road and out of here in less than thirty minutes.'

'I'm not comfortable, you know, with the idea of splitting the column.'

'Both Captain Trainor and I agree that doing so is best,' Kozak countered. 'He'll take his Marines and lead off, taking the ambassador and what's left of his staff out along the most direct route out of town. I'll stay here until he's reached the outskirts of the town. If he gets stopped before that, I can either come to their rescue with B Company or hold the embassy open as a safe haven for them to return to.'

'You,' Dixon said looking over to her, 'will of course be here until the very last.'

'Of course, General. I was, after all, trained by a rather hard-core tanker who always insisted on doing the same. I believe he was quite insistent about ensuring that all his officers understood what his "first in, last out" motto meant.' This caused Dixon to chuckle. She did likewise before turning serious. 'There's no way I can persuade you to leave now and go north where the rest of your staff is, is there?'

'So long as the ambassador stays, I stay.'

'What,' Kozak asked, 'does he hope to accomplish from here? It's all over, isn't it?'

'Like me, Nancy, he's a hard case. And like me he knows it isn't over until the fat lady sings. Though I don't believe in miracles, not anymore, he still does. And so long as the President of Colombia remains in Bogotá, he stays and, ditto, so do I.'

Folding her arms across her chest, Kozak shook her head. 'You know your presence is only making my job harder.'

He smiled. 'Well, as you know, I've always been interested in providing all my subordinates with challenges commensurate with their abilities.'

Though she heard his words, her mind was already drifting off to a new thought. Without looking away from the trucks, Kozak asked Dixon with no preamble, 'Do you think Hal Cerro knew what he was doing?'

When he had been told of the circumstances surrounding Cerro's death, Scott had asked himself the same question. More pointedly, he wondered if Cerro had in any way engineered the situation that resulted in his death. After several days of deep reflection, Dixon had finally come to the conclusion that he hadn't. Cerro was simply too good a soldier for such foolishness. And at that he had let the matter rest, until now. Looking over at the Bogotá skyline, then over at the trucks again, he watched the young soldiers as they went about their duties. Finally he spoke. 'Hal Cerro was a soldier, first, last, and always. He did what he did that day outside of El Frío, because he saw no other choice.'

Kozak thought about Dixon's answer for a moment, then mused half to herself, 'If I have to go, that's the way I want to go. In battle, at the head of troops, just as the battle turns to our favor.'

When she spoke those words, there was, Dixon thought, a clear note of wistfulness that shone through. He studied her face for a moment. In the glow of the lights from the temporary motor pool, he could see the dream-like quality in her eyes, as if she were lost deep in a daydream that pleased her. Had she, he wondered, become so jaded by her experiences in this war, especially the death of a man she so admired and a court-martial that was so trivial in nature that she was . . .

Without any need to continue, Dixon moved around Kozak until he faced her. 'Listen, Captain Kozak. I know these past few months have been hell on you. Though they've been tough on everyone, believe me, I know that you and, before his death, Hal Cerro were put through hell. There is nothing I or anyone else can do to make good the wrongs that have been done against you. Even if C. B. Lane is brought to justice, we'll never see Hal Cerro again. He's dead. And wishful thinking or your death will not make that fact any more palatable.'

Rather than being upset or repentant, Kozak looked up into Dixon's eyes. For a moment, she saw the same fire that he had seen in hers on other such occasions. No wonder she admired this man so much. Both he and Hal Cerro had been tempered by the same fire, the fire of war.

'Do you, sir, remember the story of General Garrnett of the Confederate Army?'

'The one who commanded the Stonewall Brigade at the First Battle of Kernstown and was killed later at Gettysburg?'

'Yes, sir, the same. Do you remember how he felt being charged by Stonewall Jackson for disobeying an order but never having a chance to clear his name and how he went into Pickett's charge mounted, the only mounted officer in the entire attack?'

'Look, Nancy, I better than anyone else know what's going on in your mind. I know that you are just as anxious to attach some value to Hal Cerro's death in order to make it worthwhile as well as clear your own honor. But I have learned that when a soldier dies, he doesn't ascend to a higher plane or become something more than he was before. He's just dead.'

'Are you trying to tell me that Colonel Cerro died for nothing? That he gave his life up for no good reason?'

'No. Like I said before, he made a conscious choice

when he was faced with a whole host of bad ones. In reality he probably didn't even have a choice between living and dying. He probably just picked the agent of his death. You, on the other hand, have a choice. And so long as you do, I hope that you pick life, for this world would be a damned sight less exciting without you.'

'The court-martial, regardless of what happens, is the death knell of my career.'

'Then,' Dixon shouted, throwing out his arms, 'start another. Jesus, woman! You're still young, not much over thirty. You have done nothing wrong and you have no sins, either real or imagined, to atone for. To throw away your life just because you think you can't be a soldier anymore doesn't make sense. Not one bit.'

Though she wanted to find some way of countering his argument, she couldn't. He was right, at least as far as what she had been thinking. The idea of finding an honorable and noble end had more and more crept into her tired mind. And despite what the general said, Nancy Kozak in her heart knew that Cerro had done exactly that, sought and found himself a death befitting the warrior leader that he was in thought, word, and deed.

They were still standing there, Kozak going over in her mind what Dixon had just said, and Dixon looking at her while he waited for a response, when Wally Frazier found them. In his usual style he blundered forward without regard for what was going on. 'General Dixon, sir. Colonel Delhue needs to see you right away.'

For a moment Scott neither moved nor spoke. Instead he continued to look into Kozak's eyes. He hadn't, he realized, made an impression. Not in the least. With a sigh he looked away to his aide, who stood off to one side shifting his weight from one foot to the next, like a little boy that needed to go to the bathroom but wanted to finish what he was doing first. 'What seems to be the problem, Wally?'

'Sir, the Colombian President, as well as his entire cabinet, has resigned. They up and pulled out of the capital an hour ago headed for some other country.'

'And we're just finding out?'

'The ambassador is just as pissed, sir. The only way he found out about this was when Colonel Marco Agustin, commander of Bogotá's garrison, sent one of his staff officers here a few minutes ago with a personal message from his colonel.'

'Did Agustin's message say where he and his command stood?'

'Sir, Colonel Delhue told me to tell you that the staff officer carrying the message was wearing a red band on his left arm.'

Looking over to the trucks, Dixon thought for a moment before he turned back to Kozak. 'Okay, Nancy, the time has come to get your people and Bill Trainor's Marines mounted up and ready to roll.'

'Then we're going by land?'

'Yes. The ambassador's been stricken with the same phobia everyone in Washington has about leaving the capital in a helicopter off the roof of the embassy like the people in Saigon did in '75. Seems everyone is under the insane impression that it's more dignified to leave in a limousine.'

Kozak shook her head and said nothing.

'As soon as I can pry the ambassador away from that beautiful mahogany desk of his, we'll get this circus on the road.'

Turning, Kozak began to walk away with a rapid pace, calling over her shoulder as she went, 'We'll be ready.'

Watching her go, Dixon wondered who else out there in the darkness would be.

Realizing that there was now nothing he could do to stop the first convoy of trucks and jeeps that had suddenly spilled out of the American embassy onto the dark streets of Bogotá, Julio Nariño contacted his company commanders and made sure that they understood that he would not tolerate another oversight such as that. Though he doubted that he would have another opportunity such as the one that had just passed, he ordered a roadblock thrown across the route used by the fleeing Yankees. Though his men were tired and grumbled about the foolishness of closing the door after the horses had escaped, the platoon commander charged with this mission kept them at the task. 'This,' he told his men, 'will soon be over. And when it is, and you have returned to your fields and shops, you will look back to this night and all the others we've shared with great fondness and longing.' Though none of his men believed a word he said, they continued to work, hauling whatever material was handy over to their makeshift barricade.

Impatiently Scott Dixon sat in his humvee listening to the steady grinding of the engine as the convoy snaked its way through the deserted streets. Never a good follower, Scott hated being stuck in the middle of the column with nothing more to do than keep track of where they were on the small city map that had been issued to every vehicle, and to enjoy the ride as best he could.

Further up in the line of march was Nancy Kozak's vehicle. Though she was in charge of the overall movement, she found herself, like Dixon, with little to do. Lieutenant Dan Krammer, the commander of Company B, was in charge of the actual movement. All Kozak had to do was monitor the silent radio net and hope that their luck, like that of the Marine convoy before them, held.

Just as the lead vehicles turned a corner up ahead, the radio speaker mounted to her front and connected to the radio next to her that was set on the convoy frequency came to life. The call she heard coming in was from the lead platoon leader. That broadcast, however, wasn't finished when outside her humvee the rip of automatic rifle fire drew her attention away and cut the transmission short. Instinctively she reached behind her to grab her rifle. Fighting the urge to jump out of the humvee, Kozak stayed put and waited for the initial reports to come in. She knew Dan Krammer would report as soon as he had something to report. So she sat there clinging to the stock of her rifle with one hand while grabbing the radio hand mike with her other, fighting the urge to call Krammer and ask for a report. 'He'll send me one,' she kept repeating to herself, 'as soon as he has one to give. He'll send it.'

As if in answer, the radio came to life again. 'Skyrider Three, this is Bravo Six. We have a roadblock up ahead, covered by fire. I'm dismounting my First Platoon and going forward with them to check it out. Will advise you as soon as I know the score. Over.'

Anxious to get in touch with Krammer before he dismounted and was away from his radio, Kozak keyed the radio hand mike and spoke into it. 'Bravo, this is Three. Is there a bypass? Over?' The silence, however, told her that she had missed him. Seeing no point in trying again, since his response would have been immediate if he had heard her, Kozak let the radio hand mike drop and looked down at the street map on her lap. In a flash she could tell that the Farcees had chosen their site well. Any bypass at this point would take the convoy through the narrow and twisting streets of a slum district. Besides, she realized as the sound of M-16 rifle fire began to drift back to her, by now Krammer was heavily involved in a standup fight and chances were they weren't going to be able to break it off too easily. Deciding the best thing to do right now was to bring up the engineers and prepare to bull through, Kozak turned to her driver, yelled to him that she was going up to see what was going on, and disappeared into the darkness.

*   *   *

Further back in the column, Dixon heard the same report and, like Kozak, looked to see if a bypass was possible. He too, however, soon dismissed that idea for the same reason that Kozak had. Unlike Kozak, there was even less that he could do. To start with, though he was the division commander, he was so far out of the chain of command that any efforts on his part to influence the situation at this moment would be counterproductive. Besides, his wounds, though healing nicely, limited the amount of running and ducking he could do. If he, like Kozak, ran forward, he would present a large, slow moving target. As much as he hated doing nothing, that for the moment was the only logical course of action open to him. Reaching over to his side, he unsnapped his holster and pulled his nine-millimeter pistol out. Jerking back on the upper slide, he let it go when it reached the stop on it. Sliding forward, it chambered a round. Throwing the door open, he remembered his speech given to Kozak less than two hours before and wondered what he would do if things didn't work out this time. Forgetting all the bull he had given her about there being no honor in death and that she needed to forget silly notions of such things, Scotty Dixon made up his mind then and there that he would not allow himself to become a war trophy.

When she reached the corner, Kozak lowered herself as far as she could before peeking around it. The vehicles of the lead platoon, Krammer's First Platoon, were stopped in the middle of the street, where they had been when the firing had started. On either side of the street she could see soldiers of the First Platoon crouching low in doorways or behind the corners of buildings. Emerging from behind their cover only briefly, they would fire a three-round burst and then duck back before their efforts brought down a hostile response. The Farcees, she thought, were no doubt doing much the same thing. If that was true, that meant that they were involved in a stalemate, something that Kozak knew they would eventually lose once the Farcees started funneling reinforcements into the fight.

Looking about a minute, she noted where Krammer was across the street. Bracing herself like a runner ready to do the hundred-meter dash, Kozak leaped up, sprinted across the street, and made a wild dive for cover as her movements began to draw fire, allowing herself to roll on the pavement in order to avoid breaking anything. Dan Krammer started rendering his report before she had time to recover. 'We have one man down, wounded I think, and can't do anything from here. They have us pinned, big time.'

Gathering herself up, Kozak threw herself against the wall that Krammer and two other troopers from his company were sharing and thought for a minute. So far, she thought, it seemed as if they had gotten off lightly. If the Farcees had meant to ambush her column, then someone on the other side had blown it. But if all that the people up ahead were supposed to do was hold them until reinforcements arrived, then they were in deep trouble.

Finally, without looking over at him, she began to speak. 'Dan, this is no good. We can't stay here for very long. If these people are already here in place and set up like this, you can bet that they have friends nearby.'

'Yeah,' Krammer shouted as he leaned around the corner, squeezed off three quick rounds, and then pulled his head back. 'And you can bet every one of their smiling little faces is headed this way.'

'Dan, you stay here and keep those people occupied. I've already got the engineers coming up, just around the corner, waiting to clear the barriers. I'm going to head on back, gather up the Second Platoon, and make an end run to the left. I'll take a radioman with me and contact you as

soon as we're in place. Once the firing has stopped and the
engineers have cleared the road, don't wait for me to give
you the word. Start pushing the trucks through. I'll have
the Third Platoon move forward while we're maneuvering
around the roadblock to the head of the column. Once
everyone is on the move, Dan, hop in your vehicle and
get the convoy and the First Platoon out of this city. The
Second Platoon and I will bring up the rear as soon as
everyone is clear.'

With no more words or orders necessary, Krammer
looked over to Kozak. 'Will do. We'll be ready and
waiting here. Good luck.'

As before, she prepared herself for her return across the
street by balancing herself on all fours. When Krammer
and the troopers with him were ready to spring around the
corner and cover her move, he yelled, 'Now,' and Kozak
was off.

By the time she reached the portion of the convoy where
his humvee sat, Scott Dixon had managed to pull himself
out of the passenger seat. Standing next to the vehicle,
holding the door for support, he saw Kozak running
down the line of trucks to his front, gathering up the
soldiers who had already dismounted and stood ready
to fight or flee. Making his way up to where she stood
giving instructions to the platoon leader with her, Dixon
heard the last of her instructions. Only after the platoon
leader nodded and turned to issue his own orders to his
squad leaders did Dixon come up to her. 'How bad is it,
Nancy?'

Taking a moment to catch her breath, for the first
time since dismounting her own humvee, she watched
the platoon for a minute before turning to face Dixon.
'Well,' she managed between pants, 'I've seen worse.'
Then as an afterthought she added, 'But not tonight.'

Her little stab at humor at a time like this told Scott

that she had the situation well in hand. 'You going to go with the flanking force, Nancy?'

She nodded. 'Yes, of course. Need to get this circus moving. Dan Krammer is up front and will push you through as soon as the road is clear.'

While her mind was too cluttered with details and her system too charged up from the rush of adrenaline, Dixon's was clear and quite reflective. She, and not he, despite his star and title, was in charge here. She was giving all the orders and for the first time he was little more than a spectator. It was, he realized, almost as if this were some kind of strange change-of-command ceremony, with him handing over the future of the Army to this young, hard-pressed infantry officer. Though Jan had on several occasions told him that it was time for him to start looking beyond his career as a soldier, this was the first moment that he finally realized that he was closer now to the end than to the beginning, or even the middle. The Army, his Army, now belonged to Kozak and others like her.

When she saw that the platoon leader was finished and the squad leaders were beginning to lead their people off, Nancy Kozak turned to Dixon. 'You'll have to excuse me, sir. I need to go.'

Recovered from her initial exertions, she spoke with confidence and determination. Dixon, facing her, did not know what else to say. He wanted to warn her, to tell her to keep their little talk earlier that evening in mind. But this was neither the time nor place for such talk. Instead he smiled. 'Captain, take charge and move out.'

Stepping back, Kozak rendered the sharpest hand salute she could manage and turned away. With the poise and confidence of the leader she was, Kozak moved to the front of the Second Platoon, raised her hand, then dropped it in a forward motion. The troopers of that platoon, arrayed in two files, followed her, weapons at the ready, into the darkness.

Though they were gone from view within a minute, Scott Dixon watched where he had seen them disappear, listening to the thud of their boots on pavement until that too had receded into the darkness. Finally, when the only sound he could hear was that of rifle fire coming from the roadblock, Dixon turned away and began to make his way back to his humvee.

Slowly making his way along the trucks halted in the middle of the street, he felt a pang of melancholy. This, he realized, would probably be his last battle. Even if they survived, and he had little doubt that he would, Dixon knew in his heart that he would never again be asked to put his life on the line. For just as Kozak knew that the charges brought against her by Lane would always mark her, no matter what she did, for the rest of her life, his career was as good as over too. No one, after all, remembers or promotes generals who lead retreats, no matter how brilliant those actions are. Just as well, he thought. I'm getting too old for this anyway.

That a second convoy would come popping out of the embassy and use the exact same route as the first pleased Julio Nariño. Now his fighters manning the barricade he had insisted be built would have a second chance against the troopers of the 11th Air Assault who were headed his way. His only regret was that he had delayed sending reinforcements, reinforcements, Nariño hoped, that would be sufficient to handle the Yankees.

Moving as rapidly as Kozak deemed prudent through the dark streets and alleys off to the left of the stalled convoy, the Second Platoon made good time. Guiding on the gunfire of the standoff between the Farcees at the roadblock and Dan Krammer's holding force, Kozak slowed as they neared a broad street that ran perpendicular to their front. While the troopers of the Second Platoon continued to move forward, hugging the buildings on either side of the street they had been moving along, Kozak stepped out of the file she was in, away from the buildings and into the open. As she slid her left arm through the sling of her rifle, she pulled the street map out of a pocket on her right thigh. Flipping on a small penlight, she stopped and looked down at the map in her hand to see if the street to their front ran into the rear of the Farcee position they were trying to outflank. Engrossed in her quick check of the map, Nancy Kozak didn't see the mass of figures running across their path on the street in question.

The troopers of the Second Platoon, however, did. Before she knew what was happening, half a dozen rifles and squad assault weapons cut loose. In seconds the rest of the troopers of the Second Platoon joined in, just as the first volley of return fire, aimed blindly at their unexpected assailants, answered. It was a mad minute of wild and blinding fire, punctuated by an occasional hand grenade. Then, as quickly as it started, the sudden fury was over. Only a handful of Farcees who had been at the end of the relief column managed to escape the punishing fire that the Second Platoon had unleashed. Scampering back up the street they had just come down, the survivors threw themselves into open doorways or ran down alleys between buildings. As a fighting force and a factor in the battle in progress, they ceased to exist.

Shaken but still in control, the young lieutenant in command of the Second Platoon stood up, looked around, and marveled at the fact that he had somehow managed to survive his first firefight. Though he had made no decisions, issued no orders, and had won the short, violent engagement by the mere fact that his people saw the enemy first and reacted properly, he considered this a great personal achievement. He had, after all, faced fire and lived, without disgracing himself or his unit. Yelling out to his squad leaders to sound off with their reports, he listened as each one responded that they had negative casualties. As the smile on his face grew larger and larger, he looked to the left, then to the right, blinking his eyelids all the while in an effort to get rid of the spots that friendly and enemy muzzle flashes had burned into his eyes. He needed to find Captain Kozak and determine what she wanted him to do next.

It was at that moment, after calling out her name twice, that he realized that she was gone. It was his second squad leader, off to his left, that found her. 'Hey, Lieutenant, over here. She's down. The captain's been hit.' Panicked, the smile left the platoon leader's face as he raced over to where a medic and two soldiers were huddled over a prone figure. They were just about to roll her over onto her back when the platoon leader arrived. 'Is she dead?'

The question brought no response, at least not from the soldiers gathered about Kozak. Instead Kozak provided the answer herself, though she didn't realize it. Hit twice, once in the right shoulder and a glancing blow on the side of her head, the image of another night attack carried out long ago in distant Mexico came to her raddled brain. When she spoke, her speech was slurred and her words barely audible to soldiers who still had ringing in their ears from their engagement with the Farcee reserve force. 'Sergeant Maupin,' she mumbled, 'fix bayonets and forward at the double.'

Looking over to the medic who was leaning over her checking her wounds, the platoon leader asked, 'What did she say?'

Busy with his efforts to save Kozak, the medic simply repeated those words that he had understood. 'She said, "Fix bayonets, forward at the double," or something like that.'

'Are you sure?'

Anxious to be rid of the lieutenant so that he could find out where all the blood that was spilling onto the street was coming from, the medic shouted, 'Yeah, I'm sure. She said fix bayonets and forward at the double. Now leave me be or I'll lose her for sure.'

Standing up, the young officer looked down at Kozak for a moment, not realizing that the order that she had just issued had belonged to another battle fought in another time and place at a time when she had been as young as he was now. In the darkness that engulfed them, surrounded by enemies in a foreign city, and engaged in a life and death struggle as real as Nancy Kozak's, there was no time to reason or question everything, especially a clear order such as the one that he thought Kozak had just given them.

Looking over at his squad leaders as they and the troopers in their charge huddled behind any cover they could find, the platoon leader decided that he had no choice. He had to comply. Drawing in a deep breath, he yelled out. 'You heard the order. Fix bayonets and forward at the double.' By way of getting things going, the platoon leader jerked his own bayonet out of its scabbard, stuck it on the end of the warm rifle barrel, and called out to his platoon as he turned and began to race down the street they had just cleared of enemy soldiers, 'Second Platoon, follow meeee!'

With the exception of the medics and two soldiers left by the nearest squad leader to provide security and assist in Kozak's recovery, the rest of the Second Platoon rose and madly rushed down the street behind their platoon leader. It wasn't a very brilliant maneuver. In fact, had anyone stopped and thought about it, they would have realized that they were in the process of doing exactly what the Farcee unit had been doing when they had all but annihilated it. But they were young soldiers, each and every one of them. Fired up with adrenaline and a blood lust that drove them beyond all human constraints, they could not be held back.

Nor, as they rounded the corner and fell on the rear of the Farcees covering the roadblock, would they be denied.

EPILOGUE

January 9

Item by item, Scott Dixon cleared each object and file from the desk before him. As anxious as he was to get out of Washington, especially the Pentagon, he wanted to make sure that everything, including the borrowed desk he had used for the past two weeks, was in order. When he arrived at Fort Campbell, Kentucky, all he wanted to do was lose himself for a while in the task of rebuilding the division that he had led out of Colombia less than a month ago.

When he completed the sorting and filing, Scott stood up and looked down at the last item on the desk. Arranged neatly in a blue folder was his report on the combat operations of the 11th Air Assault Division in what was now being called the Colombian Affair. As with other past military adventures, especially those that had gone astray, there surfaced a need to call it everything but what it had been, which was a war. Though he knew that this one, like the other wars he had been in, would always be with him, right now all Scott wanted to do was put some distance between it and him.

Deep in thought as he stared down at the blue folder, Scott didn't notice General Fulk as he entered the room. 'Ready to leave us for good, Scotty?'

Looking up, Scott made no effort to gather himself into the position of attention or in any way acknowledge the entrance of his superior. Instead he glanced down at the blue folder again and replied in a low faraway tone, 'I've been ready to do that for months.'

The smile that had been on Fulk's face when he entered slipped away. Walking over to a chair in front of the desk, the Chief of Staff of the Army sat down and let his arms drop over the side. 'People told me before you came here last year that the Pentagon was no place for you. Seems it took a war to prove them right to me.'

Scott ignored Fulk's comment. The losses they had just suffered were still too fresh in his mind to make light of them. Instead he walked around to the front of the desk and leaned against it. 'I believe, sir, that this report,' he said, indicating the blue folder behind him, 'will serve you and the Army staff until my staff has an opportunity to settle in at Campbell.'

Fulk raised his hand. 'I'm sure it will do. You always deliver, no matter what.'

'I was hoping,' Scott countered, 'to have it finished before the new division commander arrived and took over, but I don't think that's going to be possible.'

Not knowing if he was complaining about the appointment of a major general to come in and take over the 11th, leaving him to drop back to the position of assistant division commander, or not, Fulk tried again to relieve the concerns Scott seemed to be having. 'I talked to Bill yesterday. He isn't due to take charge until mid-February. By then, I'm sure, you'll have everything as squared away as that desktop you're leaning on.'

'Talking about taking care of unfinished business, sir, I know that you have other concerns, and this issue is still rather touchy, but I would appreciate it if the recommendation for Nancy Kozak's award could be acted upon before I leave. I was hoping to make a personal trip out to Lawrence, Kansas, before reporting back to Fort Campbell. I wanted to deliver the medal to her in person while she is still convalescing at home.'

Fulk nodded. 'I'll take care of that right away. All that we lack is the Secretary's signature and that action is on his desk right now.'

'I appreciate that, sir.'

'Why,' Fulk asked, 'isn't she waiting until she returns to duty to receive it? After all, it's not every day that a soldier is awarded a second Distinguished Service Cross for valor. I would have expected that you would have liked to make a big deal out of this whole affair, especially in light of what Lane had been trying to pull. It would in a very visible way complete her exoneration.'

'We discussed that, sir, the other day over the phone. She feels rather embarrassed, as it is, that she is receiving any award for her actions on the morning of December seventh. According to her, she doesn't even remember being hit, let alone ordering a bayonet charge.' Then, dropping his voice, he added, 'Besides, Nancy isn't the vengeful type, not really. All she wants to do is to get back to a unit and lose herself in her duties.'

'Just like you.'

This last comment caused Dixon to smile. 'Yes, sir. Just like me.'

Standing up, Fulk offered Dixon his hand. 'I'm headed out tonight on a trip to Europe for the NATO conference. That's why I came down here to say my good-byes. Is there anything else you need from me before we go our separate ways?'

For an instant the question intrigued Scott. Yes, he thought to himself, there were some things he needed from Fulk. Scott wanted to know why, for starters, Fulk had said nothing last spring when the administration had recommended sending the 11th Air Assault to Colombia despite the fact that everyone who had bothered to look at the situation knew that Colombia, like Yugoslavia, Somalia, Vietnam, and other such adventures, was a bottomless pit that defied quick, easy solutions. He wanted to know why people like C. B. Lane were allowed to build their careers over the broken bodies and careers of fellow officers. He wanted to know why good people like Hal Cerro and the men and women who had followed him into Colombia had been so casually thrown into a war simply because the polls showed that the American public favored, for the moment, such an action. There were many things that he wanted to know, so many questions.

But in the silence that followed Fulk's question, Scott asked none of them. Instead he looked down at his shoes and shook his head. 'No, sir.'

Fulk smiled, reached out, and took Scott's hand. 'Well, best of luck to you, Scotty. Say hello to Jan for me and take care of yourself.' With that, Fulk turned and walked away, leaving Scott to pull his life together again and get on with the business of soldiering.